To Ukraine, With Love

Cosmic Roots & Eldritch Shores

Benefit Anthology
for
Ukraine

COSMIC ROOTS

&

Eldritch Shores

To Ukraine, With Love

Cosmic Roots & Eldritch Shores

Benefit Anthology

for

Ukraine

Edited by
Fran Eisemann

First edition

Credits for each author and artist's work appear at the end of their work and in the Acknowledgements at the end of the book.

Library of Congress Catalog Card Number:

ISBN: 979-8-9871931-0-5 black & white illustrated paperback
979-8-9871931-2-9 illustrated reflowable epub
979-8-9871931-1-2 black & white illustrated fixed layout epub

Book Design and Composition by Fran Eisemann

Published by Cosmic Roots & Eldritch Shores

https://cosmicrootsandeldritchshores.com/
editor@cosmicrootsandeldritchshores.com

Printed in the United States of America

Cover illustration by Artur Rosa

To the Dead
And the Living, and the Unborn, Country-
men of mine, in Ukraine, or out of it,
My Epistle of Friendship.

Taras Shevchenko, from *The Kobzar of Ukraine*

TABLE OF CONTENTS

INTRODUCTION

SCIENCE FICTION

FANTASY

Myths, Legends, & Fairy Tales

Eldritch

Young People of All Ages

Acknowledgments

INTRODUCTION

To Ukraine, With Love is a varied anthology of fine science fiction, fantasy, myth, legend, fairy tales, and eldritch stories, poems, and artwork that was donated by about fifty generous writers and artists, most of whom have been published in the pages of our online magazine, Cosmic Roots & Eldritch Shores. Charities benefitting Ukraine will receive 100% of the profits from the sale of this book.

Unless one is in the midst of a war, it is almost impossible to understand the magnitude of the damge it causes. And long-lasting damage. In 1954, two Air Force fighter jets on a training mission collided mid-air. The pilots did not survive, and the airplanes crashed into woods on property I now own nearly seventy years later. I can still find fragment of shredded plane parts.

And in Ukraine? The wrecks of many thousands of exploded, burnt, and crashed planes, helicopters, tanks, trucks, missiles, artillery systems, mines, drones, and other equipment have been strewn across the land, leaving ruined cities and blasted infrastructure. The physical, mental, and emotional carnage upon the Ukrainian people from the torture chambers, abductions, mass killings, the nuclear threats, and the damge to wildlife, land, water, air, and crop fiields.

So this anthology is being offered as one small form of support for Ukraine as it fights its way through and recovers from the present hellish times upon it, defending its very existence and picking up the shredded pieces of lives, cities, and homes. This is also in gratitude for the fact that Ukraine fight for survival is also shielding the world from Russia's long-term colonizing efforts.

We'll send copies to Ukraine where possible. We hope the stories, poems, and artwork in this book will provide some small respite of just pure enjoyment. We hope to publish further benefit anthologies in the future, and hope you will join us on the journey

Slava Ukraini

Fran Eisemann
Cosmic Roots & Eldritch Shores

To Ukraine, With Love

Dedicated

to

Ukraine

and to all peoples and nations
whose freedoms are under assault

SCIENCE FICTION

Abraxas Conjecture

Akua Lezli Hope

What he saw was the contrast
the dark void, a maw   not a womb
of creation   the absence of what
strikes the lit bulb

of our wet globe   a blue jewel
and yet all is illusion   this darkness
full of light   traveling   full of light
traveling   full of what his eyes cannot
perceive, the dark empty he said

but here on the ground we see hope
each night emptied of our hungry burnings
empty of our primitive exhalations
empty of the killing ways
we glow full

speckled heaven aloft
winks blinks shines
spinning   singing to us
can you hear
it   can you hear
it   is not empty
it   is full   can you hear
it is full
for now
radiating sound light sound

We were seeded from the sky
We were elsewhere conceived
Sift the dark noise
It will happen again
Read another spectrum

We landed and bloomed
It will happen again
Feel another vibration
Depths of the next dimension
Dare to comingle the intersections
Meta morph
this welling up
taste another sound

this sacred seeding
She births a chaos of information
from compassion
feeds it her milkyway
Annunciating:
It will happen again
It will happen again
It will happen again
All Sleepers awaken
By the Light

Akua Lezli Hope uses sound, words, and materials to create poems, patterns, stories, music, sculpture, adornments, and peace. She wrote her first speculative poems in the sixth grade and has been in print since 1974 with over 400 poems. Her collections include *Embouchure: Poems on Jazz and Other Musics* (Writer's Digest award winner), *Them Gone, Otherwheres: Speculative Poetry* (2021 Elgin Award winner), and *Stratospherics* at the Quarantine Public Library. A Cave Canem fellow, her honors include the NEA, two NYFAs, an SFPA, and multiple Rhysling and Pushcart Prize nominations. She has won Rattle's Poets Respond twice and launched Speculative Sundays, an online poetry reading series. She is the editor of the record-breaking sea-themed issue of *Eye To The Telescope #42*, and of *NOMBONO: An Anthology of Speculative Poetry by BIPOC Creators*, a first of its kind, from Sundress Publications (2021). She won a 2022 New York State Council of the Arts grant to create Afrofuturist, speculative, pastoral poetry. She exhibits her artwork regularly, sings her favorite anime songs in Japanese, practices soprano saxophone, and prays for the cessation of suffering for all sentience, from the ancestral land of the Seneca, the Southern Finger Lakes region of New York State.

The Resonance of Light

Geoffrey A. Landis

"𝔉ull many a gem of purest ray serene..."
𝔗homas 𝔊ray, 1750

"We can concentrate any amount of energy
upon a minute button... which glowed with a most
intense light.
To illustrate the effect observed with a ruby
drop...
magnificent light effects were noted,
of which it would be difficult to give an adequate
idea."
Nikola Tesla, 1897

When I think of Nikola Tesla, I see the pigeons.

He was always surrounded by pigeons. I think, sometimes, that the pigeons were his only real love, that he lavished upon these pigeons all the romantic affection we ordinary mortals have for the opposite sex. Certainly he had a way with them. He would whistle, and they would come, as if from nowhere, surrounding him like an electrical aura, fluttering quickly like the iridescent discharge from an ethereal fire.

"Pigeons," I once told him, "are the scourge of the city, spreading filth and disease. They are no more than rats with wings."

That was, I think, back in 1912 or 13, before the long shadow of coming war stole across the world, and we could gaily talk about pigeons. Nikola Tesla looked at me with eyes of fire, with that intensity of soul that I have seen in no other man, before or since. "Surely you are but teasing, Katharine," he told me, "yet some things should not be taken in jest. Look at them! Ah, they soar on wings of angels." He was silent for a moment, watching, and then continued, "Do you believe, then, that men are so pure? The scourge of cities? Would you not say that for every disease that pigeons spread, men spread a plague? The scourge of man is most certainly man, Kate, and not the harmless pigeon. Do doves slaughter doves in vast wars, would you say? Do they starve one another?"

"Men build cities," I said. "Men have art in their souls, and aspire to higher things, as mere fowl cannot."

"Some men, perhaps," he said. "But few there are, few indeed, that raise themselves above the mud." He sowed a handful of his peanuts forth, and the air exploded into frantic motion, birds wheeling overhead as others waddled on the ground like winged pigs, shoving each other shamelessly for position to peck for their supper.

Nikola, however, seemed not to notice this greed. "It may be the feathery tribe builds no cities, but neither have they the need," he said. "As for art, can you say that a pigeon has no art, nor aspirations? What do you know of the feathered heart? Are not they, perhaps, the embodiment of art, the very winged soul of art incarnate? Say no more of pigeons, then, for I tell you that a pigeon can feel, can even love, as a man can."

And, as bidden, I was silent.

Surrounded by his pigeons, Nikola Tesla would forget himself, and be as delighted as a child, and how could I begrudge him that loss of self?

Do you think that I was myself smitten with the prodigal genius? Of course I was, but then, no women who ever met him was not. Still, I believe that I was his closest female companion, indeed, his closest companion of either sex, for despite all his personal magnetism, Nikola was not a man who easily allowed himself to open up to others.

Robert, of course, could see my infatuation with Nikola; I was ever quite transparent to him. But we had long ago made an agreement our marriage was to be a loose one. In that bygone gay era when we were both young, we held to the ideal of a partnership of the soul, and we promised to understand and forgive each other wanderings of the flesh. Over the years it was Robert who most took advantage of that looseness of bonds, and I, holding to our long understanding, never took him to task for the girls he took as mistresses, nor the young men.

Robert quite encouraged my companionship with Mr. Tesla, and even urged us closer. I think he too was smitten by Nikola's tremendous personal magnetism, although if that were so, Mr. Tesla seemed oblivious to any overtones.

Tesla had his playful side. But then he had too a tendency to hold his inventions secret, remembering perhaps all too well the controversy over priority for invention of wireless telegraphy. But to me he had shown many of his inventions, judging me, I think, too little schooled in the sciences to accidentally reveal his secrets.

One day he admired a pendent that I wore about my neck. This was unusual for Tesla, who usually disdained jewelry of all sorts. "It is a ruby," I said, "a small one, but well colored, and prettily cut. A gift from Robert." I think Robert had intended it as a silent token of gratitude for my forbearance, or mayhap for forgiveness. He had given it to me while he was conducting a liaison with a woman by the name of Miss Kurz (a coarse young woman quite unworthy of his attention, in my opinion, but I made no indication of such belief to Robert, who in any case became bored with her attention after another week or two.)

Tesla smiled a mischievous grin. "If you should like to come up to my laboratory," he said, "I will show you to what purpose I employ such a mineral. I believe that you shall be amazed."

"I should be delighted," I said.

His laboratory was upon the third floor of a building with windows that looked down across Forty-Second Street. It was early evening, and the electric streetlights were just beginning to glow.

As always, his laboratory was cluttered with electrical equipment, from enormous generating dynamos to tiny crystals bedecked with wires thinner than a mouse's whiskers. On the workbench in front of the window he had a ruby of his own, but rather than a jewel, this was cut in the form of a small rod, about the size of a cigarette. In the shape of a cylinder a ruby becomes quite ordinary, looking like nothing other than colored glass, for it is the gem-cutter's art that gives a jewel its sparkle. I had never before seen a gemstone cut in such a shape, and commented on it.

"It is not of a gem quality," he said dismissively, "but it is a mineral specimen adequate for my purposes."

He had earlier showed me an invention of his which utilized a high pressure spark in a rarified-gas lamp to produce a sharp blue-white flash, brilliant as lightning. This momentary illumination is quite startling, having the illusion of stopping time in a frozen moment. Now he placed the ruby cylinder into a mirrored box, surrounded with the flashlamps, with more mirrors to concentrate the flash upon the ruby cylinder, and attached the entire apparatus to a system of condensors and coils.

He then darkened the room with black velvet over the windows. "Watch the wall," he said, indicating not the box with the ruby within it, but the empty white wall a dozen yards across the laboratory.

With a turn of a rheostat, there was a sudden snapping noise. A flash of white seeped out from the box that held the cylindrical gem, but this was not the light which captivated my attention. Upon the wall opposite the workbench had appeared a sudden glowing spot of a brilliant, pure red. I clapped my hands in startlement, and Tesla smiled in pleasure.

"What is it?" I cried.

He triggered the electrical flash again, and again a mysterious glowing spot appeared. It was a crimson so intense, of a hue so unalloyed, that it seemed to me every color I had hithertofore considered to be red was a muddy, washed-out shade compared to this pigment of unblemished purity. I remarked on the color to Mr. Tesla.

"Your eye is quite accurate," he said. "If you were to take the finest spectroscope, and analyze the color of the ray I have produced for you, you would find it to be a single shade indeed. All other lamps produce a spread of spectrum, but my new beam is a ray of unalloyed purity."

With that he set the ray to flashing automatically, and the dot now appeared as an unmoving, although flickering, spot of brilliance. He passed his hand in front of it, and the spot on the wall disappeared, moving to his hand, which now seemed to cup the glowing spot in his palm. For a moment I had to suppress a gasp of fright, for the spot was so bright I worried that it would burn a hole entirely through his hand.

"No need to worry," he laughed. "It is mere light."

He lit a cigar, and the smoke curling up from the cigar made the beam visible, a ghostly line of crimson. "The secret," he said, "is resonance. I have contrived to trap light between two parallel mirrors, so that it must resonate against itself as a standing wave, and so intensify until it escapes."

His explanation made no sense to me, for as I have said, I have no training in the sciences, but still I nodded my assent, as if he had clarified everything. After a bit of coaxing, I was persuaded to put my own hand in front of the beam, and although it seemed too bright to look at directly, it was completely intangible-- the beam had no force to it at all. I bent to look directly at it, but before I could put my eye to the ray, Tesla seized me and pulled me away.

"The eye is a delicate instrument," he said somberly, "and my ray is a thousand times, no, ten thousand times brighter than the sun. You would not look into it a second time."

Although we had known each other for many years, we had never before touched. His arms had quite surprising strength, considering that he was slender and almost womanish of figure; I could still feel the heat where his hand had been upon my arms.

I placed my hand upon the spot where his hand had been, and tried to feel again how he had touched me. Mistaking my gesture, he looked down, and said, "I apologize most humbly for my ungentlemanly conduct, Mademoiselle Kate. I acted only by instinct, I assure you, worried about your safety."

"I take no offense," I said, "indeed, I thank you for your protection."

He stared down at the floor for a moment, and then, seeming to forget the incident entirely, said to me, "Look! Let me show you what my ray can do!" With that he drew aside the velvet drapes and raised the dusty window wide open. The windowsill was stained with bird droppings like a thick spill of white paint. Outside, the city was now cloaked in night. In the distance, the silhouette of the Woolworth building was clearly visible, a newly-erected colossus of the skyline.

"Do you carry a mirror with you?"

I produced a gilt-backed hand mirror from my handbag, and Tesla secured it upon the workbench in front of the ruby apparatus with a clamp. He adjusted the mirror until it was angled to his satisfaction, then once again set the ruby to flashing.

And the tiny dot of light suddenly appeared upon the facade of the building across the street. What must passersby think, I wondered, of this mysterious dot of light above their heads? I thrust my head out to look down, but of the few pedestrians below, none thought to look up. Tesla adjusted the direction slightly, and then angled the mirror to point over the rooftops.

To my astonishment, the crimson spot appeared on the Woolworth tower itself, although it must have been half a mile or more distant. "The beam does not disperse," he said proudly. "I could bounce it off of the moon; I could send it to Mars."

"Can anyone see it?" I asked.

"Certainly," he said. "They will see it, and be puzzled indeed." He laughed, pleased with the thought. "I believe that none of them will guess at the origin of the miracle in a humble laboratory distant across the town."

Following that, he disappeared into his laboratories, and although Robert and I both attempted to entice him out with invitations of dinners and garden parties, he was hard on one of his ideas, and would not be seen again for several weeks, save only as a furtive figure, walking through Bryant Park in the early morning with a handful of peanuts to feed to his beloved pigeons.

On an afternoon some months later, the weather that July of 1914 had turned suddenly sweltering, and Robert and I were prepared to insist that Mr. Tesla must join us in our excursion to see the fireworks at Coney Island. "We will bring him with us by force if necessary," Robert said, "but come with us he must, for he will ruin his health with excessive work."

I came to Nikola's apartments at the Waldorf-Astoria to deliver our invitation, but found him already seeing a visitor in the anteroom of his suite. The door was open, and without turning he gestured me to enter. His visitor was perhaps sixty or seventy years of age, and despite the great heat she was dressed in long skirts and a laced-up white linen blouse covered with several shawls, and had a scarf over her head in the style that I have heard called a "babushka." She was pleading with Tesla in her own language, and Tesla was answering her with a calm, soothing voice in the same language. I took this speech to be Serbian, Nikola's native tongue, for I speak a few phrases of Russian, and could understood enough words to recognize it a kindred tongue.

After they'd spoken further, Tesla stood to his full height, and in a voice of momentous tone, made her some great pledge. And such was his personal magnetism that even I, unable to understand a word, understood completely that whatever it was he had promised her, not heaven nor Earth should prevent him from accomplishing. At this pledge, his visitor fell to her knees and attempted to kiss his feet; although Tesla moved back slightly, just enough to avoid her touching him. Something had transpired, although I did not know what.

Later, when I talked with Tesla, he explained that she was a Serbian woman, of whom his family was acquainted, for she was native to the same small village as he. She had come to plead for the lives of her thirteen grandchildren.

"For war is coming, Katherine, a great and awful war, and it will sweep over Serbia like a tide of destruction, leaving only death behind."

"Surely it will not be so bad. We are civilized now, Nikola--"

Tesla's eyes were cold fire. "You understand nothing, my darling Katherine, nothing at all. We Serbs know what war is like, as you innocents do not. For five hundred years we have lived in the paths of armies, and when the rest of Europe looked away, we stood down the Turks, and died for it. Armies have washed over Serbia for years, like tidal waves, like plagues of rats, diseased and crazed with aggression, ravenous and destructive, and leaving only corpses behind. Before, at least some survived, but in these days of Gatling machine guns and poisoned war gasses, war will be total-- there will be no survivors, I fear, in little Serbia."

"It will not be so bad, Nikola, I am sure of it. What did she ask of you, that woman?"

"She asked if I could help her sons, and their wives, and children, to come to America to avoid the coming war. She asked me for money to pay the passage, and promised that she would herself work day and night to pay me back."

I winced inside, for I knew of his straitened circumstances. A genius he most undoubtedly was, but for all his invention, his genius had not made him rich. "And you said?"

"I told her I could not do that, but I would do something else for her."

"How can you help her? What will you do?"

"I told her that I would stop the war."

"What?"

"I have given her my pledge, my word of honor that I, Nikola Tesla of Smiljan, will stop the coming war."

I was amazed. Tesla was a prodigy, the greatest genius of our age, possibly of any age, but this was more amazing than anything I had yet seen. "But how will you accomplish that?"

"I don't know," he answered. "It will require, I believe, some study."

We sailed across to Europe on the Cunard liner Lusitania. She was perhaps somewhat less elegant than the late doomed Titanic, but still quite richly appointed, her interiors lavish with columns, artworks and tapestry, mahogany paneling and gilded furniture. More importantly, she was fast; the greyhound of the seas. Tesla said that making the passage quickly was of the essence, and worried that even the six day passage to Liverpool would be a crucial delay. Lusitania also had capacious holds, enough to carry the crates of mysterious electrical equipment that Tesla paid to have shipped across with him.

Tesla had brought with him piles of newspapers, in perhaps a dozen languages, proposing to use the time of the passage to study the situation. The headlines spoke of the coming war. The first day of the voyage he spent on inspecting the ship's steam turbines, and the radio shack; following that, he divided his time between reading, and pacing along the promenade deck, staring across the water and watching the gulls, who apparently lived on the ship, and soared in updrafts of the ship's passage.

All during the passage I dreamed of icebergs, although Tesla laughed, and said that in July it would be unlikely for us to be lucky enough to even see one.

"I should like to see an iceberg," Tesla told me. He was standing on the main deck, at the very bow of the ship, gazing into the horizon. "I am told that they are a most startling shade of blue, and I would like to see this myself." The day was warm, but the wind of passage ruffled Tesla's ascot and blew strands of his hair across his face, despite the tonic he had combed into it to avoid just that. He tossed his head to free the errant strand from his eyes, just like a young girl, probably not even noticing he did it.

"I have been designing an invention that will remove the threat of icebergs forever," he said. "A ship will broadcast high-frequency electrical waves, and from reading the reflections of the waves, will instantaneously know the location of all of icebergs to a distance of hundreds of miles."

"And so chart a course to avoid them," I said.

"Yes, avoid them. Or, when I am done, if they prefer not to deviate from their path, they will simply melt the iceberg out of their path."

"You can do this?" I said. "Oh, with your new ray! Can it be made powerful enough?"

"The ruby? No. It is a toy, nothing more." He shook his head, the errant strand once again swinging like a pendulum. "But the principle of light amplification by resonance-- ah, now that is something very wonderful indeed." Tesla smiled. "I have produced some improvements, and through combining it with certain features from my earlier work, have now made something quite-- interesting."

I shuddered involuntarily. Was this, then, how he proposed to stop the war, with a new death ray? If so, his quest was doomed, for I knew that, once started, armies were not so easily stopped. Tesla's ray might even level battlefields and set aflame all of the capitals of Europe, but the war would go on.

But when I mentioned this to Tesla, he merely shook his head. "In war, I think, as in physics, the key to effect must be to chose the right place to apply a force. It is not the magnitude of the force, but its precision, that is most critical. Resonance, Katherine, resonance is always the key-- if an action is placed in the correct spot, it will be amplified by circumstances into a great effect. If we but knew enough, I have not a doubt that a single flap of a pigeon's wing would be enough to change all the course of history."

"And your many boxes of equipment? Are they perhaps filled, then, with pigeons?"

Tesla laughed in delight. "Ah, Katherine, wouldn't that be rather cruel, to so confine such noble birds? No, I would that I had the subtlety of knowledge to be able to apply so gentle a force, but I must make do with lesser knowledge, and so apply a greater force."

An electrical ray, then, I thought. A death ray.

The Lusitania arrived in the port of Fishguard, and we then shipped immediately to Paris. From France I had expected Tesla to book passage on the Orient Express toward the Balkans, but instead he surprised me by taking rooms for us on the Seine. He spent his days reading newspapers. The headlines of the French papers were entirely given over to the murder trial of Mme. Caillaux, the wife of the French minister of finance; a subject which fascinated me, but which held not the slightest interest for Tesla, who immediately flipped past to find the war news. Afternoons and evenings he spent simply sitting in cafes, and talking earnestly to people he met long into the night.

I have always loved Paris, but that July the weather was beastly hot. I had expected the mood of the city to be somber, anticipating the looming war, but instead I found there was almost a visible eagerness for battle, with all the young men of the city excitedly discussing their idea on the coming conquest of Germany. Not a single one had even a casual thought that perhaps the Germans had other plans. "It will be over in a month," one of them told Tesla. "We will bring the Kaiser to heel, and wipe out the arrogance of the Prussians. The occupied territories of Alsace and Lorrain will again be French, and Germany will be made to pay dearly for their arrogance."

"Viva La France!" was the cry, and no one talked about death. Or if they did, it was a romantic image of death they pictured, all heroic poses, with no actual pain or dying involved.

Tesla's questioning was about the diplomats, and by what means they were endeavoring to stop the war. It gave me great cheer that he still had some hope for diplomacy, although the young men he spoke with seemed visibly disappointed at the prospect of diplomacy thwarting their desired war. "Austria will declare war upon Serbia; the honor of the Habsburg emperor allows no other course," one of them said. "And so Russia will come to defend their ally, and then Germany must certainly attack Russia in defense of their ally, and when they do, as Russia is our ally, we will defend them-- and thus we will invade Germany! Viva La France!"

"Serbia," Tesla said. "Austria, then Russia, then Germany, then France. And then Britain, I am sure, and then America will be unable to stay out of it."

"Yes," I said. The coming sequence reminded me of the chains of dominoes with which we had often played, in happier times, at parties. Each country falling into war would bring in the next one in the sequence, until the whole world was at war.

"Indeed," said Tesla, when I told him of the dominoes. "And that is the key. If we can remove one domino..."

"Then the chain will stand, and another day, the slight touch of a wind will set off the reaction," I said.

"Perhaps," Tesla said. "Or, if I calculate correctly, perhaps not. The engines of commerce are slowly but inevitably drawing Europe together, and if the war can just be postponed, I think that soon Europe will be so well entangled in commerce that there will be no France, no Germany, no Austro-Hungarian empire, only a prosperous and peaceful Europe." At my evident skepticism, he said "Observe the table you sit at."

He picked up the glass sitting in front of me. "Sparkling water, from France," he said. "It is in a goblet of Czech crystal, sitting next to a plate of Dresden ceramic, with English silver, and a napkin of Italian lace. On the table is a Chinese vase, holding a tulip grown in Holland. And so, as you see, even the least cafe in France is international."

A table setting seemed to me to be a rather weak guarantee of peace, but I did not say so, and in a day we left Paris, and set forth for Russia.

To embark by train across Germany would have entailed too many uncertainties, so from Paris we went by ship first to Rotterdam, then from Rotterdam to Riga, and from Riga we arrived in Saint Petersburg. Tesla's crates of equipment followed half a step behind us.

Saint Petersburg was a surprise to me. I had always pictured Russia as grey and cold and uncultured, but the summer climate was swelteringly hot and humid. The lazy evening twilight was long and delicious, though, and pleasingly cool. In the evenings the city was bright and gay, with the sky still aglow well into the night. Saint Petersburg seemed filled with treasures of art and sculpture, with golden-domed cathedrals and palaces of marble. The people were quite cultured, and although my Russian is so poor as to be nearly useless toward being understood, I discovered to my delight that a great number of the Russian citizens spoke quite good French, and reveled in the possibility of conversation with foreigners.

Tesla found us apartments near the Troitzky bridge, with windows that looked out across the Neva toward the Tsar's summer palace and the Field of Mars. Petersburg was not as well electrified as New York, or even Paris; the streetlights here were gas lamps, and not electrical. With the long evenings, though, streetlights were little needed. The lack of electricity drew disapproval from Tesla, but he set up in his rooms an electrical generator of his own, using a small but powerful turbine he had designed, and soon he had in his rooms a miniature electrical laboratory.

He was still reading piles of newspapers, turning the pages so quickly that I wondered how he could absorb any information at all. His questions, now, had turned to a single purpose, to learn the movements and activities of the Tsar. I cautioned him that the incessant questioning would most certainly tag him for a foreign spy, and that he would be arrested, or worse, but my fears were groundless. We shortly discovered that all the Russians loved nothing more than to gossip about the affairs of the Tsar (and more particularly of the Tsarina), and so we were soon swamped with rumors, speculation, and the most scurrilous innuendo about the movements and motives and intentions of the imperial family.

The conflagration we were all dreading was fast coming upon us. On the afternoon of July 23, Austria had delivered an ultimatum to the Serbian embassy. Confident in the support of Russia, Serbia had rejected it.

I put down the paper, where I had been puzzling out the Cyrillic characters in the headlines. "The war has begun," I said. "The Austrian armies are on the move. We are too late."

"Not quite yet," Tesla said.

Tesla, at last, had the information he had sought. He knew precisely the movements of the Tsar.

"At two-fifteen tomorrow afternoon, Tsar Nicholas the Second will arrive from Peterhof," Tesla told me. "After he and his intentions have been at the cathedral, he will appear to the public to declare the support of the Russian empire for their ally state Serbia, and instruct his generals and his people that the war has begun." Tesla pointed to his crumpled map of the city. "He will stand here. The Tsar has a great fear of assassination, and so he will appear on a balcony, out of the range of a thrown bomb, and no one will be present who has not been searched, to make sure none has a gun."

"I fail to see your point," I told him. "Unless... perhaps you intend to assassinate the Tsar?"

"As he stands, he will grasp this brass railing," Tesla continued on, ignoring my comment, "which I have ascertained is electrically grounded."

"And?" I said.

"I have made reservations for us to leave Saint Petersburg at noon on a ship bound to Helsinki. I expect all of Russia to be in chaos by then, but I believe that the ports will not yet be closed."

"You do intend an assassination," I stated.

Tesla lowered his head, and did not respond.

"And so," I said, "for all your exalted talk about removing a single domino from the chain, I find now that you intend no more than a common assassination. Surely you know that this entire situation is the result of a political assassination? Has any assassination, at any time, ever produced any positive result? Nothing good can come from such a deed, I believe, not a thing."

Tesla turned away. Without looking at me, he said, "Ah, Katherine, your idealism is as great as your beauty, and I cannot deny the depravity of my intended deed, but I simply have no more time. This once, we must hope that good can come out of evil. Russia is the critical link; once the Tsar mobilizes the Russian army, no force in the world could stop the war. How many people are in the armies of Europe, do you think? Five million? Ten?"

"Perhaps twenty million, as I count it," I replied, slowly, for I was averse to following his reasoning.

"And what fraction of those will die, if the coming war is allowed to take place? Half?"

"Ten percent," I said, and then reluctantly added, "in the war. But disease and starvation follow war, and those will kill twice that number."

"Six million, then," he said. "Tell me, then, is the life of one man worth so much?"

His plan was simple. He had affixed a mirror near to the field. With his ruby beam, he adjusted the inclination of the mirror until, by bouncing the beam from our apartments onto the mirror, the crimson spot appeared exactly where the Tsar would stand. Then he had cemented the mirror to fix it in its position.

The ruby beam, however, was too low in power to have any useful effect. For his needs, he had made a much larger apparatus, working upon the same principle of concentrating light by resonance, but this one using an electrical discharge in a blown-glass tube of rarified gas. And this more powerful beam would, he told me, actually break down the air itself, turning it from an insulator into a conductor.

"And so?"

He pointed behind him. I had seen high-voltage generators before, of course, in his laboratory in New York, but had not paid attention to the fact that he had set one up in his chambers here. "Ten million volts," he said. "It will discharge along the path of the beam."

And at this, I had nothing at all to say.

It dawned a clear, cloudless day.

Tesla had spent all the night and morning working on his apparatus, adjusting and tuning every piece. I had hoped against hope that something would go wrong, that the day would be grey with fog shrouding the city, or the Tsar would change his mind, but exactly on schedule, the Tsar, wearing a blue infantry uniform bespeckled with gilt and medallions, appeared on his balcony to address his generals and his people.

The railing of the balcony was draped in red silk, with a single bare spot: the railing before the place where the Tsar was to stand. Below him, thousands, perhaps tens of thousands of excited, earnest people thronging before the Winter Palace, pushing almost into the river, waving all manner of pennants and flags, and holding up saintly icons painted in bright colors upon wooden boards. The heat in the crowd must have been brutal, but when the Tsar appeared, with the Tsarina at his side, they raised such long and continued cheering as to be heard clearly across the river: ìBatiushka, Batiushka, lead us to victory!î

The generators whined like dogs eager to be unleashed, and the air was filled with the bite of ozone from the high-voltage generator, and the smell of the heated oil from the transformers. My hands were trembling so much I could barely hold a pencil, and I sought desperately for something to say.

But Tesla was ice steady. He watched the spectacle across the river for a minute, judging exactly where the Tsar stood. Tsar Nicholas moved forward to grasp the brass railing, and my heart went still, but Tesla did not move. Why, why didn't he fire his machine? Had he a sudden change of heart?

Then a pigeon sitting on the far end of the brass railing spread its wings and flew off. As if this were his signal, Tesla said, very softly, "now."

He fired the beam. An instant later, the high voltage triggered, and a horizontal lightning stroke reached out to cross the river with a dazzling blue-white flash followed instantly by a clap of thunder.

Rather than following the straight path of the beam, the lightning stroke at the last furlong diverged, curving upward in a jagged arc, reaching over the green copper sheeting of the summer palace roof to strike a gold cupola above. A golden eagle on the point of the cupola exploded into a shower of sparks, spraying molten droplets of gold, and then the copper roof began to burn.

The Tsar looked around for a moment, puzzled, but then turned back to continue addressing the generals.

My ears were ringing from the thunderclap.

"Failure!" Tesla cried. "Again!"

It took nearly a minute for the generator to recharge the condensors, and in that long minute we agonized. The crowd was clearly distraught, half of them still watching the Tsar, who continued to talk, oblivious, while the other half had craned their necks upward to watch as the flames on the rooftop of the summer palace slowly died out. Tesla frantically adjusted the apparatus.

"Now," Tesla shouted. Again the beam of light shot out. A moment later the electrical arc, a blue-white lightning and a clap of thunder. The lightning bolt curved across the river, flashing down a dozen secondary strokes into the river, each of which puffed up in a small cloud of steam. The lightning crackled up and down, dancing now toward the bridge, now playing over a huge statue of some ancient Tsar mounted on a horse.

The living Tsar, untouched, stopped speaking and stared up at the spectacle.

Behind us, with a great snap the overloaded condensors burst into flames, and the lightning faded to nothing. Cursing in his own language, Tesla turned to beat the flames out with a blanket before they set us on fire.

I turned back to gaze at the spectacle across the river. The beam and its ten-million-volt generator were dead. He should have tested it first, I thought. But it was too late to offer him that advice now.

The air was stinking of vaporized copper wire and the burning wax insulation.

Sitting on the workbench beside me I noticed the small ruby beam apparatus, which Tesla had long ago demonstrated for me. There was no trick to operating it, once it had been set up, and Tesla had set it up earlier to check the alignment of his mirrors. I turned the rheostat to set the ruby to flashing. The beam went out across the room, and I took my handmirror out of my pocketbook, and carefully angled it, as I had seen Tesla do, to direct the beam across the river, and to the Tsar.

The beam was harmless, as I well knew from having put my hand in it. A toy, Tesla had called it.

The glowing crimson spot appeared on the Tsar. The beam jittered up and down, looking almost alive, for I was unable to hold the handmirror perfectly steady, and flashes of impossibly bright light from the medals that bedecked the Tsar's chest threw dancing glints in all directions. Even from across the river, I could hear the awed voices of the crowd. The Tsar moved left, and then right, but I followed him with minute motions of the mirror, and the crimson spot stayed fixed to his chest.

And then the Tsar kneeled down, and stared directly into the beam.

Tesla destroyed his gas-discharge tubes, pounding the glasswork into sand until he was convinced that there would be no possibility of anyone ever reconstructing his work. The electrical generator and its equipment he donated to the Academy of Sciences, for he believed that they would have no visible connection to the events of July, and the Russian engineers, he judged, would benefit from the equipment.

The Tsar was blinded. The monk Rasputin proclaimed that the events of the day had clearly been a sign of God's wrath. A horizontal lightning bolt from a clear sky, a fire of no known origin in the palace, a glowing bloodspot upon the Tsar's chest: these miracles could signify nothing other than the anger of God with the Tsar's warlike nature, and the fact that the Tsar had merely been blinded, and not killed, was an indication of God's mercy.

And so the Tsar postponed his plans to mobilize his army. Then, remarkably, over the next few days his eyesight returned, although for the rest of his life he would complain of a missing spot in his vision. The monk Rasputin declared the return of his vision to be a sign of God's pleasure at the Tsar turning from war.

Tesla took out his pocket notebook and wrote: "Flash blindness: temporary in effect. Apparently clears up in two days." Then he looked at the note, ripped the page out of his notebook, and burned it.

Faced with the undivided might of the Austro-Hungarian empire, and with no allies, Serbia acceded to the ultimatum, and eventually allowed itself to be peacefully absorbed into the empire. As Tesla had predicted, once war had been averted, the forces of commerce eventually overrode the dissections of Europe, and a new union of all of Europe emerged, rivaling the United States in its size and power, a great force for world peace. Even Germans and Frenchmen, once the greatest of enemies, now sit together at a common table in perfectly peaceful conversation, and together make business plans for the greater prosperity of all mankind.

Would peace have come if, as we had planned, we had killed the Tsar of all the Russias? I have turned this thought over and over in my head, considering every aspect of the question, and have come to no certain conclusion. But on the whole, I think not. I think that a murder, no matter by what good intentions motivated, would have lead the world into even a greater war than the one that had been impending. I now believe that the monk Rasputin, although he did not know it, had been right, and it was the hand of Providence directly that prevented us from murder, and saved Europe from war.

Before he smashed it, Tesla removed the tiny ruby cylinder from his apparatus and presented it to me. "I know you are fond of jewels," he said. "Perhaps this mineral specimen could be cut into gems. I have no further use for it."

I did not cut it up, however, but kept it to remind me forever of the day. I had it strung on a silver chain, so I could hang it from my neck to replace the ruby pendant.

I have it still.

Geoffrey A. Landis is a science-fiction writer and a scientist. He has won the Hugo and Nebula awards for science fiction. He is the author of the novel *Mars Crossing* and the story collection *Impact Parameter (and Other Quantum Realities)*. As a scientist, he works for NASA on developing advanced technologies for spaceflight, and is a member of the Mars Exploration Rovers science team. He was the 2014 recipient of the Robert A. Heinlein Award "for outstanding published works in science fiction and technical writings that inspire the human exploration of space." Hiis web page is http://www.geoffreylandis.com/

Glory Whales

Marc A. Criley

Mars gleamed above the curving ceramacarb hull of the *Gracious Balaenoptera*. We'd swung past and it had receded to a garnet nestled in velvet blackness strewn with the light-year diamonds of a sparkling Milky Way. But here, blazing twenty kilometers to port was our interstellar visitor, comet 172I/DSCS. Barely visible from Earth, here it churned slow-motion glitter. Ripples, curlicues, backlit streamers of gray and silver rain. Crepuscular cosmic rays and the nebulous electric blue glow of the ion tail.

Deep Space Comet Survey astronomers had spotted the comet as it crossed Jupiter's orbit, its hyperbolic trajectory confirming its interstellar origin, marking it as a rare temporary visitor to our solar system. It had unexpectedly remained intact through a near-miss of Mars, ripping its way through the tenuous upper atmosphere and altering its course. It was now projected to end its journey with a dive into the Sun.

DSCS asked if we'd tweak our homebound Martian slingshot to pull up alongside for some data collection and to grab a sample if we thought it safe. As if we would miss a chance to greet this visitor on its one and only appearance in our solar system.

We'd slotted into a parallel course this morning, keeping safely ahead and offset from the dusty nucleus. Once on station, we killed rotation, hitched up mag boots, and hiked out to gawk.

Already now streaming out more than a hundred thousand miles, the comet's blue ion tail rippled in the solar wind, and the dust tail glittered white in reflected sunlight.

"Well," I said, "how's this rate for anniversaries?"

Maya crossed her arms and looked up. "Not bad. And you arranged it all for me?" There was a grin in her voice. "It *may* just edge out Sputnik Planitia." She reached over and hooked a suited arm around mine. Leaned in a bit. We bumped helmets, took a sip. A '37 Syrtis Amore waited back in the galley, but it was strictly sippy water on EVA.

For our tenth we'd swung an ultra-long haul out to the Pluto/Charon system. We'd nitrogen ice-boated out for six days at the most isolated resort in the solar system.

"Y'know, sweetie," I said, "fifteen years in, and I still don't know why you married me. I was so afraid you'd say no. Wasn't sure I actually heard 'yes'."

Her gloved hand squeezed my arm. "I had no choice. You offered up the glamor of freight hauling, deep isolation, and giving up the earth below my feet. And maybe I was nuts about you. Still might be."

We bumped helmets. I squinted past the reflected comet dazzle on her visor. Yep, there was the smile that outshone Mars, this blazing comet, and the incandescent golden jewel of the sun. A smile that's taken me from one end of the solar system to the other.

"Maya! Dominic! RiskCon 2! RiskCon 2! Maya! Dominic!"

I snapped awake. GRACIE, the ship's cybernetic executive, slid the lights up. I ripped open the sleep web and heard Maya tearing out of hers.

"Status?" she said.

The wall monitor flickered on. We paused just for an instance to stare. The glowing, dust-puffing comet that yesterday we toasted fifteen years of togetherness alongside was today coming apart at the seams.

GRACIE said, "172I/DSCS breaking up. Fusion torch warm up has been initiated, yawing to reduce cross section."

I grabbed the bedbar, flipped out of the zeroG sleeper, somersaulted to the door. I kicked off the frame to hit Command two doors down. Maya right behind. I hooked the grab bar and swung into the room.

Maya yelled, "GRACIE, start rotation! Push to two RPM!"

As I arrowed towards the engineer's station the exterior views came up. Visible we already saw; infrared was blocked by the dust cloud; radar showed comet chunks crumbling like a dissolving sand castle and tumbling away. We were way too close.

"Dissolution commenced seventy-three seconds ago," GRACIE said. "Exceptional volatiles. Explosive vaporization driving high velocity jets. But impacts expected prior to torch zero."

"Debris mass? Timing?" Maya called out from the emergency cabinet as she snatched a pair of lifesuit canisters. She flung one at me.

"Centimeter and below debris in eleven minutes," GRACIE said. "One to ten meter impacts possible in fifteen."

I intercepted the lifesuit bundle. "GRACIE, preflate suits."

The suit popped and unfurled, hinged forward at the midriff. I shoved my legs in down to the boots and worked myself up into the torso until my head popped the helmet collar. "Seal," The upper and lower portions magnetically aligned, locked, and contracted to form fit. I left the visor up. As I looked over, I saw Maya's head pop up into her helmet. Then her suit sealed and contracted.

"You okay?"

"I'm good," she replied, staring at a monitor.

Two sparkling, radar-bright streams spiraled out from the comet.

"GRACIE, radar monitor. What's spraying from the comet?"

"Highly reflective cylinders. Radar cross-section estimates all are of a uniform 25x50cm size."

"How many?"

"So far, estimating four thousand."

Maya and I stared at each other.

"Maya," GRACIE said, "first impacts in nine minutes fifty seconds."

"Right. Strap in. RiskCon 1. Whatever those cylinders are they'll have to wait."

This wasn't what we'd signed up for heading out from Saturn with a load of ring ice. The comet had remained intact plowing through Mars' upper atmosphere. Why was it self-destructing tens of millions of kilometers later?

Every sensor was compiling data in real-time. Bringning in torrents of information, expanding the frontiers of cometary science. I just wondered if we'd live through it. But ceramacarb hulls can take a hellacious pounding. Cargo bays were mostly empty and depressurized, just a couple million tons of ice headed for Luna. Rotation spread out the damage, yawing cut our profile, though it takes time to turn a whale like the Gracious. Nothing to do but reduce vulnerability cross section and watch the approaching hail storm.

"Dom?"

"Maya?"

"Was this an extra anniversary surprise?"

"Well, didn't want things gettin' all stale. Fifteen years, y'know, and boredom sets in."

"Initial debris impacts within one minute," GRACIE announced. The reactor torch power countdown dropped below eleven minutes.

GRACIE reported first impact.

We both smiled grimly.

First impact of many. Many. But the Gracious, at six hundred by three thousand feet and taring a quarter-million tons, could survive this. GRACIE tallied impacts and severity. Most baseball-sized and under. Took damage. Lost comms, most sensors. Only a tiny fraction of the comet cloud impacted us across twenty kilometers of empty space. But Gracious was a big target, and thousands of tons of sand, gravel, and increasingly bigger rocks were crashing into us. We watched the clock. Sweated hull integrity.

"Two hundred ton low-speed impact in… three minutes," GRACIE announced.

"Why didn't we see that?" I yelled.

"We only have two sensors even marginally functional, and they are obscured by dust."

"Where's it gonna hit?" I said.

"Calculate impact at the engine block, anticipating major damage. Emergency safing reactor and coolant systems now."

My chest hollowed out. I started panting, my vision sizzled.

"*Stop*," Maya whispered.

I ground my teeth, shook my head. Cleared it. Five more minutes and base power would've torched us out of here. Maya and I sealed up.

Impact. Creaking bulkheads, power dropped out and returned as electronics rerouted and rebooted.

I headed down *Gracious'* core spire to triage. The reactor access shaft running through the engine block now sported a passage leading directly to open space, the other end a jumble of boulder, debris, and solidified NaK reactor coolant. Struts, cables, ductwork, bulkwork, shredded metal, and composite furred the hole the rock had punched into the ship.

The reactor and containment chamber were untouched, so we still had power via the redundancies. But primary NaK coolant system was obliterated and the secondary system was trashed as well. Tertiary came through okay, but that was for minimal circulation in drydock. Even at full stir the reactor was limited to two percent.

It didn't take a nuclear propulsion expert like me to see that this couldn't be fixed out here in deep space. But I had to figure something out, and soon. Shadowing a sundiving comet would not end well.

The next three days I lived and worked out of the airtight twelve by twelve by sixteen foot engine block habitat, the "space rack", to avoid the quarter-mile zero-gee slog up the spire each day for meals, washing, and resupply. Primary goal was getting to our cometary vandal and strapping it down tight. We couldn't have this rock banging around under acceleration. GRACIE ran a half-dozen spiderbots alongside me, cutting out junk they carried away and stuffed into an empty cargo bay.

"Dom!" Maya radioed.

"What?"

"Behind you."

I spun and saw a spacesuited figure floating about ten feet away, steadying herself on a torn strut. Maya had been checking hull integrity and working on the antenna and comms units.

"You've been running eleven straight hours, and you only got four hours of sleep last night. I brought cookies and some Ol' Smoothie. And I need to show you something."

I looked back at the plug of debris, then over at the cutter-armed spi-derbots clipping pipes and struts and hauling away debris. "GRACIE," I said, "I'm going to take a break, hold when you've got a visual on the rock and call me."

After equalizing pressure the rack's inner door slid open and Maya rushed in, pulling me in after her. "GRACIE, bring up the cargobot video stream from where I marked it." She turned to me and lifted her visor. Eyes and smile wide, she said "Watch."

I popped the can of root beer and sippy sleeved it. Then bit into an excellent vegan chocolate chip cookie. And watched.

On the wall monitor a small spot slowly flickered like a silver star, then turned into a tumbling oblong shape.

"One of those silver things," Maya said, "drifting at a couple meters per second. It was going to pass within a hundred meters so I sent a cargobot after it."

"You get it?"

"It's in a bio hold isolation unit now."

"*On board?*"

"In vacuum, at 40K, should keep it inert. GRACIE, display and zoom in on the cylinder."

I stared speechless at a series of incised lines running along the side of the cylinder. Entwined and crossed like a DNA double-helix. Below that were line drawings. The smaller ones I couldn't make out, but the large one looked like a *whale*, despite the vertical fish tail. Long pectoral fins swept back from behind its jaw, and another pair of "fins", side-by-side short triangular ones, rose from its forehead. A stippling of dots flanked it from jaw to tail.

"GRACIE's running ambient spectroscopy and sonography right now," Maya said. "Slow speed and non-invasive. Also programming a few cargobots to survey what's left of 172I."

"But... there's only short-range docking comms, she won't be able to fly them."

"Dead reckoning. Send them on a pre-programmed course. Whatever they see they'll store for GRACIE to analyze."

"And grab more of those?" I waved at the cylinder on the screen.

"They'll try, if they find any. And I'll continue hull scans and system diagnostics and simulations so we get out of here in one piece."

"You're the crack pilot, you'll get us out."

We stared at the image of cylinder. I brushed my glove against the screen. "And that's coming home with us."

I headed back to work. The other maintenance conduits the boulder had punched through looked clear, so GRACIE's spiderbots and I spent about thirty hours clearing down to the two hundred ton extraterrestrial visitor wedged deep in Gracious' engine block. We carbon strapped it into immobility.

Gracious's hull remained mostly intact, if heavily pitted. But steerable antenna units had been obliterated, leaving us with only the short-range comms normally used for docking. We could transmit, but not receive.

Maya and GRACIE plotted an unavoidably sun-grazing course to put us into an Earth-bound freight lane. We were running on fumes, so we skipped nutri-bars and hauled ourselves to the galley to nuke some lasagna, pop a bag of Martian red, and get GRACIE's analysis of the cylinder and whatever the cargobots found.

On screen a sonogram outlined a perfect cylinder; it was ten inches in diameter by almost twenty tall. GRACIE put up a contrast-enhanced, algorithmically boosted interior rendering. Parallel curving diagonal streaks led to a sharp seam about two inches below one end of the canister; almost certainly a screw cap. Three concentric shadowy layers nestled inside, a container in a container in a container -- GRACIE tagged it on the screen as a dewar flask, with the inmost one enclosing two stacked racks of tubular shadows, like vials, eight each. GRACIE cautioned some of this was just provisional pattern matching.

Then the hi-res of the DNA and fish graphic. Just the double helix above the minimalist rendering of the creature.

"Whale," Maya said.

"But," I said through a mouthful of lasagna, "vertical tail."

"Fish or whale, aquatic."

"And that smaller graphic?"

"Maybe its food web?"

"That double helix looks like DNA," I said, "but what're the odds of alien DNA?"

"Amino acids are all over space, and all those Martian glacial lake viruses figured out RNA. With hundreds of billions of planets in the Milky Way alone, what are the odds of DNA *only evolving once*?" Maya paused. "It's tremendously flexible. If that's anything close to DNA a genomic AI could analyze it, tweak it, and a bioreactor could build it out."

"And what? Drop it in the ocean? Not so sure about the wisdom of that. Could it even survive in a terrestrial ocean?"

"Maybe a genomic AI could adapt it for our environment." Maya's face gleamed with excitement.

I laughed. "I love you."

Then she lit that smile. "I love you too." She turned to the screen. "GRACIE, what did the cargobots find?"

"No additional cylinders were retrieved. Two of the cargobots have not returned and are presumed lost."

"Uh-huh," Maya said. "Maybe we don't do that again. What else turned up?"

GRACIE displayed the view from cargobot 5's cameras, panning until a large curving metallic shard embedded in a chunk of rock hove into view. Long beams, like trusses, extended through the rock and emerged out the opposite side. "Cargobot 5 observed a portion of a spherical shell and an apparent reinforcing structure within the comet body."

Maya gasped. My jaw hung open. GRACIE tagged the dimensions of the beams and shard and wireframed a ten meter sphere tangent to it, then packed in fishcan sized cylinders. "Preliminary estimates of structure's volume indicate possible capacity of 10,800 cylinders."

I closed my mouth. "Did they bury a seed vault, or I don't know, an ark, in a comet and send it out to find a new home? Maybe programmed it to flyby and assess likely stellar candidates? And then it ends up almost hitting Mars. Which should've torn it apart."

"Maybe systems were just failing after eons of radiation, cold, and vacuum. Nothing lasts forever," Maya said. "Got too close, gravitational stress could've initiated a slow-rolling microfracture cascade. Our comet stayed together as long as it could. And then it couldn't."

"'Our' comet?"

Maya grinned and shrugged. Then she lost her smile. "But now it's a sundiver."

I dropped my head into my hands. "We've got to get more of those cylinders and get them away from here. We owe it to whoever sent this. It may be all that's left of that world. Maybe a whole ecology, their own DNA, records, "golden disks", whatever, just floating out there. We can't just let it all fall into the Sun."

"There's no time," Maya said. "Every day we're three million miles closer to the Sun. We have to give it a wide enough berth so that Gracious can handle the heat. It's going to be close. We have no sensors left to find canisters with, and we lost two out of six cargobots just looking. We have to get out of here as soon as we possibly can or we get cooked."

Maya took my hand and squeezed it. "But the cylinders are easy to spot in visible or microwave frequencies; their expulsion from the comet may have put some of them out of the sundiver trajectory, maybe along with some shards of that vault. I'll have GRACIE extrapolate from initial data and transmit what we can of their trajectories. They'll be out there just waiting. If not for us, then for someone else. Orbital mechanics, baby."

My wife the pilot.

"We'll miss the sun by thirty-five million kilometers," Maya said, "well inside Mercury's orbit. Then eight weeks or so coasting to the closest space lane."

"Gracious can stand up to that heat despite the damage, can't it GRA-CIE?" I asked for the tenth time.

"If proper thermal management is maintained there are adequate safety margins." GRACIE responded.

"We just spit roast for a few hours at closest approach," Maya said.

I tightened the seat harness, though two percent torch acceleration is hardly noticable. Monitors for reactor, coolant, electrical system, and life support showed green across the board. We were suited, visors up. Hardly necessary, but remote possibility failures kill you just as dead. On the main monitor a diffuse cloud rippled around us in the solar wind. We were now literally inside what was left of the comet's coma. Too bad Earth and Venus were on the far side of the sun, the dusty remains were putting on a heck of a show.

"Alright GRACIE," Maya said, "let's go."

One bar, two percent, on the torch thrust stack lit gold. Floating dust, stuff sensed but not really seen, drifted past, settled behind us. Fraction of a gee. On our way.

And then we were not. I changed from flight to EVA suit and went scrambling down the spire to see what had killed the torch and redlit every propulsion indicator ten minutes after we'd cleared the coma.

Carnage. Apparently when the rock plowed into us a half-ton chunk calved off and punched itself into a storage locker down a side passage. Out of sight. I'd missed it. Working too hard, too long. When we kicked on the torch, the rock jarred loose, careened down the nearest access passage and plowed into the last working heat exchanger. NaK everywhere. We were out of backup coolant systems. No more torch. No more delta-V.

We hurtled past Mercury's orbit. I'd pilot lit the reactor and jury rigged it, just doable with some scavenged coolant. No plasma thrust, but enough power to keep us warm and cool. until it couldn't. Gracious rotated to even the heat, but hull temp climbed with every passing hour. We didn't need that much lateral velocity change, but ten or ten thousand meters per second is equally unreachable without a torch. Venus and Earth spun on the far side of the Sun, Mercury retreated. Even at maximum torch it would take a fast rescue ship nearly five weeks to reach us from any of them, and GRACIE estimated she could keep us cool for only one more.

I'd thought about overloading the reactor and going out with a bang. *The Gracious Balaenoptera*, though, was just too massive to come apart that way. Some other thought was hiding behind that, but whatever it was, it was biding its time.

We'd transmitted everything we had on the comet, what little we'd learned of the fishcan, along with our theory about 1721's disintegration. We recorded our goodbyes, and told GRACIE to send them on after we were gone.

We made zero-gee love one last time.

"I'm gonna miss all this," Maya said in the afterglow. Tears had been shed, but those were dry now as we floated together. Maya's hair tickled my chin as I held her against me. "You'd've thought year after year out here would've driven us nuts."

"Certain family members, on both sides, were convinced it did."

"Yeah, well, certain family members never base jumped the Rupes, or hot soaked on Europa, or sailed under a full Charon."

"Or methane skied Titan." I said. "Though mainly for me it's the stars out here, the Milky Way, Andromeda. Diamonds in the sky, like I never saw back home. And being the only humans in ten million miles. That is some solitude. It just worked for me, but it worked best with *you*."

Maya lifted her head to mine, kissed me hard. Okay maybe not the last time.

In the warmth, and darkness, and quiet, and a brain at peace for a few short moments, something clicked. The comet came apart. The *Gracious Balaenoptera* can come apart, in theory.

I'd thought about overloading the reactor until the containment field collapsed, triggering an explosion, which would wreck the engine block, but not destroy the ship. But dumping most of *Gracious*, and then cranking up the reactor? Then a controlled containment field collapse? I blinked as I ran numbers, doing estimates and round offs in my head.

Numbers, plasma flux, megatons, mag fields, joules...

I started murmuring, got louder. "Overdrive the containment field... max the burn rate...beyond redlined. Massive volatile dump--we've got ice, tons of ice. A *directed* containment collapse could, *could*, do a vectored blast."

Against my chest Maya said, "That's what you're thinking about right now? Going out in a blaze of glory?"

My brain sizzled. "No, really. If we were strapped in the space rack when it went up... We might live through this."

Maya leaned her head back, and we locked eyes. Dead on serious, I told her, "We need to blow up the ship."

"Eight.. seven..." GRACIE intoned.

All that's left of *The Gracious Balaenoptera*, the engine block, is shaking and shrieking. By the nanosecond GRACIE makes magnetic and EM adjustments trying to keep the raging stellar core caged for just a few seconds more. We're exhausted. Two days spent jettisoning cargo bays, structurally reinforcing the space rack to hold it together under insane gees, slathering it with ceramacarb to rigidify and seal it. Charging full batteries and oxygen, detaching and pushing off the core spire, our home for fifteen years.

Now counting down.

To a megaton fusion containment breach.

Seconds away.

A hundred fifty feet below us.

"Six... five..."

We had thick gel crash cushions on the floor, placed perpendicular to the detonation vector, us lying dead flat to prevent a limb being torn off by the explosive acceleration. GRACIE estimates forty-plus gees, which stress models contend the ceramacarbed rack, and us, can survive, briefly, very briefly. We set up automated nutrient and hydration IVs that might keep us alive if we and the equipment survived the blast. We snapped an archive of

GRACIE and embedded it and the fishcan in a block of ceramacarb. We broadcast our plan and detonation vector, hoping there'd be someone out there to hear it. Or find some pieces to pick up.

"Four... three..."

All power thrown into the containment field, bottling up nova grade plasma until the last possible microsecond, until the chamber's flooded. And everything shaking so bad I can't see straight. The panels of green, yellow, and red status indicators now just arcs of color.

"Two..."

Everything smears red.

"One..."

"Breach," GRACIE blipped.

I closed my eyes.

"Oh God." Me or Maya, or both, couldn't tell.

"I..."

The rack deck smashed into us.

I remember being very thirsty.

I remember hearing a Martian-accented voice: "Oh my God they're still alive."

Another voice, same accent: "Grab that block of carb, it's marked. Add it to the collection."

One more: "It's gettin' hot in here! Let's go, let's go!"

I remember a sting on my neck, and a wave of cold washing through me. And then nothing.

The rain had stopped, though leaden clouds looked ready to unleash another cold Scottish downpour. The waves in the small bay surged against the sandy beach. Barely any movement out where Maya waded, jeans rolled up above her knees. Outside the small bay the waves heaved, cresting and breaking as they contended for entry. Beyond that, halfway to the horizon a large patch of choppy water gave away the location of a swarm of skittish bala shrimp.

"Can you feel your feet?" I asked.

"Not a bit," Maya said. "For a change." She smiled as she pulled her rain-spattered hoodie tight around her shoulders. She kept scanning the gray horizon. "I love knowing they're coming this way... "

"It was eighty-five years ago today," I said.

Maya grinned over her shoulder at me. "Dom. We really helped start something, didn't we?"

A few minutes later my mobile vibrated. I checked it. "GRACIE is saying we oughta head up." I nodded towards the headland rising up to a plateau a couple hundred feet above the sea. Maya turned to me, then picked her way back to the beach. I helped her sit as she stepped onto the sand. I brushed her feet off with a hand towel. "Chicken foot," I said. She smiled.

I slipped wool socks over her feet, velcroed her sneakers. I creaked back up and helped her stand. "Gracie says it's that way."

Hand in hand we headed across the sand. I spotted an old, corroded "Scenic Overlook" sign. An arrow pointed to a rough trailhead that passed up and around out of sight.

"Let's go, old man," she said.

I grinned, middle-aged maybe, not old yet. Though sometimes it felt like it. And more so lately.

A half-hour later we reached an old picnic table. We grinned at the gleaming alloy tabletop, it's surface decorated with the now iconic graphics from our recovered cylinder. A weatherproof visitor log was chained to the the table. We signed it.

We dropped down onto the bench. We ached. People in their one forties are usually still pretty limber. We haven't been limber for a long time. A century of medical advances prolonging and improving life still couldn't fully restore the shattered bones and shredded muscles of that bare second of forty-six gees. The report from the medics on the Martian corvette that had raced after and finally caught up with us estimated we'd only had a few hours left.

"Is that them?" Maya asked. She stood and pointed out to sea, to the north.

A few miles out the bala shrimp swarm sensed something. The huge patch of choppy ocean settled, smoothed, stilled to an iron gray mirror. We held our breaths. A line cut the patch, became a rippling vee, followed ten yards further out by another.

"Yessss," Maya whispered.

I hauled myself up and grabbed Maya's hand. Within seconds a pair of thirty-foot fins, blazing coruscating neon red/gold fins, rose up. Then beyond those another pair came carving up through the surface, triangular exploding cascades of prairie storm violet-blue lightning. Around each pair the ocean warmed gray to gold, flashed to green to blue to red to silver-white to black and back to gold. Rainbows exploded.

Balaenoptera astra gloria. Glory whales.

The more distant pair of fins rose further, pushing up a mound of water. Rivaling the length of an ancient aircraft carrier, the whale broke the surface, erect tail ruddering the pallid sea. Light detonated across its back, a fireworks/laser light show mash up. And across the back of its mate wove patterns of color; rhythmic, arrhythmic, sparklers, frenzied electronic dance flow schematic twisting shooting sparkling spinners, actinic silver red gold morphing into blue and white and shocking pounding bursting blasts of life and stars and god damn supernovas.

And then…

"Oh my God!" Maya shouted, jumped up and down, pointed. I saw it too. A small black--midnight velvet black--shape popped up between the two beasts. A calf, maybe two months old and nearly the size of a blue whale, born up North at the height of arctic summer. Black, black as space, silhouetted against bioelectric lightstorm furies.

The more distant swimmer winked out and submerged. The calf dove after. The remaining creature rolled on its side, a fifty foot fin skating sparks off the iron sea. From jaw to tail, a galaxy of stars. Gold and silver, piercing, diamond stars rippling, fountains whorling in crashing waves of gold and froth. It slid down into the dark.

Glory Whales.

"Welcome to Earth," I whispered.

Maya hooked her arm around mine, leaned in and whispered, "Best anniversary ever."

END

Marc A. Criley began writing in his early 50s, and his stories have since appeared in Cosmic Roots and Eldritch Shores, Beneath Ceaseless Skies, Galaxy's Edge and elsewhere, so one can rest assured it's never too late to start writing. Marc and his wife "manage" a menagerie of cats in the hills of North Alabama. He maintains a blog at marccriley.com and carries on at Mastodon as @MarcC@Wandering.shop.
Slava Ukraini!

Spicer's Modest Success

Jared VanDyke

"This has been Rockin' Ron's Evenin' Attitude. You're listening to Parma's home for classic rock: 98.5, The Drive. Stay tuned for The Séance, sorry, The Science of Romance, with 'Doctor' Spicer and his toaster, aka his robot."

Ron smirked heavily but Dr. Benson Spicer remained cool. In his tweed jacket, his perfect posture could cut diamonds, and in his close-cut coif of gray-sprinkled hair, he stood ready to take off for the stars. In his arms his robot Copper -- toaster sized and studded with Christmas tree lights – spun its wire limbs.

"Making a joke of my show again?"

"No, you do that for me," Ron said. He smoothed down his Megadeth

"Rust in Peace" t-shirt. "You know you don't have to dress up, right? This is radio. Nobody will see you. Fortunately."

"I dress for visitors," said Benson. "I dress for success."

"This is success?" Ron gestured expansively to the studio walls cracked with multiple layers of faux wood. A third-place award for best local radio station hung askew by the control booth's window, where Grace, the Parma Community College intern, sat in her 'PCC's the Pits' t-shirt and guzzled from an unmarked bottle.

Benson surveyed the perfection of his small-town radio domain. "No somnolent PCC students, no sullen teaching aides, no close-minded deans railing against robots in the classroom. I haveve a direct line to those who'll actually benefit from my instruction. So, yes, success at its highest!"

"Inn-Core-Wrecked," blared Copper.

Benson gave his lie-detecting cohost a stern look. Copper innocently spun its arms.

Ron stood up and conceded his spot with a deep mocking bow. Benson acknowledged the bow and occupied the swivel chair throne.

"By the by, Ronald, how fares our new satellite? I have heard we're reaching farther than ever."

"The new dish isn't new, 'by the by,' just an old government rig we salvaged from the quarry. Great range, but lots of interference."

Benson paused, grinning like a child about to explode from a secret held too long. "Are you sure the interference wasn't your music?"

Copper's tin-speaker blared triumphant mariachi music.

"Is this the wit that promoted you from part-time to glorious full-time volunteer? Another decade and maybe you can afford a real cohost instead of a talking trashcan."

"Hey, now! I built Copper from my family's first radio, and he still remains a stellar cohost and companion. You may mock me, but I'll thank you to leave Copper his dignity."

Ron hissed and hooted as he grabbed his coat and headed for the way out, waving a dismissive arm behind him.

Benson called after his retreating figure. "So how are we dealing with the interference?"

"… a pro like you can figure it out." And Ron was out the creaking studio door.

Benson adjusted his and Copper's headphones like a preening parrot. "Well, I can manage perfectly well on my own."

"Inn-Core-Wrecked," said Copper.

"Your faith is duly noted."

Benson opened his show outline and reread the portions that weren't doodles of rockets or 80s song lyrics. The margins overflowed with notes, condensing his lecturing experience and psychology PhD into talking points for sobbing callers. He patted Copper's side, hummed the last bars of the fading commercial for Mabel's Country Kitchen: home of the best roadkill specials, and leaned into the microphone.

"Good evening, and welcome everyone to The Science of Romance. I'm Dr. Benson Spicer, the Love Scientist with a PhD in psychology and matrimony. Tonight's topic is -"

"A-Lee-Inz."

"Not quite Copper, the topic's commitment. Are you ready to pop the question? Wondering if your relationship will last? Call 555-393-LOVE and let Dr. Spicer give you the formula."

Benson pulled up the pending call line on his monitor. All twelve slots remained empty. So did the "next track" line. He threw a fistful of pens at the control booth's window before Grace startled awake, took a swig, and plugged in a tune.

"Tonight we lead off with Mr. Vandross and Ms. Carey in 'Endless Love.' You're listening to The Science of Romance on 98.5, The Drive."

Benson pulled Copper closer as ultra-smooth R&B pipes filled his headphones.

"What's wrong buddy? You could speak well before we came in."

He flipped open Copper's back panel and fiddled with the interface. His effort was met with mariachi music.

"...did you 'explore' the toilet again? The gate is there for your own good. It's not a challenge, or-"

"We got a problem."

Benson sat up straight in surprise. He'd never known Grace to use the intercom, or do anything beyond load songs and choke down bags of potato chips.

"A million calls are coming in," said Grace. "They aren't queuing right, and most just hang up when I try and screen."

"Must be the new satellite interfering..."

"Ron is pretty good with this stuff. I can call him back."

"We can manage quite well without Ronald. We'll cold answer and use the delay timer if a call goes sour."

"Running near live?" said Grace. "Hope the boss doesn't find out."

"He would only be impressed with my initiative."

Grace guffawed out potato chip particles.

Benson raised his head high and waited as the last "Looovvve" came drifting like velvet across the airwaves.

"Welcome back to The Science of Romance with Dr. Benson Spicer..." he stared briefly at Copper, idly poking one of its cellophane eyes. "...and my brilliant robot co-host, Copper."

"Cah-Purr!"

"Thanks for joining us Copper. Now, before the break I floated the topic of commitment..."

Benson's monitor flashed a roulette of waiting callers, and no amount of refreshes or adjustments would exterminat the digital ants crawling the interface. Benson randomly selected line three and a 'Kth Ornsthoon' jumped onto the active call.

"...so let's bring our first caller into the arena of Love, Kth... Kathy? Kathy O! Remember Kathy: Copper can spot a lie, so speak true and let me know how I can help you."

Blasts of static broke the response into chunks."Dr. Spice... pain... my masters... ...feel the wrath... my tentacles... will not survive the ordeal..."

Benson slammed the dump button. Plenty of delay time remained.

Meanwhile, Copper was tipping off his stool. Benson steadied his spinning companion and selected another number. A chaos of consonants splayed across the active call field. He didn't attempt a pronunciation.

"Looks like we have a new caller! You've reached Dr. Benson Spicer on The Science of Romance."

The crackling line went static-free as the caller intoned in a hollow whisper.

"We fear the Dark Star."

"The dark star, ay? Forbidding, but not the strangest pet name I've heard, I assure you."

"There are no pets, no names. The Dark Star consumes our sun, yet the Seventh Priestess says we are One with the Dark Star. She is enamored with its unending hunger, and our people's sanity dies with the light of day. I am doomed. We are doomed. Save us, Dr. Spicer."

Benson dumped out again and hung his head.

His PCC students had never been so creative in their joking. But a crank call is a small price to pay for success at its highest...

A little under a minute remained on the delay timer, and Copper was halfway down the stool again, flashing its Christmas lights for attention.

The good doctor hauled him back up and randomly picked another incoherent name from the call list.

"We've a new caller joining The Science of-- "

"A mate no longer warms my chamber!"

"A-a serious issue." Benson scanned quickly through his outline for communication issues, which breakups often stemmed from, and read from his notes. "'Sometimes commitment takes work. We often grow apart unless both partners stay attentive to, and honest about, each other's needs.' Has your 'mate' left for good, or have they vanished for the night?"

"I consumed him as the Pit Lord commanded! His flesh sustains me, yet I am saddened by his absence! Comfort me, Dr. Spicer!"

The remaining delay timer read twelve seconds as Benson dumped yet again.

Grace was tapping her phone against the booth window with Ron's number dialed and waiting. The sation's 3rd-place award fell from its hook and split to pieces on the cracked linoleum floor. Copper flailed in the exit's direction and a cellophane eye popped loose. Benson held him steady, and wondered why his chaotic little robot wished to decamp.

He flipped a mental coin. Chance pranksters a fourth time or face Ronald's know-it-all smirk.

He bit his lip and picked another name as the delay timer ticked into live time.

"...hello?" he ventured.

"Excuse me? Have I reached the right coordinates?" The voice chimed in clear and calm, like a veteran secretary at a day spa. "I seek the Copper and Spicer."

"Oh! W-why yes, you've reached The Science of Romance. What is your name and how may I assist you?"

"You may call me Allora. I have questions about commitment. My partner is very... strong-willed. The Fifth Council holds him in high regard, but he focuses on his career at the expense of all else."

Benson leaned back and exhaled, relieved to have a sane caller. Even the digital ants on his monitor had slowed down. Grace turned gratefully back to swilling her label-free beverage. But Copper remained perfectly still and dark save for a whimpering vent fan.

"On a council, eh? That can be difficult. Those in positions of power often have trouble letting go when home."

"Exactly!" said Allora. "I only see him a few times a cycle. And he's always on about his Planar Forge. He thinks his is the biggest."

"Well, we all like to think that. But have you told him how you feel?"

"Once," said Allora. "It did not end well. He's focused on his duties more than ever, and he will no longer lock horns with me."

"'Lock horns'! An interesting way of putting it. But you've already taken the first step, so-"

"WHO IS IT DARES DISRUPT MY HOUSE!? I SHALL OBLITERATE YOU!"

Benson yanked off his headphones as hellish roars and screams filled the feed. Grace cut the line and cycled in a round of advertisements for Mabel's Country Kitchen: home of the roadkill special.

He yelled to Grace "She's under attack. I'll think of something for airtime after I alert the police."

He clutched his cell phone and ran outside for a better signal. The nip of snow flurries, a wash of pine trees, and a crust of splintered rock surrounded the mountainside work shed, aka radio station. Far below in the valley, Parma's crosshatch of streetlights illuminated six bars, nine gun stores, and enough churches to cover consciences the morning after. Late at night, off-duty timber farmers gathered in bar parking lots. They stood around flaming barrels, drank discount slurry, and blasted oversized radios perched on the back of pickup trucks. He wondered if they listened to his show. Not tonight he hoped.

He dialed Parma's Police Department. The dispatcher came in through crackling static.

"I'm Benson Spicer at 98.5 The Drive. One of my callers is under attack. Her name is Allora, and I..."

Benson dropped the phone as a gigantic undulating mat of space metal descended towards Parma.

Thousands of spiral mechanical arms filled the sky, dropping down through winter clouds. Illuminated by moonlight they waved about like huge metal seaweed fronds rippling through an ocean, propelling a central crystalline pod larger than a skyscraper. Within it stood the seething form of a giant more goat than man. The hundreds of spiky mech hands planted themselves along the shaking mountainside, suspending the pod to hover closer and closer over the radio station.

The pilot's eyes were great orbs of fire bisected by horizontally slit pupils, focused with murderous intent on the speck of a man in a tweed jacket.

Benson ran into the station.

Grace was already gone. The cycle of commercials no longer played, and every screen cycled incomprehensible symbols.

In the midst of the shaking, the technological hijacking, and the multi-tentacled deathship piloted by Baphomet's gigantic cousin, Copper sat limply on the stool swinging its arms.

"O-kayyyy!"

Benson picked up his co-host and dashed out the front door. One massive hoof pounded down right where the station's parking lot – and Grace's car – had been. The ground quaked, flipping Benson into the air and sending him rolling down the mountain. A giant goat hoof broke his momentum.

"Cower before Illum of The Fifth Council! Illum, keeper of its Planar Forge! You twist my betrothed's mind. Explain!"

Benson stayed curled into a ball, Copper tucked under his jacket, until the thunderous din subsided. Shakily he stood, and looked up to find the goat man bending over him, his silhouette blocking the sky.

Copper tried escaping the jacket, but Benson stuffed his cohost back out of sight.

"I'm a, ah, ah…. I meant no harm." Only the gust of the colossal goat's breathing answered, so Benson tried again. "Allora told me… she's not happy with you working all the time. I advised she let you know, that's all!"

Illum snapped his jaws in earsplitting ire and the tassels along his horns rang a dire chorus through the valley.

"You know nothing of my work." Illum flicked his massive head towards his vessel, the chiming of his tassels eliciting neon pulses from the ship's anchored limbs. **"With the Planar Forge I disable dark stars so lesser systems may know safety, so The Fifth Council may reign. I am needed; I am supreme!"**

'Inn-Core-Wrecked' shot from within Benson's jacket.

"You doubt my power?" said Illum. **"I think perhaps a little display is in order!"**

"No, nonono," said Benson. "He's only kidding. Right Copper?"

Benson's hands shook as he lifted the toasterbot to eye level, silently pleading with it to back him up.

He turned Copper to face Illum, raised it on high, and heard:

"Inn-Core-Wrecked!"

He threw himself down the mountain before Illum could react. The James Bonds and John McClanes made it look so easy, but Benson Spicer clipped every rock and stump on his way down the slope. Illum stomped, and the shockwave popped Benson into the air. At the apex of his flight he spotted his trailer home at Parma's edge, the football stadium PCC built instead of his robotics department, and the valley's premier diner -- Mabel's

Country Kitchen: home of the roadkill special.

He landed in a giant snowbank as Illum's massive hand scooped him up, snow bank and all, and hoisted him up among the clouds.

"What is your 'advice' for this situation?" roared Illum. **"Should I crush you like a drazgul, or drop you to the ground which spawned you?"**

Benson's mind raced through the stacks of psych journals littering his trailer for a suitable placatory response. But despite all the preparation, blind confidence, and margin notes he had no answer for escaping an angry giant goat being from light years away.

Copper – dented and sparking – blinked a Morse code of S.O.S.

A retreat, a cry for help, a surrender for the first time in decades.

Benson took the hint. "I... don't know."

Maybe it was the extreme height, or falling down a mountain, but his chest lightened as he repeated himself.

"I don't know what to do; I don't know everything! I'm just puffed up, and stubborn, and insensitive, and... !"

Copper played a garbled celebratory tune and hugged him. With care, and his face away from the sparking bits, Benson returned the hug.

"And I've neglected my friend. I'm sorry, Copper. I'm a real dummy, huh?"

"Inn-Core-Wrecked," said Copper.

All the while a giant flaming goat eye observed their reconciliation. **"Why does this machine forgive your weakness?"**

Benson flinched under the booming echo. Illum looked down at him, his shaggy ears hanging, head tilted, trying to understand the oddity in his palm.

"I made Copper to be my friend, my advisor, and I... haven't listened for decades," said Benson. "But now Copper knows I know better and I want to change." He tried to stay balanced in the giant furry palm as the alien weighed his words.

"And this intent is enough?"

"It's... it's a start. J-just listen to Allora, spend time with her. Think about it: she reached out across, what, light years? All for advice on how to fix things."

"Your advice, not mine!"

"Well, ah, perhaps, notice how... how you, ah, reacted." Benson flinched, preparing for a long drop to the parking lot, but Illum only dipped his horns and contemplated. "She wants things to work, she cares for you, but you have to listen to her."

Copper sparked and flashed its remaining lights in approval. Benson coughed into his hand, embarrassed by the parallel.

Illum turned about sharply and carried them up the long ramp of his many-tentacled spaceship. In the valley below hundreds of doors and windows were filled with staring faces. Parma locals stared as surges of neon light reflected off Illum's armor, and his voice rolled down the valley like thunder.

"I will not kill you, Benson Spicer. Though you are but a tiny creature from a primitive planet, you have wisdom. Together we will go to Allora and... listen. But if your way fails I will crush you beneath my hoof. Understood?"

"O-kayyyy," said Copper.

Benson opened his mouth to register a polite protest, to cry fear for the horrors of space and impending death by giant hoof. But Illum carried them into his ship and commanded it to swim away, while Copper blared mariachi music.

Ron spun himself away from his console as his outro cracked into synth wankery. The PCC student technician waved for attention, a film of sweat on his forehead.

"What, Jimmy? What's the problem now?"

"Look... look at the screens!"

Ron stomped into the tech booth. Skittering across every screen was shifting jibberish.

"It's just the feed messing up. I'll fix it during the break. Forward a call for now and I'll answer it cold. We'll dump out if any crazies get through."

"No, nonono-NO," said Jimmy. "Grace was in my class. First the monitors scramble, then the host goes missing, then you get stomped by an alien! She was in the hospital for- "

"Grace was a drunk who fell in the parking lot."

"The parking lot is shaped like a hoof!"

"Just forward a call!"

"I-I-I- "

Ron slammed the booth door. The 3rd-place station award, patched together with wood glue and hope, fell and shattered again. Ron kicked it and spun to the microphone.

"Annnnnd welcome back to the Evenin' Attitude with Rockin' Ron on 98.5, The Drive. Hello caller! Where ya calling from and what's your request?"

"This is Dr. Spicer calling from Kresge 07. How about something from 'Buddhist Peach' or 'Depth Leathered?'"

Jimmy ran from the studio and off into the forest, screaming his fear of hoof stompage.

Ron strangled the microphone. "You hack! Think you're sreally clever running off and leaving me with ALL your shifts?"

"I do apologize."

"You'll never work in radio again!"

"Oh. Drat."

"And by the way, Mabel turned your trailer into a roadkill shed."

"How lovely. I'm just calling to tender my resignation. I'll still be checking in from time to time. But don't worry, I'm sure you'll do splendidly without me."

And as Ron crushed the splinters of the 3rd place station award into dust...

from his hoverchair thousands of light years away Benson Spicer pressed the disconnect button.

His office, a hollowed cyan crystal with luminescent furniture in trendy Galactic Post-Modern, looked out over Kresge 07's wide, scintillating skies. Hundreds of spiring towers rose up through the clouds, flying the flags of the 293 space-faring civilizations allied to The Fifth Council. Vessels sleek and shining slipped through the billowing cloud layers like lunar octopi and whales.

Animated holo-vids of clients filled the crystal sphere's gleaming walls. Central among them all were Illum and Allora, her sleek magenta armor shimmering to scarlet as Illum rubbed horns with her. Other clients smiled and waved gratefully -- Third Pit Lords kicking their unproductive practice of eating mates, enshadowed Seventh-Level Priestesses breaking hereditary engagements to dark star crawlers, Twelfth Legion warbeasts exploring the taboo subject of peace, a chitinous, eight-limbed aardvark analog longing to take a beach vacation.

Copper hovered close, toaster body and arms now cutting edge tech. Its voice issued from below a spherical liquid interface display. "Pleasant conversation with Ronald?"

"Earth business finished."

Copper rattled off congratulations in 293 languages, sonic, subsonic, and far ultra-violet.

Benson brushed a hand through his long, loose hair and smiled.

"It seems I'm a success."

"Incorr-"

"I mean, *we're* a success."

"Correct!"

"I wonder if Mabel would like to open a branch on Kresge 07…"

Jared VanDyke is a deaf librarian who met his true love through Japanese crime dramas. He earned his MFA in Creative Writing from Goddard College, which taught him how to write the fun, quirky, and touching tales featured in Cosmic Roots and Eldritch Shores.
Feel free to contact him at WriteVanDyke@gmail.com regarding any collaboration or information requests.

Tau Ceti, Giovanni Palumbo

Watchers

David A. Gray

Around Husker, the Eyrie was hushed, and the night shift expectant -- high-eyes were fielding ten incursion attempts an hour, subsea moles snaring scores of marine diversion drones.

From the second tier of stations Murphy grinned and shot Husker his usual greeting. "Evening, granny".

She glanced back at him. "Evening, ratings rat."

The stocky blond man grinned. "Rumor has it Anti-Mesh Corps is taking another shot trashloading every mind in the Mesh."

Husker grimaced. "With enhanced neural scrubbers. Twenty years of memory gone in one burst."

Murphy grinned again. "Another run-in with them, bet we'll peak 12 billion shadows global."

"One Flask shootout on top of Security Central vault is enough."

Junior members listened closely to the banter while pretending to be otherwise occupied. Murphy and Husker were the only two of the shift with the particular skillsets needed to Flask, to ride the input tide of millions of minds and datastreams measured in zettabytes, take in all the street-level physical inputs of the smooth as silk flask body, and not end up with an electrical storm for a brain.

"You just got your sights on the Sea Habs," Murphy said. "They missed sinking the Atlantic barriers but they definitely sunk your ratings."

"I've got a special 'welcome back' worked out for the gilled rats next time they try putting a few thousand more square miles under the waves. They want waves – they'll get them."

Husker settled back in her chair with a shrug. He was a ratings rat but she wouldn't want anyone else as a Flask partner. She finished her coffee, shook off her shoes, flexed like a bow, and shot her mind off into the

Mesh. She let the night city currents take her, and the Mesh pulled her to the biggest crowds, the rawest concentrations of emotion. She scanned a football game through 49,989 pairs of eyes, felt the vertigo, brought in noise and low-level emo. A roar, a primal excitement, pouring from every Feed at once.

A sharp tug, over to the east side, where a small crowd gathered around a crash on the maglev highway. She looked down from 23 changing viewpoints as a man named Jonas bled out and died in the wreckage, surrounded by an intense gamut of emotions from horrified to aroused. He gaped in horror at the circle of hungry faces, choking on a torrent of strangers' emotions, desperately reached into gawkers' Feeds for sympathy that didn't come. Husker hesitated, then slid into the dying man's Feed, felt his pain, and whispered.

"I'm Husker," she said, "I'll wait with you, Jonas."

The man heard her as a subliminal murmur, more of a memory than a voice.

"I… know you," he gasped softly. "I shadow you." His mental voice quavered, surreal wonder warring with pain and a growing chill. Am I on?"

"You are live on my Feed," Husker said. "And …" she flickered an icon on in her vision. Jonas' Feed surged from 232 horrified family and friends, as a portion of her own shadows toggled back and forth between Husker's Feed, the emotionally impenetrable, omniscient Feed of a legally sanctioned Watcher, and Jonas' own raw terror, overlaid with bitter thrill at the attention.

"You have engagement just passing 80k," she murmured.

Husker logged onlookers whose appreciation of Jonas' death was the most palpable, cross-filed with other violent and public deaths, got one re-peat pattern, sent a scuttler through the woman's Mesh history, buried a snare in her Feed, and tagged it back to the Eyrie for a trawl. Observing the woman through Jonas' misting eyes, Husker saw her blink, pale, and walk off hurriedly as her Feed merged with official Eyrie Watchers.

Husker drew back from Jonas as the end came, muted the emo, and registered the Feeds coming in on an approaching med-hopper. "Too late," she cast, picking up the medics sense of failure.

She was at 218k, ha bit igh for a pre-shift warmup. She searched for something to make her feel clean and calm before her shift started proper. A street fiddler, playing to a small crowd on a hyperloop platform. They were loving it, marveling at the dancing bow, feet tapping. Husker dialed up the sound and emo, the sense of belonging.

Then one Feed -- a sly hand reaching in to a woman's bag. Husker cast them a "stay put", and of course they fled, trying to dial down their sense input below Mesh level. Too late: Husker had tagged them. This was small, not requiring a Flask; on-ground security would track and apprehend.

Husker took a virtual breath, knew her body back in the Eyrie would be doing the same, and in a heartbeat, was totally immersed. Submerged in the sights, sounds, and feel of 37 million open Feeds. One of these nights she might decide not to come back, just dissolve into the Mesh, like many old Watchers did, leaving behind an empty vessel to be quietly removed from the tower.

She was soaring. She tasted the Feed clusters, focusing on the trademark pattern analysis that had helped her gain a top-ten rating. She strummed a thousand data hooks she was teasing invisibly through the Feeds, snagging the oddest of overlapping events.

There. A sharp-eyed overseer on a crane on the Red Hook pontoon docks had spotted a fleeting movement on a floodlit slab that should have been occupied only by robot lifters. When he'd tried to zoom through the crane's cams, they'd glitched. A request for a repair team, and a check on the dock's pressure sensors had been routed into a dead loop. She gusted into the crane operator's Feed. In the corner of his vision a silhouette darted across a slab slick with ocean spray.

Husker slithered over to the Feed from the pilot of a veetol-bird lifting off the pier. The pilot's vision was darting, shifting randomly. Husker pinged a rote instruction to the pilot's controller: *Suspected F-forward junkie, mandatory bloodworks.* She stabilized the Feed, isolated a glance at the thermal node looking over the cargo pods, ran the grainy fragment through a scrubber and got a flicker of a runner, therma-shielded but visible for a moment as their suit caught the wash from the veetol-bird's engines.

Layering the dock plans with the floodlight cams, cargo pod e-eyes, the crane operator's visual -- nothing. She started an auto-analysis of the 302 people on the boulevard abutting the dock. She filtered out the main focus, patched a dozen backgrounds together, caught a crucial split second as a stealthy figure turned its lope into a confident night-out swagger. No face, just shapes, impressions. Might be Corps.

She ran a check on the whereabouts of the rest of her shift, looking for Murphy. His Feed registered from a mile away atop a glass comm spire looking through it's hi-res sensors. She opened her Feed to him and cast him a standby call in case she needed back-up.

Just say the word Granny. I'll be there.

She cut short a replythe target was off the dock. She followed as it moved onto the street, merging into the stream.

She merged hundreds of citizen Feeds hurrying along the rain-soaked boardwalk, set overlap instructions and queried the six that came back marked anomalous. Three religious exemptions walked together, logged and treble checked against the database. Two shuffling punishment cases, denied the Mesh, alone and insane in the crowd. Husker tagged them as public and interesting just in case, and knew her shadows would track them, happy to be part of the game.

The sixth Feed was an Incognito icon: a higher-up, most definitely not anyone's business. Husker frowned. She paused, and 576k shadows held their breaths. *Too many questions might invite some unhealthy phantom interest in all our Feeds,* Husker cast. A tide of complicit delight and a sudden drop of 24,989 shadows. Husker sent a tiny storm of prepared scuttles after them, with an eye out for patterns.

But since when did I avoid trouble? she cast, pinging multiple "Watcher requesting ID" waves, that pattered off the blank Incognito like raindrops against the Eyrie windows. Like a swarm of hornets they kept trying. She played a composite of the Feeds of a dozen people near the mystery figure, still showing a 360° view with a fuzzy hole in the middle.

"We'll wave goodbye for now," Husker whispered onto her Feed, and hundreds of thousands of shadows laughed, thrilled to be in on the joke. She mentally stepped back from the Incognito.

She fired off a crosslink to the walking style she'd caught a glimpse of. Nothing came up. So either the target was openly mimicking a citizen or was blocking Feeds from picking them up.

Time for the sledgehammer, she cast. And within a heartbeat of that she passed 600k shadows.

She flitted back to the crane operator, logged an over-ride and ordered him to drop a ten-ton pod 50 feet down to the platform. The crash turned every Feed. For a second, they all stopped moving. Except one. *There*: a slim figure in liquid-camo, a face that didn't register in viewers' consciousness. A cutting edge Dazzler then, that fed a thousand changing features a second onto a sensor-adapted face, only punishment cases and religious exemptions would see the true appearance.

I have you, Husker whispered, and her rating soared past a million.

She tagged the figure, setting an auto cascade on the Mesh. The figure bolted. People stopped and stared, or gave chase, their Feeds showing a running blank. Then Feeds started dropping off, evaporating with a flare.

The intruder was using a Zapper on them, and around one in ten wouldn't get up again. Husker' stomach dropped. The Eyrie might call in an orbital, and that would put an end to her Feed.

Husker queried for the nearest Flask, and was routed to one on ready in its booth a block from the end of the pier.

Husker still felt the rush of excitement and fear she'd had with her first decanting. She hit the mental button and with a wrench she was in the Flask, taking in the city through the cyber-frame's senses layered over her Eyrie feed. She hit the street at a run, seeing through the Flask's eyes, feeling rain-slick cobbles under composite feet, smelling the night air, feeling the thrum of the underground mag levs, the wash of electromagnetic energy and the smooth potential of the artificial body she rode.

5.9 million shadows now.

People stared, queried, and joined her Feed.

Husker was almost at the boulevard when the intruder rounded the corner, saw her, and stopped. The Dazzler effect fell away to reveal a slim figure in Shroud. Wired for combat, high-tech insertion with advanced physical kit. Anti-Mesh Corp.

Murphy cast *Backup time?*

Threats of heavy violence and requests for reinforcements always brought increased ratings. *Wouldn't mind it.*

ETA two minutes.

She ran an inventory of her Flask's armament: just stunners, flares, pulses. Nothing that would stop a Shroud.

The imminent threat of Flask destruction was doing her rating no harm: 15 million. But it would mean her own death, if the feedback shock exceeded buffer capacity.

The intruder paced forward slowly. He stopped before her, cleared his visor, and smiled confidently.

"Just so you can see whose killing you," he drawled. "How're your ratings, Watcher? I'm at 20 mill, with a couple mill more in black feeds. You'll die a star!"

Husker threw everything at him before he finished: the night flared incandescent and lightning arced around the invader like a mad halo.

He laughed, and waved a hand, casually. Tiny matter specks ripped holes in the pavement, catching her Flask and throwing it through the flimsy bodywork of a parked bus. Alerts screamed as she slammed against the big slab of the battery charging from a street pad below the vehicle. Her eyes flicked to the indicator, almost fully charged.

Wait for it, she sent to her followers, now an extra ten million of them since careening through the bus.

Updates flashed: an orbital was 100 seconds out, and Murphy had Flasked down close by. She could feel him getting closer in the increasing humming, vibrating feedback loop between the two Flasks.

A spray of flechettes shredded the bus and ripped holes in the Flask's outer armor.

"Kinda pitiful if that's the best show you can put on," she called.

"Wait for the finale. Which is you," he barked. A salvo of hi-ex tore the side off the bus and she scrabbled back along the center aisle. The bus creaked as the Shroud hopped on.

She peered up as he stalked towards her.

"Give me a nice closeup," he crowed, "and smile goodbye."

He raised a bulky arm and Husker detected a thermal flare as tiny fission slivers warmed their missiles.

"That should do it," she said out loud.

He cocked his head to one side. His visor darkened again and he took a cautious step back.

Your showboating might just have got yourself killed, she thought. But then she was thrown tumbling back through the shredded rear wall of the bus as its batteries ruptured and exploded under the force of the timed flares she'd pressed onto them.

When Husker stopped rolling, she looked back through her Flask's stuttering visual sensors. The bus was raining down in fragments. But the intruder was still standing.

He raised his arm and aimed again. "And that's all folks."

"We have you covered! Get down!"

Murphy.

The Shroud swiveled to send a spray of flechettes but Murphy's heavy weaponry left a dark, ragged figure lying amidst flames in the street.

Then Husker registered the "we" and rolled her protesting Flask to its knees, staring towards her colleague.

His shock rifle was just angling away from the still Shroud. And at his side was the shimmering haze of the Incognito, the request hornets still swarming.

Her skin crawled. "Murphy! Look out!"

"'Sokay granny. This is special agent Losowsky. Top level backup."

Husker felt nauseous. She had no weapons left.

"That's right, I'm a very special agent."

The shadowy figure patted Murphy's shoulder, leaving a disc flat against his flask's silver skin.

"Hab disruptor!" Husker said.

Murphy reached for it.

"Touch it and I'll explode it. You don't want to gamble on what the feedback shock does. Relax Murphy. The end is near. It'll feed a viral along the link to Central Mesh. Oh, and a grubber back up to your body in the Eyrie. Soon as I press the switch."

Murphy could see Husker scanning the explosion rubble for a likely projectile. He shrugged at the Incognito. "So toast either way. Got a record audience though... any words?"

"The Sea shall return. It will wash away your Mesh, your cities, your existence."

The Incognito gestured dismissively at the ragged Anti-Mesh Corps Shroud prone in the street. "We tracked this fool's clumsy insertion and took advantage of the distraction. We're infiltrating your Mesh... we can already hide from you in your own cities, mimic your designations." With a sneer down at Husker, the Incognito pulled out a stubby neural pistol. "You had me tagged as a government spook, didn't you?"

Husker's hand closed around a jagged shred of battery casing. Her Flask could hit with speed and deadly accuracy, but before the Incognito could pull the switch on Murphy? Nobody would blame her for killing a deadly agent even though it meant a fellow Watcher's life became collateral damage. It was duty over friendship. The public loved that. She'd be a star. They'd make a vee special. She'd be played by someone fitting the teev's notion of a Watcher -- young, shaved head, sparkling (unnecessary) skull nodes, sculpted musculature tweaks, eyes swirling mercury silver, flippant amd reckless.

"No, I had you tagged as a gilled rat Hab commando." Husker sent the casing flying in one sharp movement. It hit target, slicing through and shattering the limpet as a broad surge from the neural pistol half fried both her and Murphy. They swayed, senses dropping offline one by one.

"Nice. *And the sea shall reclaim you*. *Now...*" the Incognito paused, then juddered.

"About time," Husker grated. "You must have some very fancy tech to have resisted that request wave for so long."

The Incognito's Hab camouflage flickered, went off, and revealed a young woman wrapped in a complex web of tendrils and pin projectors. She looked around in mute, pale anger and shock.

"It contained a little welcome back I devised after you made a fool of me last time," Husker said, feeling her Flask totter, warning icons flashing. "It should be all the way through your systems by now. You'll live, if you're not too wired in, and be a vee villian."

"You couldn't have known," the woman hissed through seizing jaws. "I mimicked Incognito signature perfectly…"

"There is no Incognito in *my* Mesh. So I knew, the moment I couldn't id you."

Husker's Flask juddered, her senses dwindling.

As the cold came, Murphy cast. *98 points global, over 15 billion people watching.*

Great if we survive the neural shock. Ratings rat. As Husker faded out, the netstorm roar of relief, concern, admiration, arousal, carried them off into the dark.

ENDS

"Watchers" © David Gray   First published December 15, 2017 in Cosmic Roots & Eldritch Shores.

David A. Gray is a Scots-born creative director and writer who currently lives in Brooklyn, NYC. His first novel, *Moonflowers,* came out in 2019. He doesn't tweet, and is too private to be a natural with The Facebook, but his Instagram account (david_a-gray) is an obsessive compilation of random things he finds in the streets as he wanders Red Hook and environs. Also, of the real-life locations that end up in his stories and novel.

Artwork: *Tau Ceti,* by Giovanni Palumbo

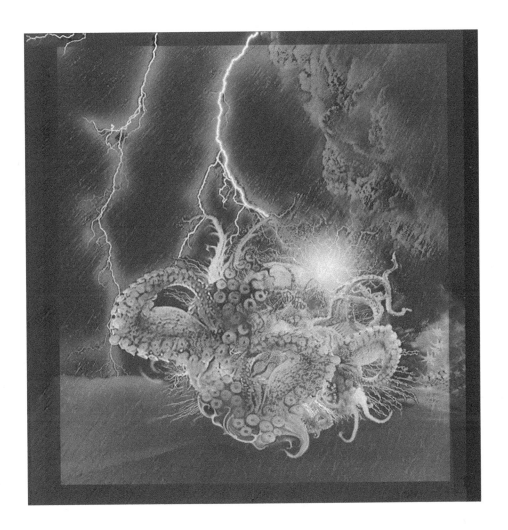

One Good Turn...

Alan K. Baker

Steinbach and Varin stared down at the fizzing nav panel.
Biting his nails, Steinbach mumbled, "So where are we?"
Varin shook her head. "Nav data was corrupted when the system
went down. We could be anywhere between Procyon and Beta Pictoris."
Steinbach clambered across the tilted deck to the viewport. "Oh!"

"What?"

"It's gorgeous – beaches, bars, an advanced dry dock that could put cutting edge everything in this old bucket."

Varin hurried over and looked out to a tortured landscape strewn with bizarrely wind-sculpted boulders and ugly, slump-shouldered hills, spattered and smeared with varying shades of grey. Rain sleeted past the viewport in near-horizontal sheets. Steinbach turned on the external comms and they heard thrumming like metal pellets as the rain drummed the ship's hull, driven by roaring, howling winds. Above the twisted horizon, thick banks of gunmetal clouds seethed like smoke from monstrous fires, sculpted into outrageous shapes by the relentless wind.

Varin swiveled her head slowly and stared motionless at Steinbach through narrowed eyes.

He shrugged. "We don't have the credits for cutting edge scissors even. Just trying to lighten the mood."

"If we had an engineer who wasn't constantly 'lightening' his mood, maybe we wouldn't have gotten shat out of bulkspace into this nameless hellhole."

The commlink crackled and a slurred voice roared. "I heard that! The nav computer failed! It's older than my grandmother. Protocol dropped us into normal spacetime. It's not my fault *where*. Or how. We just didn't have the angular momentum for stable orbit. At least we landed in one piece."

"No, Wayman, we buckled a landing strut. You and Steinbach will be going out to repair it. And looking at the atmosphere…" Varin bent over a console. Sensors tasted the outside air, detected various bacteria and other microscopic organisms, pondered the sundry chemical flavors, and reported air within safe operating parameters. "Oh, look's like the air and rain'll corrode you the first minute out."

Steinbach waved his hands. "Hey, that hill just moved!"

Varin snorted. "'Look, a diversion?'"

"No, really!"

"Sure. Okay, so no corrosives in the air. Nothing to compromise hull integrity or airlock seals. Or suits. But winds about Beaufort scale 8, and temp about 4°C – a picnic."

"Funny, Varin. I'll go check the cargo and prep the suits."

"And don't test any of Wayman's 'rocket fuel' on the way."

Steinbach slunk off.

Varin looked again through the viewport. She was just turning away when something caught her eye. She leaned forward, face almost touching the port. She could have sworn one of the hills *did* move... growing briefly and then diminishing again, like a grey, warped balloon slowly inflating and deflating ... or a lung breathing in and out.

She shook her head. Nah. *A trick of the wind and rain.*

Steinbach descended the narrow companionway to the cargo hold, thumbed the control stud and waited while the hatch creaked open in fits and starts. Like a multitude of other things on the ship, repairs awaited luck deciding to be on their side for a change.

Positive attitude, Ray, he told himself. *She'll get us out of this.*

He didn't like to admit it, but Freya Varin was definiftely the brains of their operation. It was Freya who had negotiated the fee for hauling the consignment of CO_2 scrubbers to the private research station on Sidaris; she had filed their flight plan with Procyon Traffic Control, coding the entry to fool the AI into thinking their ship was carrying duty-free cargo. She had hustled them up and down the Orion Arm for the last ten years, keeping their small enterprise afloat.

Contrary to their usual luck, the cargo was in good shape: no slippages or breakages, the sturdy duralene containers still sealed and strapped down properly. He checked and prepped the EV suits, then headed aft toward the engine room to smooth things over with Wayman: the drive probably *was* older than his grandmother. And maybe there was time for a test of that 'rocket fuel' Wayman brewed.

Varin was at the viewport, stock still, staring out at the landscape, when Steinbach ambled back im.

"Varin?"

"Come look at this."

"Okay, I don't... ... oh... It's moving! I told you it moved! Why the hell is it moving, Freya?"

"I thought it was a trick of the wind and rain, but it happened again, and now..."

And now the hill, perhaps a hundred meters distant, was pulsating in a way that made Steinbach's skin crawl. It was rising, falling, expanding, contracting, quivering now and then, as if it were...

"Alive!" Steinbach shouted. "It's alive!"

"Indigenous life form," Varin whispered.

As they watched in appalled fascination, the sides of the pulsating hill began changing color. Weirdly prismatic hues flashed, bleeding into each other, combining and exploding in bizarre flowerings that flowed together like glowing liquid.

"It looks like..." Varin hesitated.

"What?"

"Chromatophores."

"Cro... ?"

"Light-reflecting cells with colors that the organism can change. Most planets with life have them."

"So why has it started to change color? Has it *noticed* us.? Does it... want to *eat* us?"

A vision swam into his mind of the hill oozing across the boulder-strewn landscape and engulfing the ship, dissolving the metal, reaching the soft meat inside...

And then he thought of the ship's only armament, an ageing plasma cannon. "Is the cannon online?"

Varin checked. "Yes. Why?"

"So we can blast it."

"You want to attack it."

"Hell yes, I want to attack it! Before it attacks us!"

"Without knowing if it's hostile. Without knowing if it's even capable of hurting us. Without knowing if there are more of them out there, and how they'd react to one of their buddies getting fried?"

Steinbach shook his head. "So you want to just wait for it to... to... do whatever it's going to do? And with our luck you know what it's going to do."

"It may be trying to communicate," said Varin. "Some animals use chromatophores to show anger, fear, contentment... the desire to mate."

"I really wish you hadn't mentioned that last one. We should blast it."

Varin sighed. "We're not going to kill something just because it looks weird. How about you just complete the diagnostics on the ship's systems and see if there's anything else we need to worry about."

Steinbach nodded glumly and turned to finish his work, while Varin continued to repair the panels and observe the 'hill'. The strange shapes and colors continued to chase each other across its surface. If that *was* the creature trying to communicate, what might the message be?

Welcome to my world?

Stay the hell away from me?

What do you taste like?

She gave silent, ironic thanks to Steinbach for that last possibility; and grudgingly conceded that yes, it was a possibility they would be wise to keep in mind.

She looked at the hills farther off, too obscured by wind and rain to tell if they were like this one.

How many of you are there? And what are you? A single, massive organism? A colony of smaller ones, like coral?

She glanced at Steinbach, who was bent over a large display screen, muttering to himself. Then she fired up the ship's ground-penetrating radar, angling the transmitter towards the hill.

The big survey ships had elaborate and sophisticated sensor tech, but even after centuries basic GPR was still a trustworthy method of subsurface imaging. And basic was all Varin and Steinbach could afford.

The GPR completed its cycle, and Varin stared at the results.

The hill had a massively complex internal structure. She enhanced the image as much as the software would allow, but the intricacy of the hill's interior went beyond the GPR's imaging capability. All the same, she could discern countless filaments, pipes, nodules and fractal-like shapes hidden within the object's huge, mounded bulk.

She poured over the image, noting three roughly spherical structures, each nestled within a branching network of delicate filaments.

Brains? Does that thing have three brains? Or... stomachs?

The screen showed thick tendrils extending into the surface regolith from the object's gently-curved underside. Drawing nutrients? Like a plant analog... or fungus... There might be thousands or millions of these things dotted across the planet's surface.

Still pondering, Varin went back to the viewport. She gasped.

An opening had appeared in the side of the hill. It was long and thin and vertical, and fringed with delicate, quivering fronds of pink and purple. Varin gazed at it in fascination.

It reminded her of...

Unconsciously, her hand drifted slowly toward her crotch.

Something appeared in the opening, widening it, slowly squeezing its way through...

"Nebulas!"

She hadn't heard Steinbach come across the flight deck to stand beside her, and his voice in her ear made her start.

"It's giving birth!" he said with a mixture of wonder and disgust.

"That's what it looks like," Varin said.

A multicolored glob flopped to the ground in front of the hill. And the vertical orifice that had disgorged it closed and resealed itself.

But the glob wasn't just a glob. There were flailing tentacles and clusters of slowly waving cilia, twitching, frond-like antennae, and black, glassily shining nodules that might be eyes. The thing appeared to be completely encased in a glistening, transparent membrane, like a birth caul. It was still connected to the parent entity by a thick, pulsating cord.

"What a nightmare," Steinbach whispered.

"No," Varin said. "Just *very* differentn from us. Did you complete the diagnostics?"

"Yeah. We're in better shape than I thought. Internal framing is slightly warped, but integrity's at 98.73 percent. Autonomous flight systems were knocked out by the energy of the impact. It'll take maybe an hour for them to reboot and auto diagnose..."

"What about the nav system?"

"Wayman's making headway. He's actually a pretty decent engineer..."

"When he's not drinking what he brews. How long before it's up and running?"

"A couple of hours, maybe."

"Okay, so in two hours or so we'll be spaceworthy. It may not be the best idea to go outside and repair that buckled strut."

"Amen to that. You think the lifters can compensate?"

Varin looked down at the tilted deck. "We're not *too* far off center."

Steinbach looked out the viewport. "Um..."

"What?"

"Your little friend's coming toward us."

Still trailing its umbilical cord, the hideous glob had lifted itself up on several tentacles and was slowly approaching, cilia and antennae twitching and whipping back and forth, its black, glassy eye nodules apparently fixed steadily on the ship. It wavered and paused frequently, lowering itself to the ground and then rising again on wobbling tentacles, moving unsteadily from side to side.

"It looks as if it's weak," Varin said.

"Well," said Steinbach. "if it's only just been born...Maybe we could give it a quick blast from the starboard lifter. Just to let it know not to come any closer."

Varin stared at him. "It's just been born and you want to incinerate it?"

"Just *warn* it."

"It's flesh. We don't know what *kind*, but flesh all the same. Even a half-second burst would turn it to ash."

The glob was now within ten meters of the ship. It appeared to hold back for a few seconds, then continued.

"It's going to try to get in," Steinbach said. "It's just been born, and it's hungry, and it knows we're in here!"

"Shut up, Ray."

"But--"

"Shut up and let me think!"

The glob had now moved out of sight beneath the lower edge of the viewport.

"It's under the ship," said Varin. "External cameras online."

They threw a few switches, and the main viewplate flared to life. They could see the glob approaching the buckled landing strut.

"It's going to try to get in through the strut well." Steinbach turned to Varin. "You should have let me blast the son of a black hole."

"It's a newborn," said Varin.

"It's at least two meters across!"

Wayman's voice came through on the commlink. "Guys... um... I've got some bad news."

"Oh, that's different!" said Varin. "What is it?"

"Looks like I was a little wrong about the nav computer. The ai just underwent a cascade collapse."

Varin and Steinbach looked at each other.

"And that means it can't be fixed? Does the entire matrix have to be replaced?" asked Varin.

"It's fried. The quantum pathways have completely de-cohered. It couldn't even be repaired in a dry dock." He paused. "So ... um ... how are things going up there?"

"Great," Steinbach replied. "We've got a large and probably hostile alien life form trying to get in through one of the landing strut wells."

"Really?"

"Yeah, really."

"But why doesn't it use the hatch?"

Varin was thinking furiously. How to gently make it back off the hull... One of the few things spacecraft had in common with ocean-going vessels was hulls had to be periodically cleansed of remnant magnetic fields.

Maritime vessels also picked up magnetism, from the planet itself. Spacecraft accrued it through plasma turbulence in the electrically charged soup of ions and electrons that permeated space. A strong enough magnetic field could interfere with a spacecraft's electrical systems, so...

She turned to Steinbach. "Are the degaussing coils still operational?"

He frowned at her. "You want to degauss the hull? *Now?*"

Varin waited for the penny to drop.

Steinbach let out a slow "Aaaah." He checked. "Yes, for once we're in luck."

"Start with a short pulse and low current. A mild shock. *Mild.*"

Steinbach set the current to 0.01 amps.

"Ray! Something that wouldn't be painful to a human."

He shrugged, reset the dial, and flipped the switch.

Varin looked at the main viewplate. The creature had twisted several tentacles around the landing strut, as if to start climbing. She saw it react as the degaussing field pulsed. It quivered, appeared to hesitate, and then resumed its efforts.

"Increase the amperage," she told Steinbach. "Increments of point one. Another pulse."

Steinbach complied. "Anything?"

She shook her head. "Again."

Another pulse, stronger.

The creature released its grip on the landing strut.

Varin smiled. The smile faded as it threw even more tentacles around the strut.

"By the way, even if this works, we're still down one nav computer. We can't enter bulkspace without it and we're stuck out here in the middle of nowhere."

"Once we're off planet, we'll send a distress signal and wait to be picked up by Procyon Search/Rescue or Traffic Control."

"What!?" said Steinbach. "They can search ships in distress. And we've got a hold full of CO_2 scrubbers not on the manifest. That's heavy fines; maybe license suspension."

"Not if we dump the cargo and vaporize it."

"So we'll have to pay for the rescue team, and refund our haulage fee..."

"And we'll have to reimburse them for the scrubbers," added Varin.

"We'll have to take out a loan on the ship," said Steinbach.

"And, we haven't paid off the last one."

Wayman's voice boomed directly in back of them. "Do I still get paid?"

Steinbach jumped. "Why aren't you... fixing something?"

"Nothing fixable left, and if aliens are coming I don't want to be the guy left alone getting eaten."

Varin eyed him as he wavered slightly and stared out the port. "You're safe unless they like their food soaked in rocket fuel."

Steinbach increased amperage by point zero one and gave the glob another jolt... "It's clinging on even tighter!

"Maybe it *feeds* on electrical current."

"You mean we're making it stronger?" Steinbach shouted.

"If it's energy it wants," said Wayman, "there's a hell of a lot more in our batteries than in the degaussing coils. They could drink us dry, and we'll never get off this rock."

"Then let's hope we're giving them all they want," said Varin. "Just keep increasing the amperage.

She watched closely as pulses of current surged across the ship's outer hull and undercarriage. Yet still the creature kept its grip, quivering and pulsating in downright unspeakable ways. She noticed that the umbilical cord had also begun to pulsate, as if it were feeding electrical energy back to its parent.

There were many extremophiles across the Arm, metabolizing some truly outrageous chemicals in environments lethal to most carbon-based life forms. Bacterioids that consumed and excreted electrons. But they were usually microscopic. Varin had never heard of life forms of this size with such abilities.

With each increase in amperage the thing threw more tentacles around the strut, and the umbilical cord pulsated more quickly.

"Come on," Varin whispered. "Eat your fill and leave us alone!"

Something moved just at the edge of the camera's field of view. Varin angled it over, and watched in dismay as another entity joined the first. From the viewport Wayman announced the hill had disgorged a third glob, which was also making its way toward the ship.

Freya ran another cycle on the GPR, and saw that the hill no longer contained the three spherical structures she had seen earlier.

They weren't brains, and they weren't stomachs. Were they offspring? Or maybe ... occupants? Was the hill a creature that had just given birth, or was it a dwelling? But if the first creature was pumping energy back to it through the umbilical cord...

"It's a ship," she said.

"Are you crazy?" Steinbach laughed. "How could a glob covered in tentacles build a ship?"

"What's so crazy about a life form nothing like us, using ships nothing like ours? We haven't explored even a billionth of the galaxy, Ray. There are probably billions of planets with life on them. We have no idea what's really out there."

The second entity clung to the landing strut with equal tenacity. The third disappeared from view. Varin searched the other external cameras.

"Oh no."

"What?" demanded Steinbach.

"The third one's up on the hull. It's at the main airlock."

"It's messing with the controls!" said Wayman. "It's trying to open the hatch!"

"Yah, we're breaking out the plasma pistols," said Steinbach, "Or would you rather I just went and waved hello?"

Varin sighed. "Go ahead. But set the plasma at minimum -- if those things eat energy, I'm not sure how much good they'll do. And you'd better get going. It's just opened the outer hatch."

Steinbach and Wayman moved slowly along the corridor towards the main airlock.

The inner hatch opened with a quiet hiss. The glob slithered in.

Shouting incoherently at the top of their voices, they fired.

The creature stopped, and absorbed the glowing red bolts as if they were rays of gentle sunshine, and began to move toward them.

Wayman dropped his gun. Steinbach set force to maximum and shot again. The glob continued toward them. Wayman held his hip flask out to it, mouth open in a rictus of terror.

Steinbach ran, yanking Wayman along with him. They nearly fell as the deck lurched. Nebulas! he thought. *They're toppling the ship!*

Varin's voice came through on the commlink. "Ray! Wayman! Don't shoot it. The two outside just repaired the landing strut."

"What?"

"Notice we're level now?"

They stopped running and looked down at the deck.

"The globs... extruded things... tools, I guess. They realigned all of the pistons--"

"That's not possible."

"But it happened. Maybe they're enhanced, biomechanical... Where's the one that got in?"

Steinbach took a peek around the corner. He saw his own reflection in one of the glob's black eye-nodules, about an inch away from his face.

"Not far," he whimpered.

"Get out of its way and let it do whatever it's going to do."

"What if what it's going to do is eat us?"

"They consume energy, not flesh. We gave them what they needed, Ray," she said. "Now, maybe they're giving us what *we* need."

The creature moved slowly through the ship, tentacles slapping on the deck plates, antennae twitching and quivering, as if tasting the air...

Or maybe, thought Varin as she joined the others following the glob's progress, *looking* for something?

"It's heading for the stern," whispered Steinbach.

"Toward the drive section," Varin replied. "And the nav computer."

"A nav computer isn't fixed like a landing strut," said Wayman.

"All the same," said Varin, "let's just leave It be."

The glob continued through to the drive section. It paused to test, then suck dry, the contents of an ill-hidden distiller, ignoring the strangled gurgles of protest from Wayman. Then it went straight for the squat drive cylinder at the center of the room. The cylinder's screens and status lights were dark.

The creature settled its bulk down onto the deck, its antennae and cilia waving back and forth slowly, gracefully, like ribbons of seaweed in a gentle ocean current. It extruded delicate pseudopods which split apart and revealed a bewilderingly complex network of glittering filaments.

As they watched with increasing amazement, the creature's filaments extended out to and penetrated the side of the cylinder. The creature shifted a little, and its eye-nodules turned this way and that, as if pondering what it had found.

"It didn't even open an inspection panel," said Wayman. "Those things went straight through the duralene casing."

"Like some kind of molecular manipulators," Varin mused.

After a few moments, the computer's display panels and status lights winked on. The glob rose up on its tentacles and left the drive section.

Steinbach and Wayman rushed to the computer and stared down at the displays.

"Freya... the quantum pathways have re-cohered... the glob *fixed* it."

"Re-plot a course for Sidaris," Varin said. "We're back in business!"

"No. Wait," Steinbach said. It didn't fix it. It made it better."

"Better?"

"Better than cutting edge better. And... and not just the nav. All our systems We're better than... anything out there!"

They followed the glob back to the main airlock. As the inner door slid shut, they all called out, "Thank you!"

The glob ignored them.

<>

<>

<>

The Palkamshett, the Maderaal, and the Almugota watched from the planet's surface as the freighter fired its lifters and began to rise into the stormy sky.

<A noble species,> said the Almugota over their subvocal link.

<But a strange one,> replied the Palkamshett. <Difficult to believe that such a limited physical form -- with a primitive endoskeleton, if such a thing can be believed! -- should be capable of constructing a star-walker.>

<Star-walker?> said the Maderaal. <That thing is barely a star crawler; but I concede your point. All the same, their level of intelligence is rather low, wouldn't you say?>

<I would remind you that their level of intelligence saved us,> said the Almugota. <Although I am not certain how they knew we were stranded, that our energy reserves had become depleted, or knew how to replenish them for us. Their sensing technology would appear to be unequal to the task. How did they know what we needed, or that we could gather it from the outer skin of their star-walker?>

<A mystery,> declared the Palkamshett. <But they gave it freely, and liberally, that much is certain. Perhaps we shall meet their kind again, in the fullness of time, and a great and long-lasting friendship will develop between our species.>

<Perhaps,> said the Maderaal. <They did share a very refreshing liquid chemical concoction whose formula I have stored for future use. But I suspect their physical repulsiveness will be difficult to come to terms with.>

<I take it that their simple artificial navigator was easy to repair,> said the Almugota.

<A trifling matter,> replied the Maderaal, <as easy, doubtless, as the repair of the the outer damage.>

<Indeed,> affirmed the other two.

<And what of this world? Our first acquaintance with it has been rather unfortunate, but there is no denying its beauty.>

<I believe we should certainly report it as fit for colonization,> said the Palkamshett.

<Agreed,> said the Almugota. <I shall be sorry to leave here, and fully intend to return soon, for it is indeed an exquisite world.>

END

"One Good Turn" © Alan K. Baker. First published April 27, 2021 in Cosmic Roots & Eldritch Shores.

Alan K. Baker is a British expat living on Florida's Gulf Coast. He's published six novels with independent UK presses, including *The Lighthouse Keeper*, a supernatural thriller inspired by the real Flannan Isles mystery; the Blackwood and Harrington Steampunk mysteries; and *The Martian Falcon*, a Dieselpunk noir adventure. His latest novel, the SF thriller *Dyatlov Pass*, was published by Lume Books last year. His short fiction has appeared in Analog.

Boomerang Zone

Robert Dawson

"It's not that simple," said Melissa Pratt, coaxing a hex nut into place with fingers made clumsy by her pressure suit. She floated, a meter from the space station *Myriad*, steadying herself against the space scooter's mooring cradle. "Scheduling a wedding isn't easy. Pass the twelve-mill wrench?" She reached out a hand to Declan Adair.

Days before, the anti-meteor lasers had missed a pebble smaller than a pea. It had struck the parked scooter with the energy of an armor-piercing bullet. Now they were awaiting replacement parts from Earth, and working extra shifts in the meantime to fix what they could.

"Yeah, Pratt. Sure." He held the wrench handle while she snapped the lanyard around her wrist. "Your sister knew you had leave coming up, and she still planned her wedding for while you were off planet. Sounds like a cop-out to me."

Pratt began to tighten the nut. "How?"

"Think about it. This way she doesn't have to tell you not to bring Suzanne. She wouldn't want the bridesmaids getting lesbian cooties, would she?"

Damn him! "Ahhh, she probably thought she was doing me a favor. Getting me out of a bind. There. Last one."

"Good enough. Race you back to the airlock."

"No way. And use the safety line, okay?"

Most of the *Myriad's* hull was cluttered with solar panels, telescopes, anti-meteor lasers, cooling fins, and unidentifiable boxes jumbled together. Obsolete experiments were rarely removed: to ship them back to Earth, or even incinerate them on a re-entry orbit, would have used precious fuel. But a rough rectangle around the scooter cradle was kept clear. Even the network of safety cables did not extend into the landing zone.

"It's only twenty meters."

She bit back a sharp response. "We've been out here for six hours. A few more minutes won't hurt."

"Nervous?"

"No!" *Yes*, she thought, *of course I'm nervous. Space is big and merciless and you don't get second chances. But if I told you that, you'd never let me forget it.*

"We're astronauts, not zero-gee car mechanics. And we need to keep in practice. In case of mishaps, you know?" But he smiled and clipped onto the thin synthetic cable and launched himself toward the metal forest.

Pratt clenched her fists, then tried to relax and admire the fat blue crescent of Earth, its twilit inner edge soft, its outer edge hard and bright.

"Damn!" Adair's voice was harsh. "It won't shut off!"

He was attempting to slap himself on the back, perhaps hoping to unstick the valve, as he accelerated towards a rack of solar panels. But he collided with a strut, awkwardly, shoulder-first. Pratt winced at the crunch on her radio. Then there was silence. The solar panel canted drunkenly. And, beyond it, Adair was still moving, tumbling like a dropped doll toward the vast bulk of Earth. The safety line, cut on some sharp edge, drifted in a loose arc.

"Adair! Adair! Can you hear me?" she called. There was no answer. She switched channels. "Mayday, Mayday, Mayday! *Myriad*, this is Pratt –

Adair's thruster has malfunctioned. His safety line is broken. Approximate vector, Earthward. His radio has been damaged. Over."

She kept her eyes on the receding figure of Adair, alternately brighter and dimmer as he rotated.

The watch officer's voice crackled in her ears. "Pratt, return to the airlock immediately. We have Adair on radar and visual, and are trying to read his suit GPS remotely."

"I say again, his suit radio is damaged. GPS may not be possible." Her eyes lingered on Adair. Was he conscious? Could he get his thruster working again? Did he have enough propellant to get back? She strained her eyes to follow the distant speck. Was his course changing? He seemed to be moving across the face of the earth, towards the middle of the disc, still receding.

"Pratt, this is *Myriad*. Return to the airlock, ASAP."

The tiny white spot shrank to nothing.

Pratt floated behind Li Chang, peering anxiously at the video screen and trying not to drift over into the Old Lady, aka Station Commander Isabella Verdi.

"Zoom that and run it again, Chang," ordered Verdi, her voice kept neutral.

The pattern of glowing lines expanded. "Looks as if he's using his steering thrusters," Chang said. "That blast must have drained his main tank."

"He wasn't even trying to get back," said Pratt. "He just accelerated towards Earth." *Trying to end it more quickly? No, Adair was a fighter.*

"That's it!" Chang said. "He's trying to get into the boomerang zone! Maybe there's a chance."

"Boomerang zone?" asked Pratt.

Chang looked at her. "You didn't do the weapon systems course, did you?"

Pratt shook her head and shrugged. A 2034 ruling of the International Space Commission had granted space stations limited anti-piracy defenses, without expecting they'd ever need to be used. For reasons of economics and physics, piracy couldn't make the tramsition from ocean waters and science fiction to reality. Adair and Chang had taken the weapons training course anyhow, and spent hours playing with the simulated attack responses while the rest of the class studied air plant maintenance, the fire control simulator, and hydroponics.

"Well," Chang continued. "Orbits are periodic. Say you throw a wrench off a satellite, its new orbit and the satellite's orbit both keep passing through the point where you threw it."

"But they don't come back at the same time."

"Not usually,. For some directions the wrench comes back too early, for others too late. But in between there are directions where it will come back at the right time and clang into your hull! It's first-year calculus, the intermediate value theorem. Our instructor called it the boomerang zone. The math is messy for high velocities, but at Adair's speed the sweet spot's about ninety degrees to the orbit."

"Has anyone ever been rescued this way?" asked Verdi, gazing at the viewport.

"We've never lost anybody before. The boomerang zone's just where the instructor said not to fire missiles. Not a good direction to throw trash, either."

"But you mean we can rescue him?" Pratt asked, trying to keep the tight tension out of her voice.

"Slow down, Pratt," Verdi said. "Adair aimed for the boomerang zone, but that doesn't mean he made it. Chang, have you been able to get a otten a fix on him yet?"

Chang's voice was slow. "Yes. Yes, I have a fix."

"And?"

"He came pretty close. Maybe twenty meters per second Earthward, and only a bit more than one forward. Either his suit navigation system is still working, or he's one lucky guy. I've got the computer predicting his relative position." The stereo screen showed a circle, feathered with green vectors. One red arrow crept along the circle, growing longer as it moved.

"How far is he now?" asked Verdi.

"About eighty-seven kilometers," Chang answered. "Still increasing at a few hundred meters per minute."

"*Merda!* Too far. Without the scooter, we cannot go there."

"But he gets closer again. Look." Fingers danced across keyboard, and the shorter arrows turned blue. "In about an hour, he'll get within twenty-five kilometers. That's our only chance. With an extended-range suit thruster, I think we can do it."

Pratt's stomach knotted. *Maybe it could happen.* Her left arm ached. She realized that she was holding the grab bar in a death grip, and tried to relax.

Verdi chewed on her lower lip. "Does he have enough air?"

Chang thought for a moment. "It's going to be tight. He's a big guy.

He went out seven hours ago, our orbit is a hundred twenty-seven minutes. He's got a Mark Six suit?"

"Yes," said Pratt.

"Eight hours air. If he stays very calm, doesn't breathe too hard, there's probably enough. And once somebody gets there they can give him more oxygen."

"What about thrusters? We don't keep many of the extended-range thrusters now that we have the Scooter."

Chang tapped the keys. "We used four with the scooter repair. One left, twenty on order. Plenty of short-range, but there's no way to change or refuel them outside."

"All right, Chang, we'll try." said Verdi. "Run ballistics for Orlov's body mass – he's the next shift and has enough EVA experience. I'll page him."

"Can I go?" said Pratt. "I have as much EVA as Orlov does, and I weigh less."

The commander cupped her chin in her hand and looked at Pratt speculatively, as if trying to find a reason to turn her down. Finally she sighed and shrugged. "Okay. Pratt will go. Pratt, you'll need a freshly charged suit, and mine's the only other one in your size. Chang, calculate mass for my suit: Mark Four size small, extended-range thrusters with full fuel. And Pratt, remember, you're doing this under instrumental guidance. No second guessing."

Ten minutes later, Pratt was struggling into Verdi's space suit, while Verdi held it to stop her drifting into the suit racks. The inside of the suit had the usual odors: sweat, air-pump lubricant, and the harsh chemical smell of the cleaning solution. And something else, lemony and floral – the Old Lady's soap? Pratt heard a far-away voice and hastily switched on the suit's external microphone.

"...already worked a long shift. Andrei could do it."

"No." *When she'd came out in the second week of Basic, half her family said pray to God for a cure, the other half told her see a psychiatrist. Adair just said 'You're into girls, huh? Good choice!' and slapped her on the back.*

"He's my partner," she said shortly, and looked at the head-up display. The suit was ready.

"I see." The Commander glanced at the clock. "Time then to go bring him back. Remember, Chang and the computer will talk you through everything. Do exactly what they tell you. You won't have reserve propellant for seat-of-the-pants flying."

Pratt undogged the inner airlock door. Through the thick fabric of the suit, she felt the Old Lady's hand on her shoulder.

"Good luck, Pratt. *In bocca al lupo!*"

You didn't work with Verdi without learning the response to that.

"*Crepi!*" Pratt said, and pulled herself into the steel coffin.

Chang's voice crackled urgently in her ear. "Pratt, this is *Myriad*. You're drifting. Please correct. Over."

The flight path indicator in her HUD was flashing red against the brilliant tapestry of stars, the crosshairs off-center in the circle.

"Wilco." The thrusters hissed, and after a few seconds the rebellious indicator turned back to green. She looked at the propellant gauge; it still read eighty-six percent. But that was misleading; on the trip out thrusters were only moving her own sixty kilo mass and the suit. On the return trip they would be pushing more than twice that load. In this case mass was a liability to an astronaut.

Adair didn't see it that way, of course. The way he saw it, the meek could inherit the earth if they wanted it, but space belonged to hard-driving, practical-joking alpha males; and if it took a bit more fuel to lift them, that's what fuel was for.

No, that wasn't fair. He was there when it mattered. Like when a drunk driver knocked Suzanne off her bike... *the hospital had phoned late at night, Suzanne was unconscious in the ICU. She'd asked Adair for a ride to the nearest Greyhound station, told him why, and he just handed her the keys to his Mustang, his baby, fifty years old and still looking new. But she couldn't drive an old standard, and he'd rolled his eyes, said Neil Armstrong would be turning in his grave, then shrugged and drove her the seven hours, stayed with her 'til the doctor had said Suzanne would be okay, and drove her back to base again.*

The radio broke in. "Stand by to kill thrusters in fifteen seconds."

"Wilco. Out." Her instincts screamed for more acceleration, to get back there as fast as possible. But following the flight plan would get her to the point of closest approach at the right time. Patience! She found the palm switch and waited.

"Kill thrusters in five, four, three, two, one. Cut." Sudden silence.

"Turn yourself around and prepare for deceleration in approximately two minutes. Out."

Will he have enough air? she wondered. *Will he stay calm? Would I? If it were me I'd be praying.* But Adair was a stubborn son of a bitch. He'd fight. If he ever prayed – which didn't seem likely – she knew it wouldn't be when he needed a favor.

She turned herself with tiny puffs of the steering thrusters. The stars wheeled around her, Earth coming up on her left. She located the space station, a tiny irregular blob of light overhead, in Taurus. Isolation washed over her like an icy wave; she fought it down before it could turn to fear.

"Pratt, this is *Myriad*. Stand by to decelerate. And be careful, you've been using propellant slightly faster than predicted. Out."

The display showed eighty-four percent. She could do it on that. She would have to, she thought grimly. On command, she triggered the main thruster. The suit pressed gently on her feet, buttocks, and underarms, maybe a twentieth of her Earth weight. The propellant level dropped slowly, inexorably. Seventy-nine... seventy-eight...

"Pratt, this is Myriad. Look down. You should have visual contact." She looked towards her feet; a blue ring swam up into view of her head-up display, static against the moving glass, as if projected from the phantom floor she felt beneath her soles. In the middle of the ring was a white dot, slowly brightening. She flicked the radio to suit-to-suit with her chin.

"Adair, this is Pratt. Do you read me? Over." There was no response. She called again, her throat tight with fear. Then she remembered his radio was dead, and relaxed a little.

The white dot grew into the familiar shape of a space suit and drifted slowly past her, maybe fifty meters away. More seconds of maneuvering, and she had matched position and velocity. She grabbed Adair's arm, and turned him so she could see through his faceplate. One side of his face was in ink-black shadow, the other ghostly behind the coated glass. The blood-oxygen gauge beside his faceplate was in the low yellow; his suit's reserve was near zero.

She put her faceplate against his so sound could travel between their helmets, and raised her voice. "Hey, Rocket Man. The Old Lady sent me to bring you in for flogging." She clipped a linking strap onto his suit.

His eyes opened. "What kept you?" A long, hungry breath. "An' why aren't you on a safety line?" One arm went around her shoulder in a feeble half-embrace.

"You idiot." She was not going to cry. Not in a space suit. She changed channels. "*Myriad*, this is Pratt. I've got him. He's alive, and he's conscious. Initiating oxygen transfer. Out."

She put her faceplate against Adair's again. "I'm going to get you some air." She tugged on his shoulder, turning him to get at the top of his life support system. He grimaced at her touch: she let go and mumbled unheard apologies. *Broken shoulder?* His suit suggested that the impact must have been bad: the radio antenna was sheared cleanly off, the sheet metal housing of the life support system was badly dented, and the emergency oxygen socket had almost been knocked inside the housing.

She tried plugging the connector of her suit's buddy hose into the socket: it went in about half way and jammed. She applied more force, bracing Adair with one hand and pressing the connector with the other, and it clicked into place. There was a vicious hiss, and her suit's oxygen reserve came up in flashing red on the HUD, the minutes counting down so fast that she could hardly read them. Five hours, four hours thirty, four hours… Shouldn't pressure equalize soon? She looked at Adair's suit status display. What was his reserve up to?

Nothing was changing.

Her skin grew tight. *Please, no!* But there was no other explanation. The tube must have broken when he hit the strut. A safety valve somewhere had protected him from immediate death, but the break was venting her precious oxygen uselessly into space. She disconnected the buddy hose.

"Sorry, Adair. It's not working."

His voice was almost inaudible. "Then let's get the hell out of here."

"*Myriad*… This is Pratt. Adair's suit is damaged. Unable to transfer oxygen. I've lost some oxygen trying. Over."

"Your propellant level?"

She swallowed. "I'm at seventy-three percent."

"Good for now. But you've got very little margin for error. Adjust your heading and stand by to accelerate in two minutes."

"Wilco."

She turned herself until the crosshairs were green again, then braced herself against Adair, his suited body huge and awkward in her arms.

"Accelerate, full thrust, in five. Four. Three. Two. One. Now."

She started her thrusters. The familiar feeling of weight came back, but this time her arms were full with a load bigger than herself. Under the slow push of the thruster, Adair weighed no more than a baby; but she weighed even less, and his weight was in front of her, tipping her off balance into a slow helpless forward somersault. The stars began to drift upward: the HUD crosshairs followed them and turned red.

The radio crackled. "Pratt! This is *Myriad*. You've gone off course.

Correct immediately. Over."

Sweat stung her eyes as she adjusted steering thrusters, attempting to cancel the torque. Adair's spacesuit twisted on the shackle, as if they were wrestling in slow motion. The thrusters hissed behind her. Caught between, she tried to balance, finally found her equilibrium. She took a deep breath – with a pang of guilt that she could not share it – and chinned the transmit switch. "I'm back on course."

"Okay," said Chang. "But I'm concerned about your propellant level. You used a lot just now, and you're still burning it faster than the computer predicted. You're at fifty-two percent. Can you balance without the steering thrusters?"

She ignored the fist of ice closing around her heart. "Best I can do."

"Change in flight plan; you're going to coast on this leg too, to keep a little reserve to maneuver when you get back. You'll just be a little later."

"How much later?"

"About an extra fifteen minutes."

"Wilco."

For another eternity she tried to mediate between the stubborn push of the thrusters and Adair's randomly moving weight. He didn't seem to be conscious, but every so often he jerked weakly, like Suzanne sometimes did when falling asleep. Steering was like balancing a peacock feather on her finger – it required almost no force, but if her attention wavered for an instant the errors would cascade.

Ahead of her, the space station came into view, almost imperceptibly growing closer. Every so often, as Adair moved around, she glimpsed his slack blue lips. His blood-oxygen gauge was dropping into the red.

Finally, the order came through. "Stand by to kill your thrusters in thirty seconds. Over."

She swallowed. "*Myriad*, this is Pratt. That's a negative. Adair is hardly breathing. We do not have time for the slower trajectory."

The next voice she heard was the Commander's. "This is Verdi. You are ordered to cut thrusters immediately. Acknowledge. Over."

She ignored it. She was out here on her own. The laws of physics made her master and commander of her one-woman craft until she was back through the airlock. After that the Old Lady could ream her out for disobeying a direct order, confine her to quarters, and send her back to Earth in disgrace; but not until then.

So how fast could she get back? When she'd turned around, the tank had been at seventy-three percent. She could use half of that to accelerate, but no more; then she would need the other half to match velocity again. And she had better keep fuel to get to the airlock with. She looked at the gauge: forty-five percent. Just then it dropped to forty-four.

"*Myriad*, this is Pratt. Killing thrust at thirty-eight percent. Request recomputed flight plan. Over."

Chang's voice, in the background: "Commander?"

The Commander, even more faintly: "Give it to her." Did she sound angry?

Chang, full volume: "Pratt, this is Myriad. Recomputing. Wait one. Out."

She glanced again at Adair. He was deathly pale, his eyes were closed. A froth of saliva at the corner of his mouth stirred periodically. *Come on, we're almost home.*

The gauge dropped to thirty-eight percent; she killed the thrusters. "Myriad, this is Pratt. I am coasting. When do I begin deceleration? Over."

"You have ninety-five seconds before deceleration. Can you manage that?"

"Affirmative. Out."

She turned Adair's head. "Adair! Can you hear me?" His lips moved, but she could hear nothing. "We're half way back now."

No time to say more. She turned herself about by hand, awkwardly counter-rotating Adair's body against her own to save propellant.

"Pratt, this is *Myriad*. Full thruster deceleration in… Five. Four. Three. Two. One. *Now!*" Behind her, the thruster roared its response, and once more she began her slow-motion acrobatic dance with Adair.

Eighteen percent. Seventeen. Her arms and back ached.

At ten percent, the numerals on the fuel display turned red. Eight percent. Seven percent; but she was almost there. Six percent. Five. The space station was coming towards her, growing visibly as she watched.

Without warning, Adair thrashed out, his arms and legs flailing. The force of the convulsion pulled him out of her grasp, and twisted her out of line. By the time he went limp again, she was facing the looming Earth. She stopped the main thruster, grasped Adair again, and began reorienting herself.

"Pratt, this is *Myriad*. Are you having problems?"

"We're under control. I think." The head-up display said she was on course again.

She ignited the thruster one more time. It was going to be close.

"Pratt, this is *Myriad*. Reduce thrust to fifty percent of maximum."

Three times she tried to restart it, twice with voice control, once with the palm switch. "*Myriad*, this is Pratt. We are out of fuel and drifting." Her voice seemed remote, as if she was speaking at her own funeral. *Hey, God? I know you don't do miracles. But I could use a little courage right now...*

"Pratt, this is *Myriad*." It was the commander's voice. "Orlov is on his way to bring you in. Stand by and wait for rescue. And then maybe arrest. I haven't decided yet."

She watched the station slipping relentlessly past. Where was Orlov? Her relative velocity was five point one meters per second, according to the suit's GPS. Not nearly as fast as Adair had been going; but this time their relative velocity was in the wrong direction, nowhere near the boomerang zone. And Orlov would only have a short-range thruster, and three people's mass to bring in. If he couldn't reach them in time, they would drift forever.

The station wasn't sliding past any more, it was shrinking, falling away; and her slow rotation was dragging it off to the side of her faceplate. She tried to do a cat-twist, to keep it in sight, but she was bone-tired, and Adair's limp form kept getting in the way. After the station had finally gone out of sight to her left, she had still seen no sign of Orlov. What was wrong?

She moved Adair so that she could see his face; his eyes were closed, his breathing almost invisible. There was a comradeship, an odd intimacy, in dying together.

The huge disc of Earth drifted in front of her. Most of it was dark, a circular void in the stars broken by an uneven dusting of gold and silver lights. It was hard to see the lit crescent for the glare of the Sun, but she knew that they were over Asia. Her air would last long enough for her to see North America again, measure a couple finger-widths north from Florida to find Suzanne in Atlanta, spot the ragged tan triangle of desert that marked Wyoming and her family.

Myriad would be coming back into sight again soon. She strained to see around the edge of her faceplate. There it was, shockingly small – but that tiny dot there, yes, that was surely Orlov! She looked at Adair's slack face, and pressed their helmets together. "Did you see that, Adair? We've got us a ride home! And if you give up now, I'll *kill* you!"

Pratt and Orlov stuffed Adair, limp as a sack of potatoes, into the one-person airlock. For an eternity they floated, holding the grab bars, as the lock cycled. Finally the light showed green. Orlov opened the door and gestured her in.

A minute later she stepped through the inner door to the sound of cheering; half the crew were gathered in the little airlock vestibule, floating by any available hold like bats in a cave. Adair's helmet was off, and the medical officer, assisted by one of the technicians, was giving him oxygen. Adair opened his eyes and smiled weakly.

"Hey, Pratt," he said, "thanks f' the lift."

"I owed you one," she said.

The air was cold against her face. She wiped sweat out of her eyes, pushed clinging hair away from her forehead. Somebody was helping her undo her suit seals. Laboring like a moulting insect, she wriggled out of the suit.

Behind her, the airlock cycled again.

Orlov stepped out and removed his helmet. "So, you are back with us, Adair! I was afraid you would not make it. Well done, Pratt!"

"Thanks, Orlov," she said.

The oxygen was bringing color back to Adair's face. He smiled, more himself now. "Hey, Pratt – you were right. It can get dangerous out there."

Adair had been floated off to sickbay for observation. Pratt took the Commander's suit to the storage room, swabbed it out carefully, drained the sump, and disconnected the oxygen bottle and lithium hydroxide scrubber cartridge. The familiar routine was calming. She attached the suit to the wall with shock cord, and reached for the recharging cable.

"Pratt?" It was the Old Lady, her tone so abrupt that Pratt almost stood to attention.

"Ma'am?"

"You disobeyed a direct order out there. This is not the military, but as captain I'm in charge."

"Sorry Ma'am."

"I am putting an official reprimand in your record," Verdi said. "It will, however, go next to the commendation for rescuing Adair. I shall make sure that the commendation is more strongly worded."

"Thank you, Ma'am." Pratt braced to push off.

"Before you go, Pratt. I'll have to write a report on this incident, and I'm wondering -- for his oxygen to last as long as it did, Adair must have managed to stay calm for a whole orbit. For two hours of drifting in space, with no radio contact."

Pratt relaxed a little. "I was fairly sure he'd make it, Ma'am."

"Why?"

Why *had* she been sure? For a moment she was silent. "Ma'am, when I was little, they used to tell me when things got tough, faith would get you through. I guess you've seen enough of my psych files to know I'm not a very regular member of my church these days, but I still believe that. Sort of."

"But Adair?"

Pratt laughed. "Adair must be about the least religious person I know. But using the last of his propellant to boost *away* from the station - that shows real faith in *something*. In the laws of physics, at least."

Verdi nodded. "And in you."

"Boomerang Zone" © 2015 Robert Dawson   First published in Cosmic Roots & Eldritch Shores February 27, 2016

Robert Dawson teaches mathematics at a Nova Scotian university. When he isn't teaching, doing research, or writing science fiction, he enjoys hiking, cycling, and fencing, and he volunteers with a Scout troop. He is an alumnus of the Sage Hill and Viable Paradise writing workshops, and on the executive of SF Canada. He believes that the world needs more bicycles."

Make a Wish, digital painting © Karim Fakhoury. We first used this work to illustrate this story for its initial publication. Karim Fakhoury is a 29 years old illustrator and designer based in Montreal, Canada. Over the past 13 years, he has turned his passion for the world of visual arts and design into a profession. He specializes in image making, digital illustrations, and branding identity.

Astronaut with Tether: Image and caption courtesy: NASA: During the Gemini 4 mission on June 3, 1965, Ed White became the first American to conduct a spacewalk. The spacewalk started at 3:45 p.m. EDT on the third orbit when White opened the hatch and used the hand-held manuevering oxygen-jet gun to push himself out of the capsule.

The EVA started over the Pacific Ocean near Hawaii and lasted 23 minutes, ending over the Gulf of Mexico. Initially, White propelled himself to the end of the 8-meter tether and back to the spacecraft three times using the hand-held gun. After the first three minutes the fuel ran out and White maneuvered by twisting his body and pulling on the tether.

In a photograph by Commander James McDivitt taken early in the EVA over a cloud-covered Pacific Ocean, the maneuvering gun is visible in White's right hand. The visor of his helmet is gold-plated to protect him from the unfiltered rays of the sun.

In the original photograph, the tether was, of course, Not broken.

WEATHERBUNS

Diana Hauer

"I crave something extreme. Awe-inspiring. Powerful."

Sandra looked up from the half-frosted three-layer cake. "Sure, I'll be with you in just a moment."

She set her spatula aside and cycled through the readouts for each layer of the Perfect Autumn Day. Virtual numbers superimposed themselves over the cake as though projected on a pane of glass only she could see. They showed her the balance of each segment: temperature, humidity, air pressure, and so on. The first layer had thick morning fog that was gradually banished by sun. The second layer was a crisp, cool afternoon with sparse clouds. Sunlight would kiss the earth and ward off the chill. Evening, the third layer, brought clouds in slowly to make a spectacular sunset and to keep the heat of the day from bleeding off into the atmosphere. The code was interwoven through a carrot cake matrix and topped with cream cheese initiation frosting. More frosting made the transitions between the segments move smoothly. This was the most complex weather pastry she had ever created. Sandra hoped her mentor, Weatherman Fawkes, would be pleased. His standards were forbiddingly high. With hard work, he might judge her ready for the Journeyman test in a year.

After she wiped her hands, Sandra smiled and turned to look at her customer. Spiky hair, piercings, chains and metal spikes all over his clothes. Tattooed lightning crept out from under his shirt and climbed partway up his neck, like it was trying to strangle him. He made a beeline for the storm section.

"What did you have in mind?" asked Sandra as she walked over to the case that housed their most complex weather concoctions. "We have Sandstorm Soufflé if your reality pocket has arid settings, or Blizzard Baked Alaska if you favor cold. Either of those set things up nicely for sandsurfing or snowboarding after the weather program ends."

He tugged at the ear gauge that expanded his earlobe as large as a mouse's hula hoop. "Not enough."

She forced herself to keep smiling and tried not to groan. Master Fawkes had warned her about this sort of customer. "I am required by law to advise you that all of the goods at Weatherman's Bakery are intended for safe, recreational use in your private reality pocket, with proper precautions and shelter in place before activation is begun."

That advisory had become a requirement after it became clear that people were unleashing giant-sized lightning storms in small reality bubbles, not even pockets. Sometimes in little more than a grassy field with some sky. Every school child learned that lightning seeks out the tallest thing to ground itself on. But obviously a few eventually forgot.

Black fingernails released the earlobe to flick dismissively in Sandra's direction as the customer peered into the Wild Weather Case.

"You will have to sign a waiver and safety agreement before I can sell anything from that case," she said, holding grimly to the bright smile and professional demeanor that Weatherman Fawkes had drilled into her in the first weeks of her apprenticeship.

"Tyr Typhoonmaster" signed without bothering to even glance at the document. Sandra had a sinking feeling she knew what he wanted.

"I want a hurricane." He licked his lips. "A wicked one."

Sandra gestured at a tall, elegant creation. "Hurricane Flower Cake." Layers of spun sugar wound around each other like petals. White in the outer layer, the petals darkened gradually as they went deeper. The innermost layer of the flower was storm-cloud gray, so dark it was almost black. "Vanilla cake with black raspberry filling. The deeper you cut, the stronger the storm. Outermost layers are a tropical storm. If you cut all the way to the middle it will be Category 3."

Tyr placed both palms on the case and leaned in so close that his breath fogged the glass. "What if I cut it in half?"

Sandra swallowed hard. "It would be a category 5 hurricane, but we don't recommend that."

"Does it come with lightning? I want lots of lightning. Ball lightning, if you have it."

"Not in this cake, but we do have Banana Crème Thunderstorm Pie. The two should be compatible if you don't cut more than halfway through either."

"I want them together."

"That would be a special order. I can get one started for you though if you like."

The entry bell chimed as Mrs. Johnson and her four-year-old son walked into the bakery.

Sandra shot her a sincere smile and a nod. "I'll be right with you."

Mrs. Johnson took Peter by the hand and went over to browse the Lovely Day Case.

"Can't you just add them as sprinkles or something?" asked Tyr.

Sandra shook her head. "Weather confections need a very delicate balance. If it were a Sunshine Bun, no problem. They're just sunlight, flour, water, and sugar. But a hurricane pastry combines pressure, humidity, and a dozen other factors. Altering a finished item of that complexity could make the whole thing collapse into a mess of corrupted code and frosting. I do have some Ball Lightning Cupcakes, though. They require the presence of cumulonimbus clouds, such as from the Thunderstorm Pie or one of the tornado items."

"Oh, all right." He pouted. It was not a good look with the tattoos and chains. "I'll take hurricane, thunderstorm, and Ball Lightning."

"I'll have those right out to you."

Sandra boxed up Tyr's order and activated the items. As she rang him up, she smirked inwardly at the black-clad punk guy carrying pretty pink boxes around. Tyr didn't notice. He had eyes only for the storms.

"What might it be today, Mrs. Johnson? A few hours of sunshine?" After a questioning glance at his mother, Sandra slipped Peter a plain sugar cookie to chew on. Tiny clouds materialized in front of him. He giggled and batted at them with the hand that wasn't holding the slobbery cookie.

As Mrs. Johnson debated the cheaper options (with effects lasting one to three hours, small to medium coverage) versus the more expensive and complex options (four hours minimum, large enough to fill extra-large reality pockets), Sandra realized that she hadn't heard the door chime when Tyr left. She stood on her tiptoes and looked around. Tyr was in the corner, hunched over one of the display tables. Was he rearranging his boxes so they would be easier to carry?

Sandra walked towards the door to get a better look. The cookie boxes she had arranged yesterday were now shoved off to the side. Empty, pink boxes were on the floor. She stood frozen for a moment, realized the dire implications, and ran for the gate between the cases. "Sir, please, what are you doing? I must insist you stop right now."

Air pressure dropped. Humidity rose.

Tyr turned to her and grinned. He set the cupcake atop the pie, which sat atop the cake, making a baked pyramid. The pie had disturbed the cake frosting, starting the hurricane program.

Sandra flicked her wrist to activate her VR weather code programs, desperately hurling cancellation codes at the cake. The display flashed red. She was too far away to affect the goods on the table. Tyr drew a large knife and grinned at her.

"You can't activate a major weather effect in shared reality!" screamed Sandra, forcing herself to breathe so that she didn't choke on panic. "Weatherman, help!"

Tyr raised his knife and cut straight down through the pastries. Frosting and cake exploded everywhere as three distinct weather programs activated at once. Sandra could see the code, carefully infused within the matrix of each delicious confection, unfurl chaotically, mixing and merging in unintended ways. The bakery ceiling disappeared behind a layer of storm clouds, pregnant with rain and ready to birth lightning.

Sandra swore. Avoiding indoor manifestations of major weather was one of the first safety rules taught to a would-be Weatherperson; right after making sure effects activated discretely, one at a time, to avoid precisely what she was witnessing now. The air pressure plummeted, and winds whipped through the store. They hit walls, bounced off, then circled around, taking the clouds with them.

Tyr spun and capered, cackling in ecstasy. He raised his arms to the clouds as if inviting the lightning to take him. Naturally-formed hurricanes took hours to build up. Indoors, everything was condensed. She and the customers were about to be right in the middle of a concentrated hurricane.

Weatherman Fawkes was in the back room. Sandra didn't know if he'd heard her yell. Hopefully he would hear the storm; her mentor tended to play music while he worked.

Mrs. Johnson and her son huddled against the Wild Weather Case. Whether they had been blown there or were trying to take shelter in the shallow overhang, it was about the worst place they could be. If the case shattered, shards of glass could cut into people as well as the pastries. The more dangerous baked goods were kept inert until sold, but the buns and cheaper items were active. If their case broke, Tyr's "perfect storm" would seem like a pleasant Spring day.

Or a perfect Autumn day...

Sandra stopped trying to fight the wind and let it shove her back into the employee area. She snagged the kitchen doorknob and struggled to open it, but the wind and pressure held it shut. Probably it held the door to the Weatherman's workroom, too, she realized. She fought her way to the back of the cases, crawling over debris, dragging herself toward the weatherbun case. Sandra yanked open the door, scooped some buns into her apron, and slammed the door shut before the wind could wreak havoc with the rest of the contents. She scrambled over to her worktable and was relieved to see that her half-decorated cake was untouched behind its work shield. She flipped open the cover and hurriedly set two Sunshine Buns and two Windcalm Buns on the top. Habit and training made her arrange them symmetrically, so the cake would look nice.

Slamming a plastic display dome over the cake to protect it, Sandra curled her body forward as she struggled against the unpredictable winds that battered her like the world's largest cake mixer. Cake mixers always miss a little bit on the bottom and sides, Sandra realized, and she dropped to her hands and knees. She crawled with one arm wrapped protectively around her little carrot cake, inching her way towards Mrs. Johnson and Peter. The wind roared between them. Gusts ripped at Sandra's hair and clothes, threatening to sweep her away. Time for desperate measures.

She pulled a Windcalm Bun out of her apron pocket and ripped it open with her teeth, praying that she wasn't making things worse by adding more code to this debacle. The air around her instantly stilled, but she could see the code clashing and roiling as effects fought against each other. The weatherbun's effect was no match for the complex cake and pie systems. They started to rip it away like layers of phyllo dough off a baklava.

Sandra got to Mrs. Johnson and Peter just as the storm systems had finished devouring her little bubble of calm. There was no time for finesse. She set the cake between the three of them, flipped the cover off, and ripped it and the buns apart with her bare hands.

Calm burst out from the cake like the opposite of a bomb blast. The riot of wind and clouds immediately stilled and started to disperse… on her side of the bakery. Fog swallowed the view from the windows outside. She heard pounding on the door – Weatherman Fawkes trying to get into the bakery. Ugly purple clouds swirled faster and tighter on the other side of the room, between her and the front door. Her program dueled with the storm, order against chaos, a momentary stalemate. Sandra pulled up her control panel and desperately twisted the weather code, urging the storm towards the front of the bakery, clearing a path.

Autumn sunlight broke through the clouds and caressed the work room door. It burst open and Weatherman Fawkes stood scowling in the doorway. His long, gray hair had escaped its usual tight braid, and his thick, bushy eyebrows cast shadows over his eyes as he surveyed the scene through his glower.

Tyr was standing on the edge of the two systems, one side in the calm, the other in the storm. "Isn't this amazing?" he yelled. His eyes were open wide, wind and rain plastered his clothing against his skinny body. "I am the lightning god!"

Weatherman Fawkes laughed as his fingers flexed and he tapped intricate commands into his VR control panel. Sandra couldn't tell what he was inputting -- her panel was apprentice-level. Whatever he was doing was far beyond her skills.

"Rudolph, is that you?" bellowed the old man. The wind started picking up again, blowing his baker's apron behind him. Sandra could see the code of her Autumn Day shredding under the power of the storm. And the bubble of calm was shrinking fast. "I hoped I'd be the one to bring you down, lunatic. Now here you are, in my bakery." Weatherman Fawkes laughed and strode forward, unconcerned as the clouds closed in on him. "And it's not even my birthday!"

Wind recoiled from the Weatherman's scowl. The dark, rolling clouds cringed away like frightened puppies. They huddled in corners, as far from the angry Weatherman as they could get, until he dispersed them with a wave of his hand.

Tyr/Rudolph snapped out of his ecstatic trance and turned to flee. Weatherman Fawkes raised a Lightning Cupcake to his lips. He must have snagged it from the case on his way, thought Sandra. He bit into it when Tyr was almost at the door. Sandra watched in awe as the weatherman activated the cupcake while spinning code to simultaneously direct and weaken the bolt of electricity that struck Tyr. The sodden punk collapsed in a heap.

Weatherman Fawkes turned to consider the weather programs still battling for supremacy in his bakery. With a few deft swipes, he enhanced Sandra's Perfect Autumn Day code, spreading its influence to every corner of the bakery. It wiped away the gathering storm and fog as if they never existed.

"I'll call the Weather Authority, explain what happened and have them send someone to pick up Rudolph, there." He jerked his head at Tyr, still twitching on the ground. "If you ever wondered what happens when an apprentice Weatherperson goes bad, there you go. Rudy was my greatest failure."

Weatherman Fawkes looked at the windblown shambles that was his bakery. "Close the store and get started on this mess, Journeyman. I'll be out to help once I finish my call." He grimaced. "Believe me, yours is the easier task."

Sandra gaped at him. "J-journeyman? But Master Fawkes, I haven't tested. I've barely finished half my apprenticeship!"

The old man looked over his shoulder and gave her one of his rare, true smiles. "I'm promoting you to Journeyman, because if this doesn't count as a field test, I don't know what does. See to Mrs. Johnson and then get to work. I'll cook something nice later to celebrate."

Sandra beamed after him. "And maybe I'll make dessert," she said softly.

She helped Mrs. Johnson up from the floor and fetched towels from the kitchen to dry them off. Peter was still sobbing, wet and miserable, until

Sandra handed him a Sunshine Bun.

"Thank you, Weatherwoman," said Mrs. Johnson as she basked in the warm sunbeams.

"Someday," said Sandra wistfully, "but today I'm just a Journeyman Weatherperson. Can I wrap you up something warm before you go?"

"I think we've had enough of weather systems for a while, said Mrs. Johnson as she wrung her clothing. "But I'll take a dozen Sunshine Buns."

"On the house," said Sandra. "Have a lovely day!"

Diana Hauer is a writer of words, both technical and fantastical, who lives in Beaverton, Oregon, with a dog and a fiance, both of whom she adores. When she's not writing, she enjoys gardening, reading, gaming, and martial arts.

When the Chancellor of Mars signed the nonaggression pact with the First Speaker of our Jovian Collective, I was tickling Nishka's baby. I had apprenticed for Donyo two years in his tiny dome on Europa, and Nishka--well, Donyo called her "My little peasant girl." Everyone in the solar system loved Donyo's sensorized versions of the old 2d's (save those purists who called them abominations). This was for "Three Men and a Baby."

Babies are so pure of feeling, so elegant. No subliminals to filter. This naivete infected me, for that day, with Donyo in a jovial mood where I felt I could say anything (and knew I shouldn't), I had the hubris to remark how fortunate I was the Collective assigned me this job. It didn't matter that the dome's cold numbed my fingers to uselessness, my eyes crackled with long hours, or that I was so addicted to sense euphoria I endured sleep like a cougar writhing in a steeljaw leg-trap.

I marveled that the Planning Ministry's infinite wisdom hadn't left me an ice-hacking longshoreman like Nishka or sweating away my whole, worthless life mining one dinky asteroid and dying young, like so many of my childhood dome-mates.

Even Jovians called him Master Donyo, though only a handful of Earth films were approved for local experience (the rest showing, case in point, deviant behavior like parents rearing their own children). I stood tall among Jovians. Donyo's Apprentice.

Donyo shook his pipe and growled good-naturedly through his black, gray-flecked beard, "Never tempt fate, Haig. No good can come of it. Now work, you have a baby to tickle."

As today I stare down death's gaze, I wish I had not stood so tall.

Donyo was right, of course. One must never tempt fate. No good can come of it.

While the Martians and our Glorious Jovian Army were invading the asteroid belt, to split it fifty-fifty and effectively declaring war on Saturn, I was filtering out 'yech' from Nishka's baby's first encounter with solid food. You can't find a Newness/Surprise feeling more genuine than an infant's, and we would merge it tomorrow with Donyo's own connoisseurial taste of real beans. This was for "Blazing Saddles."

'Filtering'-- I dislike the word. It implies science where only there is art. Filtering is what Radio Collective does, as I have learned from listening to Voice of Earth on the unrestricted radio Donyo secured to keep his work 'lifelike.' Filtering a Sense is more like sanding the finish on fine wood. At the time I was no master, but had glimpsed perfection like Monet's Water Lilies flashing through a kaleidoscope's chaos -- and I wanted more.

Thus, restless and unable to sleep due to the effects of my sensoria habituation, I had snuck from my sweat-stunk dorm across the ice sheet.

The ice was slushy from recent tectonic activity, eerily lit beneath Jove's immensity in the sky and the flashes of lightning as gas-packets smashed into our atmosphere, replenishing it. Fighting stomach pains of anxiety, I slipped into Donyo's studio. The air fresheners hissed, covering my foot-steps, though they never removed the smell of stale body odor. I picked my way across piles of old 2d canisters. I dodged the replica of the centuries old film projector that had gone out of style in the twenty-first century when 2d's gave way to the holos. I could have walked across Master Donyo's junk-cluttered dome blind and still tapped each of the rusting old support girders that loomed above us like a bloodied rib-cage, the ceiling sheets stretched between them like skin.

I lay on the firm plasticrete floor and rested the black silk editor's skullcap on my head. The stomach pains melted away as I silently smoothed and polished the baby's feeling of Newness/Surprise while (I had assumed) Donyo slept in the next room.

"No good will come of this!" I heard Donyo suddenly bellow, and moments later thwacked aside the partition door. Nishka huddled with him under his imported Alpaca blanket, her eyes ablaze and mouth set defiantly beneath tousled brown hair. Donyo scowled, and looked toward the baby in the incucrib. My first hunch (after my stomach flinched, preventing me from making the retreat I suddenly prayed for) was that Nishka wanted to keep her baby. I suddenly saw the baby's resemblance to Donyo. The same eyes. Donyo's baby.

Nishka gave me a quick sympathetic smile before returning her lips hard to face Donyo.

I expected Donyo to throw me out then raise cracks in the thermal roof tiles explaining to her that no matter how immensely the Collective profited from his work, even the Great Donyo had not the power to prevent Youth Services from taking the boy tomorrow. They would take it, name it, and assign it a Nurturing Dome and trade as Jovians had done for centuries. I imagined him thundering that it was a miracle and perhaps a mistake he'd called in favors to keep it so long for his projects.

"Parents are Evil," I recited the Collective's mantra. I remembered with angry, downturned eyes how dirty I felt to have met my grandfather, how that strange man with the same red hair and hazel eyes and sharp nose should never have sought me out during play periods to tell me stories of his immigration from Mars and excursions to Earth. I looked at Nishka's baby in the incucrib and wished him spared that shameful, dangerous fate.

But instead of shouting down the dome, Donyo paused on seeing me, only a moment, then repeated, "No good will come of this! Haig, take off that fool thing and make us all tea."

Holding my knotted abdomen I clambered to the basin that doubled as kitchen and lavatory sink.

"No, Donyito," she whispered to him as I squeezed thinly colored drops from well-reused tea packets. "I will free my son from this life, Donyo. If the Martians attack us, I will join them."

Despite the cold I felt flush. My stomach tightened more. I grabbed the counter for support. Instinct told me to run, not walk, to the nearest Foreman and report Nishka's treason, for which she should rightfully be drawn and quartered. Yet I stood transfixed, tingling with electricity, just as the time I watched Dorm Monitor Lozaki on Io beat my friend Timo to death for sneezing too loudly. I had winced with pain in my belly at every blow, as if I were being struck, so horrified was I that I could neither stop the abuse nor make myself look away.

Donyo waved dismissively. "Fools surround me! Haig, tell me, would you rather live as an 'Impure' in a Martian death camp?"

Years of Dorm Monitor induced silence brought a catch to my tongue. And shame at secretly being Martian, and knowing it.

"Of course not!" Donyo continued, to my relief, with a pause long enough for his thin lips to test the temperature of the luke-warm tea as if it might actually be too hot. "Would you rather be a fat, hypocritical Earther, hating outplaneters, raising your own children, spewing egalitarian tripe, but not stooping to help us, so long as we wait her table? Of course not! Be proud to be Jovian. The Collective is fundamentally good. This oppressive regime could fall even in your generation. You stand with your mother planet. Change from inside. Now drink your tea."

Nishka glanced at me, then glared a "This isn't over yet" at him.

Donyo threw up his hands. "Fools!"

He was right, of course. No good came of it.

When that Martian madwoman declared the Jovian Collective to be 'impure', and annexed our outer moons, I was recording a boy playing with toy soldiers for "Toy Story." They were only old powercells that he 'killed' with slingshot ice. Tactiles are my least favorite to record, especially those of touching people, though Donyo tells me with a smile this feeling is easily overcome. I grumble that I should report him for that, but I never do.

The boy, Feder, was on loan from Nurturing Dome 437, across the Nile River. Well, we call it that, but it's no more than an ice floe of a darker color. (Of course, we call them Nurturing Domes, too. We're a people filled with irony.)

Nishka spent progressively fewer evenings with us since Youth Services exchanged Feder for Nishka's baby. She-d named the child Emmeth and even taken to calling him that in public. I assume Donyo pulled strings with the constable's office, as she was never arrested for this crime--she faded toward invisibility of her own accord. When the war started, we heard that a group of miscreants had sabotaged a local port, hijacked an asteroidal transport, and gone to join the Martian military. Donyo never mentioned Nishka's disappearance. Like a good Jovian I asked nothing.

"I'm going out. Keep the heater off," Donyo grumped at me, as he had taken to doing.

He never said where he went. I didn't ask. But I don't think he cared that I one time followed him across the frozen waste to the local Martian Relocation Dome. I hid behind the tangled wires of a power tree lest some Foreman recall that I have Martian blood. I covered my nose from the cold and stench of burnt insulation.

Ostensibly just another black-tiled and windowless dormitory dome, albeit hastily constructed, the Martian nationals and Naturalized Jovians of Martian Origin who were moved there were never seen outside. In my innocence I assumed Donyo had another "little peasant girl" inside.

I should have been inside there as well. I should have turned myself in, learning as I had in that unclean way that I was also of Martian descent. But my shame at having met a grandfather prevented me. And fear of what might lie inside.

Donyo stayed longer each time, and the time I followed him I had shivered there an hour before crunching my way back. So much work to do. I was by now doing most of Donyo's sensorization. If anyone on Earth (blissfully ignoring our "little war") could smell the difference, I never heard. I remarked to myself more than once that I was on my way to becoming Master Haig.

Such heady thoughts.

If only Master Donyo had been there, to tell me once again that no good would come of it.

When the Martians whacked Earth's moon with a "stay out of this fight" rock the size of a solo-dome that they'd launched years before, I was meshing a local boy's first adolescent Urges with "The Graduate."

As Donyo had told me so long before he had moved into the small hut near the Martian relocation dome, back when we joked and I thought coyly that if having a father was like this, then the idea might not be so bad, back then he'd said Desire is a tricky thing.

Donyo was master of emotional recordings; even on Earth sensorists and scientists were years behind Donyo and his Art. He'd never told the Collective how much emotional control Limbic Cortical Recordings could give them, how he'd stumbled on a subliminal hammer the Collective could wield against the experience-hungry Earthers on an anvil of Sensies.

But he told me.

On pain of death, he shook his fist, and I swore a child's oath that I would die before revealing his secrets. Desire, he told me, was among the easiest to mold. An aphrodisiac. A dangerous subliminal.

I did not know any Earthers, but I was relieved to hear on Voice of Earth that the Collective abandoned its imminent plan to round up local Earthers as they had the Martians. Alliances shift like clock hands. Earth was now our ally. Earthers still despised our "assembly line" society, but such is life. I both love and hate our society, and that too, is life.

I was relieved though that we wouldn't be incarcerating the local Earthers, because rumor had it the Martians were tortured in the relocation dome, though rumor here is as unreliable as the sun is for warmth. I'm shamed to admit that I secretly wished this rumor were true, as I forced myself to chew and swallow the NutriRations the Collective had mandated because of the "Martian Threat" and uncertainty of resupply.

I wished Donyo was in their drafty dome playing unfiltered Anguish to them, making them feel unclean like my grandfather had made a certain child feel, his hand lightly resting on the boy's shoulder like a iron weight, filling his memories with the ale-breathed tales of family that he must not hear... I wished them pain because I knew I was Martian like them.

Surely the Collective must know as well. I vowed, very silently, that I would go straight-backed when they came for me.

How soon, I wondered?

Everything Is Known. As Donyo would caution, no good can come of that.

When the Jovian space forces obliterated all life on Ceres -- some miners, two Martian Divisions and the Jovian Resistance Brigade, Nishka's unit, I was amplifying an Earth soldier's Anger over a "Dear John" letter. My first love, he'd said. "She swore she'd wait forever. God damn your war," my ally said. By the time he'd arrived from the garrison his reaction had cooled from white-hot, but I restored that, much as we amplify slaughtered rats for death scenes. This was for "The Ten Commandments."

I worked sloppily, my stomach in a painful knot. Earthers, Martians, Saturnians, they must feel like this when they lose a sister. I had known Nishka for more than my few years with Donyo. We had been dome-mates when I first arrived, while she still worked the Pahu Hau ice docks, though we rarely spoke. I had dreams of the collective selecting us as breeders, and it was on my recommendation that Donyo requested the collective assign her to him as "research material." The docks had given her a hard edge, but like ice insulating a sapling in winter. I was too shamed to ever speak more than a few words with her, yet I sensed from her acceptance of me in their private conversations that she knew we both held Donyo's best interests at heart.

Donyo stamped in that day, shaking frost from his parka. I had not seen him for weeks. His hair was far grayer, more gray now than black. When had that happened? Wrinkles creased his face like Europa's fault lines.

Why today, of all days, I cried silently? I'd just heard the newsflash on his radio. I knew he could not yet know about Nishka.

"I will not do it!" he said in icy greeting. "If Foreman Bargasa comes here, tell him I will have no more part of this. I am moving back here."

My throat tightened. Jovians do not tell Foremen; Foremen tell you. "You are cold, Master Donyo," I said. "I will make you tea."

"I'm always cold. The Collective is cold. The Collective is Hell, and Hell is cold."

I opened a new tea bag, the one he didn't know I knew about, hidden beneath the trivet some Earther had sent as a token of gratification, and which the Collective had let him keep presumably because of the ironic uselessness of a stand for hot dishes in a place where dishes never got hot.

I told him the news.

He sipped his tea, nodded slowly. Blinked back tears, snuffled. "Jove eats her weak alive, like Europa's ice eats craters.... This damnable cold," he said.

The buzzer announced a visitor. Donyo waved me to his bedroom, my stomach fluttering with fear that they'd come for me. Donyo would lie, say that I was not here. I hoped.

Foreman Bargasa flowed into the room along with two guards. He casually removed his thermals, revealing an immense belly that said "I am well fed" and thick biceps that said "I need no stave to kill you."

Donyo and Bargasa talked in quiet, forceful tones while I peeked. I imagined they spoke my name, and said "Martian," and I thought of the relocation camp. Donyo punctuated his conversation with negative jabs and waves. Bargasa: slow, placating, invisibly threatening. The guards surveyed the room with raised noses and cow-like eyes, too good for such menial work.

Head hung, Donyo donned his parka and followed Bargasa toward the door. "We must all make sacrifices," Bargasa said loudly, patting Donyo on the back.

Donyo turned before he left, and I could see him saying with his eyes, "No good will come of this."

When the Earth transports delivered Europa's first contingent of Martian POW's -- so gorged were Earth's POW camps with their victories that they had to fill ours -- I was recording my own hatred of the Collective; this for "The Godfather."

Parents are so much trouble. The Collective is right to deny children their knowledge. Yet that displaces the rebellion a child must feel against his nurturers if he is to be free. Of course, the Collective does not want us free, and for that I hated them doubly. Triply, for allowing my own grandfather to infect me with knowledge of who I am. I shuddered with rage, hoping he was rotting in a relocation dome on Io, simultaneously shuddering with fear that he should be spared, that he was as kind and gentle a man as Donyo.

Deep in my terrified soul I knew better. I'd heard the news: Donyo was dead. They would come for me.

The buzzer sounded. I imagined two guards outside the door.

I looked to Donyo's sleeping mat. To his table. Nowhere to hide.

The guards shuffled in without a second buzz. Three of them.

"Apprentice Haig?" one asked.

I nodded meekly.

"Come with us." They hurried me out, still fumbling on my parka.

The room they locked me into at the relocation dome was larger than I expected. I imagined sharing ten beds among twenty people, and only five blankets. But this room was small, austere, adorned only by a cot, a table, two chairs -- and a Limbic Recorder. It was an interrogation room, I realized.

I sat at the table and, in a flight of fancy like a condemned man who was enjoying a last meal, I rested the editor's cap on my head. I played the short session last recorded on it. I remember the events as if they are still happening---

--- *I feel* a man's hot breath on my/his face. Eyes closed. Face in hands. Wet hands. Crying. Trembling.

"I must record this," he says, with a Pulling Himself Together feeling, and blowing his nose. He is alone, in this room. This chair.

"At first I felt I had no choice. Do you understand? At first we tried rats. I told them it would not work. Death is elusive, too terrible a weapon. There may indeed be a way to record it perfectly, but I refused, to myself, to consider it. It failed. The rats lived. Then they connected a detainee. They said they would kill him whether I recorded or not."

'This is war and you are a Jovian,' Bargasa told me.

"I pretended to record but left the machine off. They noticed, and my God, they killed another. Just so I'd record Death. Then they demanded I play Death to a detainee, a woman I'd seen at the commissary. They're not even prisoners of war! They're our own people. Who cares if they have Martian blood?"

Someone comes in -- I feel my/his head turn. A medic. "You must sleep, Master Donyo, you are upset."

"Of course I'm upset! Leave me be!"

The medic leaves.

"I refused to play the recording. They killed her anyway. 'See?' they said, 'it does not matter. Play your recording.' They think it a weapon, that they can magically broadcast Death to the enemy. It is absurd, but I refuse, to myself, to try it. So I said yes, but played something else, Harmony, and said, 'Look, it does not work.' And they said, 'then you must record again,' and they killed him.

"I broke the machine. They produced another, saying if I damage it again they will torture and kill them until a new machine is found. As soon as you give us what we want, we will stop, they said. I stalled, saying how difficult each recording is to prepare, to edit. But they know it cannot take forever, and they have a guard watching my every move and when I can no longer stand his staring at me I tell them it will not work anyway and they kill another. They killed them slower. Faster. Alone. In groups. Men. Women. Boys. Girls. Babies. One after another, and I cannot stop it!"

"Today I am done for," Donyo records. "Nishka is here," he says with a sigh. "There were survivors from Ceres. Earth 'repatriated' them. Did Earthers not know what would happen to Jovian traitors? My God, they even asked for asylum on Earth. I cannot go on!"

The recording stops amidst racking sobs. He has disconnected the recorder. After a pause of blank recording, he reconnects.

"They know about us, Nishka and me. Our child. And if I do not succeed with one last nameless detainee, Nishka is next. A painful death, they promise, for best recording. Then our baby. Emmeth; they remind me she named him, and that I said nothing. Emmeth."

I feel him fumble in his pocket, swallow something.

"At least I came prepared," he says. I feel his life drain away, like a golden-red sunset, then a fade-to-black. ---

The recording ends and I sit with my head in my hands, breath reflecting hot on my face. I had so thought of my own fears I had been blind to Donyo's life force, slowly ebbing away, day after day as he trudged in silence to the relocation dome, ultimately forced to live there. A Jovian's answer to a problem is always, "Work Harder!" Foreman Bargasa was a Good Jovian.

I want to cry for Donyo, with Donyo, for myself, but I can no longer remember how. I hear footsteps shuffling in the corridor.

I am ready to die.

Foreman Bargasa enters the room, fills it. "So, this is Master Donyo's Apprentice," he says. "The boy who does all Master Donyo's work."

I want to spit, but years of instinct prevent me.

"Not so cocksure now, is he?" Bargasa says, laughing with the guards.

I stiffen my back. I am ready to die. I must not show weakness.

Nishka is escorted in. She is connected to the recorder. And to the Interrogator.

"You know how to work this device?" Bargasa asks, pointing to the recorder, and I take a deep, shuddering breath. I am not to die.

Nishka's eyes are harsh, defiant. Daring me to kill her. I narrow my eyes. What is she to me? A sister? A traitor. A dome-mate? A hateful Martian-lover. She deserted Donyo. She killed him. I search for the quick smile she used to throw me, for any sign of the sapling under the ice. Her face is an avalanche of hate. She wants to die. I must not show weakness.

Bargasa sees the anger and anguish in my face. From the guard he takes the Interrogator's control, extends it to me. "A setting above nine is fatal," he says.

I take the unit.

Nishka stiffens.

Bargasa smiles.

The image of Dome Monitor Lozaki comes unbidden, beating Timo to death. Of how I watched.

I throw the unit down.

"Foreman Bargasa," I say. My stomach knots up. "I cannot do this. When I was a child, a Martian visited me. Told me tales of his family. I am shamed I did not report him. I am his grandson. I am a Martian."

In my head I could hear Donyo saying, "You see! No good has come of this!"

Having sealed my own doom, I doubled over in the white-hot pain of self-hatred.

When the Martians surrendered, several years later -- though how many I wasn't sure, since we prisoners made a pact not to count the days -- I was imagining myself recording Agony. In fact, Bargasa's guards were thrashing me with an ice rope. They did this to us Martians routinely, for no particular reason. Perhaps it was because we wouldn't count the days? It helped to depersonalize the pain, as if I were merely reviewing another prisoner's beating. We had become as close as brethren, us Martians.

I forgave the Collective nonetheless. Deep down I was Jovian. They had to purge me of my sins. The longer I stayed in the relocation dome, the closer to my brothers I became, the greater my sins, the more we deserved the rope. We shared our pain together as we shared everything else, twenty people to ten bunks and five blankets.

Soon after the war ended they released me. Bargasa himself led me to Donyo's dome. "Do good work, Master Haig," he said, and stung my back with a slap.

I resolved to prove Donyo wrong, that on the contrary, some good might come of this.

When Mars issued a formal apology for the war of fifty standard years ago, I was reviewing my apprentice Carlista's recording of Love for my re-sensorizing of "Snow White." I have had other apprentices over the years, and all added to the Collective's coffers. But no other apprentice has had such a talent as Carlista's. I did not ask her from where she got this Love, since ours was still very much a loveless society. But the feeling she recorded was so pure, so intense, that when the Martian Chancellor openly wept over it during the Voice of Earth broadcast, I wept too. And then memories flooded back of my years imprisoned. The random, senseless beatings. Fighting through the stomach pains and uncontrollable shaking of sensoria withdrawal. The innocent detainees and Nishka and other POWs they killed trying to force me to work on their evil project. The memory of how I almost gave in.

"What is wrong, Master Haig?" she asked. "Would you like some tea?"

I patted her shoulder. "No, thank you, Carlista. I was remembering the war. Someday I should tell you. When you are old and dying like me, you'll understand. I've lived a long life. Sometimes your memories remind you just how long."

Master Donyo's searing, twinkling eyes peered out at us from the wall-mounted holo of his bust. His name had become a legend of mythic proportion. None knew the real Donyo now, only the epic sensies.

"Do good," I felt him saying.

A rat scurried past our feet. "Ooh!" she shrieked. "How I hate them!" She sat pensively for a moment, but bit her lip.

"What is it, Carlista? I know your habits. What do you want to say?"

She gave me a quick smile. "Something I discovered, master. When you slept... the rats... I..."

"What is it, child? What?"

Her face shone with glee. "I've recorded Death, master. When I play it to them, they die!"

Ohmygodmygodmygod, I thought. My face felt hot, flushed. Stomach pain I had not known for decades seared my fattened belly. I grabbed the table for support.

Such a weapon must never be loosed. I calmed my body as I had learned in the camp, lest I should die before I stopped her. My heart is not so strong any more.

"You must destroy it, Carlista," I said, my voice hoarse. And I told her of the war, the relocation domes, of Donyo, Nishka, and their baby she had called Emmeth.

"Carlista, it is too terrible. You must destroy it and forget it forever! Take your Love instead, and add it to every 2d you do. A subliminal, as I showed you." Then I uttered a heresy. "I am too old to care if they kill me now. The Collective is wrong, based upon a rotting foundation. Parents must know their children, and love them."

I told her to insert Love of Family in every sensie she did for Jovian experience. Dislike of the Collective, also. As, I confessed, I had secretly been doing for decades. Her recording of Love was so much stronger, it would finally have the effect mine lacked. "'Work from Within,' as Master Donyo once said."

"Master Haig, do not talk of those things!" She looked about the empty dome as if someone might overhear, but she did not run. Did not report me.

"One more thing you must know, child," I said, taking her hand. "Master Donyo, that greatest of men..."

I choked up. Forgive me, Master Donyo. Some good may come of this, as you might say.

"He was your grandfather."

"Sensoria" © Andrew Burt. First published here in this anthology, *To Ukraine, With Love*, Cosmic Roots & Eldritch Shores' Benefit Anthology for Ukraine.

Dr. Andrew Burt is founder & moderator of the first writers workshop on the web, Critique.org; the founder of the world's first Internet service provider – Nyx.net; donation funded, & still going strong; CEO ReAnimus Press specializing in bringing out of print books back to life; former Vice President of Science Fiction and Fantasy Writers Association, professional science fiction writer, retired computer science professor at the University of Denver (research in AI, networking, security, privacy, and free-speech/social issues), and CEO of TechSoft https://www.aburt.com/

Danged Black Thing

Eugen Bacon & E. Don Harpe

'DEY'S A TIME TO MAKE a stand, and dey's a time to make tracks,' my daddy used to say. I didn't understand what he meant, 'cause I'd never had to do either, but the fact is, I'm a right smart gal. I took one look at the yard filled with them danged gizmos and just about hit the road.

My name is Champ McPherson, and I've seen hardware and software do all kinds of dang stuff. Viruses wiping more than one system clean, and I never had the inclination to get the hell out of Dodge. But you don't have to tell me twice. One look out the front window, and out the back door I leapt.

The first of them danged black thangs arrived at noon. I watched them from the safety of the attic (locked), knew the electric fence would do a number on them. And it did! At first! But soon the fence lay on the ground smoking, as they rattled bolts, banged at the chain link, jumped back and forth, all angry and riled, getting ready to rush the house, looking to gain an entrance by breaking down doors or smashing windows. They were fine-looking portables, laptops mostly, but from the attic window I could make out a few palmtops, desktops and a couple of mainframes chugging up steam down below. Every one of them black as ebony.

The mainframes lent muscle to the rest of the apparatus down there and, before long, they'd smash into the house. I knew.

Wasn't she something? I found her at an ancient shop in Omega Street one mild autumn day. 'Second hand,' the shopgirl said. 'Some missionaries from Mozambique. Didn't want a dollar for it, but I gotta make a buck.'

I eyed the machine in astonishment, ran my fingers across her dark silk coat. I stroked the feminine outline of her screen, the contours of which bore the silhouette of a black woman's face, lush lips, eyes like a deer's and all. She was perfect. Just the thing I needed to zing up Slade's humdrum life. 'Twas hard enough getting his notice in bed; a piece of equipment might spark more attention off him, I thought. He could use her as a journal or a word processor, or perhaps a platform upon which to test the Tec-build software for his shuttles.

Slade, he was a good boy, played it straight. Head full of tick-tock thoughts, I could read him like a watch, ever since and before we wed. He was a shuttle repairman down the South Depo. Every day he worked an eight-to-five. I never once knew him to miss a day of work, not even an hour. Soon as he was done at the factory, he'd be home like clockwork, never skipped the evening news.

Well Slade, he lit up like a Christmas tree, just soon as his eyes set on the notebook.

'Her name's Embu,' I said. 'Bought her just fer yew.'

'Yews de sweetest thang, my white chocolate,' he said to me. 'Brought me a dark truffle.' He at once powered the machine. Her screen saver had chocolate eyes full of soul and thick braided hair, all kinky. Her skin was black velvet.

'She looks almost human,' he said in stupefaction.

'Shock proof,' I said. 'Trendy, ain't she? And packs a refined graphics interface. Real time tracker too. Inbuilt. Yew can never lose her.'

Puppy eyes sought consent or authentication that he could fiddle with his new toy.

'Go on.' I smiled.

He vanished into the study, and I capped the occasion by cooking for him. This was an old gourmet recipe I got from my grandma, back in '17 before she passed.

I grabbed a couple cans of red beans and a box of instant rice from a shelf in the pantry, took a pound or so of hot sausage, some okra from the chill bin, didn't take long for the kitchen to start smelling like the old South, back when there still was an old South. A random thought crossed my mind as I set the table. Before I knew it, I had spiked a punch to set the mood right.

Slade emerged from his den with an odd look, gobbled his dinner in silence. Soon as I rose to clear plates, he gripped my arm, escorted me to our chamber. There, he lay with me with more zeal than I had ever witnessed, with more ardour than he'd ever shown, even on a mating moon.

From an eight-to-five, Slade became a nine-to-four, never mind it sliced our income. He left for work an hour late, having spent time with Embu; left the assembly line an hour early, another session with the machine before the evening news. His eyes now carried more than their pensive light. What went on inside them was more than tick-tock thoughts.

As for Embu, when I wiped her screen, her eyes were nicely smoked up, her brow smudged with colour, her ebony cheeks spread with scarlet blush to lift her complexion even more. Her braided hair was kinkier than ever, her full lips blood keen.

'Oh my,' I said to her with a tart smile. 'Aren't yew just de most darling little thang? Africa is where yew belong. Some wilderness camp or elephant graveyard in Mozambique. Don't know as I've ever seen a cuter…notebook, and I reckon Slade – well, *honey*, he thinks so too!'

A leopard-patterned petticoat, the shape of a rose, spattered with dark rosettes, glided along a velvet thigh across the screen. But what got to me was the smile, Embu's teeth like freshwater pearls. I reached for the machine with spiteful hands, ready to crash her to the floor and trample her good. And then I caught myself. Surely! This was a tad paranoid to say the least, perhaps even a smidgen over the frame. Was my mind hot and bothered with jealousy of a laptop?

There was no necessity for it, for sure, as Slade took me now each night, mating moon or not. I had something solid with him; nothing could beat that. No stupid Tec-build would take my Slade away.

He still spent a lot of time in his den before the taking, so one day I had to know.

'Dis ain't right,' I said to Slade. 'What yew do in dere? What take so long? Yew know, wit Embu? What yew doing wit dat machine?'

'Stuff, just stuff. Nothing much.'

'What kinda stuff?'

'A bit a dis, a bit a dat. Nothing much.'

I raised an eyebrow, stared at him.

'Dat's de truth, yes, love,' without flinch he said.

But with Embu's gilded brightness lighting up the house, I was now certain that no spiked punch or dinner thing, not even Slade's need for me, fit the math to make him that committed, so aberrantly savage when we were joined between the sheets, when straight from the den he took me like a demon.

He kept coming back for more but, desolate, I understood. It was nothing to do with a statement that I was unresistingly scrumptious, and everything to do with Embu, wrapping my husband with the silk of her web.

One night, after yet another of my grandma's old-fashioned New Orleans dinners, he set out as usual for the den where Embu waited. I cleared the table, packed the dishes in the spinner, set it on. By the time the dishes were done and sparkling, Slade had still not emerged. I made myself a cuppa, steaming black coffee, laced it with the last of a bottle of brandy. I cupped the china with both hands, as if holding a fragile heart, finished my coffee alone.

Only then did I give up on Slade and, with it, any hope of a tumble. I thought I heard voices behind the door of the den, one crafty and eager, the other soft and caressing. Sounds like jungle, the mews and purrs of a leopard, the laughter of a hyena. I stood outside that door, hugged myself not for warmth but dread. Was what I heard a sound card processing inside a machine, or demons in the core of my head? With profound wretchedness and legs knock-kneed with sadness, I made my way to the chamber.

Slade… He stole inside the sheets beside me as the clock inched to midnight. I counterfeited sleep but he did not nudge me to wake me. I opened an eyelid, and there was no keen look on his face, the one he wore before he dragged me into his arms at dusk. Slade lay on his side, elbow under his head, half a smile on his face. He was fast asleep. He did not want me tonight; it hit me hard as he snored away. My husband did not want me.

Next evening, I cooked for him something different. I grabbed green onions from the pantry, tossed them on top of reserve marinade chicken in a ceramic dish, spooned in some olive oil and pepper, baked everything until golden. He wolfed it down without notice and then vanished into the den.

He was even later coming to bed that night. I tossed and turned, tossed and turned again. Close to midnight, the door squealed, and he slunk into the bedroom. I sat up with riot hair, snapped on the bedside lamp. And there he stood, guilty as sin. He started to explain, something about some project or other. But I saw a hickey on his neck.

'Love at first bite, was it?'

Anger, when it arrived, came fast and hard like a thunderbolt. I leapt, cross-eyed with fury. My fist brushed past his jaw when I meant to punch his nose. I reached for his neck, proposing to strangle him, found it was sticky. I leant close, and a sickly aroma of maple syrup wafted into my nostrils. Maple! That hickey was no lean bite, no mistake: it was a premier hickey, no holdback on it. And Slade had smeared maple syrup on his neck for it. A leopard can't change its spots, and Embu was a wild one.

Finally, worn out with hitting him, I just lay on the bed and pondered slitting my wrists or shredding up Slade. But all I wanted really, I finally figured, was to shove effin Embu up his butt. The bubbles of something unformed spread inside me and rose to the surface but, before they could formulate into a plan, they were gone from my head.

This was real, how easy, a Zulu goddamn machine had replaced me.

Sobbing into my hands, I fled. Dressed in nothing but a negligee, I ran out of the bedroom, leapt down the steps and out the front door into a well-lit street.

Slade stamped at my heels in bedroom slippers, beside himself and saying over and over: 'It was just stuff. Nothing much. Dat's de truth. Dat's de truth!' His feet closed fast. 'Yew git back here. Champ McPherson.'

I turned right, ran all the way to the freeway. There, right there in the middle of the road, I lay face up, arms spread.

And though the road was dead at night and no traffic haunted it, Slade beseeched me, 'I love yew. Yews de sweetest thang. Git off de road!'

Just then, headlights rose from the distance. The red grew bigger and sharper until a turbo bus rolled into view. The driver was bobbin his head, lips pushed out like he was whistling.

Deaf to the rumble of the bus or Slade's pleading I lay silent. It took some time before I realised that Slade had stopped the bus; that the driver had raised me and tossed me onto grass at the other side of the road; that Slade had pulled me up by the arm and was leading me home.

Back in the house, I made straight for the den. But, again, Slade tried to calm me.

'Damn yew!' My fists pounded his face. I struggled with him, and was unstoppable this time. When I burst into the den, I was yelling and crying. I took hold of Embu, who sat grinning on his desk. She shuddered mildly, it seemed, as I raised her above my head and bashed her onto the ground. But her screen flew open and her face grew full of sweetness and deep secrets: vague, butter smile full of knowing, the smile of an adulteress. I flung her against the wall, and she crashed back to the floor. I was falling and kicking and sweating and thrashing. I meant to wreck her once and for all. But when I was done, she shone darker and brighter than ever, finer than new.

Embu was shock proof. Now she regarded me with a half-crooked smile. I moaned into the arm of my nightie that was torn and falling off my shoulder. I went down on all fours and cried to the gods of all ancestors when I wasn't cussing Slade.

'Godsake, Slade, a hickey!'

He drew me gently but firmly away from his den.

When he was asleep, I snuck out of the chamber and staggered right back to the den. I pushed Embu into a plastic bag and stashed her out with the garbage. Splendid thing there was a collection at dawn.

I slept until the wheels of the garbage truck woke me. I found Slade in the kitchen, his arms tenderly wrapped around Embu. He wore the defiant look of a boy protecting his toy. Her inbuilt tracking device had led him to her. He locked the den and put a security code on it.

Soon as he left for work, I ran out the garden and into the shed. I grabbed a hammer, beat down the door. I threw Embu into the trunk and sped all the way to the lake. Three big sways, *hooray!* and Embu pitched-straight up into the air and down in an arch. She met the lake with a splash.

Water closed over her head, and she did not come up.

I was bone weary when I arrived home. But elated I had got rid of that black bitch once and for all. I poured myself a cup of coffee, laced it with new brandy.

I was on a second cup when the danged gizmos arrived. Machines from hell, they were, Embu's spirits come to get me.

Before I hit the back door to the nearest telebooth, where I could call the military, get smoke, bazookas and lasers on them, I looked out the attic window at a mainframe, a large male autobot, bulk iron and face like Shaka Zulu, an intel warrior most lustrous and robust. I thought how fine-looking a specimen...

If Slade could do it, that selfish prick, heck! maybe I could.

But what I could do most with now was a plan to seduce a hunk in the middle of a riot.

"Danged Black Thing" © Eugen Bacon & E. Don Harpe. First published in Jagged Edge of Otherwhen by Interbac, July 2012

Eugen Bacon is an African Australian author of several novels and fiction collections. She's a 2022 World Fantasy Award finalist, a Foreword Book of the Year silver award winner, and was announced in the honor list of the 2022 Otherwise Fellowships for 'doing exciting work in gender and speculative fiction".
Danged Black Thing, by Transit Lounge Publishing, was a finalist in the Foreword, BSFA, Aurealis, and Australian Shadows Awards, and made the Otherwise Honor

List as a 'sharp collection of Afro-Surrealist work.' Eugen's creative work has appeared worldwide, including in *Award Winning Australian Writing*, Fantasy Magazine, Fantasy & Science Fiction, and *Year's Best African Speculative Fiction*. Eugen has two new novels, a novella, and three anthologies (ed) out in 2023, including *Serengotti*, a novel, and the US release of *Danged Black Thing*. Visit her website at eugenbacon. com and Twitter feed at @EugenBacon

E. Don Harpe has had a varied career, ranging from military service in the 1960s to industrial engineering. A published Nashville songwriter, he is a real descendant of the Harpe Brothers, America's first serial killers. Harpe has nearly forty short stories, including two in the Twisted Tales II anthology that won the Eppie Award for best science fiction anthology in 2007. Harpe lives in South Central Georgia, USA, and devotes his time to his family and his writng.

Bubbles

David Brin

1.

On planets, they say, water always runs downhill ...

Serena had no way of knowing if it was true. She had never been on a planet. Not in her brief million or so year life so far. Nor had any of her acquaintances. The very idea was absurd.

Few Grand Voyageurs ever got to *see* a planet. Yet, among them, some ancient truisms were still told.

That which goes up must fall, and will ...

The clichés came out of a foggy past. Why question them? Why even care?

No matter how far down you fall, you can always go lower still ...

Stunned and still nearly senseless from her passage through the mael-strom, Serena numbly contemplated truths inherited through the aeons from distant times when her ancestors actually dwelled on tiny slivers of rock, close to the bright flames of burning stars.

She had had no inkling, when she tunneled away from Spiral Galaxy 998612a with a full cargo, that the ancient sayings would soon apply to her.

Or do they? she wondered. Was she perhaps as far down as one could possibly get? It seemed to Serena, right then, that there just wasn't any lower to go.

Systems creaked and groaned as her instruments readapted to normal space-time. Serena still felt the heat of her passage through Kaluza space. That incandescent journey via the bowels of a singularity had raised her temperature dangerously near the fatal point.

Now, though, she realized that her radiators were spilling that excess heat into a coldness like none she ever knew before. Blackness stretched in all directions.

Impossible. My sensors must be damaged, she hoped.

But the repair drones reported nothing wrong with her instruments.

Then why can I not see stars?

She increased the sensitivity of her opticals, increased it again, and at last began to discern patterns—motes of light—spread across the black vault.

Tiny, tiny, faraway spirals and fuzzy globes.

Galaxies.

Had she been an organism, Serena might have blinked, closing her eyes against dismay.

Only galaxies?

Serena had traveled deep space all her life. It was her mission—car-rying commerce between far-flung islands of intelligence. She was used to black emptiness.

But not like this!

Galaxies, she thought. *No stars, only galaxies, everywhere.*

She knew galaxies, of course—island universes containing gas clouds and dust and vast myriads of stars, from millions to trillions each. Her job, after all, was to haul gifts from one spiral swirl to the next, or to and from great elliptical giants, galaxies so huge that it seemed extravagant of the universe to have made more than one.

She had spent a million years carrying cargo from one galaxy to an-other, and yet had never been outside of one before.

Outside! She quailed from the thought, staring at the multitude of foggy specks all around her. *But there* isn't *anything outside of galaxies!*

Oh, she had long used distant ones for navigation, as stable points of reference, but nearly covered in a swarm of nearby stars in a great galactic disk, vast because it lay all around her, a bright, restless, noisy place filled with traffic and bustling civilizations.

She had always felt sorry for the members of those hot little cultures, so busy, so quick. They flashed through their tiny lives so briefly. They never got to see the great expanses, the vistas that she traveled. Their kind had *made* her kind, long ago. But that was so far in the past that few planet-dwellers any longer knew where the Grand Voyageurs had come from. They simply took Serena and her cousins for granted. Packing her holds with treasures to carry to the next culture, in a never-ending chain of paying-forward.

No, she had never been outside before. For traveling *among* the galaxies had never meant traveling *between* them.

Her job was to ply the deep ways at the hearts of those galactic swirls, where stars were packed so dense and tight that their light hardly had room to escape, where they whirled and danced quick pavanes, and occasionally collided in brilliant fury.

Sometimes the crowded stars combined. In the core of every galaxy there lay at least one great black hole, a gravitational well so deep that space itself warped and curled in tight geometries. And these singularities offered paths—from one galaxy to another.

The great nebulae were not linked at their edges, but at their hearts.

So how did I get here? Serena wondered. *Here, so far from any galaxy at all?*

Part of the answer, she knew, lay in her cargo bay. Pallet fourteen was a twisted ruin. Some violent event there had bruised her Kaluza fields, just at the most critical phase of diving into a singularity, when she had to tunnel from one loop of space-time to another.

In disgust she used several of her remote drones in pryimg apart the tortured container. The drones played light over a multicolored, spiny mass. Needlelike projections splayed in all directions, like rays of light frozen in midspray. The thing was quite beautiful. And it had certainly killed her.

Idiots! she cursed. Nobody had informed her that antimatter was part of her cargo. In Kaluza space, the normal means for containing cargo were inadequate. She had thought even the most simpleminded of the quick-life cultures would know to take precautions.

She tried to think.

To remember.

In that last galaxy there had been funny little creatures who twittered at her in languages so obscure even her sophisticated linguistic programs could barely follow them. The beings had used no machines, she recalled, but instead flitted about their star-filled galactic core on the backs of great winged beast/craft made of protoplasm. A few of the living "ships" were so large that Serena had been able to see them unmagnified, specks fluttering near her great bulk. It was the first time she recalled ever seeing life up close, without artificial aid.

Perhaps the creatures had not understood that machine intelligences like Serena had special needs. Perhaps they thought …

Serena had no idea what they thought. All she knew was that their cargo had exploded just as she was midway down the narrow Way between that galaxy and another, diving and swooping along paths of twisted space.

To lose power in a singularity. Serena wondered. It had happened to none of the Voyageurs she ever encountered. But, sometimes Voyageurs *disappeared.* Perhaps this was what happened to the ones who vanished.

Galaxies.

Her attention kept drifting across the vault surrounding her. The brush strokes of light lay scattered almost evenly across the sky. It was unnerving to see so many galaxies, and no stars. No stars at all.

Plenty of stars, she corrected herself. But all of them smeared—in their billions—into those islands in the sky. None of the galaxies appeared to be appreciably above average in size, or appreciably closer than any other.

By this time her radiators had cooled far below the danger level. How could they not? It was as cold here as it ever could get. Enough light struck her to keep the temperature just near three degrees absolute. Some of that faint light came from the galaxies. The rest was long-wave radiation from space itself. It was smooth, isotropic. The slowly ebbing roar of the long-ago birth of everything.

Her remote drones reported in. Repairs had progressed. She could move, if she chose.

Great, she thought. *Move where?*

She experimented. Her drives thrummed. She felt action and reaction as pure laser light thrust from her tail. Her accelerometers swung.

That was it. There was no other way she could tell she was moving at all. There were no reference points, whose relationships would slowly shift as she swept past. The galaxies were too far away. Much, much too far.

She tried to think of an adjective, some term from any of the many languages she knew, to convey just how far away they were. The truth of her situation was just sinking in.

Serena knew that planet-bound creatures, as her distant ancestors had been, would have looked at her in amazement. She was herself nearly as large as some small planets.

If one of those world-evolved creatures found itself upon her surface, equipped with what it required to survive, it might move in its accustomed way—it had been called "walking," she remembered—and spend its entire brief life span before traveling her length.

She tried to imagine how such creatures had looked upon the spaces *between* their rocky little worlds, back in their early days. It was a millionfold increase in scale from the size of a planet to that of a solar system. The prospect must have been daunting.

And then, after they had laboriously conquered their home planetary system, how they must have quailed before the interstellar distances, *another* million times as great! To Serena this scale of distance was routine, but how stunning those spaces must have seemed to her makers! How completely frustrating and unfathomable!

Now she understood how they must have felt.

Serena increased power to her drives. She clung on to the feeling of acceleration, spitting light behind her, driving faster and faster. Her engines roared. For a time she lost herself in the passion of it, thrusting with all her might toward a speck of light chosen at random. She spent energy like a wastrel, pouring it out in a frantic need to *move!*

Agoraphobia was a terrible discovery to a Grand Voyageur. She howled at the black emptiness, at the distant, tantalizing pools of light. She blasted forth with the heat of her panic.

Galaxies! Any galaxy would do. Any one at all!

Blind to all but terror, she shot through space like a bolt of light… but light was far too slow.

Sense took hold at last, or perhaps some deep-hidden wisdom circuit she had not even known of triggered in a futile reflex for self-preservation. Her drives shut down and Serena found herself coasting.

For a time she simply folded inward, closing off from the universe, huddling in a corner of her mind darker even than the surrounding night.

2.

Galaxies have their ages, their phases, just as living things do. Aim your telescope toward the farthest specks, motes so distant that their light is reddened with the stretching of the universe. The universal expansion makes their flight seem rapid. It also means that the light you see is very, very old.

Yet these are the *youngest* things you will ever see. Quasars and galaxies at the very earliest stages, when the black holes in their cores were hot, still gobbling up stars by the hundreds, blaring forth great bursts of light and belching searing beams of accelerated particles.

Look closer. The galaxies you'll see will be flying away from you less quickly, their light will be less reddened. And they will be older.

Pinwheel spirals turn, looking like fried eggs made out of a hundred billion sparks. In their centers the black holes are now calmer. All the easy prey have been consumed, and now only a few stars fall into their maws, from time to time. The raging has diminished enough to let life grow in the slowly rotating hinterlands.

Spiral arms attest to where clots of gas and giant molecular clouds concentrate in shock waves, like spume and spindrift gathering on wind-swept verges. Here new stars are born. The largest of these sweep through their short lives and explode, filling surrounding space with heavy elements, fertilizing the fields of life.

Barred spirals, irregulars, ellipticals… and all the other galaxy types, sprayed like dandelion seeds across the firmament.

But not randomly. No. Not randomly at all.

3.

Slowly, Serena came back to her senses. She felt a distant amusement. *Dandelion seeds?*

Somehow her similes had taken on a style so archaic… perhaps it was a defensive reaction. Her memory banks drew forth an image of puffballs bending before a gusty wind, then scattering sparkling specks forth …

Fair enough, she thought of the comparison.

She'd lost all sense of motion, although she knew she had undergone immense acceleration. Galaxies lay all around her. Apparently unchanged.

She looked again on the universe. Peered at one quadrant of the sky, then another.

Perhaps they aren't scattered as smoothly as I'd thought.

She contemplated for some time. Then decided.

Fortunately, her cargo wasn't anybody's property, per se. *Gifts.* That was what the Grand Voyageurs like her carried. No civilization could think of "trade" between galaxies. Even using the singularities, there was no way to send anything in expectation of payment.

No. The hot, quick, short-lived cultures accepted whatever Grand Voyageurs like Serena brought, and then loaded her down with presents to take to the next stop. Nobody ever told a Voyageur where to go. Serena and her cousins traveled wherever whim took them.

So she wasn't really stealing when she started dismantling her cargo section, pulling forth whatever she found and adapting the treasures for her own purposes.

The observatory took only fifty years to build.

4.

Strings.

Bubbles.

The galaxies were not evenly distributed through expanding space. The "universe" was full of *holes.*

In fact, most of it was emptiness. Light shimmered at the edges of yawning cavities, like flickers on the surface of a soap bubble. The galaxies and clusters of galaxies lay strung at the fringes of monstrous cavities.

While she performed a careful survey, cataloging and measuring every mote her instruments could find, Serena also sought back through all her records, through the ancient archives carried by every Grand Voyageur.

She found that she had not been the first to discover this.

The galaxies were linked with one another—via Kaluza space—through the black holes at their centers. A Grand Voyageur traveled those ways, and so never got far enough outside the great spirals to see them in this perspective.

Now, though, Serena thought she understood.

There wasn't just one *Big Bang, at the beginning of time,* she realized. *It was more complicated than that.*

The original kernel had divided early on, and then divided again and again. The universe had had many centers of expansion, and it was at the intersecting shock waves of those explosions that matter had condensed, roiled, and formed into galaxies and stars.

So I am at the bottom, she realized.

Somehow, when the explosion sent her tumbling in Kaluza space, she had slipped off the rails. She had fallen. Fallen nearly all the way to the center of one of the great explosions.

One could fall no farther.

The calculations were clear on something else, as well. Even should she accelerate with everything she had, and get so close to light-speed that relativistic time foreshortened, she would still never make it even to the nearest galaxy.

Such emptiness, she contemplated. Why, even the cosmic rays were faint here. And those sleeting nuclei were only passing through. It was rare for Serena to detect even an atom of hydrogen as a neighbor.

It is better, far,
to light a candle,
Than to curse the darkness.

For a time it was only the soft melancholy of ancient poetry that saved Serena from the one-way solace of despair.

5.

To the very center, then.

Why not? Serena wondered.

According to her calculations, she was much, much closer to the center of the great bubble than to any of the sprayed galaxies at its distant rim.

Indeed. Why not? It would be something to do.

She found she only had to modify her velocity a little. She had already been heading roughly that way by accident, from that first panicked outburst.

She passed the time reading works from a million poets, from a million noble races. She created subpersonae—little separate personalities, which could argue with each other, discussing the relative merits of so many planet-bound points of view. It helped to pass the time.

Soon, after only a few thousand years, it was time to decelerate, or she would simply streak past the center, with no time even to contemplate the bottom, the navel of creation.

Serena used much of her reserve killing the last of her velocity, relative to the bubble of galaxies. All around her the red shifts were the same, they remained constant. All the galaxies seemed to recede away at the same rate.

So. Here I am.

She coasted, and realized that she had just completed the last task of any relevance she could ever aspire to. There were no more options. No other deeds that could be done.

"Hello?"

Irritably, Serena wiped her conversation banks, clearing away the small subpersonae that had helped her while away the last few centuries. She did not want those little artificial voices disturbing her as she contemplated the manner of bringing about her own end.

I wonder how big a flash I'll make, she thought. *Is it even remotely possible that anyone back in the inhabited universe might see it, even if they were looking this way with the best instruments?*

She caressed the fields in her engines, and knew she had the will to do what must be done.

"Hello? Has somebody come?"

Serena sent angry surges through her lingula systems. *Stop it.*

Perhaps suicide would come none too soon. *I must be going crazy,* she subvocalized, and some of her agony slipped out into space around her.

"Yes, many feel that way when they arrive here."

Quakes of surprise made Serena tremble. The voice had come from outside!

"Who … who are you?" she gasped.

"I am the one who waits, the one who collects and greets," the voice replied. And then, after some hesitation:

"I am the coward."

6.

Joy sparkled and burst from Serena. She shouted, though the only one in the universe to hear her was near enough to touch. And she cried aloud.

"There is a *way!*"

The coward was larger than Serena. He drifted nearby, looking to her like nothing so much as just a great assemblage of junk from every and any civilization imaginable. He had already explained that the bits and pieces had been contributed by countless stranded entities before her. By now he was approaching the mass of a small star and had to hold the pieces apart with webs of frozen field lines.

The coward seemed disturbed by Serena's enthusiasm.

"But I've already explained to you, it *isn't a way!* It is death!"

Serena could not make clear to the thing that she had already been ready to die. "That remains to be seen. All I know is that you have told me there is a way out of this place, and that many have arrived here before me and taken that route away from here."

"I tell you it is a funnel into hell!"

"So a black hole seems, to planet-dwellers, but we Grand Voyageurs dive into them and traverse the tortured lanes of Kaluza space—"

"And I have told you that this is not a black hole! And that what lies within this opening is not Kaluza space, but a door into madness and destruction!"

Serena found that she pitied the poor thing. She could not imagine choosing, as it obviously had, to sit here at the center of nothingness for all eternity, an eternity broken every few million years by the arrival of one more stranded voyager. Apparently every one of Serena's predecessors had ignored the poor thing's advice, given him what they had to spare, and then eagerly taken that escape offered, no matter how hazardous.

"Show it to me, please," she asked politely.

The coward sighed and turned to lead the way.

7.

It has long been hypothesized that there was more than one episode of creation.

The discovery that the universe of galaxies was distributed like soap bubbles, each expanding from its own center, was the great confirmation that the Big Bang, at least, had not been undivided.

But the ideas went beyond that.

What if, they had wondered, even in ancient days, *what if there are other universes altogether?*

She and Coward traded data files while they moved leisurely toward the hole at the very center of All. Serena was in no hurry, now that she had a destination again. She savored the vast store of knowledge Coward had accumulated.

Her own Grand Voyageurs were not the first, it seemed, to have cruised the great wormholes between the galaxies. There were others, some greater, who had nevertheless found themselves for whatever reason shipwrecked here at the base of everything.

And all of them, no doubt, had contemplated the dizzying emptiness that lay before them now.

A steady stream of very strange particles emanated from a twisted shapelessness. Rarities, such as magnetic monopoles, swept past Serena more thickly than she ever would have imagined possible. Here they were more common than *atoms*.

"As I said, it leads to another place, a place in which the fundamentals of our universe do not hold. We can only tell very little from this side, just that *charge, mass, gravity,* all these have different meanings. So then, what hope does a creature of our universe have of surviving there? Will your circuits conduct? Will your junctions quantum-jump properly? Will your laser drives even function if electrons aren't allowed to occupy the same energy state?"

For a moment the coward's fear infected Serena. And the closer she approached, the more eerie and dangerous this undertaking seemed.

"And nobody has ever come back out again," the coward whispered.

Serena shook herself out of her funk. Her situation remained the same. If this was nothing more than yet another way to suicide, at least it had the advantage of being interesting.

And who knows? Many of my predecessors were wiser than I, and they all chose this path, as well.

"I thank you for your friendship," she told the coward. "I give you all of this spare mass, from my cargo, as a token of affection."

Resignedly, the coward sent drone ships to pick up the baggage Serena shed. They cruised away into the blackness.

"What you see here is only a small fraction of what I have accumulated," he explained.

"How much?"

He gave her a number, and for a long moment there was only silence between them. Then the coward went on.

"Lately you castaways have been growing more and more comn. I have hope that soon someone shall arrive who will leave me more than fragments."

Serena pulsed to widen the gap between them. She began to feel a soft tug—something wholly unlike gravity, or any other force she had ever known.

"I wish you well," she said.

The coward, too, began to slowly back away. The other's voice was chastened, somber. **"So many others find me pitiable, because I wait here, because I am not adventuresome."**

"I do believe you will find your own destiny," she told him. She dared not say what she really thought, so she kept her words vague. "You will find greatness that surpasses that of even those much more bold in spirit," she predicted.

Then, before the stunned ancient thing could reply, she turned and accelerated toward her destiny.

8.

On planets, they say, water always runs downhill …
From the bottom, from as low as one could go in all the universe, Serena plunged downward into another place. Her shields thickened and her drives flexed. As ready as she would ever be, she dived into the strangeness ahead.

She thought about the irony of it all.

He calls himself Coward… she contemplated this, and knew that it was unfair.

She, and all of those others who had plunged this way, blindly into the unknowable, were the real cowards in a way. Oh, she could only speak for herself, but she guessed that their greatest motive was fear, fear of the long loneliness, the empty aeons without anything to *do.*

And all the while Coward kept accumulating mass: bits of space junk … debris cast out from Kaluza space … cargo jettisoned or donated by castaways who, like her, were only passing through …

He had told Serena how much mass. And then he had told her that the rate of accumulation was slowly growing over the long epochs.

And with the mass, he accumulates knowledge. For Serena had opened her libraries to him, and found them absorbed more quickly than she would ever have thought possible. The same thing must have happened countless times before.

Already space had warped beyond recognition around her. Serena looked back and out at all the galaxies, distant motes of light now smeared into swirls of lambent glow.

Astronomers of every civilization puzzle over the question of the missing mass, Serena thought.

Calculations showed that there had to be more mass than could be counted by measuring the galaxies, and what could be detected of the gases in between. Even cosmic rays and neutrinos could not account for it. Half of the matter was simply missing.

Coward had told her. He was accumulating it. Here and there. Dark patches, clots, stuffed in field-stabilized clusters, scattered around the vast emptiness of the center of the great galactic bubbles.

Perhaps I should have stayed and talked with him some more, Serena thought as the smeared light melded into a golden glory.

She might have told him. She might have said it. But with all of his brain power, no doubt he had figured it out long ago and chose to hide the knowledge away from himself.

All that mass.

Someday the galaxies would die. No new stars would be born. The glow would fade. Life—even life crafted out of baryonic machines—would glimmer and go out.

But the recession of the dead whirlpools would slow. It would stop, reverse, and fall again, toward the great gravitational pull at the center of each bubble. And there universes would be born anew.

Serena saw the last glimmer of galactic light twinkle and disappear. She knew the real reason why she had chosen to take this gamble, to dive into this tunnel to an alien realm.

It was one thing to flee loneliness.

It was quite another thing to flee one who would be God.

No wonder all the others had made the same choice.

The walls of the tunnel converged. She plunged ahead.

All around her was strangeness.

David Brin is a scientist, speaker, technical consultant and world-known author. His novels have been New York Times Bestsellers, winning multiple Hugo, Nebula and other awards. At least a dozen novels have been translated into more than twenty languages. See more about him at https://www.davidbrin.com/biography.html

Waiting for Mother

Glenn Lyvers

I die a little every 182 minutes,
waiting, watching her pass by
with so much life inside –
bone-white against a teal sky,

mothership in orbit. She,

no bigger than a grain of rice
from my buglike perspective –
standing on an ancient glacier,
a wind-swept ice-blue river
of brittle frozen crystals,
looking up – still waiting.
Last night, I felt the darkness stir,
timeworn and pregnant with fear;
I am here, restless in the stillness,
Look down, mother – look down.

Glenn Lyvers is a writer, editor, and head of Prolific Press. You can find out more about him at https://glennlyvers.com.

FANTASY

Allegory of Power, George Janny

A Witch's Junk Drawer

Rebecca Buchanan

The witch departs
to fetch the tea
and the tea things.

The drawer waits.

Don't open it.

(After you have opened it,
don't touch anything.)

There will be spools and snippets and tangles of thread,
red and pale yellow and gaudy blue.
These are fates not yet woven,
lives yet to be lived,
terrible memories clipped away
in exchange for a secret or a kiss.
(Be wary which thread
you tie around your finger or wrist:
that fate or life or memory is yours now.)

Shiny rocks, too,
some worn smooth as glass,
others sharp enough to cut the air.
The witch has gathered these
from the bottom of the ocean
and the bellies of volcanoes
and the birthing caves of wild rivers.
(Would you sing like a whale?
Cleave the tongues of liars?
Know the thoughts of a salmon?
Then pick a stone.)

Feathers.
Crow and raven and jackdaw,
owl and eagle.
The witch will sew these into a cloak
and fly with the north wind,
eastward around the sun
and westward around the moon.
(Take care, for corvids are known for their greed,
the wisdom of owls is a burden,
and the bravery of eagles is often fatal.)

Bones.
So many bones.
Do you recognize any of them?
Feline and canine,
rat and mouse and raccoon.
(Would you be graceful, loyal,
cunning, quiet, or clever?)

And deer antlers,
and bear claws,
and wolf fangs,
some still stained red.
(Careful, for the antlers
are a heavy crown to wear,
the claws' strength is such
as to make you untouchable,
and the fangs will leave you hungry,
so very hungry.)

And there are eyes,
of course,
polished and gleaming.
The eyes of foxes and rabbits,
rivals and lovers,
and those who looked
where they should not.
(Choose, quickly.

Would you always see
the right path? The treasures
within the earth? The truth
hidden deep in a heart? Choose.)

Close the drawer,
if you can.

Sit. When the witch returns,
tea and tea things in hand,
say thank you.
Drink the tea.
When the witch smiles,
showing teeth, smile in return.
Do not show your teeth.

Leave,
if you can.

And when you return,
clutching the thread or rock or feather
or other stolen treasure,
and beg the witch to take it back,
do not lie.
A memory or a fate or an eye,
polished and gleaming,
for looking where you should not —

Payment must be made.

"A Witch's Junk Drawer" © Rebecca Buchanan, 2022. First published 2022 in Cosmic Roots & Eldritch Shores.
Rebecca Buchanan is editor of the Pagan ezine Eternal Haunted Summer, eternalhauntedsummer.com, and is a regular contributor to evOke:witchcraft*paganism*lifestyle. Her poems and short stories have been released in a variety of venues. Most recently, she has published the occult archaeological adventure *The Secret of the Sunken Temple* (Sigil House Productions) and *Not a Princess, But (Yes) There Was a Pea, and Other Fairy Tales to Foment Revolution*, by Jackanapes Press.

The River's Daughter and the Gunslinger God

Matthew Claxton

The river's daughter heard the new sounds in early spring, when the passes into the valley were still mantled in heavy snow. Hooves crunched through rotten ice, and a voice cursed. The intrusion woke her, in her little hut of birch and pine branches. She waded through the river, catching a fish in one hand for her breakfast, whispering thanks to her father as she bit into silver scales and white flesh. She clambered up the far side of the riverbank and crept through the fern and huckleberry, her footsteps silent as the falling dew.

The voice belonged to a dwarf, the hoofbeats to his red-eyed mule.

He was an unlovely creature, with the pale grey skin of his kind, mouth set in a scowl, nose bulbous, teeth like granite. His foul temper was stamped on his features plainly. His clothes were as rough and work-worn as his hands and face, but the pistol he wore at his belt was a fine piece of craftsmanship, gleaming steel with a carved ivory grip. On one finger, the dwarf wore a ring of gold that was as fair as anything to be found in the great cities of civilized lands.

As the river's daughter followed him, the dwarf paused from time to time to draw air into his wide nostrils, or bent to sip from the cold river.

He followed the scent to a sandbar, and swirled a pan in the creek water. He ignored the glacial bite on his pale fingers, and kept swirling until he saw the bright gleam.

His kind don't smile easily, and this dwarf less easily than most, but he allowed himself a satisfied grunt. He scooped out the gold dust with a callused finger and spread it across his tongue. He closed his eyes for just a moment and let the cold metal work its way down his throat, into his guts, his blood, his marrow. He opened his eyes and there was a glint of gold in the brown of his eyes. He packed up his gear and continued upstream into the valley. He had the taste of it in him now, the flavor of the gold, and he would find its source.

The river's daughter followed.

In the long age before the dwarf came through the pass, a giant had been struck down by the blows of a fellow immortal. The jotun's death throes had gouged deep ravines, his flailing fingers had scraped out box canyons. His stony flesh had sloughed away as sand and gravel, his jagged, shattered bones had formed the mountains through which the dwarf had journeyed. At the far end of the valley, his skull still loomed, a mountain topped by the cavernous cliffs of the dead jotun's brows.

In death the giant had given life to the valley, like a fallen tree that nourishes the forest. His sinews had mated like snakes, his skin had swollen to beget monsters like man's flesh begets maggots. A great motherless river roared out through his teeth, and the river in its turn had fathered its own children.

The river's daughter had hair as long and green as eelgrass, and skin the livid white of a fish belly. Her teeth were sharp, and through her thin lips, she sometimes whispered spells and curses, for her mother had been a sorceress.

Since her mother's departure, swathed in furs in the middle of a winter storm, the river's daughter had not seen a single outsider to the valley. She spoke to the winds and her siblings the creeks, and she amused herself by practicing charms to change her shape – spending a season as an otter, another as a bird.

She had little past and less future. Destiny had put no stamp on her.

This dwarf, this outsider who moved with such purpose, fascinated her. She watched him for days, from silent concealment in the forest.

The dwarf's name was Brokkr, and if he had vices, sloth was not among them. He followed the taste of gold on his tongue to a bend in the river, and by a broad sandbar he made a tidy camp. While his red-eyed mule cropped the ferns and scanty grasses, he panned the gravel, up to his knees in the water, trout scattering as he flung away useless rock and sand.

He found a dead tree, lightning-blackened, with a deep hollow at the base of its trunk. In the hollow, Brokkr stored his gold dust in tightly tied, tightly-woven sacks.

It was three weeks before Brokkr realized someone was watching him.

He squinted his eyes and glared at the silent forest. His hand strayed to the butt of his pistol.

The river's daughter rose from the ferns, head cocked to one side, arms slack.

Brokkr put down his hand. He laid his pan down on the gravel bar.

"Who are you, and what do you want here?"

"I was born in this valley," the river's daughter said, in a voice like water coursing over stone. "My father is the river over yonder. Who are you and what do you want here?"

Brokkr bristled at being challenged on his own claim. But still he was civilized, and for all that his manners were rusty, they yet endured.

"A visitor, and one who would be your neighbor," Brokkr said. "May I offer the poor hospitality of my camp?"

They ate hard tack and drank coffee, and said little, neither being made for conversation.

"I'm called Brokkr," said the dwarf, before she vanished back into the woods. "What are you called?"

"Sigrun," she said.

She returned each day, staying longer each time. Sitting on a fallen log, tin mug clasped in her hands, she'd watch Brokkr pan and shovel, watch him hammer together a sluice where a fast-rushing creek met the body of her father. Then she began to help him, guiding Brokkr to the best sandbars, warning him of places where the river coiled around hidden snags, pointing out where its richest beds lay.

In his turn he gave her knowledge, of tool and craft.

While he built a sluice, he showed her how to hammer a nail straight, the use of plane and chisel, level and plumb bob and carpenter's square. Along with the skills carried in hands, he taught her the charms and quiet words that shaped metal and wood.

He could be gruff, on the rare days when she did not immediately grasp his lessons. But he was not cruel. He would simply repeat himself, show her again, and guide her hands until she had caught the trick of the thing. She took to the new craft like a hawk to an open sky, and before long even the stern dwarf was forced to admit that she had learned well.

Sigrun watched every day the care the dwarf took with his work, the way he combed out his mule and checked its hooves, the way he grunted in satisfaction at a board cut straight and true.

By inches, the river's daughter felt the flickering flame of fascination grow into a bonfire within her breast.

The dwarf smiled at the gold shining in the bottom of his pan, and Sigrun smiled at him, and neither one of them understood the depth of the other's infatuation.

One day Sigrun did not leave Brokkr's camp. She went with him into the canvas tent, and lay beside him in the night.

It was the dawn of summer when others began to trickle through the high passes around the valley. They came alone or in small bands, men and dwarves, elves and trolls, things with three heads or lashing tails, bald as ivory or furred like a bear. They dragged their supplies on barrows and drove teams of snorting oxen hauling heavy carts.

The valley echoed with the sounds of saws and the crash of falling trees. The newcomers also took to the streams, and if their efforts were less fortunate than Brokkr's, they were not fruitless. Gold came forth from the river and the stone, gold that had once flowed as blood in the jotun's veins and salted his bones.

By late summer, there were three hardware stores, seven saloons, and two whorehouses in the valley, clustered together less than an hour's walk from the cairns that marked Brokkr's claim.

"I suppose it doesn't seem right that the first man in the valley should live in a tent," Brokkr said one evening, when the warm wind stirred the cottonwoods.

The next day, he began felling trees. The River's daughter helped him saw the planks and level the foundation.

By the time the summer was at its height, the house was finished. It was a fine thing, oak-boned and roofed with fragrant red cedar shakes. The powerful words Brokkr and Sigrun had bound to its beams made it proof against storm, against heavy ice or snow, against rot and the gnawing teeth of vermin. But it was not finished until the day Brokkr built window frames.

"Come," he said to Sigrun that evening. As the sun sank, he led her to a clearing, where he set the frames out on the soft meadow grasses and flowers. The sky was cloudless and bright with more stars than there are stories.

Brokkr spoke a few words and reached up with one rough hand to grasp at the sky. He tugged, and into his empty window frames, he spread falling dew and starlight. He smoothed it and spoke to it, and coaxed the cool clear light into shape.

Sigrun had caught the words, and mouthed them silently along with Brokkr.

"I'll try," she said, and she too poured a handful of silver light into a window frame. The glass was as clear as meltwater.

They set the windows into the house that night. Sigrun stayed up until she saw the dawn break through glass for the first time.

Winter fell on the valley like a wolf, and carried off those too weak or foolish to prepare.

For a fortnight, no one came through the pass. Anyone there should have been dead, a larder for the bears when they awoke come the spring.

Yet the stranger appeared out of the howling gale.

His buckboard was drawn by two black bison, the wooly hair of their backs clean of snow, bronze rings in their bridles, madness in their eyes. The stranger wore a broad-brimmed hat and a long, fringed coat. The handles of his two pistols and the knife in his boot were carved from black horn. His skin was pale, his eyes black. He stabled his animals and walked into the nearest saloon and ordered a drink. He paid with an old coin, the portrait of a long-dead king worn to smooth anonymity. He produced more coins as he finished each drink, and he didn't get up from his stool for three days, exhausting the saloon's stock of whiskey, one glass at a time. Then he moved on to the next bar.

Speculations began to circulate that a god had entered the valley. The barmen took his money. Everyone else gave him a wide berth.

"He's waiting for something," Brokkr told Sigrun one night. "When it comes, maybe he'll move on and leave us in peace." Something about the stranger bothered Brokkr, put an itch between his shoulder blades.

She arrived in the spring, with the first warm breeze.

The woman alighted from the stage onto the muddy thoroughfare in front of the Serpent's Head Hotel. Ferns and wildflowers sprang to life around the soles of her white boots. Her hair was bright as molten copper, her eyes the golden brown of wild honey. Her teeth were even and white, and her lips curled up into a smile so glorious that the poor bellhop of the Serpent's Head fumbled the coin she dropped into his palm. He rushed out to fetch her bags, hands shaking, the faint floral scent of her skin working its way deep into his mind. When he died, five score years later, it was that scent that would drift through his final dreams.

The name she wrote in the hotel register was Inkeri. She said nothing about her business in the settlement, but went straight up to her rooms and closed the door.

In a saloon at the far end of the muddy street, the stranger sat up straight in his chair and took in a heady lungful of air.

He laid a coin on the counter and walked straight to the Serpent's Head. He marched up the stairs to Inkeri's room. He rapped on the door.

She sent him away.

Brokkr heard the tale when he came to the town the following day to haggle for supplies.

"The dark-haired man, the one with the bison?" said the owner of the general store. "Someone had the iron-blooded courage to send him packing. A woman!"

Brokkr grunted as he grudgingly paid for his flour, lard, and pickled cabbage. He was loading his supplies onto the mule when the shutters of the Serpent's Head opened wide to let in the fine spring air.

Inkeri turned away from the windows, and Brokkr's glance caught her in profile, the curve of her brow and nose, lips and chin. He saw her reach up and unpin that copper hair, and watched it fall down her back, like a river of liquid fire from the earth's own heart.

She moved away from the window then, and Brokkr took a step forward, as if drawn on a line. He stood there for a long moment, dumbstruck.

That night, while Sigrun slept at his side and the moon poured light through the thin curtains of his fine home, Brokkr fretted and tossed, and he arose having slept not at all.

He returned to his diggings and chipped away with pick and shovel, he sluiced the golden flakes and nuggets from the soil, and for the first time in his long life, the sight of gold could not fill the gnawing desire in his heart.

By the fine house and the rich vein of his claim, Brokkr built a forge.

In the town, the nameless stranger returned each day to Inkeri's hotel room. He knocked and stood before the door, until a servant opened it and gave him a single regretful shake of her head. The stranger stomped down the stairs, his boots burning holes in the carpet runner, his gaze hot enough to catch the hotel register alight. The staff of the Serpent's Head scattered or ducked behind the desk when he arrived, and when he left they cleared up the damage.

"I wish she'd see him," muttered the hotel manager, who was no fool and feared worse to come. "Gods!" he said. "There's no trouble like godly trouble."

After nine days and nine refusals, the stranger hitched his bison to his buckboard and followed a rough track into the hills. His pistols were at his side, a long rifle slung behind his back, and chains and ropes coiled like snakes in the buckboard.

When he returned that night, tethered to his wagon was a bear far larger than any the settlement's inhabitants had ever seen. Its claws were like bayonets, its paws the size of skillets, and its heavy shoulders supported two monstrous heads. It was exhausted, breath heaving from its red mouths, tongues lolling. Two brass collars had been set round its necks and set to chains leading to one leash.

The stranger took the chain in hand and led the creature down the dusty main thoroughfare as though he were taking a dog for a walk. All those passing by suddenly remembered pressing business that must take place behind closed and locked doors.

The stranger stood in front of the Serpent's Head. Wordlessly, he raised the leash in offering.

The curtains of Inkeri's room twitched open a finger width, then closed again.

He stood there while the sun advanced across an eighth of the sky, but when there was no answer, he led the beast into the woods.

There followed a terrible mix of roars, then a retreating crashing, which no one felt inclined to investigate.

At dawn the stranger visited the town baths, and cleaned stinging black blood from his body. He dressed again in clean clothes. He drove his buckboard out of town.

So it continued for another eight days. The stranger returned with animals the likes of which few in the town had ever seen. On the second day he brought in a white stag with curling horns of solid bronze, that knelt before the Serpent's Head as prettily as a trained pony. On the third he drew a leashed wolf with eight legs and black fangs dripping venom, on the fourth a snake thick as a telegraph pole with a forked, rattling tail.

No wild prize, it seemed, was suitable for the woman who kept her rooms in the Serpent's Head. Each refusal enraged the stranger. The air stank of blood and magic.

A young witch who had come to make her fortune at the card tables abruptly paid extra for the first stage ticket back out of the valley. "You don't know the half of it," she said when the bellhop at the Serpent's Head asked her if she'd seen something. "There's more than him and her at play here."

She tugged at the blindfold that covered her eyes, and turned her face down the valley for a moment, then shuddered.

At his claim, Brokkr heard the howls and screams of strange beasts, but he paid them no mind. He hauled heavy beams and flagstones to build his forge. His sinews were strained and his hands bloody with ceaseless effort with axe and adze. From the upper windows of the house, Sigrun watched him. She had offered to help, and he had angrily refused.

Finally the forge was ready, and Brokkr stole to his hoard of gold by starlight and weighed out a precious store of dust.

For three days, he labored in his forge. When he emerged he carried a round broach. It was a circle of pure gold, gleaming and still warm as blood. Brokkr stood on the porch of his home and blinked smoke-reddened eyes. Sigrun stepped onto the porch next to him, carrying a mug of strong coffee, and he took it from her without a word. He never took his eyes off the broach.

The circle of gold showed leaping trout and chinook, sleek otters, foaming rapids. The scales of the fish gleamed in the dawn light, achingly close to real.

Sigrun stared at the broach, entranced. Brokkr never made anything that wasn't useful. His craftsmanship was impeccable, but all the beauty in his house, in his tools, came from the clean lines of a thing well fitted for its task. He could no more have built an ugly house than he could have built a cold, drafty one.

Yet here was a thing of great art as well as great craft. She reached out her slender hand, and Brokkr finally met her eyes.

"No," he said. He tucked the broach in the pocket of his apron, and the light on the porch dimmed a little, that golden gleam hidden away.

Sigrun let her hand drop to her side, limp. She searched Brokkr's face, and found nothing there. His eyes already sought the path that led towards town.

He went inside, leaving Sigrun on the porch. When he emerged he wore his newest clothes, clothes she had mended and cleaned for him, boots she had shined and left by the door of their bedroom. He walked past her without a word.

In the river, trout leaped wildly and the rapids lashed the stones and gravel. Sigrun's eyes were dry. She knew where Brokkr was going. The winds of the valley had been her friends since childhood, and they had shared the gossip with her, the story of copper-haired Inkeri's arrival in town. Even the southern breeze had spoken of her beauty.

The winds had also told of the black-clad man, and his efforts to court Inkeri. He knew her of old, the winds whispered, and she knew him, and this was some long game played by immortals, which beings who were born and lived and died could scarce understand.

Sigrun wrapped her arms around herself, and shivered with rage and sorrow.

She went back into the house, a house she had thought built for the two of them. But now she feared she was little more than another tool to Brokkr. He fed and curried his mule, he cleaned mud from his picks and pans, he rubbed the gleaming steel of his pistol with oil and kept it clean. When he had a woman, he built a house and gave her its keys. Was there no more than that?

Softly she went to the upper floor and stared out through the starlight windows, and she saw the scorched tree that concealed Brokkr's hoard of gold. Sigrun's nails dug into the soft wood of the windowsill.

He was walking to his death, and in that moment a part of Sigrun dearly wished for the arrogant dwarf to bleed out into the mud.

But he was the first man to have held her heart, unworthy vessel though he had proven.

An instant later, Sigrun was gone and a small grey bird perched on the windowsill. It fluttered into the sky.

Brokkr caught himself on the stairs of the Serpent's Head hotel, his course uncertain for the first time in many a year. He drew the broach out from the pocket of his jacket and felt its weight, the smooth fine features of the work, its golden light, and yet it seemed to him the merest trash to lay before the woman.

But it was all he had, and he could make nothing finer. Brokkr steeled himself, took the stairs at a steady pace, and rapped on the door. A servant girl peered out and demanded to know his business.

"A gift, for your mistress," Brokkr said, and he held up the broach like a talisman.

"I'll give it to her," said the girl.

Brokkr's arm drew back. "It'll go into no hand but hers," he said.

Even in the dim light of the corridor the girl could see the shine of the thing, feel the heat of forge and magic still radiating from it. She nodded and shut the door.

Inkeri stood there when it next opened.

As best he could Brokkr stammered out some rough greeting, while Inkeri smiled serenely, then he thrust the broach at her.

She took it, her fine white fingers brushing his coarse callused ones for a brief second.

He barely heard her prettily-worded thanks, or the suggestion that perhaps they might run into one another in the tea room downstairs some day, or the entirely polite dismissal as she had pressing appointments.

The door closed, and Brokkr found himself standing in the street, mouth hanging open like a dog's on a hot day.

In the distant woods, hunched over the spoor of an elk, the stranger smelled coal smoke, hot metal, and the reek of the forge. And behind that, a fine floral scent. He ran to his wagon. In a fury he set his bison to a wild gallop, heading back to town.

The coffin maker perked up his ears at the first gunshot. He allowed himself a feral smile. Business had been slow, what with folk leaving town. Those who remained spoke politely, drank alone, and played cards honestly, all of which was bad for his business.

But the second shot was louder than the first, the third louder still, and the fourth a thunderous crash like the cleaving of mountains. Wood splintered, men and women and animals screamed. The coffin maker ran to the window in time to see the facade of a saloon collapse into the street, a pile of splinters. Standing in front of the ruined building was the stranger, a smoking pistol in each hand.

Bleeding drunks pulled themselves from the rubble and fled.

A shattered table shifted, and from under it came a dwarf, the one from down the river who scowled at everyone like he had the toothache. A gun was in his hand.

The stranger waited. He still had bullets in his guns, and the coffin maker judged that one of them would finish off this dwarf, and then some.

"We'll bury him in a matchbox, that'll be how much is left of him," muttered the coffin maker.

But the god in the broad brimmed hat stood stock still, pistols at his side. He smiled, as if at last he had found some true sport, and he did not want it to be over too soon.

Brokkr raised his gun.

But Sigrun was standing on the top floor of the livery whispering charms her mother had taught her, mingled with prayers and pleas to her father. The river had burst its banks upstream from the town and flung itself down the thoroughfare, tearing away porches and painted signs, picking up wagon wheels and water troughs, saddles and stones and mud and logs. All of them struck the god with the force of the spring freshet, the time when the snow melts and flings itself at the sea with all the abandon of first love.

The god could stand against bullets and jotuns, but a flooding river was another matter. He was swept away, gone in an instant.

Brokkr stood before a wall of water, jaw slack. He looked up at the livery and met Sigrun's eyes, as the wave receded and left the street a muddy slough.

The dwarf holstered his pistol and looked down the ruined street. The manager was fleeing the Serpent's Head, the bellhop on the back of his horse, a carpetbag of cash slung next to the saddle. The buildings that had not been destroyed by the god's gunfire and the flood were starting to smoke, threatening an inferno. Somewhere in a pile of refuse down near the livery, the god was buried in shattered timbers.

On the upper floor of the Serpent's Head, Brokkr saw the light catch on copper tresses for an instant. The curtains twitched back.

He started down what was left of the street, and turned his face away from the river's daughter.

In the distance, the river rumbled.

The coffin maker was sensibly leaving before he had need of his own wares. He had packed his money and saddled his mare, and was urging her for the pass.

He rode past the Serpent's Head, and saw the two women looking at one another, the green-haired witch on the livery roof, the copper-haired woman on the hotel's porch. Inkeri's servant girl was loading luggage onto the last stage out of town.

"You should stay to see how it comes out," said Sigrun, a challenge in her voice. "See if your man kills mine, or mine yours."

"He's not my man," Inkeri said. "Nor is the other one yours, I think."

Sigrun was too proud to let her hurt show.

"I know how it turns out," Inkeri said. "It's happened a hundred times, in a hundred lands. And always the ending is the same."

Sigrun shrugged. "Your man's killed a lot of folks, I expect. But he might find Brokkr tougher than he supposes."

The corners of Inkeri's mouth twitched. She stepped down off the porch. But the mud of the river-washed road became green beneath her feet. Mountain flowers sprang up around her boots, a whole season's growth in seconds. They withered and died just as fast, petals scattering on the breeze.

"He'll die, a bullet in his belly," Inkeri said, as calm as if she were discussing the weather. "We all play our roles."

"I ain't playing," Sigrun said.

"But you have played. A bit part." Inkeri said. "Shall I tell you your future?"

"No."

"You will rule this valley. You will be its witch-queen, its forest hag, lurking in the shadows of the pines, wise and terrible. Your kin the jotuns will come seeking knowledge of the worlds beyond death, and you will give it to them, dragging wisdom from the cold places beneath the bones of the earth. You will live long, and wax powerful. But you will never know love again."

Sigrun felt the woman's words trying to grab hold of her, like burrs greedy for purchase.

"Are you sure, ma'am?" Sigrun said. "Because you can't catch me in a false prophecy. Not here. Not in my valley."

Sigrun vanished for a moment, and a bird fluttered down to the street, and then the river's daughter stood before the goddess, heavy square-toed boots inches from delicate calf skin. "Maybe you just want to snare me into a story because you hate what you can't have."

Inkeri's lips curled in a fair imitation of a smile.

"You envy me," Sigrun said. "The way stone envies fire. I'll die, but I can make my own way. You play the same part, over and over. Courted but never caught. Always followed. Always refusing. You must get tired, lonely, just playing your game, watching us mortals die, waiting for the end of all things."

Inkeri's mouth was a thin line. She began to speak but Sigrun held up a hand. Anger mingled with sudden pity in the heart of the river's daughter.

"Shall I tell your future?" Sigrun's voice filled with old power from her sorceress mother and the stone bones of her jotun grandfather, hot in her very marrow. "Before the world burns to a cinder, he'll catch you, or you'll slip away. You'll have your heart's desire, or you'll weep until you're wrung clean out. But the long chase will end. And you'll have a chance to make your own choice."

The power went out of Sigrun.

The goddess looked at her, and something in those perfect, empty eyes flickered. Fear or hope, or both together like close-growing pines. But then wordless she turned away and climbed into the stage, which soon left the ruined town behind.

A moment later, Sigrun was gone, too. A grey bird fluttered away into the smoky chaos.

It was mid-day by the time Brokkr reached his claim. The fine house was gone. Its timbers and cedar-shake roof were a waterlogged jumble amid the pines. Its starlight windows were smashed to pieces, the shards shrinking, turning to curls of silver mist in the sunlight.

The forge, built of thicker timbers, still stood, but its roof was torn apart, silt and gravel ankle deep on the floor.

Brokkr trembled and let the mule's lead drop. He ran breathlesly to the lightning-struck tree.

The tree had toppled. The hollow beneath it had been scoured clean. Not a speck of gold remained.

"My father is quick to anger in the spring," said Sigrun. She stepped from behind a fir tree, quiet as a fawn.

"You did this," Brokkr said.

Sigrun shook her head.

"Why did you interfere?" he snapped.

"Thought you might like to live through the day." She held out one hand, in invitation and forgiveness. "Come with me. We can go away. Build another house, somewhere far from here, hidden."

But he turned from her and looked at the distant dust cloud raised by departing horses and mules and wagons. His eyes sought for Inkeri. Then he glared at the hollow tree, emptied of the gold that could have adorned the copper-tressed woman. What gifts could he bring her now?

"I'll not be chased out of this valley without my gold," Brokkr said. "Not by a foolish girl!"

And this sliced the last strands of affection binding Sigrun to him.

"You'll take your mule and leave."

Brokkr's clenched his fists in fury, wishing to unleash them on Sigrun. But even fired with rage, he feared the moment after that, the rushing of vengeful water. "I can dig it free again," he said. "I can build again."

Sigrun shook her head. "He'll come for you, Brokkr."

"He's dead," the dwarf spat.

"No. He's a god. Even my father couldn't kill a god. Even I couldn't. He'll whisper your name to the winds, send them seeking for you across plains and mountains. He'll speak to the streams, ask if you've drunk from their waters. He'll find you."

"I can beat him," Brokkr said. He grasped the butt of his pistol. "I made this gun. The bullets are the first gold I ever mined. I etched them with runes, powerful charms, to fly true, find the heart's blood and drink deep to the death."

"Maybe," Sigrun said. "Maybe you can even take away Inkeri and lock her in a tower and keep her for a time. But not here."

She held her chin high, and no hurt showed in her eyes.

"I should never have taken you to my bed," the dwarf said, his words sour as vinegar. "I should never have given you the hospitality of my fire."

"Your fire? Your bed?" Beneath their feet the pines shook and the ground trembled. "This is my valley, my home, my birthright!"

Brokkr braced himself as Sigrun opened her mouth, and he waited for a curse to fly and find him.

But Sigrun lowered her hands and looked away.

"I'll lay no spell on your head," Sigrun said. "Nothing I could do is worse than what you've brought on yourself."

Brokkr nodded grimly. He salvaged what tools he could, bridled his mule, and started walking.

Sigrun turned away before he was out of sight.

When he was gone, she cried at last. She wondered that she had been such a fool and wiped tears from her eyes. The south wind rustled her long, winding hair and wrapped itself around her shoulders like a shawl.

The valley was empty again. Ferns pushed up through the blackened rubble of the town. When winter came, sluices collapsed under the weight of snow. The river rose and washed away the town built by men for the love of gold.

Sigrun retreated to her hut, cleaned out the cobwebs and dust, and slept again on the bed she had built for herself. She added a few tools – pots and pans, knives, a hatchet. Over her bed she hung a long saw, and at night she whispered the words Brokkr had taught her for shaping wood and metal and calling down starlight.

She thought of staying, of letting Inkeri's prophecy come true. Witch of the woods, prophet of the pine forests. She could make that life her own.

But summer brought the creak of oxcart axles in the pass, more gold lovers on the way. Sigrun found herself pacing the ridgelines, looking out over the distant peaks. The valley felt too small to share again.

By the time the first prospectors waded into the creeks, Sigrun was gone. She headed upriver, leaping the rapids in the skin of an otter, flying overhead on grey-feathered wings. In her own shape she walked past the skull of her grandfather, skirting the cliffs of his cheekbones, a pack on her back.

Maybe Inkeri's prophecy would still catch hold of her, and draw her back to the valley. Maybe she would never know love.

But she would craft her own tale, before she returned.

End

"The River's Daughter and the Gunslinger God" © Matthew Claxton First published March 15, 2017 in Cosmic Roots & Eldritch Shores.

Matthew Claxton is a reporter whose career has allowed him to encounter magicians, con artists, philanthropists, lemurs, robots, stunt pilots, Mounties, live bears, and politicians. His stories have previously appeared in Asimov's Science Fiction and Mothership Zeta. He lives near Vancouver, British Columbia. He writes a newsletter, Unsettling Futures, at https://www.getrevue.co/profile/ouranosaurus.

St. George and the Dragon, © Scott Gustafson. All rights reserved.
For more information please visit www.scottgustafson.com

The Trial of St. George

Andrew Jensen

"What in blazes is this?" bellowed St. George.

Reginald Thorpe-Jones, Barrister, paled slightly. "My dear George, calm yourself. I'd have expected that as a saint you'd be rather unflappable."

The aging knight waved a document at him. "As a saint my patience has not just been tried, it's been snapped altogether. Read this and see if I don't have reason to be furious!" With a sword-like thrust he held the paper out for his barrister's inspection.

Thorpe-Jones studied the document carefully. A deep frown grew on his brow.

"I'm afraid this is actually quite serious, George. You've been charged under the new Endangered Species Preservation Act with knowlingly and maliciously causing the extirpation, within England, of Draco Vulgaris, otherwise known as the Common Dragon."

"Poppycock!" exclaimed the irate Saint. "After I killed the last dragon in England I got sainthood, and dinners, and cutting ribbons, and television talk shows. Now things have settled down, Susan and I were beginning to enjoy my retirement. And that fellow had the cheek to serve this summons at my club!"

"Unfortunately, George, it's not Poppycock. Environmentalism is all the rage now. This law was passed by Parliament two months before you slew that final dragon. I suspect this is a test case. Why don't you just go home and relax? I'll ring you up when I've developed a strategy." Gently but firmly, Thorpe-Jones esorted St. George to the door.

St. George had little idea of how to relax. He took to wandering about the castle all hours of the night. In his armor. The clanking got to be a bit much for his wife.

"George dear," said Susan soothingly, "there's absolutely no need to worry. Reg is a marvelous barrister. He's complicated things terrifically for the Crown Prosecutor."

"Yes. He's insisted I be tried by my peers. But I doubt it will be as hard as he thinks to find twelve saints to make up a jury. The Church makes out quite well on sainting people."

The jury looked on with saintly patience as the trial progressed.

"Bishop Thumbshute," said the Crown Prosecutor, "did you preside at the canonization of St. George last November?"

"I had that honor."

"Did the Church's approval of the canonization require that first a satisfactory examination be made of St. George's accomplishments?"

"Yes, of course," replied the Bishop.

"Did you conclude that he had, in fact, slain the last remaining dragon on English soil?"

"Certainly," answered the Bishop. "My staff had researched this most diligently. Destroying the last of these monsters was a cornerstone of his eligibility for sainthood."

The Crown Prosecutor swooped in on the Bishop, and fixed him with an accusing stare. "Did it not occur to you, Your Grace, that in fact you were encouraging reprehensible, morally bankrupt, and unlawful behavior by honoring a man for slaughtering the last of an entire species of one of God's creatures?"

"Certainly not," the Bishop responded coldly. "That dragon had been terrorizing my diocese. It ate only virgins. Before St. George arrived, *virgins* were extinct in my diocese."

The Crown Prosecutor was shocked. "The dragon ate them all?"

"No. These young women developed a rather clever and practical form of self defense. They…" the Bishop cleared his throat, "ensured that they were not virgins. I suspect that without St. George, the dragon would have starved to death. As it is, I can encourage my priests to promote sexual morality again with a clear conscience."

"Have you seen today's lot?" shouted St. George, clanking into the castle with an armload of tabloids.

"No, dear," replied Susan over her knitting. "And I don't think you should look at them, either. They'll play havoc with your blood pressure." And thank goodness you never learned to use the internet! she thought.

"But these are intolerable!" exclaimed the saint. "Listen:

'WHY DID DRAGONS WANT VIRGINS? Exclusive Photos of Cave Orgies on page 4.'

"Here's another:

'GIRL SPAT OUT BY DRAGON DISOWNED BY FUNDAMEN-TALIST PARENTS: "She's disgraced the family!" Says Mother.' "

"Really, George," said Susan. "I wish you'd throw those on the fire. Or at least recycle them. They're not doing you a bit of -- "

"-- Infamy!" roared the saint. "Libelous slander! This!!:

'SEXY SAINT SAVES SWEET SIXTEEN. Yorkshire girl reports she was rescued from a fate worse than death by St. George himself, who saved her by removing her virginity. "He was wonderful," she told reporters. "He saved me five or six times that night.'

"Can you imagine?" he sputtered.

"Well no, I can't," murmured Susan. "The girl clearly doesn't know anything about you."

St. George hurled the paper into the fire. "My reputation is ruined! They'll un-saint me! What am I to do?"

Susan put down her knitting and comforted her husband. "There, there, love. Why don't you go down to Reg's club, and see how things are coming along? He'll have some good news for you."

"I can't understand why things are going so badly," said Thorpe-Jones, staring into his fifth brandy.

"What do you mean?" asked St. George, who had lost count of his own brandies.

"That Crown Prosecutor, Smythwick. I've known him for years. He's a gormless idiot. He hasn't got a single ounce of native wit. But throughout this trial he's outmaneuvered me at every turn. One step ahead all the way. Anticipated every argument and countered with unassailable replies. Closed every loop-hole with great skill. If I didn't know better, I'd suspect someone in his office had suddenly developed intelligence."

"One step ahead, you say?" remarked St. George, swaying. "Sounds like fighting a dragon. Crafty beasts. Once they start talking, you're lost. You must strike immediately. Many's the knight done in by letting a dragon get a word in first."

The barrister straightened. "Like a dragon, you say? Hmm. . . . ."

"My Lord, I move that all charges against the honorable St. George be dropped," said Reginald Thorpe-Jones.

"On what grounds?" asked the judge.

"He did not kill the last dragon in England."

Smythwick shot up. "My Lord, is he... is he saying the Church, the bishop, is lying?"

"Not at all my Lord!" rapped out Thorpe-Jones, "Rather it has come to our attention that the Crown Prosecutor's Office has in its employ an individual named Bertram. I hereby submit photographic evidence, taken only yesterday, of this same Bertram, at a seriously undersized desk, in the prosecutor's office."

Studying the photographs, the judge intoned, "Mr. Smythwick, what have you to say to this?"

"Um."

"And there, my Lord," crowed Thorpe-Jones, "we have a much more typical Smythwick response. Here in this photograph we see one Bertram, a *Draco vulgaris*. And very much alive. This Bertram, having been hatched in Cornwall, is by law an English dragon, despite Cornish political ambitions. St. George has not caused the extinction of the English dragon."

Smythwick's mouth opened and closed several times before any words came out. "I never really spoke much with Bertram... He looks different in person."

The judge frowned down at him.

Smythwick wilted. "The Crown is prepared to drop all charges."

Susan found her sainted husband leaning out a crenelation, gazing far off across the moon-lit woods. "Come down to the ballroom, dear," she said. "Everyone wants to congratulate you on winning your court battle."

"What's the point?" said St. George. "There's still a dragon out there. If I don't slay it, I'll lose my sainthood. If I do slay it, I'll end up in court again."

He gazed even further off.

"Ahem!"

St. George and Susan turned around. "Bishop Thumbshute!"

"The church also has a slight conundrum. If our research is infallible, then there are no English dragons left. And yet, there is… Bertram. I've spoken with the Archbishop. He has ruled that the dragon's employment in a legal capacity has made this a special case. Bertram's depredations as a lawyer will be no worse than those normally found in the legal world. He is no longer your concern."

St. George looked at the bishop with amazement. "I don't have to slay this dragon? I can keep my sainthood?"

"In the eyes of the church, you have nothing to slay. By becoming a lawyer, the dragon became extinct, morally speaking. Your job is done."

Susan reached out. "Now, George, will you come to the party?"

St. George smiled. "Yes. I believe I will."

As they descended the turret, he remarked "But you know, doesn't that mean that there might be even more dragons lurking about?"

Bishop Thumbshute shook his head. "Our research is always quite infallible."

"The thing is… " St. George continued, "instead of fights to the death, sometimes, a dragon and I would come to... more civilized arrangements."

"I don't think I quite heard you -- over the sound of all those people waiting to congratulate you," the bishop replied mildly.

St. George paused, then accepted his fate with saintly forbearance and continued on down the turret.

The End

Andrew Jensen lives in rural Ontario with his family and too many dogs and cats. He is the minister at Knox United Church, Nepean. Over twenty-five of his stories have appeared in the USA, Canada, the UK, and New Zealand. Andrew plays trumpet, impersonates Kermit the Frog, and performs in musical theatre. You should have seen him as Henry Higgins...

Andrew grew up in Terrasse Vaudreuil, near Montreal, during the Cold War. Many of his neighbours were from Ukraine, Latvia and Estonia. They worked tirelessly for years to help the folks "back home" living under Russian occupation.

Andrew is proud to have "The Trial of St. George" included in the *To Ukraine, With Love* benefit anthology.

Lingering in the Golden Gleam, Artur Rosa

Cloud Tower Rising

Ian Pohl

Hungry and claw-scratched, Devlin flitted like a shadow through the twisted trees. The air was dense with rotting vegetation, but a mountain breeze rilled in from up ahead. The light looked brighter there too, less strangled. *Just a little further,* he told himself.

Soldiers had pursued him from the Brass Duke's fortress up to the tangled branches and gnarled roots of the wood. They had watched him disappear into its dimness then turned back, laughing. Now he knew why.

Rustling from behind caught his ear. He shifted into the shadows of a rotting tree. Something low, long, and pulpy slithered through the brush, sucking and snuffling as it tracked him. He caught a glimpse of pale, swollen flesh and massive coils. Another of the vat-born, twisted wizardly creations, voracious and starving now that their masters were gone.

He swore soundlessly and drew a small bundle of porcelain and wire from his belt. He clicked a tiny switch and it unfolded and formed into a dragonfly. The wings fluttered and blurred, then it rose and sped after the vat-born, circling it, distracting it.

Devlin leaped from hiding and sped for the light. He won precious steps before the creature oriented and arrowed after him. He dodged, drew his short sword and slammed the blade against its hide. A crackling net of blue sparks flashed across its skin, leaving it twisting and coiling. He whirled and ran, breaking into the sunshine. But where the trees ended so did the ground, and the creature was already recovered and slithering after him. He looked down at the long steep slope, then turned to face the vat-born as it came roaring out of the trees and reared to strike. Devlin stepped back into the void. His hands traced the rock face as he slid, the creature above raging at the loss of its prey.

Devlin came to a stop on a ledge. Below, granite slopes curved down gently now to a valley. He patted the silver chain beneath the sash at his waist. Castle wall or rocky slope, so far it had secured his hold on whatever he climbed.

He sat, swinging his aching feet over hundreds of feet of empty space. He relished the cooling touch of mountain air. He set his short sword down, letting the obsidian-flecked scabbard charge in the sun.

He'd entered the Wood far less prepared than he'd planned. His love of books had betrayed him. Instead of a rushed study of the maps of the old wizard satrapies, he'd lingered in the Brass Duke's library. Not, it turned out, a good place to be found uninvited. But he'd discovered accounts supporting the tantalizing stories of this region from before the Wizard's Ruin.

What the maps *hadn't* shown was a forest crawling with the vat-born, misshapen things of mushy flesh or rigid scale, lidless eye or poison tentacle. He shivered. He hoped his coming here proved worth it.

He pulled his seeing-glass from his pack and surveyed the valley, with increasing astonishment. He'd expected a wasteland. Instead there were rich farmlands surrounding mounded earth, palisade walls, even stonework. Veiled by wood smoke, he glimpsed not rubble but shops and homes. And above the gabled roofs rose a steeple whose clockface glinted bronzed light.

He looked further, to the cumulus clouds growing on the noonday thermals, billowing above the mountains. A sparkle on one cloud's shoulder caught his eye. He glimpsed white walls and slender towers of ivory and pearl rising with the blossoming cloud.

Devlin whistled softly. The cloud castle, a wizard's stronghold, had survived, and it looked unscathed.

He the loathed wizards. They'd ruled and robbed for generations, bleeding the land of coin and learning, smashing universities, stealing books and art, lighting innocents into screaming human candles, banishing rebels to the Demonic Planes. Their war amongst themselves left nothing save broken works in a haze of smoke and chaos.

But magical objects fascinated him. He'd roamed far hunting for them, thieving them from the newly risen petty warlords. Most he sold. A few he kept. His far-seeing glass. His short sword that soaked up sunlight and struck blows like lightning. The cloud castle might still hold a trove of such treasures.

Devlin brushed away what signs he could of his days in a forest of nightmares. Then he slung his sword across his back, hoisted his pack onto tired shoulders, and started down.

Nearing the town, Devlin slowed and studied it. The entrance gate was set in a wall of stone between tall towers. The fine strong stones looked taken from a wizardly structure. The walls were being rebuilt, rough wood palisades coming down to make way for stone.

He rubbed his stubbled jaw. Most towns these days were feral with confusion, disorder filling the void left after the wizards had annihilated one another. Warlords had risen, former servants taking power with violent excess and greed.

Yet here in this fertile valley, rounded by a protecting of snow-bright mountains and the horrors of the woods, was an oasis. Governed without the fear and blood writ elsewhere. The people were looking to the future, rebuilding with vigor and hope.

Though his heart leapt for their renaissance, still he silently urged the wall-builders to hurry. After all he'd seen, he doubted their secret would keep. They would need those walls.

He merged with the farmers and tradesmen entering through the gate. Within spread a broad plaza edged with brightly colored stalls. The ancient clock tower, from an age before the wizards, stood on the far side.

He drifted among the stalls, drinking in colors, lively conversation, the enticing aroma of good food sizzling in the fresh air. When had he last been in a cheerful market? Black Firth stank of rotten seawater, bloody chains, and slavery. Wind Home's great square held only the skeletal wind-rattle chime of starving people who'd dared to steal bread. The Duke's streets were filled with dull eyes in wasted faces, the wet-gasping miner's cough, drowned by roaring forges.

What must it be like to stay, safe in such a place? To be a welcome part of a good community, building, supporting, protecting, instead of wandering in, avoiding the horrors, lifting warlord's treasures, and hoping to leave still alive and in one piece?

Valuing the new and unknown over home and hearth, he'd lived as a wanderer, a finder and trader of curiosities and lore, slipping through the cracks, avoiding entanglements. He'd told himself his travels made him a living book, that he'd written his life in the ink of wonders the wizards couldn't steal.

But if his life were a book, it had gone unread.

He shook his head. *Focus, you fool!* He needed to resupply and leave without attracting attention. He shopped quickly, paying with old Imperials, grimy and scored from their travels.

"Good coin, this," murmured the last merchant. "Haven't seen many Imperials since the wizards torched each other." His appraising eyes swept over Devlin. "Between the Rotting Wood and the Silver Peaks, Cloud Tower is an island. Strangers don't just wander in."

"I slipped through the wood by luck," Devlin answered carefully. "Nor was I planning on staying. The West is in flames. The Brass Duke is arming for pillage. I'm looking for a quiet part of the world. I have no taste for war."

"None of us do," said the merchant, his eyes hard. "We can guess how bad it is Outside. We aren't going back to that. No more cowering down as playthings of wizards or slaves of warlords. It's been sweat and blood regaining our town. We don't need anyone from beyond the pale stirring up trouble... spying."

"Good policy," said Devlin. "Good day, friend." He grimaced a smile, then quickened his step for the edge of the square. He didn't need to look back to see if the Guard was being called.

Slipping into a side street, the market's bustle faded. He dashed down side lanes, turning into ever narrower passages between walls of rough stone and wood until he found a deserted alley. He leapt for handholds, scuttling up, lizard-fashion. At the roof edge he spun round and jack-knifed up and over. Startled crows hopped away as he piked into their midst. He rolled into a crouch, listening for sounds of pursuit.

He heard only his own breathing. *I'm getting too old for this,* he thought.

Devlin hid on the rooftops the rest of the day. He laid his sword in the sun and ate a small meal. He listened to the sounds of the town and studied the castle atop the clouds.

He found the town's sounds soothing. There were children playing, peddlers calling, matrons gossiping. Not once did he hear a whip's lash, or a scream, or the plunging creak of a gallows. What had the merchant called it – 'Cloud Tower?' He liked the name. He could live here.

The thought surprised him. *Don't be a fool. You're here only to take what you can from that castle. Nothing else.*

After dark, Devlin slipped out of town, spending the night in a hay pile in a barn. He slept fitfully, stirred by distant thunder and pattering rain. Before dawn he rose and headed for the mountains.

Walking through pastureland, then up wooded heights, he reached the tree line at sunset. Here the wind blew chill from high ridges black against the crimson sun. He was near the looming edge of the tower cloud. Through his seeing-glass he could make out the curtain wall and towers high atop a rounded shoulder.

He gathered firewood as thunder rumbled, then took shelter beneath a rocky overhang. When evening rains came, he had a small fire burning, screened within the hollow.

After eating, he checked his gear. He sharpened his blade, cleaned his tools, and sorted his climbing rack. Last, he lay his chain on his lap, checking the harness buckle that allowed him to wear it like a belt. The chain was smooth, silvery links of a light wizardly metal. An engraving wound about it, like waves rolling before the wind. He'd found it looking for treasure in the sunken ruin of a wizard's sailing craft. He suspected it was part of the anchor. Over time he'd discovered its gift.

Tomorrow would be its greatest test.

He rose before dawn. The rain had stopped and the air was still. The tower cloud hid the sky, lapping at the mountains. He limbered up and ate, then built a bonfire out under the open sky. Nursing the flames to a ruby coalbed, he slipped on his sword and pack then tossed a tangle of sodden green alder wood onto the coals.

Smoldering plumes rose. He reached high, grasping the thick dark smoke. It stayed firm in his hand, like desert-warmed sandstone, hot and gritty. He pulled himself up, feeling with his soft boots for smoky footholds.

He climbed quickly, weaving hand and footholds from the curling smoke. He had only as long as the wood smoked on the coals.

The air grew cool and wet. Dawn found him just below the nebulous lower banks. He reached for the next handhold, but found nothing.

Fear knifed through him. The smoke in his hands was dwindling, no longer billows but wisps, bending in the breeze, swaying with his weight. He was far above the earth now, and the fire was nearly out.

He searched and found one more solid handhold. It was cold, like grasping icicles. But now the smoke gave way beneath his feet. Plunging his other hand into the cloud he found icy purchase and chinned himself up. A high-kicked heel, a toehold, and he was climbing into the thick mist of the shifting, flowing mountain-cloud. The holds were soft, some no more than the tiniest of ice seeds swirling in mist.

He climbed, losing sense of time and place. The holds were tenuous, the cloud chilling. His hair and clothes hung wet against his skin. He began to shiver. His cold-stiffened hands were losing their grip when at last he broke through the cloudtop to brilliant, warming sunlight. Patchwork lands below drifted in and out of sight beneath swirling mists. Above him the sun streamed between cumulous pillars like a ruined, snow-softened temple.

Climbing round a billowing cloud serac, the castle revealed itself, its white walls and slender towers sparkling. The cloud beneath him slowly grew firmer. He poured on his strength, climbing 'til he heaved himself up onto a misty ledge.

The castle gate stood open before him. Within lay a courtyard: bright, sunlit, and still.

Approaching over the gentle cloud drifts, the walls above glinted like white granite flecked with quartz. Higher the tower cloud blazed against a sky of noon-washed blue. He put a hand to the barbican wall. It felt solid, stone bathed in sunlight and lofty airs.

Past the gate lay a winding series of courtyards, each larger than the one before, like a chambered seashell. In the innermost courtyard stood a tree of pale metal, its finely crafted leaves fluttering and chiming softly.

Beyond the tree rose the castle's keep. High-paned windows of stained glass poured color upon the paving stones. Beneath them stood a pair of tall, narrow, ornate wood doors three times his height.

Devlin stood before them and put a hand to them.

The doors swung open, utterly silent, onto a hall dark with sullen brooding. Cautiously he stepped in, and the doors swung shut behind him. Stained-glass windows cast colored shafts of light like fanned buttresses of prismatic stone. He slipped quietly to the end of the hall, to a darkly lustrous high-backed chair atop a dais. Beside it on a table stood a golden goblet and an unopened bottle of dark wine. Dust lay thick on everything.

A massive tapestry covered the wall behind the dais. It was skillfully woven with threads of red and orange and noxious green on a field as black as a hole in the night. It held his gaze and chilled his heart. The lines in the tapestry swirled, not in the soothing fashion of a river's flow, but with nausea and despair. It was a rendering of the Lower Planes.

The Demonic Planes.

He averted his eyes, but still its message slithered across his mind like a tentacle...

The wizard will send you down to a place of corrupted power and malice, a place of Torment Eternal...

"The wizard is dead," he whispered.

There was a door to each side of the tapestry. He drew his sword. Blue sparks danced along the blade and disappeared with a snap. He went to the door on the left, gently opening it onto a dim, windowless room filled with tables and tools and alembics. A faint glow pulsed at the far end. He drifted towards it.

Weak candlelight pooled atop a desk strewn with parchments and books. Slumped over them lay a man in heavy robes.

Devlin froze. The man's tangled grey hair lay like strips of flensed skin across the desktop, his cheek resting atop a book. There was a faint rise and fall of his chest, and dark red sand scattered around his chair.

Scarcely breathing, Devlin backed away. Just then his sword sparked and snapped, matched by an answering crackle as a crimson hemisphere surrounding the wizard flared then faded.

The wizard stirred, raising his head. Seeing Devlin, he hissed like a scaled beast.

Freezing cold gripped Devlin, crackling down from the top of his head inwards and down. Heart hammering, he could still breathe and move his eyes but was frozen in place.

The wizard blinked sunken, lamp-like eyes.

"It feels an age since I've thrown a basilisk curse." His voice drifted like cobwebs on a hot wind. "Yet I snared you with ease."

He straightened slowly, grimacing with pain. He squinted down at Devlin's sword.

"Fool artificer. Do you not know me? I am Pallius! Your toys can never match my Arts."

He rubbed his brow. "I've been gone so long... such demon-haunted dreams..." His head arced up and he stared hard at Devlin. "Who sent you? Tinian? Seeking to finish me off?" He coughed.

I am not an assassin, Devlin thought at him. *I thought the castle empty...*

He gasped in shock at a sensation like cold hands rummaging through his mind.

"Hmm... so you are after all just a trinket-hunting fool... ...as you frequently tell yourself."

His sifting brought him to the fact of the Wizards' Ruin. He swayed in his seat. "How can this be? Your little mind doesn't show me..."

His head sank into trembling hands. "I've not yet the energy for this," he murmured. "Tinian's attack weakened me despite my shield..."

He waved a hand, and the crimson hemisphere flickered; he snapped his fingers and it disappeared. "And now it seems I may be the last wizard left...?"

He frowned. "I need time to recover." He tilted his head, thinking aloud: "...and if I am the last, I must establish my rightful rule. Over all!"

His form grew more substantial, frightful, gloating. "But first things first -- best rid the castle of vermin. So you thought to rob me, little fool thiefling? You will serve as the first example of my new rule."

Taking up an onyx-dark staff, the wizard rose up, taller and taller, looming like a storm cloud. He stared down at Devlin, holding him tightly immobilized, compelling him.

Devlin had never been so close to these monstrosities of power. He struggled against panic so strong it froze the breath in his lungs.

"What do you fear?" whispered the wizard. "What do you loathe? See it. Feel it. It's rising, forming, approaching. What you create shall be your fate..."

Devlin's mind bent beneath the power of the wizard's will. He could not fight off approaching darkness, or imagine something safe. Then his mind locked on the tapestry.

The wizard laughed, the sort of sound that soaks into a torturer's work table. "Excellent! I hung that tapestry to bring terror upon all who sought audience. Well done, fool! You've chosen Torment amongst the Demons."

With a long thin fingernail, Pallius sliced a line along his left wrist. Blood-colored sand whispered to the floor as he turned in a slow, full circle. He let fall a final drift in the circle's center. With a long pale finger he traced symbols in the sand. Then he flicked the knife along his right wrist and dark red blood fell upon the drift of sand. Up twisted a dark red candle.

Pallius whispered a word. The candle flared to red life, throwing the chamber into crimson shadows. He began a harsh chant, guttural, arcane words rising and falling, echoing off the chamber's vaulted ceiling. In the darkness the red flame reflected off the wizard's shining eyes and the glinting silver runes of his robe.

Devlin felt he was a stone statue in a vast, dark cavern. Rising from beneath the driving chant, he heard a swelling rustling like thousands of insects rasping over one another. Past the edges of the light, twisted dark shapes pulsed and jittered.

Pallius straightened, raising his staff aloft, and bloody light flashed, sweeping at the creatures like a ruby blade. The rustling retreated in alarm, then edged forward again. The candle flickered low, then flared brighter. There was a pressure, pushing and probing the boundaries of the wizard's circle. The staff flashed, and again the chitinous buzzing scraped through the darkness.

"You threaten me at your peril, demon," hissed the wizard.

A thin voice thrummed like a cockroach's wings from the darkness. "You are brazen, Pallius, to summon me."

"You are a mere servant of the Greater Torments. Remember your place, lest I teach it to you." Again the staff blazed, like blood lightning.

"What do you ask of me then?" The voice's fury resonating in a low, grating hum Devlin could feel in his chest.

"What news of the Wizards' War?"

"The Wizard's Rule is over, the Wizard's Ruin well begun. Your world is shattered. You stand alone. And weak." The voice drifted closer.

Pallius raised his staff and blood-red light flashed. The harsh roar of the insects swelled then dwindled, sharp with frustrated hunger.

"Insect!" he spat out. "You presume to lecture me on my place in the world? I shape the world to my desires, now and forever!"

But Devlin heard in the wizard's voice an undertone of struggling for control, power far from full.

"The only reason you are not an agonized meteor, screaming through the Under-Dark, is that I wish an errand boy." Pallius gestured toward Devlin. "I pass down this little plaything as a token of my return to power, for the Demons to amuse themselves with as they will. Convey him below."

"I await the incantation then," said the voice, amused.

The wizard's chant began, now high, now deep, echoing through the chamber.

Horrified, Devlin felt insect legs climbing up his boots, swarming up his legs. He felt himself sinking into freezing water. His skin begin to crawl. He tried to scream. But when the swarm and the cold reached the chain at his waist, there was a pause; chitinous chittering rose to a crescendo, then fell. There was the roaring of a wave collapsing and rushing away. The cold receded.

"No," the wizard croaked hoarsely. "No!"

Then the screaming started. Pallius fell twisting beneath a swarming tide of black insects. A pale hand emerged, reaching, clutching at the table edge; then it was buried under the carapaces. Slowly the heaving, tortured mound dwindled away.

Devlin felt stabbing needles through his body as blood flow returned. His sword slipped from his hand to the stones with a clang and a flash. He collapsed onto his hands and knees. Shaking, he leaned slowly back on his haunches and drew a shaky breath.

There was no sign of insects or crimson candle or wizard. Only the staff remained.

A spider the size of his hand, body thick with bristling hairs, lowered down before him, hanging on a strand of midnight silk. A multitude of aquamarine eyes stared into his.

"The last surviving wizard makes a better toy than a simple thief," said the spider, its voice like clicking mandibles. It dropped to the floor and scuttled up his thigh. It circled his waist, then climbed to sit on his shoulder. "But perhaps not so simple a thief after all. That is no ordinary chain you wear. But you know this."

Devlin struggled to find his voice. "I learned over time," he said, his voice shaky. "Since it held me well to whatever I wished, I hoped it might hold me in this world."

"Most intriguing…" murmured the spider. Its long thin legs moved, feeling the arcane resonances around Devlin. "It is fascinating to see how old enchantments play out in the Ruin. They weaken, or strengthen, or transmute. But now I must go to watch a wizard pay for his hubris." The spider sounded satisfied.

A wind grew in the darkness, and as the spider's weight dissolved from Devlin's shoulder he heard fading words. *"This cloud castle remains in the sky through strong enchantment. But keep your chain close, thiefling, lest you step out of bounds. I shall watch your self-education with interest…"*

And then, he was alone, in a pool of candlelight.

It was some time before he found the courage to move, taking up his sword and stumbling back to the audience hall. He pulled down the tapestry of the Demonic Planes. Backing away from the cloud of dust, he paused by the slim right hand door, limned in clean, cleansing daylight.

Opening the door just slightly he saw a library, light streaming in dusty beams through floor to ceiling windows. The comforting smell of books wafted out, thick and rich. Graceful, curving staircases mounted on tracks rose from the floor to the high vaulted ceiling.

He went in and wandered among the towering bookcases, now and then touching a spine, reading a title: *Mastering Your Mind and the Minds of Others. On Flying. The Art of Siegecraft. The Control of Weather. How to Build the Rule of Law, and How to Break It.*

Sinking into the high-backed chair, he gazed at the thousands of books and scrolls rising in shelves from floor to ceiling. He'd thought there was nothing left behind of the wizards except broken works and monsters. But it seemed valuable knowledge had survived.

He sat deep in thought through the afternoon.

As the blush of sunset tracked across the wall opposite the windows, he stirred. Leaving the library he walked out through the courtyards and stood at the gate. He gazed down on the darkened land, glimpsed through the air pools between clouds. The lights of the town shone warmly far below.

He was wary of wizardry, but perhaps with the wizard's books he could help Cloud Tower rebuild and defend itself. The library was a huge wellspring of knowledge; pried loose from the wizard's grasp, he could share the good from it with the wider world. Be part of the town, but keep his life of discovery. He'd have to be wary of thepull of such power.

He looked back at the walls and towers, the clouds rising above them. Moonlight frosted the edges and cast curving shadows across the courtyards. The castle held mystery and purpose, and a path to fellowship.

Devlin's breath streamed out in the high, cold air as he whispered, "Home."

He had much to do. He walked back into the library, and began.

Ian Pohl grew up on a homestead in Alaska surrounded by books, snow, tree forts, and northern lights. Today he works as an oceanographer in the Pacific Northwest. When not diving or at sea aboard research ships, he is typically reading, writing, coding in Python, or messing around with cameras above and below the water. This is his first fiction publication.

Artwork: *Lingering in the Golden Gleam,* © Artur Rosa

Love Potion

Anne E.G. Nydam

Xyblik's Cosmic Emporium had stood for as long as anyone could remember at the corner of Elm and Hillside. The proprietor was one of the Old Ones, all writhing tentacles and slime, who bubbled cheerfully at his customers and loved nothing better than a good gossip with anyone coming in to buy bags of moondrops or packets of eldritch biscuits. Abby Dimmock took this into consideration when pondering the best time to purchase a love potion, although time often ran strangely in Xyblik's shop.

He would chat if she came when the Emporium was empty, and she was in no mood to chat about the sorry state of her love life. But better that than asking for a love potion in front of fellow townsfolk on a busy Saturday afternoon.

She winced as the cracked iron bell over the heavy doorway clanged, announcing her entrance. So much for subtlety. She looked around and saw no other customers amidst the shelves of dusty bottles, lead-sealed urns, dark orbs, mysterious curios, and occasional bright and entrancing items such as the ineffable feathersquid, where her gaze lingered longingly.

"Ah, Dear Lady Dimmock!" Xyblik greeted her brightly from the high counter of polished mahogany. The multiple quivering air sacs within his semitransparent greenish body swelled and pulsed as he spoke, amplifying his voice to a volume and timbre suitable for Dark Proclamations. "And what service may be rendered unto you on this fateful day?"

"I'm looking for a love potion, please," she mumbled.

"What's that? A Potion of Inexorable Love?" the Old One bellowed, making Abby grateful she was indeed the only customer in the shop. "Surely you need not such uncanny power to sway the heart of man."

Abby thought wistfully of Charlie Godwin, the new math teacher at the high school, who seemed so sane and sweet and funny... and so diffident. The chance that he would approach her, or that she could engineer a better acquaintanceship with him, seemed dismal.

These dispiriting reflections made her a little blunter than usual. "Dear Xyblik... I'm 42, it's been years since my last real date, I don't like bars or the men who hang out in them, and the thought of being endlessly swiped over by potential internet stalkers does not appeal. Now I've finally met a man I like, and I do not want to waste this opportunity. So I would like a love potion, if you please."

The Old One oozed forward confidentially and lowered his voice to a softer boom. "Pray tell, what man is this of whom you speak?"

"I'm not sure that's any of your business!" Abby returned tartly, "And everyone knows you're the world's worst gossip!"

A fountain of bubbles rippled up inside Xyblik. "Verily, you speak sooth, Lady Dimmock," he chuckled. "Guilty as charged. Yet I have known you for most of your years on this Earthly plane, and my only desire for you is to further what happiness such a brief span as your mortal life may encompass."

A sympathetic tentacle writhed toward Abby and the deep voice grew more plangent.

"For many long millennia have I observed the love affairs of mortals, and I judge not that this unnatural elixir will bring you True Happiness."

Abby frowned. "Xyblik, I don't need a life coach. Please just sell me the love potion."

A disapproving gurgle shook Xyblik's gelatinous frame. "I should be loath to see you destroy your peace with such a baleful brew. Consider well whether you could truly be content, ever fearing that the love you were given was yours only by compulsion. Surely true happiness can come only with the love of free hearts freely bestowed."

"So why sell love potions if they're so 'baleful'?"

"Alas, even one such as I am not mighty enough to withstand the insidious force of Expectation. Who would respect a Cosmic Emporium that trafficked not in arcane tinctures, cryptic tomes, dark talismans, and otherworldly relics?" He waved a dripping tentacle at the rows of shelving around him. "Marketing, Dear Lady. Marketing. But I repeat that surely you need not such uncanny power to sway the heart of man."

Abby sighed. "All right, Mister Dark Lord of All Advice, what do you think I should do instead? Because I want to get this right."

A phosphorescent glimmer twinkled across the expanse that would be Xyblik's face, if Old Ones composed of tentacles and slime had faces. "Disclose unto me, Dear Lady Dimmock, which item of all that may be found within this wondrous Cosmic Emporium would truly give your heart the most gladness?"

"Oh, so you do want me to buy *something?*" But the Old One's most earnest and meaningful voice made Abby give his request the consideration he clearly sought. "I don't know, you have a lot of 'wondrous' stuff. The tenebrous hand lotion is so soothing. The Cimmerian peanut butter is the best I ever tasted..."

Her eyes travelled around the dark, crowded shop, over all the strange and fascinating items that lurked in the shadows and had tempted her through the years. Scrolls teaching arcane knowledge or magic skills... cloaks of power granting invisibility or armor plating or eternal warmth... intricate crafts from other planes of existence... Then her gaze stopped. "I've always wished for an ineffable feathersquid, but I'm afraid I couldn't care for it properly."

Xyblik nodded and his air sac swelled and thrummed as his voice rang out sonorously, "I proclaim to you now, Miss Abigail Dimmock, with all the oracular authority of my chthonic soul, that if an ineffable feathersquid is what you desire, then verily an ineffable feathersquid you shall acquire!"

He added slightly less portentously, "I shall instruct you most carefully as to all its requirements. Such as misting it regularly, exposing it to baths of fresh moonlight, and showering it with affection to cultivate its naturally sweet temper. And they do enjoy treats of Cimmerian peanut butter."

"Really?" Abby laughed and shrugged off some of her unhappiness. "Honestly, Xyblik, I don't know why you think this is preferable, but... If you won't sell me a love potion, I'm going to be alone the rest of my life, and if I'm going to be alone, better be alone with an ineffable feathersquid for company."

Several minutes of instruction later she was walking out of Xyblik's Cosmic Emporium gently carrying a hollow crystal sphere about the size of a basketball, peering at the glowing turquoise fluffball within, making kissy faces, and crooning, "Who's a precious little cutie?"

Focusing her attention to her new little friend, she nearly ran into a man on the sidewalk outside. It was Charlie Godwin. She blushed furiously, remembering that she'd hoped to slip him a love potion.

Then she noticed that he, too, was holding a crystal sphere. And that within it glowed a soft orange fluffball.

"Morning, Abby," he said with a shy smile, "It looks like Xyblik's been doing a good business in ineffable feathersquid today. Just got this little guy."

"But I bought mine just now too. How could we both...?"

Charlie shrugged. "I don't know. They say time's a bit out of kilter in Xyblik's shop. But yes, he talked me into one after I dropped by looking for... something else." He suddenly blushed.

"Same with me." She smiled.

Abby and Charlie quietly watched their ineffable feathersquids for a few moments. The little fluffballs had sidled up close to the sides of their spheres and were gazing fondly at each other through the crystal. They chittered eagerly, while luminescent waves of color flickered over their long whiskers, and their long, plumed tails fizzed like sparklers.

Abby looked up and her eyes met Charlie's. She blurted, "Xyblik said they like Cimmerian peanut butter. Want to come over to my place and give them some treats?"

Charlie smiled. "Yes," he said, "I'd like that very much."

Anne E.G. Nydam has brought worlds to life in art and writing since she could hold a crayon. A former middle school art teacher with an undergraduate degree in linguistics, she makes relief block prints celebrating the wonders of worlds both real and imaginary, and writes books about adventure, creativity, and looking for the best in others. Her most recent book is *On the Virtues of Beasts of the Realms of Imagination*. See her art and books at NydamPrints.com.

Artwork by Anne E.G. Nydam

The Memory Bank & Trust

Patrick Hurley

The girl in Vanan Quick's Memory Bank & Trust wore the dark robes of the desert nomads. Perhaps fifteen, she was thin, with vacant eyes, and hair shorn close to the skull. Not the usual class of client Vanan Quick served in his shop on Varrowmind's elite Street of Sorceries. And not, he was sure, an applicant for the valued position of apprentice.

But he was ever the professional. "What can I do for you, young miss?"

"You are the memorist?"

Vanan blinked in surprise. Not at the question, for he was indeed a master memorist, having graduated at the top of his class from the Gray School before setting up shop in fabled Varrowmind. It was the sepulchral voice in which the girl spoke that gave him pause.

He reached for the jade amulet at his neck. "I am. And what, pray tell, are you?"

"A jinn, in need of your services."

"Perhaps you are," said Vanan. "But we have laws in Varrowmind prohibiting forced possession."

The girl's head tilted to one side, studying Vanan. "I will pay well." The head tilted to the other side. "And the vessel is willing."

"Of that I would require proof."

"As you wish." The girl's brown eyes quickened to life, and her body relaxed.

"And who, pray tell, are you, young lady?"

"Serefina." The light voice whispered like a desert breeze.

"A merchant took my sister Ela and me as payment for our family's debt. I escaped. The jinn found me and promised help freeing Ela if I would but host him. A deal I chose freely."

"Just a moment, Serefina." Still holding his amulet, Vanan took a small loupe from a vest pocket and affixed it over his spectacles. He focused it and examined the girl.

"It would seem you're telling the truth, Master Jinn," said Vanan eventually. "You've relinquished control of the young lady's essence. She could cast you out if she chose."

The girl's eyes unfocused and her posture stiffened once more. "So, Vanan Quick," the jinn's deep voice returned, "we can do business?"

Vanan released his amulet. "Yes. And your name?"

"Never will you know that, memorist. But call me La Nar."

"Very well. I rarely work with jinn, but most of the usual services are possible -- memory extraction, duplication, preservation, recovery."

La Nar was long silent. "I am old for my kind," he finally said. "So old, my body of flame has extinguished, leaving me a being entirely of memory."

"A Flameless Jinn! No other beings on this plane hold such accurate and vivid memories."

"But mine have been poisoned. I opened forbidden knowledge -- the location of the god Lokonos's hidden treasure temple -- and it brought down a curse upon me. It spreads through my mind, devouring memory like a ravening beast, corrupting all it touches, blurring and tangling everything I know into nonsense. Victories become defeats. Delights become nightmares. I am weak and in agony. You must remove this curse before I lose all."

Vanan stared. What sound, taste, or scent could coax forth the cursed memory of a Flameless Jinn? Would arthane scalpels sever it from his mind? What receptacle could secure it? No bell jar nor sea conch nor iron-bound chest could long hold it fast. In a human it would die with its host, but who would take on such a burden? And what preservative would accord with the memory... amber, wine, living blood? Vanan spread out his hands helplessly.

"Master Quick, you are the best of the Gray School." The jinn's voice wavered. "If you can't save me, I'm doomed to torment until I fade utterly."

Such confidence in him from a fabled Flameless Jinn, ancient spirit of vast memories, was not without effect.

"I could try... but the materials for extraction and preservation alone would cost more than my shop."

"I am old and was once powerful. For thousands of years I amassed treasure... it is at your disposal."

"But I could not guarantee the result. And the risk is great."

"But worth it, I think. In payment I offer you memories. Memories of such wonder all Varrowmind will line up at your door to sample them."

Vanan kept his face and voice impassive. "I've heard this promise from many adventurers in need of coin. Yet I find their slaughter of mythic beasts distasteful and dull."

"Bah! Such things are dust to the ancient memories of a Flameless Jinn! I've seen the birth of civilizations and their cold, dark death. I watched as the foundation stones of Varrowmind, City of Steam and Crystal, were laid down. I stepped into the fabled paintings of Saramando. I read the lost Books of Night of the sorcerer Degyr. If you aid me, once I am free, one of these memories will be yours, for yourself and for others to sample to your great profit."

Vanan placed a steadying hand on the counter. The ancient origins of Varrowmind were fiercely contested; primacy would deal out supremacy or destruction to its competing factions. It was said Saramando's paintings opened gates to other realities. Degyr had risen to attain the might of a demigod, so powerful his name was still whispered with respect, and fear.

"Each memory is a gem. Yet," Vanan paused, "there is great risk, and I will have to close the shop during this work. I would ask for all three memories."

"Done."

Vanan blinked at the speed of the jinn's acceptance, and a tendril of wariness curled up inside him. "And what of Serefina? What treasure did you promise her?"

"She will be amply rewarded."

"I would have her speak for herself."

"As you wish."

A moment passed. The girl's form and face relaxed.

"Freedom," she said, "for my younger sister. Soon the old merchant will want more than just labor from her. La Nar will give me his memory of hidden treasure, and I can free her."

A dark suspicion fluttered through Vanan's mind. A *cursed* memory?

"Cost is no object," boomed the jinn, with new and sudden energy. "And I can stay here and acquire whatever you need. Master Quick, do we have an accord?"

Jinn and girl stared expectantly at him through the same eyes.

Well, one step at a time. He put up the Closed sign on his shop door. "My workroom is in the back. We have much to prepare."

The work went slowly. When Vanan needed to hire artificers, La Nar and Serefina would leave and return with the necessary funds within hours. At first they had brought treasure, but too many ancient coins and fabulous jewels raised more questions than Vanan wanted to answer, so now they brought unquestioned coin of the realm. And when sent to purchase rare ingredients, Serefina was a fierce haggler.

After one of their expeditions, Serefina came back with a cut lip and a bruise under one eye. It was then Vanan learned jinn and girl made quite the card-playing pair.

"A Varrow princeling took offense at getting out-played by a desert rat," she said as Vanan applied a poultice to her eye. She squared her thin shoulders. "He'll think twice before attacking another rat."

One day Vanan allowed Serefina to watch as he referred to a book of glowing runes for inscribing protective wards, and she asked, "Why do you put memories in a vault?"

Vanan straightened and looked at her. "Because memory is the most precious coin there is. More valuable than gold, more vital than bread. What are those compared to the memory of a first love? Or the soft voice of one's mother singing in the gentle evening? The jinn aren't the only ones made of memories, child."

"When you store memories, do people forget them?"

"I leave a copy if I can. Memories may fade with age, but well stored, they stay as pristine as the day they were decanted. If a memory is at risk, a client may store it in my vault and return to view it as often as they wish."

"But you can remove memories," Serefina asked, her voice soft. "Make it as if something never happened?"

Vanan paused. "I am not of the School of Oblivion. Removal leaves holes in one's being, gaps in the structure of the mind. And the destructive effects of the memory live on, invisible, past knowledge or control, and it overshadows one's whole being. No, I am a Restorationist. On the whole, it makes for a healthier life."

"But… " and then her voice deepened to that of the jinn's.

"May we get back to the work? My mind's time is limited and this cursed memory is painful."

As he returned to warding the containment vessel, Vanan wondered what memory the girl wished to forget.

Filling half the room, the crystal containment sphere was inscribed with ancient and powerful memory wards. To a panel on the sphere were attached long heavy sleeves ending in heavy gloves. Inside the sphere were arrayed the most potent instruments to be found in the memorists' trade: crystal arthane scalpels, and tongs of iron and silver.

Tall glass cylinders held swirling aether. Prepared from blood rubies crushed in Elysium wine heated over spirit fire from a blue salamander, the aether was meant to cling to the cursed memory down to its slenderest wisp.

Vanan put on a protective coat and purple-lensed shielded glasses. Serefina sat in a heavy chair with coils and tubes running to the sphere.

"In case there are convulsions I must strap you in."

She simply nodded and closed her eyes. He connected the tubes to her temples with suction cups. He turned a lever, and white light flowed along the tubes into the sphere. Serefina shuddered and twisted. Her eyes rolled back and she struggled to breathe. The sphere grew brighter, the jinn's light filling most of the space, and becoming almost blinding as the last traces of La Nar entered it. Serefina sagged in relief.

Even with the glasses Vanan could hardly face the light. Brilliant rays illuminated every corner of the memory-filled workroom, and little spirits that had lived quietly in the darker corners for ages flitted behind vessels for refuge. Vanan studied the jinn's mind with amazement. Most memories were random nodes in chaos. More organized minds had a memory house, and the most gifted had palaces. But the jinn's mind was a whole country of fascinating, wildly varying landscape. This was the light and mind of a weakened jinn?

Vanan opened the valve on the pipe from the aether cylinders, and purple aether swirled into the crystal sphere. As it touched the jinn's mind it thickened and darkened, transforming into jagged lattices weaving their way through the webbing of the curse. Now he could see the curse infecting the heart of the memory country and spreading outward.

Eyes blazing in concentration, Vanan slipped his arms into the gloves, flexed his fingers, selected a scalpel, and began to cut. And nearly pulled back out in shock as the memory attacked.

Usually, these were soothing operations; the subject relaxed, sipped their drink, and told a story while he worked. The arthane scalpel was rarely necessary. The right trigger of scent, taste, or tale called forth the memory and Vanan contained it in a proper receptacle.

But this memory shifted away from Vanan's blade, tendrils twisting and lunging, ensnaring his gloved hands. He excised the tendrils but noted they left marks on his gloves, regenerated almost as quickly as he cut them, and attacked again. So he cut again. And again the tendrils regenerated.

Reflexes from his days as a fencer served him as he parried and slashed. Flashes of forbidden knowledge crashed against the crystal sphere and faded, but to his horror the protective gloves began to wear thin. Would the gloves, treated with the sandworm ichor, give out before the curse?

Hours passed before he cut away the very last traces, his gloves now barely gossamer. He had left uninfected memories intact, but even so the jinn was much reduced. Vanan sealed off the tubes and filtered the purified jinn into a smaller globe. He wiped the sweat from his brow and sank down trembling into a chair.

"Sir jinn, rest. The memory is removed. How are you?"

La Nar, a much smaller whirling country of lights, darted to the small speaker box attached to the glass globe. "I am diminished, but I am still myself. And clear again. Thank you, Vanan Quick. The memories you desire shall be yours. So… the curse is placed in the girl?"

Vanan looked grim. "So you *did* intend her to receive the curse."

"Of course. My possession of her body made her ideal. I assumed you knew this."

"Such a burden would drive her mad."

"The sacrifice of a mayfly for my eons of life."

"I've not unleashed your cursed memory into the girl," Vanan said.

There was a pause.

"And why not?"

"I dislike dooming young women to madness and death. A small quirk of mine."

The containment globe shuddered slightly. "What then have you done with the memory?"

"I have countless receptacles in my vault. One of them will suffice to hold the memory."

"A non-living receptacle will break down. And then Lokonos's curse would seek me out."

"It will never escape my vault."

The globe shuddered again. "While you live. But for me, that is the barest flicker of time. I require a more permanent solution."

"We could find a person soon to die and promise to pay their heirs..."

"Wait for a human willing to give themselves to cursed madness? The girl is here. Use her."

"I cannot accede to that request," said Vanan softly. "Master Jinn, I will find a way to destroy the curse. And I will settle for just one of your memories, instead of three."

The globe dimmed and hummed. "A far better alternative suggests itself."

"And that is?" Vanan kept his voice steady.

"I seize your body and use it to place the memory in the girl."

Vanan reached for his jade amulet but lost his grip as the jinn burst out of the globe and slammed into him like a bolt of lightning.

The memorist shuddered and collapsed, falling through hot ice, drowning in a whirlwind of freezing dark.

"You forget," the jinn's voice filled the room, "I move as quickly as thought."

Vanan reached again for his amulet, but his hand froze.

"I'm aware of your pathetic little amulet, memorist of the Gray School," La Nar mocked.

Vanan's mind was crushed beneath the torrent of the jinn's ancient intellect. The room grew dim. His rows of gleaming shelves, filled with the preserved memories of generations, faded from his sight.

As darkness took him, a cool, smooth stone was slipped in his hand. His fingers could move now. He traced the amulet's warding sigil, and warmth coursed through him. With a thunderous roar the jinn's mind poured into the amulet. It began to grow hot.

Sound and light came crashing back to Vanan. He lay on the floor, Serefina crouched over him, shaking him, a fierce focus on her face.

He slowly forced his stiffened fingers to unclasp the burning amulet. From within, the smooth jade, now an angry dark red, smoldered.

"Not such a pathetic little amulet after all, La Nar," Vanan said, his voice a cracked wheeze. He would have to find safe receptacles for both jinn and curse.

"Serefina. How... did you break free?"

"I learned long ago how to escape from such bonds," Serefina hissed grimly. "Perhaps even vile memories serve a purpose. I should have known better than to trust La Nar. Now I have nothing."

The memorist studied the fierce girl. "I've been looking for the right apprentice."

The desert nomad raised an eyebrow. "A good trade, this, but I am no fancy Gray School graduate."

"Stay and I will teach you."

She closed her eyes and shook her head. "No. I have to save Ela. I'll steal her back. We'll run."

"And be caught. Here you will be safe, trained, paid well."

"While my sister lies helpless with a depraved merchant? A cursed memory indeed!"

"Memories can be removed."

"Better I die with her in the desert."

Vanan smiled slowly and nodded. "Good. I value loyalty. I will pay your family's debt, buy your sister's freedom, and sponsor an apprenticeship of her choice. Perhaps beside her sister, learning from a fancy Gray School graduate."

He could see her gaze taking in the measure of him in a long slow study.

Serefina nodded and smiled. "Now this is a memory I can live with."

"The Memory Bank and Trust" © Patrick Hurley First published on April 30, 2019 in Cosmic Roots & Eldritch Shores

Patrick Hurley has had his fiction published in Factor Four, Deep Magic, Paizo's Pathfinder, Flame Tree Press, and Abyss & Apex. Patrick is a graduate of the 2017 Taos Toolbox Writer's Workshop and a member of SFWA. Find out more about his work at www.patrickhurleywrites.com.

CAT AND MOUSE

L.C. Brown

So I'm out front of Jaxon's, down in the French Quarter, singing for my supper. Jaxon's been good to me, you know? For some fool-headed reason he lets this old cat sit on his doorstep and wail on her trumpet, just like in the old days, even though both of us could get taken for it. They don't get seen again, them's that get taken. Jaxon knows it; I seen all them pictures behind his bar. And don't me and my brother know it, too.

Where was I? Oh, yes. Singing for my supper. At least, my trumpet is. Me an' my trumpet, making the magic them tourists wanna hear. People want happy tunes, these days. They don't want no sad songs no more. They want blues that sounds more like yellows and greens. So that's what I give 'em. I give 'em happy blues, and they give me a couple credits, and we all walk away happy.

But not today. Today, the Silence finally finds me.

Oh, honey, I know who they is, even if they ain't dressed up in them dumb old elephant ear hats. They always got the Look about them, you know? That frown line right between the eyes, like they listening just a little too hard to what's around 'em, but not hard enough to what's in front of their noses.

This one's just a baby, he is. Fresh outta Silence school, or whereever the generals mint 'em. He's dressed like a tourist, in his tee shirt and floppy sandals, but please, this ain't my first rodeo—he's got that Look. So I know who he is, and he knows who he is, but I don't know if he knows I know who he is, you got me?

But I can tell the crowd around me also know who he is, because all a sudden they start finding all the rest of Bourbon Street real interesting, and nobody in their right mind thinks Bourbon Street is interesting at one o'clock in the afternoon.

So I'm caught, right? I'm a fish on a hook. The kid sees the trumpet before I can either put it away or sing up a spell to make it look like a vape or a Coke bottle or whatever else they haven't banned yet. So of course he knows right away that, one, I make music outta magic, which only those Confeds is supposed to do; two, if I'm here it means they ain't caught me yet; and three, I could be his ticket to a bigger, shinier badge.

I put my trumpet back in its case real slow-like, bell side down, no sudden movements. He comes right up to me. I play it cool, because, heck, what else am I gonna do? I know sure as anybody that if they catch you Busking, they break your instrument, and we ain't just talking about your trumpet, no. The Silence makes mimes outta musicians. And this one might be a kid, but he still got that bully stick and that badge on him somewhere, I'm sure of it.

"That's quite the lovely song you were playing, citizen," he says.

Now I'm thinking, that's how we're gonna play this? This cornpoke squirt can't even give a girl the dignity of an outright arrest. No. No, first he gotta pretend he's some kinda cat and I'm the mouse. But of course I don't show none of that, not to him. I just smile, sweet as pie.

"Thanks, sugar."

"What song was it?"

"Don't got no name, sugar." I give him a nice, flirty up-and-down. He's built like an oak tree, and he look fast too. I don't think I could outrun him, even if I was half my age.

"You made it up?"

He frowns, and I wonder if that's a crime now too.

"Naw. Momma used to play it. She was in a second line band, before the war. Living Music Brass Band, you heard?" I pick up my trumpet case and don't bother waiting on no answer. "Excuse me, sug—"

He catches my shoulder, and it's everything I can do not to bolt. "Just a minute, citizen, if you please. May I see your papers?" When I don't move or say nothing, he goes on, "Any citizen can freely ask to see another citizen's papers, you know. It's our right, by Confederate law."

Lord. Who done let this chicken outta the fryer before he cooked? "Reckon you right, Sir."

I pull out the ID card we all gotta carry on us these days and give it to him. He look a little disappointed. Joke's on me, though, 'cause it's a fake, and if he catch it? Well, I'm just hoping he's too green at this job yet to spot the difference.

Of course I don't got no real papers. You kidding me? Momma came over before the Fall of the States, and then she done spent the rest of her life trying to get herself and me and my brother out again. She only ever managed one of the three.

I'mma get you two out too, baby girl, just as soon as I can.

Yeah, sure you will, Momma. Sure you will.

He gives the card back just as I start to sweat. Smiling wide, like he trying to be charming, heaven above. "Tell me, citizen, have you heard of the Nightingales?"

I shake my head as hard as my old bones will let. "I want nothing to do with no Nightingales, Sir. Revolution ain't my tune. I just wanna get home to my cat."

He chews that over a spell; I think he expected I gonna play dumb instead. He leans in. "I hear there's a secret meeting of these Nightingales tonight."

"If you say so, Sir."

"Tell you what. If you tell me where this meeting is, I'll overlook your unlicensed use of magic on public grounds." A little smile crooks up his cheeks. "Or didn't you know that Busking could get a person taken away?"

I ain't sure what the best answer is, so I stay silent. Anything I open my mouth with just gets me in deeper.

Quiet's the wrong answer, though, 'cause now he look mad enough to spit. "Tell me."

"I don't know nothin' about no meeting, honest."

He steps closer. I can smell that sour-stink hotel coffee he had for breakfast on his breath. He licks his lips.

"Tell me, or I'll shred your lips to ribbons."

"I'm telling you, I—"

Then the kid does the thing, the one thing I was praying he ain't gonna do: He opens his mouth, so wide that all's I can see is teeth and tongue and pink, and out of that empty hole comes... nothing.

The sounds of the street go dead. Can't hear no tourists talking, no cars honking, no bike bells chiming. All of it, gone, just like that.

Everything is silence.

And it hurts. Good Lord, does it hurt. The nothingness crawls over and under and through my skin like it's sucking up my magic through a straw; and it builds and builds till I feel like I'm gonna burst.

Lord, I swear I ain't proud of what I do next 'cause my Momma, you know she taught me never to raise a hand in anger. But this ain't no hand, it's a trumpet case, and I whack him upside the head with it just about as hard as I can swing.

THONK.

It ain't magic, but it does some kinda magic for me, 'cause he goes cross-eyed and staggers around like some kinda drunk, and I think, now he really look like he at home on Bourbon Street.

All the sounds come rushing back. But this ain't no time for relief. It's time to go.

So I run. I run as fast as my old legs will go. That ain't so fast these days, but I got the up on him: He's just some dumb kid, fresh from the farms, and I been living in the Quarter half my life. I know the streets and how they twist up on you, and I also know where a local can go so they ain't gonna be seen.

I beeline 'round Preservation Hall, not looking behind to see if the kid's after me, and now I'm down the alley behind the Cabildo, and I burst on through to the Square proper. I run by Jackass Jackson, leering down at everybody from his pedestal after they took him down and put him up again.

Past him is a crowd full of tourists, standing five deep. They watching the street performance, you know, the one that goes on every hour on the hour? It's got all them official Confederate jugglers and jumpers and crap. You can't even hear yourself think over that corny, state-approved jinglejam they piping in, much less let out any noise of your own.

So with my fingers I plug up my ears best I can, then whistle a low little tune. My magic starts running through me. All a sudden the long hair goes short, the brown eyes go white, and I look completely different, like some maw-maw out from the sticks come in for a wild weekend in sinners' city before she croaks. My trumpet case turns into one of them big straw handbags, the kind little old ladies like to hide knitting needles in to stab at little hands gone looking for sweets.

Nobody even sees me change. Or if they do, they don't say nothing; maybe they just think I'm part of the show.

I walk right back the way I came, easy as you please. The kid's over by Jackass Jackson now, scowling up a storm. He got his bully stick out, oh yes he do, a big mean thing like a timp mallet the size of your leg; and don't he look ready to smash everybody and anybody that get up in his business?

But he don't notice ol' Maw-Maw, no. The Silence can't see through our kinda magic—not yet anyway. They just like everybody else. That's what makes 'em so mad.

The Silence, you know, they act so high and mighty, like they the only ones got the power to shape things how they see fit. But our kinda music--the rough kind, the magic kind—shows 'em up for the liars they is. Of course they gonna chase us. As long as we around making noise, their lie ain't never safe.

But then again, neither am I. And I just wanna live, thank you very much. I just wanna live.

I go home. Just as soon as I open the door to my apartment and drop my trumpet case, out she come running, my sweet little girl, my Clementine.

That fat ol' tabby tangles herself up in my legs like Mardi Gras beads, tail whipping this way and that, until I can't hold the spell no more. My skin shivers, and I look myself again. She wants a song, I know she do. She always do.

"Not now, Clem," I nudge her off. "I ain't got it in me right now."

More howling.

"Don't let no Silence catch you talking like that."

But she don't care. Of course she don't care. She just a cat. And the Silence don't care nothing about her.

But me, well. There ain't no sneaking from the Silence no more. Not now, not ever again. Maybe there never was. They the ones with the bully sticks and the badges and the boys built like oak trees. Me, all's I got is luck and a song. And one day soon, they both gonna run out.

I fall on my couch, heavy as a stone. I get to thinking, about living and not living and everything in between. I think of Jaxon, about all them faces behind his bar. I think about my brother, too. His picture ain't behind that bar, you know. He never made it so far as New Orleans. But trust me when I tell you, he had an angel's voice. He was fifteen and beautiful, and he could make a statue cry with that voice of his. That voice I can't even hear in my head no more, no matter how hard I try.

If the Silence gets what they want—a world with only jinglejam for weddings and parties and funerals, where the blues don't even got no yellows or greens in 'em no more, just a bunch of greys—well, I get to thinking, then maybe my brother got taken for nothing.

I get up and take out my trumpet, 'cause, well, I don't know why. I got something to prove, maybe. And even before it's outta the case, Clementine, that ol' diva, she starts getting her yowl on. She's gonna let it all out, ain't she, no matter what kinda man or mice be listening in.

Clem's got the right of it, that's what I think.

I pick the old girl up and love on her tight.

"C'mon," I tell Clementine. "It's time for you and me to find us some Nightingales."

"Cat and Mouse" © Lara Crigger.   First published on May 30, 2018 in Cosmic Roots & Eldritch Shores

L.C. Brown lives with her husband and two kids in a secret volcano lair just outside New Orleans, LA.

Maggoty Meg Flies Up the Mountain

Jonathan Lenore Kastin

They called her Maggoty Meg because her skin was sallow, her arms and legs thin as matchsticks, and her hair was the color of sickly carrots. But to herself she was just Meg, and she was tired of being ugly.

The village children would follow as she went about her many chores: mucking out the stables, watering the horses, running errands for the cross innkeeper's wife. Though Meg was nearly nineteen and taller than any of her tormentors, that didn't stop them from chanting rude rhymes and throwing stones at her back until she was bruised from shins to shoulders.

The beautiful children were the cruelest. The baker's son and the butcher's daughter with their hair like corn silk and their eyes the color of clear water, skin always rosy and unblemished. They knew how lovely they were and with whispers and smirks they made Meg feel worse than the worms that crawled in the dirt.

It had been raining as she left the market with apples for the horses and a basketful of eggs. The rain made her hair slick and stringy, and the muddy streets splattered her skirts, but it kept her tormentors away. Then the rain stopped and soon a chorus of "Maggoty Meg" followed her.

As usual, she turned sharply to give them an earful, but slipped in a puddle and fell. The street filled with laughter, even from passing adults, while the butcher's daughter, arm in arm with the baker's son, pointed a perfect finger at her, an ugly curl to her rosy lips.

Meg righted herself and shook off the mud as best she could. But then a stone stung her hip and another grazed her cheek. And another. And another. She took a deep, racking breath. She was cold, she was miserable, and she was not going to let them terrorize her anymore. She left her basket back at the inn and fled. It was time to see the witch.

The children and their stones followed her past the edge of town, but when Mad Annie's hovel, leaning precariously toward the mountain, came in view, the crowd behind her grew quiet and still.

Meg paused at the broken gate. Afraid. But she had had enough. She turned and stared at the children and put her hand on the gate. They shrieked and ran away.

Her triumph faded as she gazed at the dark hovel. Wispy smoke came meandering at odd angles out of the chimney, and the windows were dim. She shivered and her knees wobbled. But she was sick of being laughed at, sick of the stones and the insults. She drew her shawl close, tip-toed through Mad Annie's overgrown garden, and knocked on the door.

"Who's there?" croaked a voice.

"It's Meg," she said. She was the only Meg in the village.

At first, nothing happened. Then the door yanked open and a small toad of an old woman squinted up at her and harrumphed.

Meg could clearly see that if she was not beautiful then Mad Annie was uglier than the Devil himself. She had a long red nose that became rounder at the end like a doorknob and her face was covered in brown spots. She was barely half Meg's height and hair sprouted like tufts of gray weeds on her face.

Mad Annie looked Meg up and down and croaked out, "I know what you'll be wanting so I'll save you the trouble of asking. I can't make you beautiful, don't even ask. I'm not that sort of witch."

Meg's shoulders sagged. "I wouldn't mind so much but for the stones they throw."

Mad Annie nodded her shaggy head. "I remember those. They don't dare throw stones at me anymore."

"Can't you make me a tiny bit beautiful?" she asked, unwilling to lose hope so soon.

"Not even a tiny bit."

Meg sighed. "I must find someone else then."

"Wait a minute," said the old witch, huffing and puffing for breath. "I said I couldn't make you beautiful. I didn't say I couldn't do *other* things."

"Like what?"

Mad Annie stepped aside and gestured her into the hut, dim and smelling of earth, full of who knew what horrors. Meg hesitated, but she had come this far, and a fire glowed in the hearth.

Mad Annie beckoned her to a stool by the fire and plopped down beside her. She leaned in close and waggled her eyebrows. "Have you ever considered becoming one of us?"

"Us?" Meg drew back, startled.

"A witch, child! A witch!"

Meg shuddered. "Everybody says…"

Mad Annie spat and poked at the fire. "'Everybody says?' Ha! Just jealous, is what they are. Saying we fly naked up to the mountain, and eat babies and bats' wings, that we kiss the backsides of billy goats. As if any witch worth her warts would sail through those frigid mountain passes with not a stitch on. And for what? To show her sagging breasts and knobbly knees? Certainly not! It isn't like that. And I can show you." She crossed her arms over her lumpy chest and snorted like a sow.

"I won't sign my soul over to no Devil, if he be up there."

Mad Annie stamped her foot impatiently. "The only devil you need fear is right down here in the hearts of half the village. Up there we each of us get our own special what everybody calls 'Devils'."

Meg wrung her hands, images of horned demons looming in her mind.

"There's nothing to fear! Come along at the dark of the moon. You'll never need to be *beautiful* again. See for yourself."

Meg nodded before her courage failed her. When the moon hid its face again she'd return and fly with the old witch up the mountain.

This time, as Meg walked through the rain she held her head high, her heart lighter than it had been in years. It seemed as if there were fewer shouted insults, fewer bites of stone against her back. She had a secret and a purpose and maybe that was better than straight white teeth and flaxen hair.

A fortnight later Meg rode sidesaddle behind Mad Annie on her crooked broom, shivering in the cool spring air as they flew over the fields toward the mountain. She tried not to look down. If she fell to her death only the horses would miss her - who else would braid their hair and feed them apples? She wished she could have ridden *them* up the mountain.

"Nearly there!" Mad Annie shouted.

Meg could just make out the orange light of a bonfire. The dizzying voice of a fiddle wound up to them on the breeze. She held her breath and clutched the broom tight, peering into the darkness as she searched for the black cauldrons and the terrible, twisted shapes people were always warning about, but she couldn't see a thing. Then Mad Annie snapped her fingers and the scene below lit up as if from a flash of lightning.

A crowd of witches had gathered on the mountain, yes, but they looked just as human as Meg. Only they were clothed in luminous spider's silk and velvety flower petals instead of rags. Some danced about the fire, some on chairs of glittering crystal round a banquet table, feasting and drinking and laughing.

"Not quite what you were expecting, is it?" said Mad Annie as they landed with a thump. Meg was startled to find her guide suddenly dressed in a gown of lupin blossoms, her weedy hair swept into a net of silver cobwebs.

Meg gasped, and looked to see her own rags turned into a dress of green moss, her hair woven into a loose braid twined with golden feathers, and her feet were clothed in slippers as light and soft as sea foam. A laugh bubbled from her lips for the first time in many a dreary month and she grabbed Mad Annie's hand and pulled her toward the table.

"Steady, child," she cried. "My legs are never so young as yours."

There were two crystal chairs waiting for them. The people there were mostly strangers, but a few she recognized from the village. Addled Tate, the town drunk, sat across from her, looking like a fine lord in a frock coat of ivy and holly. The almswoman and the Merchant's son, who was thrice as ugly as Meg, sat at the end of the table. And Tommy Brown, who'd come back home from the war with one leg gone and was always jumping at shadows, sat two witches away.

"Is this… is this real?" Meg asked.

"Aye, child. Those of us cast aside. All here for a modicum of solace. And fine solace it is, too." She lifted her goblet in a toast. "Try the wine, dear. You'll never taste its equal back at home."

The wine tickled its way down her throat, warming and enlivening her. Platter after platter was passed around. Soups and stews, chestnuts and oranges, pastries of almond and lemon curd, steaming goblets of melted chocolate rich with spices. Cheese and bread and honey. Nuts and berries. She was always hungry at the innkeeper's table, but here she feasted.

"This is better than being beautiful," she cried, munching mince pie.

Mad Annie nodded in agreement, her mouth just as full.

But no sooner had they filled their stomachs with food and drink than a cry rang out and everyone started whispering, "The Devils! The Devils! They're coming!"

Meg thumped down her goblet, shaking. The horrors would come now, surely. She tried to get up, but Mad Annie pulled her down again.

A green mist filled the mountain valley, dark shapes forming within. Oh, why had she ever come? Of course the food and fripperies had all been a trap to lure her from her good sense and now she would pay the price.

Then Mad Annie rose up out of her chair and pointed into the mist. "There he is! There's my captain."

Meg stared, clutching at the table. She searched the mist. Then, yes, striding out of the mist came an older gentleman with sea green eyes and a tangled beard, swathed in fishermen's nets. He smiled at Mad Annie and swept her into his arms.

"My Devil!" She swung her arms around his neck and gave him such a kiss Meg blushed and turned away.

It was as though Mad Annie were a fairy tale princess. Meg shook her head in confusion. This was no pointy-tailed Devil, no terrible horror.

She looked about her, searching for gruesome horns or sharpened talons, but these Devils looked no more harmful than wild rose brambles.

Addled Tate rested his balding head on the bosom of his dead wife, gone these five summers past. The almswoman was running her hands through the black curls of a woman covered in red butterflies. Two girls with skin shimmering like the scales of a fish led the merchant's son toward the trees. And Tommy Brown was dancing one-legged in the arms of a young man with alder leaves spilling down his back. Mad Annie danced spinning round the bonfire with her sea captain, cackling and whooping.

But there was no one for her. Of course. She sank down into her chair, excitement and terror both draining out of her.

Then there was a soft voice behind her. "Meg?"

She turned to find a young man with eyes as gold as wheat fields in August and a pair of goat's horns peeking out from beneath brown curls. She had never seen him before and yet she felt as if she had always known him. As a child, maybe, or in dreams, or as an image in the back of her mind while she tended the horses and forgot for a time that she was ugly, that the villagers were cruel.

She nodded. "Are you my Devil?"

He held out his hand and smiled. "I am." There was dirt under his fingernails and he smelled of pine needles.

Meg shut her eyes. "This can't be true. I'm just *Meg.*"

He brushed his fingers against her cheek and pressed his lips to her ear and whispered. "And you are beautiful Meg. In your very soul."

She shook her head, face burning.

"Let me show you." He took her hand and kissed it, a featherlight brush of lips that shook her like thunder.

Her hair swirled about as in a whirlwind. Wildflowers sprang from the ground where she stood and ivy climbed up her dress, twining through her hair like green lace. She could hear the wind and the trees whispering their secrets. She could feel the underground rivers carrying treasures to the sea. Her skin burned in the moonlight and her heart beat with sap.

She drew back and looked at her hands. Her skin was still sallow, her hair still the color of sickly carrots. But she stood tall now, chin tilted high. For the first time, she felt strength and beauty within her.

She smiled, and took her Devil's hand in her own.

When she woke the next morning she lay in her own lumpy bed, her clothes mud-stained and tattered once more. She stared up and saw just the dark cob-webbed thatched roof above her, and tried not to sob. A dream, it had all been just a dream. She turned to bury her face in her straw-stuffed mattress, then sat up, astonished. Tangled vines climbed the walls and a blanket of pale flowers lined the floor. The room smelled sweet as honey-suckle. She broke into a laugh and leapt out of bed, scooping up handfuls of petals and tossing them into the air to fall like snow. The whole world seemed lit with a secret fire.

She *had* signed the Devil's book last night, but it hadn't been one of hate and horror. She'd signed it in kisses and good food and a soul free as a butterfly. When the witches next rode she'd go back up the mountain and do it again.

That afternoon she carried oats to the stable, a gaggle of beautiful tormentors chanting "Maggoty Meg" at her heels. The little devils were lobbing lumps of coal at her.

With a flick of her wrist Meg turned the coal to roses.

END

"Maggoty Meg Flies Up the Mountain" © Jonathan Lenore Kastin.
First published February 25, 2022 in Cosmic Roots & Eldritch Shores.

Jonathan Lenore Kastin (he/they) is a queer, trans writer with an MFA in Writing from Vermont College of Fine Arts. His poems have been published in Mythic Delirium, Goblin Fruit, Liminality, and Abyss & Apex. His short stories can be found in Cosmic Roots and Eldritch Shores, On Spec, and Galaxy's Edge, and the anthologies *Ab(solutely) Normal, Transmogrify!*, and *We Mostly Come Out at Night*. He lives with two mischievous cats and more books than he could ever read.

THE QUIET

George Guthridge

Though we often lacked water we were not unhappy. The tsama melons supported us. It was a large patch, and by conserving we could last long periods without journeying to the waterholes. The Whites and tame Bushmen had taken over the /Gam and Gautscha Pans, and the people there, the !Kung, either had run away or had stayed for the water and now worked the Whites' farms and ate mealie meal.

There were eleven of us Gwi, though sometimes one or two more. !Gai, the bachelor, was one of those who came and went. /Tuka would say, "You can always count us on three hands, but never on two or four hands." He would laugh, then. He was always laughing. I think he laughed because there was so little game near the !A Ha !O Pan, our home. The few duiker and steenbok that had once roamed our plain had smelled the coming of the Whites and the fleeing !Kung, and had run away. /Tuka laughed to fill up the empty spaces.

Sometimes, when he was trapping springhare and porcupine, he helped me gather wood and tubers. We dug !xwa roots and =koa, the water root buried deep in the earth, until our arms ached. Sometimes we hit the n=a trees with sticks, making the sweet berries fall, and /Tuka would chase me round and round, laughing and yelling like a madman. It was times like those when I wondered why I had once hated him so much.

I wondered much about that during !Kuma, the hot season when starvation stalked us. During the day I'd take off my kaross, dig a shallow pit within what little shade a =/uribush offered, then urinate in the sand, cover myself with more sand and place a leaf over my head.

The three of us – /Tuka, Kuara, and I – lay side by side like dead people.

"My heart is sad from hunger," I sang to myself all day. "Like an old man, sick and slow." I thought of all the bad things, then. My parents marrying me to /Tuka before I was ready, because, paying bride service, he brought them new karosses. /Tuka doing the marrying thing to me before I was ready. Everything before I was ready! Sometimes I prayed into the leaf that a paouw would fly down and think his penis a fat caterpillar.

Then one night /Tuka snared a honey badger. A badger, during !kuma! Everyone was exited. /Tuka said, "Yesterday, when we slept, I told the land that my !U was hungry, and I must have meat for her and Kuara." The badger was very tender. !Gai ate his share and went begging, though he had never brought meat to the camp. When the meat was gone we roasted /ga roots and sang and danced while /Tuka played the //gwashi. I danced proudly, not for /Tuka but for myself. N/um uncurled from the pit of my belly and came boiling up my spine. I was afraid, because when n/um reaches my skull I !kia. I see ghosts killing people, and I smell the rotting smell of death, like decayed carcasses.

/Tuka took my head in his hands. "You must not !kia," he said. "Not now. Your body will suffer too much for the visions." He held me beside the fire and stroked me, and n/um subsided. "When I lie in the sand during the day I dream I have climbed the footpegs in a great baobab tree," he said, "I look out from the treetop, and the land is agraze with animals. Giraffe and wildebeest and kudu. 'You must kill these beasts and bring them to !U and Kuara before the Whites kill them,' my dream says."

Then he asked, "What do you think of when you lie there, !U?"

I did not answer him. He smiled. His eyes, moist, shone with firelight. Perhaps he thought n/um had stopped my tongue.

The next day the quiet came. Lying beneath the sand, I felt n/um pulse in my belly. I fought the fear it always brought. I did not cry out to /Tuka. The pulsing increased. I began to tremor. Sweat ran down my face. N/um boiled within me. It entered my spine and pushed toward my throat. My eyes were wide and I kept staring at the veins of the leaf but seeing dread. I felt myself go rigid and shivering at the same time. My head throbbed; it was as large as a /ga root. I could hear my mouth make sputtery noises, like Kuara used to at my breast. The pressure inside me kept building, building.

And suddenly left. It burrowed into the earth, taking my daydreams with it. I went down and down into the sand. I passed =ubbee roots and animals long dead, their bones bleached and forgotten. Then I came to a waterhole far beneath the ground. /Tuka was in the water. Kuara was too. He looked younger, barely old enough to toddle. I took off my kaross. The three of us held hands and danced, naked, splashing. There was no n/um to seize me. No marrying-thing urge to seize /Tuka. Only quiet, and laughter.

The Whites with Land Rovers came during !ga, the hottest season. The trucks bucked and roared across the sand. /Tuka took Kuara along and hurried to meet them. I went too, though I walked behind with the other women. There were several white men and some Bantu. !Gai was standing in the lead truck, waving and grinning.

A white, blond woman climbed out. She was wearing white shorts and a light brown shirt with rolled up sleeves. I recognized her immediately. Doctor Morse come to study us again. /Tuka had said the Whites did not wonder about their own culture, so they liked to study ours.

She talked to us women a long time, asking about our families and how we felt about SWAPO, the People's Army. Everyone spoke at once. She kept waving her hands for quiet.

"What do you think, !U" she would ask. "What's your opinion?"

I said we should ask /Tuka. He was a man and understood such things. Doctor Morse frowned, so I said SWAPO should not kill people. SWAPO should leave people alone. Doctor Morse wrote in her notebook as I talked. I was pleased. The other women were very jealous.

Doctor Morse told us the war in South Africa was going badly; soon it would sweep this way. When /Tuka finished looking at the engines I asked him what Doctor Morse meant by "badly." Badly for Blacks, or badly for Whites. Badly for those in the south, or those of us in the Kalahari. He did not know. None of us asked Doctor Morse.

Then she said, "We have brought water. Lots of water. We've heard you've been without." Her hair caught the sunlight. She was very beautiful for a white woman.

We smiled but refused her offer. She frowned but didn't seem angry. Maybe she thought it was because she was White. If so, she was wrong. "Well, at least go for a ride in the trucks," she said, beaming.

/Tuka laughed and, taking Kuara by the hand, scrambled for the two Land Rovers. I shook my head. "You really should go," Doctor Morse said. "It'll be good for you."

"Land rovers are something for men to do," I told her. "Women do not understand those things."

"All they are going to do is ride in the back!"

"Trucks. Hunting. Fire. Those are men's things," I said.

Only one of the trucks came back. Everyone but /Tuka, Kuara, and some of the Bantu returned. "The truck's stuck in the sand," !Gai said. "The Whites decided to wait until dawn to pull it out. /Tuka said he'd sleep beside it. You know how he is about trucks!" Everyone laughed. Except me. An empty space throbbed in my heart.

Then rain came. It was !ga !go – male rain. It poured down strong and sudden, not the even and gentle female rain that fills the land with water. Rain, during !ga! Everyone shouted and danced for joy. Even the Whites danced. A miracle! People said. I thought about the honey badger caught during !kuma, and was afraid. I felt alone. In spite of my fear, or perhaps because of it, I did a foolish thing. I slept away from the others.

In the night the quiet again touched me. N/um uncurled in my belly. I did not beckon it forth. I swear I didn't. I wasn't even thinking about it. As I slept I felt my body clench tight. In my dreams I could hear my breathing – shallow and rapid. Fear seized me and shook me like the twig of an in=I bush. I sank into the earth. /Tuka and Kuara stood slump-shouldered in steaming, ankle-deep water at the waterhole where we had danced. Kuara was wearing the head of a wildebeest; the eyes had been carved out and replaced with smoldering coals. "Run away, mother," he kept saying.

I awoke to shadows. A fleeting darkness came upon me before I could move. I glimpsed !Gai grinning beneath the moon. Then a hand was clapped over my mouth.

Kuara, my son, the Whites have stolen the moon. I have awakened again. Outside the window the sky is black. A blue-white disc hangs among the stars. It is the Earth, says Doctor Stefanko. I wail and beat my fists. Straps bind me to a bed. Doctor Stefanko forces my shoulders down, swabs my arm. "Since you can't keep still I'm going to have to put you under again," she says, smiling.

I lie quietly.

It is not Earth. Earth is brown. Earth is Kalahari.

"You are on the moon," Doctor Stefanko says. It is the second or third time she has told me this; I have awakened and slept, awakened and slept until I am not sure what voices are dream and what are real, if any. Then something pricks my skin. "Rest now. You have had a long sleep."

I remember awakening the first time. White. Everything white. The room white, Doctor Stefanko white, a white smell, white cloth covering me. Outside, blackness and the blue-white disc.

"On the moon," I say. My limbs feel heavy. My head spins. Sleep drags at my flesh. "The moon."

"Isn't it wonderful?"

"And you say my husband, /Tuka is dead."

Her lips tighten. She looks at me solemnly. Her hand, cool hand, strokes my forehead. "He did not survive the sleep."

"The moon is hollow," I tell her. "Everyone knows that. The dead sleep there." I stare at the ceiling. "I am alive and on the moon. /Tuka is dead but is not here." The words seem to float from my mouth. There are little dots on the ceiling.

"Sleep now. That's a girl//. We'll talk more later."

"And Kuara. My son. Alive." The dots are spinning. I close my eyes. The dots keep spinning.

"Yes, but −" The dots. The dots.

"About a hundred years ago a law was made to protect endangered species - animals which, unless humans took care, might become extinct," Doctor Stefanko says. Her face is no longer blurry. She has gray hair, drawn cheeks, sad eyes. I have seen her somewhere − long before I was brought to this place. I cannot remember where. The memory slips away. Dread haunts my heart.

!Gai, wearing a breechclout, stands grinning near the window. The blue-white disc Doctor Stefanko calls the Earth haloes his head. His huge, pitted tongue sticks out where his front teeth are missing. His shoulders slope like those of a hartebeest. His chest, leathery and wrinkled, is tufted with hair beginning to gray. I am not surprised to see him, after his treachery. He makes n/um pulse in the pit of my belly. I look away.

"Then the law was broadened to also include endangered peoples. Peoples like the /Gwi." Doctor Stefanko smiles maternally and presses her index finger against my nose.

I toss my head.

She frowns. "Obviously, it would be impossible to save entire tribes. So the founders of the law did what they thought best. They saved, well, certain representatives. You. Your family. Along with a few others, such as !Gai. These representatives were frozen."

"Frozen?"

"Made cold."

"As during !gum, when ice forms inside the ostrich-egg container?"

"Much colder."

It was not dream, then. I remember staring through a blue, crinkled sheen. Like light seen through a snakeskin. I could not move, though my insides never stopped shivering. *So this is death,* I kept thinking. *An awful thing, death.*

"In the interim you were brought here to the moon. To Carnival. It is a very fine place. A truly international facility. Carnival will be your home now, !U."

"And Kuara?"

"He will live here with you, in time." Again, that tightening of the lips. Fear touches me. Then she says, "Would you like to see him?" Some of the fear slides away.

"Is it wise, Doctor?" !Gai asks. "She has a temper, this one." His eyes grin down at me. He stares at my pelvis.

"Oh, we'll manage. You'll be a good girl, won't you !U?"

My head nods. My heart does not say yes or no.

The straps leap away with a loud click. Doctor Stefanko and !Gai help me to my feet. The world wobbles. The Earth-disc tilts and swings. The floor slants one way, another way. Needles tingle in my feet and hands. I am helped into a chair. More clicking. The door hisses open and the chair floats out, Doctor Stefanko leading, !Gai lumbering behind. We move down one corridor after another. This is a place of angles. No curves except the smiles of Whites as we pass. And they curve too much.

Another door hisses. We enter a room full of chill. Blue glass, insides laced with frost, stretches from floor to ceiling along each wall. I see frozen figures standing behind the glass. I remember this place, and how sluggish was the hate in my heart.

"Kuara is on the end," Doctor Stefanko says, her breath white.

The chair floats closer. My legs bump the glass; cold shocks my knees. The chair draws back. I lean forward.

Through the glass I can see my son. I can see his closed eyes. Ice furs his lashes and brows. His head is tilted to one side. His little arms dangle. I touch the glass in spite of the cold.

I hear !Gai's sharp intake of breath and feel him start to draw back my shoulders, but Doctor Stefanko puts a hand on his wrist and I am released. There is give to the glass. Not like that on the trucks in the tsama patch.

My n/um rises. My heart beats faster. N/um enters my arms, floods my fingers. "Kuara," I whisper. Warmth spreads upon the glass. It makes a small, ragged circle.

"He'll be taken from here as soon as you've made the adjustment," Doctor Stefanko says.

Kuara. If only I could dance. N/um would boil within me. I could !Kia. I would shoo away the ghosts of the cold. Awakening, you would step through the glass and into my arms.

"This will be your new home, !U," Doctor Stefanko says as she opens a door. She has given me a new kaross; of *genuine* gemsbok, she tells me, though I am uncertain why she speaks of it that way.

When she puts her hand on my back and pushes me forward, the kaross feels soft and smooth against my skin. "We think you'll like it; and if there's anything you need —"

I grab the sides of the door and turn my face away. I will not live here in nor even look at the place. But her push becomes much firmer, and I stumble inside. I cover my face with my hands.

"There, now," Doctor Stefanko says.

I spy through my fingers.

We are in Kalahari.

I turn slowly, my heart shining and singing. No door. No walls. No angles. The sandveld spreads out beneath a cloudless sky. Endless pale-gold grass stretches, surrounding scattered white-thorn and tsi; in the distance lift several flat-topped acacias, and even a mongongo tree. A dassie darts in and out of a rocky kranze.

"Here might be a good place for your tshushi — your shelter," Doctor Stefanko says, pulling me forward. She enters the tall grass, bends, comes up smiling, holding branches in one hand, sansevieria fibers in the other. "You see? We've even cut some of the materials you'll need."

"But how —"

"The moon isn't such a horrible place, now is it." She strides back through the grass. "And we here at Carnival are dedicated to making your stay as pleasant as possible. Just look here." She moves a rock. Below, a row of buttons gleams. "Turn this knob, and you can control your weather; no more suffering through those terrible hot and cold seasons. Unless you want to, of course," she adds quickly. "And from time to time some nice people will be looking down ... *in* on you. From up there, within the sky." She makes a sweep of her arm. "They want to watch how you live; you — and others like you — are quite a sensation, you know."

I stare at her without understanding.

"Anyway, if you want to see them, just turn this knob. And if you want to hear what the monitor's saying about you, turn this one." She looks up, sees my confusion. "Oh, don't worry; the monitor translates everything. It's a wonderful device."

Standing, she takes hold of my arms. Her eyes are loving. "You see, !U, there is no more Kalahari on Earth – not as you knew it anyhow – so we've created another. In some ways it won't be as good as what you were used to, in a lot of ways it will be better." Her smile comes back. "We think you'll like it."

"And Kuara?"

"He is waking now. He will join you soon." She hugs me. "Soon." Then she walks back in the direction we came from, quickly fading in the distance. She is gone.

A veil of heat shimmers above the grass where the door seemed to have been. For a moment I think of following. Finally I shrug. I work at building my tshushi. I work slowly, methodically, my head full of thoughts.

I think of Kuara, and something gnaws at me. I drop the fiber I am holding and begin walking toward the opposite horizon, where a giraffe is eating from the mongongo tree.

Grasshoppers, !kxon ants, dung beetles hop and crawl among the grasses. Leguaan scuttle. A mole snake slithers for a hole beneath a =uri bush. I walk quickly, the sand warm but not hot beneath my feet. The plain is sun-drenched, the few small omirimbi water courses parched and cracked, yet I feel little thirst. A steenbok leaps for cover behind a white-thorn.

This is a good place, part of me decides. Here will Kuara become the hunter /Tuka could not be. Kuara will never laugh to shut out sadness.

The horizon draws no closer.

I measure the giraffe with my thumb, walk a thousand paces, stop, remeasure, walk another thousand paces, remeasure.

The giraffe does not change size.

I will walk another thousand paces. Then I will turn back and finish the tshushi.

A hundred paces further I bump into something hard.

A wall.

Beyond, the giraffe continues feeding.

Doctor Stefanko returns after I've finished the hut. She and !Gai bring warthog and kudu hides, porcupine quills, tortoise shells, ostrich eggs, a sharpening stone, an awl, two assagai blades, pots of Bantu clay. Many things. !Gai grins as he sets them down.

Later, Doctor Stefanko brings Kuara.

He comes sprinting, gangly, the grass nearly to his chin. "Mama!" he shouts, "Mama! Mama!" I take him in my arms, whirling and laughing. I put my hands upon his cheeks; his arms are around my waist. Real. Oh, yes. So very real, my Kuara! Tears roll down my face. He looks hollow-eyed, and his hair has been shaved. But I do not let concern stop my heart. I weep from joy, not pain.

Doctor Stefanko leaves, and Kuara and I talk. He babbles about a strange sleep, and Doctor Stefanko, and !Gai, as I show him the camp. I show him how one of the knobs can make a line of small windows blink on the slight angle between wall-sky and ceiling-sky. The windows look like square beads. There, faces pause and peer. Children. Old men. Women with smiles like springhares. People of many races. I tell Kuara he must not smile or acknowledge their presence. Not even the children's. Especially not the children. The faces are surely ghosts, I warn him. Ghosts dreaming of becoming /Gwi.

We listen to the voice from what Doctor Stefanko calls the monitor. It is sing-song, lulling. A woman, I think. "!U and Kuara, the latest additions to Carnival, will soon be accustomed to our excellent accommodations," the voice says. The voice floats with us as we go to gather roots and wood.

A leguaan pokes its head from the rocky kranze, listening. Silently I put down my wood. Then my hand moves slowly. So slowly it is almost not movement. I grab. Caught! Kuara shrieks and claps his hands.

"Notice the scarification across the cheeks and upper legs," the voice is saying. "The same is true of the buttocks, though like any self-respecting /Gwi, !U will not remove her kaross in the presence of others except during the Eland Dance."

I carry the leguaan wiggling to the hut.

"Were she to disrobe, you would notice tremendous fatty deposits in the buttocks, a phenomenon known as steatopygia. Unique to Bushmen (or 'Bushwomen,' we should say), this anatomical feature aids in food storage. It was once believed that —"

After breaking the leguaan's neck, I take off the kaross of genuine gemsbok and, using sansevieria fiber, tie it in front of my hut. It makes a wonderful door. I have never had a door. /Tuka and I slept outside, using the tshushi for storage. Kuara will have a door. A door between him and the watchers.

He will have fire. Fire for warmth and food and !U to sing beside. I gather grewia sticks and carve male and female then use ??galli grass for the tinder. Like /Tuka did.

"The /Gwi are clearly marked by a low, flattened skull, tiny mastoid processes, a bulging or vertical forehead, peppercorn hair, a nonpragnathous face —"

I twirl the sticks between my palms. It seems to take forever. My arms grow sore. I am ready to give up when smoke curls. Gibbering, Kuara goes leaping about the camp. I gaze at the fire and grin with delight.

But it is frightened delight. I will make warmth fires and food fires, I decide as I blow the smoke into flame. Not ritual fires. Not without /Tuka.

I roast the leguaan with /ore berries and the tsha-cucumber, which seems plentiful. But I am not /Tuka, quick with fire and laughter. The firemaking has taken too long. Halfway through the cooking, Kuara seizes the lizard and, bouncing it in his hands as though it were hot dough, tears it apart.

"Kuara!" I blurt out in pretended anger. He giggles as, the intestines dangling, he holds up the lizard to eat. I smile sadly. Kuara's laughing eyes and ostrich legs … so much like /Tuka!

"The /Gwi sing no praises of battles or warriors," the singing voice says. I help Kuara finish the leguaan. "They have no history of warfare. Though petty arguments are common (even a nonviolent society cannot keep husbands and wives from scrapping), any actual fighting is considered dishonorable. To fight is to have failed to —"

When I gaze up there are no faces in the windows.

At last, dusk dapples the grass. Kuara finds a guinea-fowl feather and a reed; leaning against my legs, he busies himself making a zani. As the temperature begins to drop, I decide the door would fit better around our shoulders than across the tsushi.

A figure strides out of the setting sun. I shield my eyes with my arm. Doctor Stefanko. She smiles and nods at Kuara, now tying a nut onto his toy for a weight, and sits on a log. Her smile remains, though is drained of joy. She looks at me seriously.

"I do hope Kuara's presence will dissuade you from making any more *displays* such as you exhibited this afternoon," she tells me. "Surely you must realize that he is here with you on a … a trial basis, shall we say." She taps her forefinger against her palm. "This impetuousness of yours has to cease." Another tap. "And cease now." Her left brow lifts.

Head cocked I gaze at her, not understanding.

"Taking off your kaross simply because the monitor said you do not." She nods knowingly. "Oh, yes, we're aware when you're listening. And that frightful display with the lizard!" She makes a face and seems to shudder. "Then there's the matter of the fire." She points at the glowing embers. "You're supposed to be living here like you did back on Earth. At least during the day. Men always started the fires."

"Men were always present." I shrug.

"Yes. Well, arrangements are being made. For the time being stick to foods you don't need to cook. And use the heating system." She goes to the rock and, on hands and knees, turns one of the knobs. A humming sounds. Smiling and rubbing her hands over the fire, she reseats herself on the log, pulls a photograph from her hip pocket and hands it to me. I turn the picture rightside-up. Doctor Morse is standing with her arms across !Gai's shoulders. His left arm is around her waist. The Land Rovers are in the background.

"Impetuous," Doctor Stefanko says, leaning over to click her fingernail against the photograph. "That's exactly what Doctor Morse wrote about you in her notebooks. She considered it a virtue." Again the eyebrow lifts. "We do not." Then she adds proudly, "She was my grandmother, you know. As you can imagine, I have more than simply a professional interest in our Southwest African section here at Carnival."

I start to hand back the photograph. She raises her hand, halting me. "Keep it," she says. "Think of it as a wedding present. The first of many."

That night, Kuara and I are wrapped in the kaross, sleeping in one another's arms, in the tshushi. He is still clutching his zani, though he has not thrown it once into the air to watch it spin down. Perhaps he will throw it tomorrow. Tomorrow. An ugly word. I lie staring at the dark ground, sand clenched in my fists. I wonder if they will watch the night !Gai climbs upon my back and grunts throughout the marrying-thing.

Sleep comes. A tortured sleep. I can feel myself hugging Kuara. He squirms against the embrace but does not awaken.

In my dreams I slide out of myself and, stirring up the fire, dance the Eland Dance. My body is slick with eland fat. My eyes stare into the dark and my head is held high and stiff. Chanting, I lift and put down my feet, moving around and around the fire. Other women clap and sing the !kia-healing songs. Men play the //gwashi and musical bows. The music lifts and lilts and throbs. Rhythm thrums within me. Each muscle knows the song. Around and around, ever dancing. Tears squeeze from my eyes. Pain leadens my legs. And still I dance.

Then, at last, n/um rises. It uncurls in my belly, breathes fire-breath up my spine. I fight the fear. I dance against the dread. I tremble with fire. My eyes slit with agony. I do not watch the women clapping and singing. My breaths come in shallow, heated gasps. My breasts bounce. I dance. N/um continues to rise. It tingles against the base of my brain. It fills my head. My entire body is alive, burning. Thorns are sticking everywhere in my flesh. My breasts are fiery coals. I can feel ghosts, hot ghosts, ghosts of the past, crowding into my skull. I stagger for the hut; Kuara and !U, my old self, await me. I slide into her flesh like someone slipping beneath the cool, mudslicked waters of a year-round pan. I slide in further. I become her once again. My head is aflame with n/um and ghosts. "!U," I whisper, "I bring the ghosts of all your former selves and of your people." Again she groans, though weaker; the pleasure-groan of a woman making love. Her body stretches, stiffens. Her nails rake Kuara's back. She accepts me, then; accepts her self. I fill her flesh.

And bring the quiet, for the third time in her life. Down and down into the sand she seeps, like !ga !go rain soaking into parched earth, leaving nothing of her self behind, her hands around Kuara's wrists as she pulls him after her, the zani's guinea-fowl feather whipping behind him as if in a wind. She passes through sand, Carnival's concrete base, moonrock, moving ever downward, badger-burrowing.

She breaks through into a darkness streaked with silver light: into the core of the moon, where live the ghosts of !kia. She tumbles downward, crying her dismay and joy, her kaross fluttering. In the center of the hollow, where water shines like cold silver, /Tuka awaits, arms outstretched. He is laughing – a shrill, forced cackle. Such is the only laughter a ghost can know whose sleep has been disturbed. They will dance this night, the three of them: !U, /Tuka, Kuara.

Then he will teach her the secret of !oa, the poison squeezed from the female larvae of the dung beetle. Poison for arrows he will teach her to make. Poison for which the Bushmen know no antidote.

She will hunt when she returns to !Gai and to Doctor Stefanko.

She will not hunt animals.

END

George Guthridge is Professor Emeritus at the University of Alaska at Fairbanks. An expert in indigenous cognition, he was named as one of America's 78 top educators for his work with Alaska Native youth. His fiction has appeared in Amazing, Analog, Asimov's, F&SF, and many other places. A Hugo finalist and twice Nebula finalist, he was co-winner of the Bram Stoker for year's best horror novel, grand prize winner in the Las Vegas International Screenplay Competition, and national finalist for the Benjamin Franklin Award for year's best book about education. He has retired and now lives in Thailand. Email: glguthridge@alaska.edu

Note: The extra punctuations are the notations for glottal stops.

Night, Edward Robert Hughes

excerpts from

The Witch of Atlas

Percy Bysshe Shelley

'Tis said, she first was changed into a vapour,
And then into a cloud, such clouds as flit,
Like splendour-wingèd moths about a taper,
Round the red west when the sun dies in it:
And then into a meteor, such as caper
On hill-tops when the moon is in a fit:
Then, into one of those mysterious stars
Which hide themselves between the Earth and Mars ...

The deep recesses of her odorous dwelling
Were stored with magic treasures--sounds of air,
Which had the power all spirits of compelling,
Folded in cells of crystal silence there;
Such as we hear in youth, and think the feeling
Will never die--yet ere we are aware,
The feeling and the sound are fled and gone,
And the regret they leave remains alone.

And there lay Visions swift, and sweet, and quaint,
Each in its thin sheath, like a chrysalis,
Some eager to burst forth, some weak and faint
With the soft burthen of intensest bliss.
It was its work to bear to many a saint
Whose heart adores the shrine which holiest is,
Even Love's:--and others white, green, gray, and black,
And of all shapes--and each was at her beck....

And liquors clear and sweet, whose healthful might
Could medicine the sick soul to happy sleep,
And change eternal death into a night
Of glorious dreams -- or if eyes needs must weep,
Could make their tears all wonder and delight,
She in her crystal vials did closely keep:
If men could drink of those clear vials, 'tis said
The living were not envied of the dead.

Her cave was stored with scrolls of strange device,
The works of some Saturnian Archimage,
Which taught the expiations at whose price
Men might from the Gods win that happy age
Too lightly lost, redeeming native vice;
And which might quench the Earth-consuming rage
Of gold and blood -- till men should live and move
Harmonious as the sacred stars above;...
;...

And wondrous works of substances unknown,
To which the enchantment of her father's power
Had changed those ragged blocks of savage stone,
Were heaped in the recesses of her bower;
Carved lamps and chalices, and vials which shone
In their own golden beams--each like a flower,
Out of whose depth a fire-fly shakes his light
Under a cypress in a starless night.

At first she lived alone in this wild home,...

While on her hearth lay blazing many a piece
Of sandal wood, rare gums, and cinnamon;
Men scarcely know how beautiful fire is--
Each flame of it is as a precious stone
Dissolved in ever-moving light, and this
 Belongs to each and all who gaze upon.
The Witch beheld it not, for in her hand
She held a woof that dimmed the burning brand.

This lady never slept, but lay in trance
All night within the fountain -- as in sleep.
Its emerald crags glowed in her beauty's glance;
Through the green splendour of the water deep
She saw the constellations reel and dance
Like fire-flies -- and withal did ever keep
The tenour of her contemplations calm,
With open eyes, closed feet, and folded palm. ....

Then by strange art she kneaded fire and snow
 Together, tempering the repugnant mass
 With liquid love--all things together grow
 Through which the harmony of love can pass;
 And a fair Shape out of her hands did flow--
 A living Image, which did far surpass
 In beauty that bright shape of vital stone
 Which drew the heart out of Pygmalion.

A sexless thing it was, and in its growth
 It seemed to have developed no defect
 Of either sex, yet all the grace of both,--
 In gentleness and strength its limbs were decked;
 The bosom swelled lightly with its full youth,
 The countenance was such as might select
 Some artist that his skill should never die,
 Imaging forth such perfect purity.

From its smooth shoulders hung two rapid wings,
Fit to have borne it to the seventh sphere,
Tipped with the speed of liquid lightenings,
Dyed in the ardours of the atmosphere: …

And it unfurled its heaven-coloured pinions,
With stars of fire spotting the stream below;
And from above into the Sun's dominions
Flinging a glory, like the golden glow
In which Spring clothes her emerald-winged minions,
All interwoven with fine feathery snow
And moonlight splendour of intensest rime,
With which frost paints the pines in winter time.   …

The Witch of Atlas lives in a cave by a secret fountain, and fashions a hermaphrodite being from snow and fire. They cast spells over people in power, causing some havoc to the status quo, as Shelley himsself may have wished to do.

During his lifetime (1792-1822), Shelley's work was little read and was generally unfavorably reviewed. His radical politics, vegetarianism, atheism, and advocacy of 'free love', much at odds with his time, added to his difficulties. A good deal of his work was left unfinished, unpublished, or published in censored or error-filled forms. It was not until years after his death that a wider audience began reading and appreciating his work.

The Witch of Atlas is considered one of Shelley's most important works, but was not published until two years after his death along with other of his poems. The editor felt that while brilliant, Shelley was "discarding human interest" and should have written poems less abstract and more in line with popular interests. -- The editor was his wife, Mary Wollstonecraft Shelley, author of *Frankenstein*.

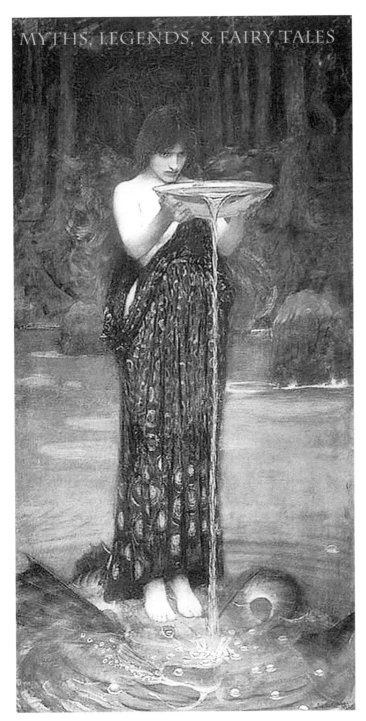

Circe Invidiosa, by John William Waterhouse

The Silver Apples of the Moon, by Margaret MacDonald MacKintosh

The Song of Wandering Aengus

W.B. Yeats

I went out to the hazel wood,
Because a fire was in my head,
And cut and peeled a hazel wand,
And hooked a berry to a thread;
And when white moths were on the wing,
And moth-like stars were flickering out,
I dropped the berry in a stream
And caught a little silver trout.

I came in through the cottage door
And went to blow the fire a-flame,
But something rustled on the floor,
And some one called my name;
It had become a glimmering girl
With apple blossom in her hair
Who rose up from the floor and ran
And faded through the brightening air.

Though I am old with wandering
Through hollow hills and lands,
I will find yet where she has gone,
And kiss her lips and take her hands;
And walk among long dappled grass,
And pluck till time and times are done,
The silver apples of the moon,
And golden apples of the sun.

W.B. Yeats was born in Dublin, Ireland, in 1865 and is considered one of the greats of modern English-language poets. He was one of the founders of the Abbey Theatre, and received the 1923 Nobel Prize for literature. Rather than identify with his Protestant background, he sought out the ancient pre-Christian traditions of Ireland.

In Irish mythology, Aengus is one of the supernatural Tuatha De Danann. He was a god of love, youth, and poetic inspiration.

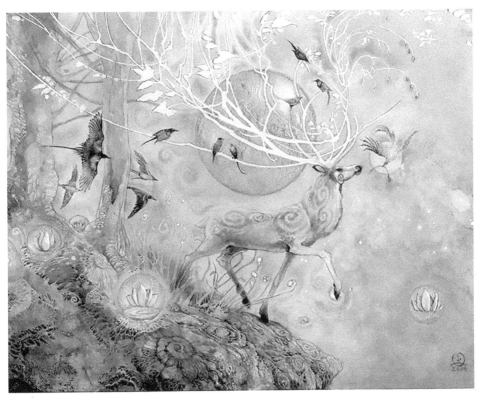

artwork detail from *Allegro* by Stephanie Law

Following the White Deer:
On Myth & Writing

Terri Windling

The act of creation, it has always seemed to me, is one of the great magics of our world -- an ancient magic, guarded by the gods, blessed (and coveted) by the fairies. In mythic cosmologies found around the globe, specific gods are associated with each of the creative arts: building, weaving, instrument making, theatrical productions, etc. And these gods must each be petitioned for aid, or propitiated against their hindrance. Ancient poets, dancers, musicians, storytellers used their gifts to cross over the boundary lines separating the human realm from the spirit realm and the lands of the living from the lands of the dead; artists performed an almost shamanic function, creating new worlds, new ideas, new realities.

In many ancient cultures, creative arts were used (both literally and metaphorically) to heal, blight, praise, curse, celebrate, lament, and renew. Inspiration could be sought through one's genius[1], which was one's own personal spirit-guide in Greek mythology -- or through the Muses, those lovely daughters of Zeus and Mnemosyne (memory): Clio (history), Euterpe (lyric poetry), Thalia (comedy), Melpomene (tragedy), Terpsichore (dance and song), Erato (love songs), Polymnia (divine hymns), Urania (astronomy), and Calliope (epic poetry).

In Celtic lands, the Leanan-Sidhe was a faery mistress who inspired poets with her touch -- but if misused, her powers could burn too brightly and lead to an early death. Likewise, the White Deer Woman of Cherokee tales inspired poetry and song, but only to those who showed her respect as she roamed through the woods in deer form.

In the fields of fantasy literature and mythic arts, many of us still seek our inspiration deep in the archetypal forest, following trails blazed through the centuries by the writers and artists who have gone before. We chase the white deer through Shakespeare's fairy plays; through the French and German fairy tale salons; through the poetry of Keats, Goethe, and Yeats; through the visionary dreams of the Pre-Raphaelites, the Symbolists, the Surrealists; and through a wide, wide range of magical writers from George MacDonald to Angela Carter.

The Muses speak to us not only through stories and dreams, but also through all the creative acts of life: making food, making love, making conversation, making community, making a poem or a prayer out of each moment lived. To some, creative inspiration comes only during life's quiet times; to others, when life is abundantly full -- and as artists, we must each learn our own individual ways of summoning the Muses.

Perhaps now, in this non-animist age, few leave out wine and flowers anymore -- but we still have our Muse-summoning rituals and talismans: the favorite pen or brand of paper, coffee in a certain mug, paints arranged just so on the palette, the email box emptied or the phone switched off or the desk surface cleared before we can work...all those small rituals we do each time, every time, in order to clear the mind, to focus, to prepare for the crossing[2] from the physical world to the realm of imagination.

That moment of crossing is a mythic moment -- as potent as the old folk tales where the hero crosses running water (once, twice, three times) to enter Faerieland. Some days it is easy to make the crossing and to lose ourselves in the creative process; some days it is much harder; and we rarely know which kind of day it will be in advance.

On the most difficult days, one can't cross at all -- as if Janus, god of the threshold, or Hermes, god of boundaries, stands firmly blocking the way. Occasionally I've recognized this "writer's block" as a necessary thing: a time to let the dry well of inspiration fill up with water once more. At other times, it feels like a banishment, and I fear that the gates might stay locked up too long.

"When I don't write," lamented Anaïs Nin (in 1966, at the height of her success), "I feel my world shrinking. I feel I am in prison. I feel I lose my fire and color. Writing is a necessity, as the sea needs to heave, and I call it breathing."

Sometimes it's not lack of inspiration but lack of *time* that interferes with one's ability to create.

In May Sarton's splendid novel *Mrs. Stevens Hears the Mermaids Singing*, a poet's struggle with her Muse is often overshadowed by a deeper, less romantic struggle: the effort to push life aside long enough to actually get to her desk.

Thomas Wolfe echoed this sentiment in his *Autobiography of a Novelist*. We can't wait for those perfect moments, he warns us, when daily life seems to melt away and nothing exists but the fire of inspiration. Those moments of grace are precious, but rare. Treasure them, he says, but don't depend upon them; for the rest of the time we must be able to work despite the bills clamoring for attention, the dog barking, the telephone ringing, and the mailman at the door.

In her inspiring essay collection *The Gates of Excellence*, Katherine Paterson wrote what is, for me, the last word on the subject of the artist's perpetual struggle to find a balance of time for both life and art:

"I had no study in [the early] days, not even desk or file or bookcase to call mine alone. It might have happened sooner [the writing of work worthy of publication] had I had a room of my own and fewer children, but somehow I doubt it. For as I look back on what I have written, I can see that the very persons who took away my time and space are those who have given me something to say."

As for me, it's the richness of life itself that keeps luring me away from my writing desk... but, conversely, provides me with tales to tell when I find my way back again. Then, like all writers, I'm faced with that frightening and holy object: the blank white page. But it only takes one sentence, one word, to begin... and then, gods willing, the Muses come.

And I'm away with the fairies...

1. https://www.terriwindling.com/blog/2015/10/the-muse.html
2.https://www.terriwindling.com/blog/2015/07/from-the-archives-rituals-of-approach.html

"Following the White Deer: on Myth and Writing" © Terri Windling
First published in The Journal of Mythic Arts, 1996

Terri Windling is a writer, editor, painter, and folklorist specialising in fantasy and mythic arts. She has published over forty books, receiving ten World Fantasy Awards (including the Life Achievement Award in 2022), the Mythopoeic Award (for her novel *The Wood Wife*), the Bram Stoker Award, and the SFWA Solstice Award. She has edited fantasy fiction since the 1980s, working with many of the major writers in the field, and co-edited *The Year's Best Fantasy & Horror* anthologies with Ellen Datlow for sixteen years. She writes fiction for adults and children, nonfiction on folklore and fairy tales, and a long-running blog on myth, nature, and creativity: *Myth & Moor*. She delivered the fourth annual Tolkien Lecture on Fantasy Literature at Pembroke College, Oxford (2016); participated in the Modern Fairies folklore and music project (Oxford and Sheffield Universities, 2018-2019); served on the Advisory Board for *Realms of Imagination*, a major exhibition of fantasy at the British Library in London (2023-2024); and has been involved with The Centre for Fantasy and the Fantastic at the University of Glasgow since its founding in 2020. Born in the U.S., she now lives in a small village full of artists in south-west England.
https://www.terriwindling.com/books/author-biography.html
For her mythic arts blog: https://www.terriwindling.com/
For her folklore & fairy tale essays available online:
https://www.terriwindling.com/folklore/   and
https://www.terriwindling.com/mythic-arts/

Artwork is a detail from the painting *Allegro*, by Stephanie Law

The Witching Hour

Oghenechovwe Donald Ekpeki

I stood balanced at the top of the oldest palm tree, the one that grew at the south end of the village. I was in my element -- pitch black night.

This was my dawn. The murmurs of glowing spirits mixed with the chitter of living insects.

The hoot of an owl reminded me there was work to be done, battles to be fought -- silent, undeclared, but raging all the same. And old Mama Ishaka was on the other side of them. With a sigh, I leapt from the tree, fell free, and caught one of the power lines that led to a human spirit. The link was strong. The call of this spirit sang the music of its soul to me. It called me back home.

We sat in my hut, bare as it was, Eijiro and I, on the even barer floor. The kerosene lamp hung from a nail on the wall, its flickering yellow light the only illumination. I didn't need much, being a creature of the night.

I had chosen my apprentice for her goodness. Shy and quiet, she was my sister's child. Like other old world witches I was glad to recruit from family, where they were cut closest to us. Blood was more than just a symbol.

She was still learning to manoeuvre the many delicate currents of the other side.

I rubbed the *ori* ointment on her eyes to ease the transition and make visible the other realm – the beauty of it along with the denizens that drive normals mad with fright. We moved freely among it all -- the souls of sleeping humans, shining shapeshifters, headless spirits drifting along upside down.

I took hold of her hands and invoked the deep black sleep that let us travel to the other side. Our bodies slumped, and we passed over. We floated, translucent and unbound by gravity. We had power in this state. A power that was intoxicating.

Eijiro moved towards the door. I smiled and pulled her toward the wall. I flowed through it and she followed. Outside the protection of my hut we felt the pull, the dreams, the thoughts of sleeping normals. Those souls connected to us pulled the most, sending out strong lines of power.

There was one we set out to find. I had established a connection with her in the physical world, and so I could now see her soul cord faintly shimmering. We flowed along it, shifting shapes, I an old brown owl, Eijiro a nightjar. We sailed swift and sure, alighting on a palm tree beside a darkened house.

I shifted back and floated to the roof. My fledgling followed. We sifted down through the thatch. I looked at Ejiro. She nodded and threw a shroud over the home's sleeping occupants, to keep them still until our work was done. She fastened on their sleeping forms and they choked, gulping for air, struggling vainly to wake.

In the morning they would say they had been *pressed* and they would shiver.

I drew close to the one we were here to help, a girl of eleven. She tossed and turned, feeling the energy of the other side but unable to wake to it. I slipped my hand into her chest and cradled the pulsing spirit heart of her being. She gasped. I gathered my energy and pulled. But her body convulsed and she held back, frightened at the pull to cross over, though this crossing was only a hair's breadth width, not the faraway world of the ancestors.

I pulled again. Her body heaved, its hold on her loosening. Again I pulled, and the body's grasp slipped away. Her translucent spirit form came away. Initiation. In this newly freed form, she floated gently, looking at us curiously.

My spirit energy was depleted, a danger especially as I rarely fed on others. I glanced at Ejiro, She was flush, glowing faintly, without intention having drained energy from those she subdued. She had not yet mastered the art of fastening and holding without feeding. She started guiltily.

We sifted up through the thatch, leaving the newly awakened one floating quietly about the house. She would explore the new realm we had opened her to. Before a coven found her we would be back to teach her and bring her into the fold.

We flew on. Owl and nightjar. We awakened other young ones. Each time I was left weaker. Ejiro unintentionally drank in life energy and spirit consciousness. If she drained too much their spirit flame would be extinguished, and they would die. But as her teacher the guilt would be mine.

Dawn was near. And we were far from our bodies. We could not survive long here without the clear spiritual focus the night imbued us with. Weak and tired, I set a course for home.

We glided along the spirit currents. I didn't notice I was falling until I hit the ground and rolled roughly. The nightjar alighted beside me, shifting into the shape of a wild cat and picking me up in her jaws. She could so easily have crushed me, leaving my contorted body bereft of spirit. But she bore me safely home.

I slept for two days, waking only to gulp down water and a morsel of food.

I awoke in my hut. A blanket covered me. Beside my mat was a cup of water and food in a covered clay bowl. The hut had been swept and arranged. I smiled. Ejiro took great care of me. I took a pull of the water. Though I wondered sometimes at the rightness of what I did, if I was any better than those we battled, Eijiro did not doubt. Perhaps I could trust the innocence and goodness of her heart if I couldn't trust my own.

I stretched and got up. I had business to be about. My small farm did not tend itself. We all had day work. Like everyone else we needed to survive in the physical world. This was why Ejiro was with me, although my sister thought her daughter helped me tend my farm. Well, she did. She just also helped me cultivate souls.

Ejiro had gone to our food stall in the marketplace. The market was a good place for recruiting, and mothers often warned their young ones not to touch or take anything from strangers. But recruiting mostly came from relatives.

Every young child had a tendency toward the spirit realm that waned as they grew and got more settled into the physical world. But giving them food saturated with the substance of the other side would strengthen the connection and in sleep the spirit strove to break free from its body and re-join its natural home. Often, the help of an initiating witch was needed. Such as myself.

This was the way, but I wondered sometimes if it was right, taking them as young as this, without their consent, as I had been taken by Mama Ishaka. She had been a family friend. She liked her recruits sweet and kind and young. So did I. But our motives were as different as palm oil from groundnut oil. You could fry with both but only one was good for yams. And the old one, she exulted in corrupting innocent apprentices, warping them into bloodthirsty hags who fed for the pure joy of the misery they inflicted.

Witches like Mama Ishaka had a craving for evil, came to it of their own strong, iron will. Such ones allied themselves with like-minded dibias and medicine men, prophets and healers, the strongest of the othersiders. They lived in both sides and with keen balance accessed either at times and ways that made us feel like normals.

The dark dibias sometimes sent their allies among the witches to carry out assassinations and other such work. My time with Mama Ishaka left me prey to the pull of their ways.

Another haunt. A night for Ejiro to train in practices of power, skills to help turn the tide in our silent battle.

I let out a hoot to signal the haunt's start, sending shivers through the spines of any beings still awake, setting them praying.

We sailed through the night in our favourite forms, owl and nightjar. We could take any shape we conjured, but the more time in one form, the more powerful we grew within it.

I led the way, swerving to avoid a copse of trees – it was a coven's meeting place, surrounded by a haze cloaking the coven's activities from other creatures and night users -- prophets, healers, even worshippers of the white Christ. They each followed their own gods or god, and drew power from the other side.

Just power. Like a knife, it was what you did with it that mattered. But I knew what many did with their power.

The nightjar's call drew me out of my thoughts. We had arrived at our first stop. We perched atop a mango tree beside the house. Normals knew a tree beside one's house might bring hauntings from creatures of the night.

I led Ejiro through the art called *sendings*. She fed to the point where the soul's hold was tenuous, at the cusp between life and death, then I helped her establish a spiritual connection, to see this person's life threads and move them gently, guiding their fate and fortune to their benefit in the waking world.

The one who turned me, Mama Ishaka, she taught me this, but she gave those she haunted terrible sendings, tortured them with nightmares and visions. Sometimes she toyed with them, gave helpful sendings they came to trust, imagining them from ancestors or kind spirits. Then she sent visions pulling her victims down to ruin and death. And so witches and dreams were feared.

She did not always take the time to be this creative. She might simply feed until their heart gave out or their organs failed. The more one fed, the more powerful one became. Seeing further into the future, taking the shape of more powerful beasts, influencing people and events more. Living longer. So some of our oldest witches radiated a powerful malevolence.

Mama Ishaka took immense pleasure in corrupting her apprentices, whom she chose from amongst the goodliest and kindest hearted. These were the ones she enjoyed breaking, pulling the good from their souls.

On our haunts she pushed me to feed until our quarry's life force gave out. But I would not. I was a most difficult one to corrupt she would say, then cackle and fly off in search of our next victim. But feeding is addictive and my craving grew. She was a patient one. She knew it was a matter of time.

Earning my freedom would require giving in to that which I hated and feeding until the victim died. But this owl outplayed her twice over. When I saw souls in difficulty, held their life threads stretched before me, glowing white lines leading towards good, the darkened lines pulling them toward misery and ignominious decease, I went down their white threads, through a cascade of images and gave them positive sendings, visions, and warnings for the future. I set many on a safe path out of the claws of Mama Ishaka.

And from another witch I learned a second way to earn my freedom - wake a new witch, create my own apprentice. When she found out, in a rage Mama Ishaka tormented the one who had taught me this.

So Eijiro and I followed power lines, sailing swift and sure, agents of the night, searching out the wretched ones of the earth, the ones that most needed good in their lives. And provided them this while feeding, an unholy exchange, rendering help to these ailing ones through a power feared and known only for misery and death.

Eventually dawn neared, and we needed to return to our bodies to cross the veil back to the world of normals. We flew for home. And into an ambush. The nightjar was pounced upon and sent careening off to slam against a tree. I was held fast in the strands of an otherside web. A spider's web. Large and thick and strong enough to hold a goat. Only an old witch, with much power could do this. And there was something familiar about that aura...

A monstrous spider dropped down before me, its huge head twisting and writhing into the shape of a human face. It was she -- the old one who had initiated me, opened me to the other side. Mama Ishaka.

She swung around me cackling, hanging upside down with her full glare on me. Even with a human face, her maw was rich with venom that flew out, scathing and burning me. I would wake sick and wounded, if I woke at all.

She lunged for my throat and pulled back, toying with me. Then she held her pincers to my head, and in that sharp vice a tunnel of dark visions and memories swallowed me. Her memories. Of people. People that looked familiar. I stared. They were the people I had helped when I had been her apprentice. But she had found me out and carried out her spiteful revenge, tormenting and killing them.

She laughed, shrill and mocking. She had undone all I had devoted myself to, all that allowed me to live with the evil I felt inside me. My anger was a fire. I tore free of the vision.

She slid a claw down my cheek, telling me that now she was content to finally let me go.

"Or,' she said, "maybe I'll stay close, watch you save spirits, watch them flourish, then pull them apart, rip them to pieces." A crooked smile laced her face and she turned to sidle up her web.

But the old one made a huge mistake that night. Perhaps because to her, goodliness only meant weakness. Perhaps she underestimated the value of those souls to me, underestimated the power of my rage, failed to see that I might freely do what all her power had never been able to force me to do. I struggled in her web of body and heart and mind, and in my fury and desperation broke free.

As a lion.

Fangs, claws, wings, power.

I shredded her strands like gossamer. She turned to face me and I leapt upon her. My claws tore into her as she tried to transform, tried to cast me off. But I held fast. Held tight with the power of my hate, my grief, my love for what she had destroyed.

Eventually she fell still. I felt the tremors from her body dying in the physical world. Her spirit form floated away and came apart, dark dust in the wind of the nether realm.

I shrank back down to an old, sad owl and flew to where my wounded apprentice lay crumpled. I transformed and cradled the small body. I wept. I had lost myself and everything I'd tried to build. The old one had triumphed. She had made me what she wanted in the end. I had run away from death-dealing all my life, never knowing I was running straight to it. I wept, Eijiro's broken body in my hands, my hated enemy regrettably dead, and the dawn closing in on me.

One could be a certain thing, but not be bound by it so long as one never gave up fighting it. I would keep fighting this thing I was, this evil Mama Ishaka saw in me, that she tried so hard to make me live out. Evil never wins until you stop fighting it.

Eijiro survived that night. I recovered my heart and resolve.

We stood at the top of the oldest palm tree in the village. The night was alive around us. Two realms were open to us. I meant for us to change things. Just two women, one almost too old, the other maybe still too young and inexperienced, two witches against a world, the set way of things. But we were all there was and if we failed it wouldn't be for lack of trying.

My apprentice looked to me.

"Perhaps good can never win," I said. "But maybe evil not winning is enough. Enough to keep us going each day. I will train a cadre of good witches. You are the first."

Eijiro nodded, and without prompting we leapt off, following the call of souls, connecting to the lines of power, soaring into the living blackness to carry out a dark goodness.

Oghenechovwe Donald Ekpeki is an African speculative fiction writer, editor, and publisher in Nigeria. He has won the Nebula, Otherwise, Nommo, Locus, British & World Fantasy awards, and was a finalist in the Hugo, Sturgeon, British Science Fiction, & NAACP Image awards His works have appeared in Asimov's, F&SF, Uncanny Magazine, Tordotcom, Galaxy's Edge, and other venues. He edited the *Bridging Worlds* and *Year's Best African Speculative Fiction* anthologies, and co-edited the *Dominion* and *Africa Risen* anthologies.
He was a guest of honor at CanCon and at the Afrofuturism-themed ICFA 44, where he created the term/genre Afropantheology. You can find him in Twitter https://twitter.com/penprince

Out of Brambles

Leenna Naidoo

"Bubble, bubble, taste of sambals," I intoned, just slightly high on chocolate wine. "Let my love climb out of brambles."

I added the bramble jelly into the pot, wondering where on earth those lines had come from.

Shrugging, I stirred my Halloween dinner. Tree branches tapped the window. I shivered. I'd never been a fan of October squalls. Time for my sweater.

My first Halloween alone.

For a creative sabbatical to write my new cookbook, I had made this old cottage in Scotland my temporary home. It was a tad lonely... and spooky. The tappings at the window increased with the gusty wind.

I turned on the radio.

"*...tale, by The Erskine Storytelling Association.*"

I sipped my wine, hoping the story would be good.

"*It was a dark and stormy night...*"

I groaned, too comfortable in my chair to move just yet.

"*...a ghostly knock on the door,*" whispered the narrator.

How could a knock on the door be 'ghostly'? Soft, tentative, loud, unexpected, maybe...

I stood up. The pot needed a stir.

"...You called for me, and now I have come," rasped a voice.

I stopped. That voice sounded different, not like the narrator at all. I turned off the radio, and plugged in my flashdrive. The distinctive sounds of The Cure merged nicely with the weather.

I opened the pot, breathing in deeply. I could almost taste the divine sweet and sour notes already.

Smiling, I put the lid back on the pot and turned around.

"You called for me, and now I have come!"

I stared into the light grey eyes of the man standing in my kitchen. His haggard, annoyed face reminded me of a man pulled out of bed for a trifle. He was handsome in a ragged way, his dark hair was back in a ponytail, and he wore simple, old-fashioned clothes.

"What will you have me do, Mistress?"

"I beg your pardon!" I wasn't anybody's mistress, and I never meant to be. What was this stranger, a man twice as heavy and tall as me, doing in my kitchen, where I was testing my newest, most secret recipes?

"Who are you? Who sent you? Have you come to steal my recipes?"

I inched towards the sink where a sharp knife and a frying pan lay.

"I am the Dark Man of Erskine. You have called and I have come, Mistress. I know nothing of recipes." His eyes slanted towards the pot. "But that smells delicious. It is surely more than haggis and neeps you cook there."

My heart softened. He must have been passing in the storm, and smelt the cooking. He looked half starved anyway. Maybe all he really wanted was a hot meal.

"It's...." I hadn't named the dish yet; hadn't even tasted it. And here was a man with an empty stomach. "...something new. No haggis and neeps; but if you'd like, pull up a chair and I'll get you a bowl and a glass of wine."

He looked surprised. "Mistress, are you sure that is all you would wish of me?"

"I don't want anything of you, and stop calling me Mistress!" I said, spooning the hearty stew into two bowls. "But, you can tell me what you think of this." I placed a steaming bowl and spoon on the kitchen table.

He raised an eyebrow. "Are you sure?"

"Quite sure," I insisted, pouring him some chocolate wine, the only wine I had left.

"I thank you, Mis...Ma'am." He sat down and picked up the spoon.

I joined him, my bowl opposite his. He took a spoonful, the smell of damp earth accompanying the scent of my cooking. What an odd man!

I tasted the stew. It was good, but...

"This is good!" He had finished his serving. And was looking at the pot. I obliged, filling up his bowl again.

"Do you like the bramble in it?" I asked.

He smiled and nodded. "Indeed I do. It is my favourite! Especially with the rose tea!"

I was impressed. I had added some rose tea. What a fine palate!

"Who are you?" I was still confused. "Are you from around here?"

He put down his spoon, well satisfied, and was turning his attention to the wine.

"You are a fine cook, ma'am. The best I've met in years, so I shall be truthful with you. I am the Dark Man of Erskine, once the Lord Erskine's wayward son, but now a spirit to be called upon by a mistress on the night of Halloween--"

"But!" I protested. "I was cooking! I wasn't..." Then it struck me. No, intoning nonsense thymes on Hallowe'en was nothing to do lightly.

He was smiling at me, a curious, amused smile.

"Are you...?" I couldn't say it. It was too preposterous! So I tried, "Just how old are you?"

His smile grew sad. "I am two hundred and twenty-seven years old, by most reckoning. Then he brightened up. "And that was the best meal I have had in one hundred and ninety years! So, I shall not take you with me."

I looked askance at him.

He explained. "When a mistress calls the Dark Lord of Erskine, she may have him do whatever she pleases for that Halloween. Then she must accompany him back to his resting place."

I shivered again. It was hard not to believe him. I had to know...

"How did you... die?"

"I was poisoned by my mistress."

I sat speechless. The wind howled, then died down to a whisper.

He continued. "Your delicious meal has brought me peace and well-being, something I have not experienced since childhood. Two more such meals, and my lonely soul shall gain peace. Will you help me, ma'am?

"Will you cook for me – just two more meals to set my soul free?"

How could I not?

"Well, I've been wanting to find a taster for my newest recipes. And with tastebuds like yours..."

His smiled beatifically. "We are agreed?"

I smiled back. "If you do the dishes."

He laughed, nodding.

My spookiest Halloween, but by far the most productive.

Besides... no gourmet goes to hell from my kitchen.

"Out of Brambles", © Leenna Naidoo. First published March 5, 2016 in Cosmic Roots & Eldritch Shores.

Leenna wanted to be a witch when she was little, but decided to be a writer instead. She loves writing cross-genre suspense, romance, and dabbles in sci-fi/fantasy. Her books include Settle Down Now and Here Be Monsters. Her short stories have appeared in Mad Scientist Journal, SciPhi Journal, and Cosmic Roots And Eldritch Shores where she is editor for the Myths, Legends, & Fairy Tales department. She also reads the tarot and tries her hand at anything vaguely artistic. Leenna's most unnerving experiences include interviewing Alan Dean Foster (even though it was via email) and teaching a hellhound how to share a biscuit. She blogs and shares updates on https://leennanaidoo.wordpress.com. Her tarot resources and videos are on Patreon: Writerstarot With Leenna, and on her website https://leennascreativebox.com. Otherwise, she wanders down rabbit-holes on the net and the real world, looking for her next story idea.

Rapunzel
A Re-Winding

Joan Stewart

A woman lived with her family and followed the common customs of the time in the common way, yet she found herself gazing more and more at the uncommon walls surrounding the land of the old woman right beside her. Surely those thick old stone walls must hold something marvelous, but she didn't dare approach the small, formidable old woman who sometimes in the early morning came out of the woods, tended to mysterious business within those walls, and then with the setting sun walked back into the woods again.

Well. When she was back in the woods, how was she to know who was peering over her wall? The woman put a ladder to the wall, climbed to the top, and looked. The whole of the place was a garden, and it was indeed breath-taking. Wondrous. It pulled at her invitingly. Well, how would the old women know who was in her garden? She slid over the wall and went floating down mossy pathways to the garden's center, where a single shining plant of rapunzel flourished, encircled by briars. The plant's tall stalk was split into two sinuously entwining spires.

As in a dream, the woman threaded her way through the thorns and caressed the plant. She took a leaf and ate it and a fresh green living blaze ran through her. She began to eat right off the plant, until overtaken by the feeling the plant wanted no more taken. She sighed, full of live greenness, lay down softly, and fell asleep at the plant's roots.

She little remembered waking and leaving, but afterwards she could see the garden in her mind's eye, as clearly as if it were before her, and it changed with the season. She shivered as in these living images she caught an occasional glimpse of the old woman, moving closer and closer to the rapunzel as it's brilliant blue flowers faded, until, as the rapunzel began to set seed, she held its stalk and looked at it with a smile...

One day the woman realized she was going to have a child, and as the time for the birth approached, the garden in her mind became clearer and more vivid. And then one day there was the old woman looking down at the seed stalk as it opened and let fall two seeds. The old women let one fall to the ground, and caught the other in the palm of her hand. She looked at it, then with a smile looked up sharply at the watching woman.

Startled, the woman gasped and went about with a fearful tremble, but not long after she gave birth to twins, and so the garden faded to the dimmer corners of her mind like the background hum of bees in a late summer garden.

The children grew and gave her much joy, and one of them she named Rapunzel for her eyes as blue as the flower in her visions. There was a dreamy distance in those eyes, and the woman sometimes fancied about her a shadow, almost in the shape of the old woman.

Then one day, for no earthly reason, it occurred to the woman that the old woman was somehow entitled to take this child. Perhaps if she renamed her she would be safe! In a panic she reached out for her little girl, sitting smiling on the grass, but a shadow fell over her. The child looked up and smiled, the woman looked up and a strangled cry rose from her heart. A dusky silhouette before the sun, the old woman looked down at Rapunzel with eyes like sunlight. Rapunzel put a soothing hand on her mother. Then she entwined her fingers through the old woman's and looked up with a warm smile and dancing light in her eyes.

The two turned and left the woman staring open-mouthed after them. Later, to explain the impossible event, she told family and neighbors her daughter had been apprenticed to a distant healer, an honor for one so young.

The dark one and the light one walked deer paths through fields never plowed to a deep forest that had never known an axe. The plants and trees looked so bright and alive, almost breathing and moving and whispering softly. Animals ran through the fields and forest. Birds flew through the air and zipped past them, singing. Rapunzel sing with them.

Deep in the woods they came to a large glen, enclosed by a long fence woven of branches. At its center was the old woman's dwelling. Rapunzel felt she had returned home and her eyes had only just opened and the real world was before her and she jumped in with joy.

How clear and unearthly yet familiar every single thing felt, looked, sounded, tasted, smelled. She played, and learned as she played. She called the old woman Old Mother, and soaked in her wisdom like sunshine and her love like moonlight. Day by day she loved her life more. She helped tend the half-wild plants and animals that lived about Old Mother' home. She loved especially brushing the horses, and accompanying them to the gate when they would gallop out at midday or sunset. Birds, such strange birds, would sit on her fingers and fling out rich and wild notes and she would try to sing back to them.

Old Mother taught her to call guardian animals when she left the cottage, and they would walk with her. One beautiful day, seeing a strange shining animal on the path a short distance past the gate, Rapunzel ran out the door forgetting to call, and was half-way to the gate when she paused. A shining paw suddenly stretched far forward toward her and then a shrieking shadow swept over her from behind, there was a darkening, a blinding flash, and when Rapunzel could see again the animal was gone and Old Mother was guiding her back inside and closing the gate. After that, unbidden, an animal was always near her, like a guardian shadow, and she felt a current of caution she had never felt before.

At times there were visitors Old Mother would meet by the gate. One such visitor would come as the sun was low and spilling bright along the path through a gap in the trees and Rapunzel would watch from a window, seeing a bright burning shape before the brilliant, shining sun. There were others who seemed to bring darkness with them, or crackling lightning.

Sometimes visitors would come to the cottage and on rare occasions Old Mother held long and friendly talks. But even some of these visitors were overwhelming, almost forbidding, so that even though she might be allowed near, Rapunzel might sit hidden, closer or further, curled up, silent, and watchful.

Sometimes at night Old Mother would go out. Often then Rapunzel would hear high wind or rumbling thunder, but the cottage stayed warm and safe. Except for one night when Old Mother ordered Rapunzel into the circle of light cast by the fire. She whirled about, gathering objects and hurling out words of command. The shutters slammed shut, the fire flared bright, Rapunzel's guardian animals drew close, and the door barred shut as Old Mother flew out into a gathering storm.

Rapunzel huddled on the hearth by the bright and steady fire. The storm drew closer and more ferocious. Like approaching monsters, winds roared through trees, tearing off limbs, beating against the cottage, sending shrieking under the door to the edge of the firelight. The air filled and filled with heaviness and a tight, sharp buzzing. It became hard to breathe. Thunder exploded and cracked and bright sizzling green and red sparked through the edges of the shutters. There were screeches, pounding, pulling, and scrabbling at the door and shutters. Her animals shivered and sparks ran through their fur. And it just didn't stop. It was unbearable. She wanted to run.

And then there was a crackling yellow flame around the edges of the door and a heavy thud against it, and it groaned and bulged inward. The fire burned brighter. Yellow sizzling tendrils began to pass in under the door and head toward the circle of light. The animals yowled with terror and protective rage and huddled close round Rapunzel. The fire burned brighter.

The yellow sizzled more violently. The wood of the door cracked and the lock and hinges whinged sharp and high. Then repeated lightning blasts lit the shutters edges blue-white and shook the cottage. A screeching bellow exploded outside the door and the yellow light fizzled sharply out with a deafening snap.

The storm raged on but the fire never dimmed, Rapunzel whispering endless wishes that Old Mother would be safe, until, after many long hours, exhausted and dazed she slipped into sleep.

She awoke slowly to silence and dim light struggling in through open shutters. The fire had burned low. It seemed days had passed. Fresh air drifted in, rain-washed and new.

Old Mother lay in a deep sleep. Rapunzel put a warm blanket over her and laid next to her and whispered more wishes for her, but it was a long time before she awoke, and she moved slowly at first when she did.

Although the world grew to feel safe once again, Rapunzel felt more open-eyed and awake. She asked Old Mother to teach her how to help when nights like that came. Old Mother seemed pleased and sad, but said the old ways were not easily learned, and it was a long wandering way to that, each moment a step, a test, sometimes too tiny to see, that changed the ways the next step could go. But Rapunzel kept asking, and finally Old Mother began to teach.

Rapunzel grew. Lean and free she sprouted up and her hair kept pace, long and strong and shining like the sun. Then, it grew faster, and when she ran across the meadow the tips of her hair would stream out behind her and brush against the flowers and stir their scent up into the air. It grew so long that she could lay on the thatched roof of their cottage and teasingly lower her hair to Old Mother as she sat on the doorstep, writing or spinning or preparing herbs. And Old Mother would smile up at her, eyes shining with love. Rapunzel's hair grew so long that braids coiled about her head still trailed to the ground.

Old Mother gave her a beautifully worked necklace that shone out sharper and sweeter than the finest silver, and a curiously decorated knife to carry always, and taught her which plants to collect, how to brew them, what they would help heal. She began to teach her about the sun, moon, and stars and how to mark their movements.

As time passed Old Mother sometimes sent her to tiny huts deep in the woods, because part of the old way came as a flower opening from within.

There was study and quiet contemplation, but sometimes in the silent spaces between questions, her mind went ringing back and forth like a bell.

Old Mother had told her that someday there would be a long time of solitude, of learning, of testing herself. When Old Mother knew the time was right she led Rapunzel through woods Rapunzel did not know, though they seemed familiar. They came to a long green valley surrounded by hills and vast forest. Far off past the forest, toward the setting sun were hazy blue mountains. To the east, nestled at the edge of the forest as if grown up out of it, was a tower of simple grand beauty. A carven tree trunk from an age when giants walked and trees towered many, many times higher than the tallest now living, a giant even among those trees, a thousand times the great-grandfather of the vast surrounding forest as far as the eye could see.

Heavy rose briars surrounded the tower except at the entrance, which was barred by a curiously wrought gate washed over with dusty gold. Old Mother took out a small golden key from the folds of her robe and unlocked the gate. It swung inwards and they entered a small stone room and climbed a winding stone stairway. It was washed all in gold and on the walls were fantastic pictures and tapestries. At each winding, the stair looked out on one side to the valley and forest and on the other side to the tower's central courtyard. At the top of the stair was a massive stone door. A key hung on the wall to the left of it. Old Mother unlocked the door and it swung slowly inward. Rapunzel stepped over the threshold.

This was to be her home through a long time of study, contemplation, prayer, spinning, weaving, brewing, singing, silence. She was free to explore the tower, the skies, her books, her thoughts, and the inspirations that would come flying in to her like birds on wings.

Old Mother would come, to teach, answer questions, and bring food. She gave Rapunzel the key to the golden gate, and a long rope with which to lower the key. As she took the rope Rapunzel paused, a fleeting smile brightening her face.

When Old Mother first came back, and called up to Rapunzel, she watched in surprised delight as Rapunzel's hair came rippling down like a shower of gold, with the key tied to it's tip. After that, when she arrived at the tower, Old Mother would sing "Rapunzel, Rapunzel, let down your hair, that I may climb the golden stair," and Rapunzel would unbind her hair, fix the key to the tip, and let it all spill down the side of the tower like molten gold. Old Mother would climb the gold-washed stairs and unlock the stone door and Rapunzel would fly happily to be enfolded in her wise old arms.

Old Mother would smile and warm, and speak gently and lovingly to her treasured child. Besides food, she would bring new things to learn and small treasures to delight her. Then she would spend long hours teaching and answering questions. And so Rapunzel slowly grew in other kinds of wisdom.

There were four rooms around the tower top, each looking out upon a different direction and having a character all its own. Windows, all lined with window seats, on one side faced out to the world and on the other side, overlooked a central courtyard filled with a garden which shifted it's colors through the days and seasons, from bright blue-white beneath a high hot sun to moonlight lavender-silver below a lunar ship sailing across the night sky lighting up stardust and trailing wisps of clouds.

Far below, in the very center of the garden she glimpsed a rapunzel plant. Though she found lower and lower corridors and windows to view the garden from, its entrance eluded her.

Sometimes, from her towertop she glimpsed smoke and faint flashes beyond the hills on the horizon and sounds like distant thunder. All near her stayed peaceful. No danger approached. But those flashes brought to her day-dreaming mind a dim image, like a very old memory, of a warrior. She saw him in the midst of that smoke and flashes and thunder, and a chill ran through her and she wished protection for him. Or she'd sing a soothing song to him as she sprinkled a simmering liquid with a mixture or recorded in careful script the concatenations of the day, and the image in her mind seemed to pause and listen.

One day she noticed that the rapunzel in the courtyard had sprouted a tall central stalk, and wishing to stand before it she again sought a passage to the courtyard. She could approach no closer than a third floor window. Without thought she dropped down from the window, expecting a hard landing but coming to rest on soft, thick moss. She rose slowly and began to wander along moss-covered paths, glimpsing innumerable things unseen from above, and plants and animals she had never seen in her life. What kind of birds could be making the sounds she was hearing? This strange courtyard had a separate life, kept a time of it's own. All it held looked so... where it belonged.

Finally she came around a tight twist in a path and caught her breath. There in the center of the courtyard glowed the rapunzel, surrounded by briar roses. Buds had just begun along the stalk. For some time she gazed. Slowy she approached, threaded her way safely through the briars, reached out, gently took a few leaves, lowered her head in thanks, and left. Below the window again, she saw that there was a heavy vine growing up around it. Gently holding the leaves close, she climbed the vine.

Back in her tower, she spread the leaves out on a wooden plate and ate them slowly, with salt and herbs, one by one. When Old Mother visited, she sniffed the air and even looked at the plate, but she only smiled slightly and seemed satisfied.

Rapunzel was drawn back to the garden many times. She saw much that she thought could not possibly be there and thought there must be a passage to the outside, but she could never find it. She collected from the garden for food, drink, and medicine, but rarely approached the rapunzel. She just glimpsed it from around the twist in the path to see that now it had flowered, and now its stalk had split in two...

One day she looked out from her tower to the west and saw that the smoke had disappeared and she heard only peace in the distance. Even on that dark, moonless night there were no more flashes on the horizon. She sat at the window, singing happily, and the darkness seemed to listen, so she sang again the next night and the next, until one night as the setting sun spilled red-gold light across half the darkening valley, and a huge moon full in the east spilled silver-blue haze over the other half, at the foot of the tower, limned in the twin lights of the sky, was a worn and dusty warrior, his face turned up towards her.

Her song ceased and she drew in a sharp breath. He looked somehow to be the warrior of her imagination. Then he called up, in a soft, deep rumble that vibrated in her soul, the last words she would have guessed: "Rapunzel, Rapunzel let down your hair, that I may climb the golden stair," and a different world began its rush in upon her.

She looked silently down, breathing deeply. She could faintly see a good-natured smile on his face.

He spoke again. "From the hills I saw a river of bright gold pour down this tower. And from the woods I saw and heard the old woman."

Rapunzel looked and looked at him, so strangely not of her world and so very the image from her heart. She reached for the key, undid her hair, and sent it tumbling down to him.

When he opened the tower door and she saw him close, wearing items she could not name or recognize - the dusty leather, the chain mail, the sword, with an air of battle still clinging to him - the unknown of it all was so strong she could hardly see him clearly. Long, dark hair framed his face, which, so recently having looked upon the slaughter of battle, was slowly overlaid with soft wonder as he looked at her. Now she could see clearly he was worn and hungry, and she made him strengthening food and drink. And while she did he spoke to her. He had led men in battle. A long hard fight had turned back the invaders, but he had sent his men on home ahead of him because there was some of the world he was wanting to see before returning. And as he wandered a golden waterfall had side-tracked him. He asked if he could come back again, and she nodded. After he left, her familiar room felt strangely different and the tower seemed to be thrumming at its very core.

He visited every day, leaving his horse with food and water at the foot of the tower. They talked, haltingly at first, then more easily. Days went by and he grew less the stranger, more a deeply-known part of her.

She sensed though, that Old Mother would know of this change and arrive early. It was best to tell her quickly. But how, she wondered, when she knew no words that might unravel all this to herself.

But the thing decided itself. He had said something to make her laugh and she had looked up smiling into his face, but kept gazing, almost startled. He stood transfixed, then looked out into the distance. His face warmed, his chest rose and fell. His eyes, bright and clear, and soft as he looked back, met Rapunzel's eyes and her breath caught in her throat and the new world overtook them both.

They stood bathed in the warm yellow-gold candlelight of the tower. An owl's hoot floated softly across the night air. They began slowly to smile and their eyes held a light new to them both.

They sat at the window, and gazed out, and waves of soft darkness swept in on them. Rapunzel felt as if they could go flying out of the tower window right then, and across the moonlit sky into the complete unknown. Silent and serious now, their thoughts, wandering new territory, slowly stilled as the candles burned low. Framed in the midnight sky they nestled against one another and fell into a deep sleep.

Rapunzel felt the room being held still and unmoving while the glow of day grew brighter and brighter through her closed eyelids until it seemed she were looking at the sun. She felt her warrior stir beside her, and her eyes flew open and she was looking up at Old Mother, standing bright in the dawn light at the doorway, taking in the scene.

After a stab of fear, Old Mother felt relief; her treasured child was not harmed. Then with terrible face she surveyed this soldier, this stranger, this interloper, stirring as if fighting to wake but unable. Rapunzel could see that she was just deciding to hold off, to allow this stranger a chance to prove himself, when he fought himself to waking and saw, as Rapunzel did not, looming in the uncertain light of dawn, a forbidding figure glaring balefully down at him with with glowing eyes anda ferocity that pierced his mind, and without a thought he reached for his sword and rose.

This was too much. In Old Mother's snapping, angry eyes here was everything she had kept Rapunzel safe from.... attacker, arrogant war dog, mindless brute invading peaceful home and holding sword to innocent throat.

Dawn turned angry red. Old Mother loomed larger, storm-like, and her screamed curse split the air like a bolt of lightning. As Rapunzel dropped to her knees to plead for his life Old Mother's arm swept out and the air sizzled and crackled and a deep boom shook the tower and a fierce wind howled through it and he was swept backwards out the window. They could hear a strangled cry of pain as he fell upon the thorns below. A sob rose up from Rapunzel's heart. She rushed to the window and without a thought leapt out after him.

Now a cry rent Old Mother's heart and she clutched desperately onto Rapunzel's hair. Without a thought Rapunzel reached up with her knife and slashed at her hair until she fell free.

Now all Old Mother could do was hurl a command to the thorns, and when Rapunzel landed it was upon soft leaves and branches. Then Old Mother flew down the stairs as quickly as she was able.

He was grievously wounded, thorns piercing his flesh, slashing his face. His eyelids were closed and blood fell from him like rain. But their protective fear for each other gave them speed. His horse came close at his call, they mounted, and the horse, eyes rolling in fear and sensing the anguish of his riders, bolted into the forest as Old Mother reached the gate.

With horrible, bitter remorse she realized what a dark moment of change had just passed over them, and as the dust settled on the path where they had disappeared into the forest, Old Mother could only send after them the most powerful protective blessings she knew.

After a time the warrior managed to stop the horse's mad gallop, and in spite of tearing pain, sat listening for sounds of pursuit. He smiled grimly at the silence, and breathed a sigh of relief when he found Rapunzel had not been hurt, but the horse had injured his leg. They slid off, and holding the halter as a guide, the warrior urged him to return to camp, and slowly limping, the horse led them to a glade circling a small, waterfall-fed pool deep in the forest. There was an old forester's hut and a shelter for horses.

Rapunzel feared that even the best she could do would not heal him, but gathered from plants growing about the clearing in startling profusion, and trembled as she tended the deep scratches raking his face and eyes.

That night, as they slept beside a small campfire, Rapunzel dreamt that she rose up like a silent-winged owl and looked down upon a small, flickering light lost amidst a sea of darkness.

There was no place to go and nowhere else to stay and no way to find their way anywhere anyway - he could not see, Rapunzel knew no paths or places in the outside world, and the horse still limped.

Her visions and dreams were interrupted and the little birds at the fringes of her mind whose messages she would not listen to out of fear and confusion would not leave her alone.

All they needed seemed ever near at hand for the gathering, and the prince healed. Except for his eyes. Through the summer, wide-eyed, he willed, urged himself to see the resin-laden pines and forest flowers he knew were there. But as flowers faded and burning autumn colors lit the forest his eyes remained dark. And as the fires of autumn went out and winter swept in, hope froze in them and lay as numbly blanketed as the snow-covered woods encircling them.

But in the silent depths of winter, one would sometimes rest their head upon the other's chest and find the comfort of a warm, beating heart, and with inner eyes see the bright glow of love, the welcoming haven of a hearth safe from all else. One night, as the power of winter seemed surely at its height, Rapunzel cradled his head in her arms and sang with soft, sweet tenderness sounds that trembled out into the still listening forest. Once he fell asleep, her notes quavered, fell, dwindled to nothing out in the darkness, down to whispers at her lips, then contracted and vanished into silence. And her tears began to fall like rain across his sightless eyes. And so she fell asleep.

She awoke next morning to find him looking up with concern at her. She stared. He touched her face to comfort her, as he had in the past, but now he was looking, looking right into her eyes. Then they both realized he could see again, but in the blaze of joy that followed, the first thing they did was close their eyes and see each other's bright, beating heart once more.

Now he could find his way, and he was in truth a prince, so it was to his father's kingdom that he brought Rapunzel. She saw a beautiful, peaceful land, and a lordly king overjoyed at the return of his son. But when the king saw the necklace Rapunzel wore he grew still, and then drew out from his robe a necklace of the same pattern. He asked then for a full telling of their story, and as they spoke he grew grave, and then alarmed.

"You have no idea of what you have done," he said softly. "In the old, old days she was my teacher. You 'escaped' her? No. No more than one escapes the noonday sun on a treeless plain. She let you run free. I marvel. In the old days.... " A chill raised the hairs on the back of his neck.

"You will go back and beg forgiveness, and so shall I, for having raised my son in ignorance....... "

They met outside Old Mother's gate.

The King and Old Mother stood separate, excluding all else, a silent, history-filled stillness between them.

The Prince and Rapunzel moved restlessly, feeling the touch of ages, mysteries beyond words, the turning of the heavens and the fall of a leaf.

As Old Mother and the king talked long into the night beside a golden hearth fire, Rapunzel and the Prince each drifted to sleep feeling the world was being reworked.

And when bright, long beams of dawning sun filtered through the green glade and through the windows, they awoke to find that yes, the world was new.

The old, old rules had rewound themselves into a new and wondrous pattern, and though the king returned to his kingdom and Old Mother abided in hers, the two young ones remained with her, to learn, and to bind the tie that now entwined the kingdoms together.

The Beginning

Joan Stewart first thought of rewinding the tale of Rapunzel years ago when she read Paul O. Zelinsky's note on his beautifully illustrated retelling of the fairy tale. She had what she thought was a flash of insight – a story can be so fundamentally altered even while retaining its essential elements, and evolve (or devolve) along with the cultures that reshape them and that they inturn reshape. But then she read Joseph Campbell's "Transformations of Myth Through Time", and even the title let her know that this fact… had been noticed long ago. She hopes her version is a good evolution and will be enjoyed.

To Em, the kingdoms, and the ties that bind them

Papa Legba Final, NiaDayo

Major Difficulties

H.B. Stonebridge

Some folks would tell you Major Graham got what he deserved for calling up the Devil. But Devil is an ignorant man's word for something he don't understand. Major just got tangled up with something he didn't know nothing about, and it bit him. You would not mess with one of them big electrical boxes if you wasn't an electrician. And neither should you try to deal with a Devil you don't know.

We like to think we know what we're doing, but mostly we don't, and don't know we don't. A wise man doesn't act out of ignorance; and a truly wise man knows he can never be sure he ain't ignorant. So wisest of all is the man who does nothing.

And I happen to have a talent for that. My aunts called it laziness, but actually, it's wisdom. And the wisest way to deal with the Devil is not to do it. I *can* do it, of course, otherwise not doing it wouldn't count. I just know better. Most of the time.

I don't live in the city. They may call it the Big Easy, but that city is too big and not nearly easy enough for me. I live out to the swamp a ways. Man was meant to live in the swamp. I reckon the Garden of Eden was very likely a swamp. There ain't no place easier for the creation of life. You leave your shovel out overnight, and in the morning there'll be worms living in the handle.

With so much life all around my house, it's downright impossible to surprise me. When a human gets within a hundred yards, the frogs and chuck-will's-widows and devil's horses all come so quiet you're like to go deaf. So I knowed it when the police was coming. If I'd had a phone, they could've called me. But that's why I don't have one.

The detective who came out was a cousin of mmine, not close but kin nonetheless. I'd seen him at family functions and such, which obliged me to listen to him, against my natural inclination. His name was Hebert, Stephen

Hebert. Whereas I was a Boudreaux - Tom Boudreaux.

I invited Stephen up to my porch and offered him a drink. I had a Sazerac myself, except I was out of absinthe. And out of bitters, so you could say I was just drinking a glass of rye with a sugar cube. Well, three sugar cubes.

Stephen declined my whiskey on the grounds he was working. If I'd ever needed convincing about the foolishness of working, that would have done it.

"There's been a murder in town," he said gravely.

"I'm most sorry to hear that," I replied, "but you have to expect that sort of thing, working for the Homicide Squad."

"Yes, Tom," and he sighed, as if *I* was the one bothering *him*. "I do expect that. But this case looks like it involved hoodoo. And that means you have the opportunity to be useful for once in your life."

"I thank you for the opportunity, but you ought to know I'm morally opposed to being useful."

"I know *that* for damn sure!" Stephen tugged at his starched white collar, getting his temper under control. "Just try doing the right thing for once."

"I have," I said darkly, "but *I* learn from my mistakes."

"Look, I ain't asking for much. I expect all you do is walk around and stare at things, recite mysterious nonsense, and collect your payment."

A wise man don't talk when he has nothing to say so I just sat there and enjoyed my drink and hoped he'd go away.

But Cousin Stephen was a righteous man and he knew if he kept standing there in the heat, with his collar wilting and the mosquitoes biting his neck, I'd be obliged to help him…

He briefed me in the car, on the drive to the city. That's what they call it, only *brief* ain't the word for it. Them Heberts love to talk.

"The victim is Major Graham. 'Major' isn't a title; that's his name. White male, forty-seven years old, five-foot-ten, two hundred and eleven pounds. Member of the local country club - one of the better ones. Mister Graham was found dead by his housekeeper at 8 a.m., in his garden. He was impaled on a sharp implement."

I nearly snorted when he called it an *implement*, like the TV police.

"No fingerprints nor footprints but his own. Nothing on security cameras, and the servants were gone for the night. He had only recently quarreled with a friend at the country club, but his friend has a good alibi and a lot of lawyers. And, as the Commissioner reminded me, he's first cousin to the mayor's wife."

The Graham house was one of them huge estates. Its garden was about the furthest thing from my swamp you could imagine. Every blade of grass the same height and color. A tiled pool with a fountain. Paths of crushed white limestone with not a spot of moss on them. A hedge maze trimmed so perfect they must have used a ruler. I reckoned Major was so rich he bought a new boat when the old one got wet.

I got a look at the *implement* what had sealed Major's fate – and it made the whole garden unreal. It was a raw, thick black line nine feet high, with a crescent moon shape up top. The police didn't know what it might be, and it troubled them. Me, I knew what it was, and it troubled me more.

"I don't think this, ah, *implement*, stabbed him to death. That don't look like a lot of blood."

"Cause of death is for the medical examiner to determine. But we can't move it. Can't haul it off. Can't dig it up. Can't cut it down."

Of course they couldn't. Sometimes an object in our world gets too close to the OtherReal, and starts acting according to its rules. They can cause a powerful lot of trouble, and to deal with them safely, you need a good hoodoo man on a good day. But this wasn't an object from our world. It wasn't even an object. It was pure symbol, and had no right standing in the crossroad of two paths in the middle of a man's garden. That place-ment, and the moon-shape on top, well, that was a Devil I knew quite well - Papa Legba. All crossroads are one to him, and he can be called at any of them. And this implement was Papa Legba's walking stick.

But why was it here? I looked about real close.

And there it was. Rolled under a hedge. A broken, empty bottle of rum. I got down under the hedge. In a little pool of rum was a half-smoked cigarillo. Cousin Stephen stared at me down under that hedge, considering whether it had been his brightest idea to bring me in on the case.

I was tempted to not tell him about the bottle. But to know what had happened here I'd have to get him off my back. And that bottle would keep him occupied. I pointed it out, and while he was making a fuss about his new *evidence*, I walked up to the mansion.

I'd noticed one of the servants, by the look of it the cook, standing outside a side door watching. I went up and tipped my hat and introduced myself, like my Momma had taught me.

Esther, as she introduced herself, said, "You with the police?"

I confessed to being Detective Hebert's cousin, and hoped she would forgive me. "Did Mr. Graham ever take a drink outside with him while he was smoking?" I asked.

"Sometimes."

"And yesterday?"

"I already told the police. He was pretty upset about some business deal. Angry, saying his partner had stabbed him in the back. He started drinking before supper, and told me I could go home early. I was just as glad. I saw him grab a bottle of rum out of the cabinet when he went out to smoke. No glass, just the bottle."

"Was Major Graham into hoodoo?"

"What do you think?"

"And you?"

"Me?! I've no business meddling in that kind of thing. Nothing good ever comes out of that. Cooking's all the magic I care to know."

"What kind of shoes was Mr. Graham wearing yesterday?"

"Brogues. Hand-made. No label," said Esther.

I borrowed a package of cornstarch and thanked her as I left.

The police had walked all over the grass, but that didn't matter as much as you might think. Major Graham, he'd died in the evening hours. Louisiana folks like to water their lawns in the evening, so the ground stays wet all night.

The smooth soles of Major Graham's brogues had left their marks in the wet grass. When the police had come along, they was wearing boots and trampling dry grass. I used the cornstarch to mark Major's footprints. Where the footprints ran across the stone path, I had to make some guesses.

Cousin Stephen was whining in my ear like a family of mosquitoes, but a swamp man learns to ignore that. I got him to stop stepping on my cornstarch, but it would have taken God Himself and three saints to shut him up. I finished and stood back to look.

"Well! Butter my butt and call it a biscuit! What does that look like to you?"

"It looks like a mess, Tom. It looks like you sprinkled cornstarch all over my crime scene."

"See the pattern? Seems Major's drunken stumbling created what we in the trade call a *veve*."

"A what now?"

"The pattern what you draw on the ground when you want to speak to a particular spirit. It's like sending a letter. The *veve* is the address. But the Post Office ain't going to deliver it without a stamp. And that stamp is a *sacrifice*."

"Human sacrifice?!"

"No call to go that far. It don't necessarily got to be fancy, just the right sort of thing. The *loa* all got different human things they want they can't do for themselves. And, you got to pay Papa Legba to get messages through to them. He likes drinking, and smoking, and cussing. And that's what Major Graham was doing.

"The *loa* really want human passion. The cook just told me Major Graham felt *backstabbed*. There's nothing like betrayal to cook up rage. And that rage called up a devil he didn't know. Papa Legba."

Well, Cousin Stephen wasn't listening properly. He was just a hound waiting to be put on the scent.

"All right, then, I want to speak to this Mister Legba. Get a statement from him."

"That's the most damfool idea I ever heard! You hired me on as an expert, Stephen, and in my expert opinion, you're someone who ought to stay far away from hoodoo."

"You're saying that because actually hoodoo is baloney, there is no Legba to call, and you'd be too lazy to call him anyway." He gave me his best smirk. "I think we're done here. I'll just tell the Commissioner—"

If this was just about Stephen, I'd have left. But, that *implement*. It didn't belong here and it was going to cause a powerful lot of mischief if it stayed.

"Now hold on! I'll help you. But you're going to need a lot of rum. Not good rum, mind. Rot-gut. And you'll need to smoke. And cuss." I sent him off, and got to work.

I've never been at ease calling on the devil. It's a nerve-racking and worrisome business. The *loa* are not human, and it's a mighty bad mistake to forget that. You don't want to start thinking you're in control. You don't *use* hoodoo, not really. Hoodoo uses you.

Cousin Stephen sent his policemen off to get some lunch and showed me the supplies he had procured. Now, for this kind of purpose, I like to use Wray & Nephew rum and Hav-A-Tampa cigars, but Stephen took me at my word and bought the worst stuff he could find over to the Seven-Eleven. The rum came in a rectangular plastic bottle, like mouthwash, and the cigars was artificial grape flavored. It was good enough, or rather bad enough. So we set to it.

"Now look here. I need to call up Papa Legba, so's he can pick up that *implement*. But you let me do the talking, understand? *Loas* are dangerous, but at least I know what I'm doing. You're my cousin, so I reckon I owe it to my dear aunt to keep you safe."

He shrugged, "I don't expect any Hoodoo gods to show up, anyway."

"Fine. But if they do, you let me handle 'em. You don't call any attention to yourself, and *under no circumstances* do you step inside the *veve*."

"Yes, yes, all right."

Well it was just the most pitiful hoodoo ritual you ever saw. Technically speaking, Cousin Stephen *was* smoking and drinking and cussing, but you'd swear he'd never done anything of the kind in his life. I would have to give him some proper motivation. Not that I took pleasure winding Stephen up.

At least that wasn't my primary motive.

"Stephen! Is that the best you can do?"

He stopped and coughed for a bit and glared at me.

"You look like a fool! Taking timid little sips of rum, coughing on every puff of them cigars. And that's the most fainthearted cussing I ever heard. You want to see Papa Legba, you got to put in some real effort."

"Oh? That's rich coming from you, Tom, real goddamn rich. I've been *putting in some real effort* my whole life. I went to Tulane on a Dean's Honor Scholarship, because my family could never have paid for it. Every night, every weekend, studying and sports and extracurriculars, to get that scholarship and keep it. And I graduated with honors, because I *put in some real effort*.

"Do you think it›s easy to become a detective, Tom? *I'm* not the Mayor's cousin. I'm a good detective. I have a folder full of commendations. But every family gathering Ma goes on about you, how you're such a respected hoodoo man. While you sit on your butt out in that rotting shack in the swamp. Well, I hope you rot away with——"

BRAHOOOOOWHAHEYYYWHAAAARRAOOOO!

And just like that the world around us burst open and the OtherReal poured in.

Stephen's curse was drowned in a cacophony of car horns and train whistles and horse neighs. My hair stung like needles in my neck.

Papa Legba had arrived.

To Papa Legba, all crossroads is the same. He's always there. Just his attention changes. So when I say he *arrived*, it was not that he came to this particular point from somewhere else. It's like we got his full attention. This one particular crossroads became *every* crossroad.

We was standing at every place in the entire world where two roads crossed. We was there, on that garden path. We was at Haight and Asbury, where them hippies hang out, over to San Francisco. We was at that real big go-round in Paris, with the marble arches. We was at a place where two dirt tracks met in the middle of a lonely desert, in a night so empty you could see the Milky Way over your head. All of it at once, and if you think that's too much for the human mind, you're right.

Then it all fell shut again and we was standing back on a garden path, but looking at a smiling old man with a long pipe, wearing a straw hat 'cause the sun down here is so bright not even the spirits want it in their eyes. He was standing smack in the middle of the crossroad with his wrinkly hand curled around his walking-stick, right next to the *implement.*. The one looked like natural wood and normal size, the other was empty black and unreal.

Direct encounter with the divine was enough to shut even Stephen up for a while. He took a few steps back and stared with his mouth open. Then, once he'd gone through being stupefied, he got just regular stupid. When in shock, the human brain falls back on what it thinks it knows.

He flashed his badge and opened his notebook.

"Detective Stephen Hebert, NOPD. Sir, please state your full name, age, and occupation."

Papa Legba chewed on the end of his pipe and cocked his head. Then he smiled a *friendly* smile.

"Damn it, Stephen! You must be outside of your mind! Stop talking!"

But Stephen *kept* talking. And that's when I realized that little bit of rum had been far too much for him.

"Where were you between 4 p.m. yesterday and 8 a.m. this morning?"

Papa Legba gestured to all the space around him.

My cousin tapped his little notebook. "Excuse me sir, this is a murder investigation. You can answer me here or down at the station!"

For a second I saw a tiny smirk in the corner of Papa Legba's mouth.

"Stephen you can't arrest something like Papa Legba!"

"He's got wrists, don't he?"

"No, he don't! The hat, the pipe, the whole body, that ain't him! That's just... politeness! He's just looking human so we have something to look at."

"Occupation?" Stephen gritted stubbornly.

"His *occupation* is standing between our world and theirs. Anybody wants to deal with Commander Agwe or Baron Samedi or Mama Erzulie, they got to give him his cut. And he always collects!"

"Well, Mister Legba, if you expect to collect from the NOPD, you need something worth striking a deal for! Now, how did Major Graham die?"

The air thickened like we was underwater. Papa Legba raised his head and looked at Stephen.

Stephen stepped unsteadily towards him.

"Don't step in the *veve!*" I yelled, and went grabbing after him.

At first, I felt solid. On the edge of the OtherReal, your body feels more alive. Every breath deeper, every object sharper, every word means more. But the OtherReal is always hungry, and whereever it touches our world, it sucks the reality plumb out of it. Dissolves it, drinks it dry. Already, the grass under my feet was crumbling into a colorless dust.

Stephen waved his finger at Papa Legba. "I want the exact events! The exact events of Major Graham's death!"

And that was all it took. No long negotiations. No tricky wording. No oaths. Just strong emotion and a hungry devil.

Papa Legba grinned.

A big old gator grin, with too much mouth and too many big white teeth.

He nodded once, his hand closed around Stephen's to seal the deal, and it was done.

~

Night fell. Sweltering night, muggy and humid. Just the light of them little lamps on the garden path to see by.

I couldn't move or breathe. I was too light. No, I just *wasn't*. Cousin Stephen wasn't. The grass and the air and the path weren't. I wished it was a nightmare, but it was the OtherReal. Never had I been in it so fully.

And then here comes Major Graham. Staggering, kicking up stones. But I saw him the way the *loa* see - a thunderstorm of emotions raging inside his skin, the eye of the storm swirling around his heart. Colors no human can name bursting like fireworks in his chest with every breath.

He came to a wavering stop dead in the middle of the crossroads, and tried to put that bottle to his lips. But he was so drunk he spilt half on the ground, and commenced to hollering and a-screaming.

The *implement* appeared, shooting up from the ground like reverse lightning, an endless streak of pure jagged blackness. It skewered Graham through his chest and gigged him like a frog.

All those nameless colors flashed brighter and fiery intense. I tried to shield my eyes, but it wasn't my eyes I was seeing with. Papa Legba's cane hit the thunderstorm raging in Graham and blew it up into a hurricane, battering the inside of his chest, pounding with every heartbeat.

Graham made a soft sound. His arms and legs twitched. He pawed at the streak flaming through his chest, but his fingers couldn't close over it. The power running through him flared up and then snapped down into nothing.

He fell stone dead.

Papa Legba had a little puzzled twist of a smile. He reached out to reclaim his cane... and his hand passed right through it...

~

Reality flashed back.

Muscles that had been wanting to move had power again. We was back in our bodies, and able to move, but only just. The OtherReal takes its toll on mortal folk, and we had been deep in there. I felt like a worn-out old man. Cousin Stephen slumped over, all wilted like. I staggered over and helped him up.

Papa Legba stood and watched us, patient as a hunter.

When he could speak again Stephen whispered. "What the *Hell* was that, Tom?"

"Seems Major Graham had the same bad luck as if he'd stumbled onto train tracks."

"I can't tell the Commissioner Graham was run over by a hoodoo train."

"You won't have to tell the Commissioner nothing. Do you see the *implement* of murder?"

Legba leaned forward, looking straight at me like a cat getting ready to pounce. If he'd had a tail, it would have twitched. I had his *attention*, that was for sure.

"Is this a trick question?"

"Yes, because you *don't* see it."

"What do you mean -- I see the damn thing."

"That's just a...a conductor that connects the OtherReal with this specific place. That's why it appears *before* Papa Legba. He can conjure a hundred of them, a thousand, all at once ... but he never leaves one behind. An open line between reality and the OtherReal? Well, somebody with the right knowledge could talk to the other *loa* directly and cut him out."

But there was another reason too, one I had no intention of speaking. Somebody with more knowledge than sense might use the *implement* to tap into the OtherReal and draw on its power.

Papa Legba followed my every breath and movement. He understood what I was saying, and what I wasn't. The *loa* don't like being disadvantaged, and he was surely calculating just how much my understanding would be costing him.

Stephen didn't understand, but at least he was listening now.

"Physically it's not here, that's why nobody can move it. We don't even see it. We see an empty line and feel it across our hearts. Major Graham's death cut it off from the OtherReal and got it stuck in our world. So this ain't a murder scene."

Stephen looked down at his little notebook. "'Impaled with a sharp implement.'"

"Is your little notebook the Bible, Stephen? Are you Saint Francis now?"
"Saint Francis didn't write the—"

"Listen, Graham's heart was full, pounding fit to beat the band! Papa Legba's signal shot enough OtherReal power into it to fill it up all over again. Major Graham died of a heart attack. There was no murder, just an angry millionaire who got drunk and cussed hisself to death."

But you don't never get nothing from the *loa* for free. I looked to Papa Legba, and he nodded. His mouth was crooked in a pleasant little smile, but his eyes were sharp as a shark's.

We were tangled in the barb wire now. There wouldn't be no getting out without some scratches. But we had us a bargaining chip. Papa Legba needed that *implement* back and he couldn't take it without help from the mortal side.

But then Stephen said "And what about *this!*" And at grabbed the staff.

I yelled, but too late. Papa Legba's hand shot out and closed around Stephen's. Stephen's eyes widened, he went pale, and sweat popped out on his forehead. He looked like a landed fish, breathing in shallow gulps.

Then Papa Legba's hand passed through Stephen's and closed around the *implement*.

For a moment the noise swole back up, a wave of sound like a brick wall. Then all felt silent.

Papa Legba was gone.

The *implement* was gone.

The OtherReal was gone.

We were standing at the garden crossroad.

Stephen rubbed his palm, then stopped and stared at it. Not the hand he'd curled around the *implement*. No, it was his right hand, the one that was still holding his badge. He'd been gripping it so hard it left an imprint in his palm. But where it should have said NOPD and his name, red marks on his flesh spelled out:

DETECTIVE
STEPHEN HEBERT
OTHER REAL INVESTIGATOR

You can't say the *loa* don't have no sense of humor! It seemed Cousin Stephen had a new job, like it or not.

He was welcome to it, I thought... for a second. Then I had to face facts. Cousin Stephen got my hackles up, but he was family. Papa Legba would want help with things Stephen didn't even know existed, things that would bring him more trouble than he could imagine.

A wise man wouldn't have got himself into this position. A crooked man would be thinking how to use it to his advantage. But cousin Detective Stephen Hebert was a righteous man. The loa would be back to involve him in their affairs, and Stephen would try to do the right thing.

And then he'd find himself in need of a man who knows how to do nothing...

...And I'd have to admit I was just the right man for that.

-END-

H.B. Stonebridge is the writer team of Helena and Byron.
Helena pursued her obsession with the magic of words by studying literature and philosophy. When she is not trying out new recipes for exotic sweets, she is reading her stories to her prime audience – her brown spotted Dalmatian. Byron is a writer, history professor, and Game Master who lives in Florida with his two sons and two dogs.

Art: "Papa Legba Final", by Nia Dayo https://www.deviantart.com/niadayo

HOW THOMAS CONNOLLY MET THE BANSHEE

JOHN TODHUNTER

Ah, the Banshee? Well sir, as I was striving to tell ye, I was going home from work one day, from Mr. Cassidy's that I told ye of, in the dusk o' the evening. I had more nor a mile – aye, it was nearer two mile to thrack to where I was lodgin' with a decent widdy woman I knew, Biddy Maguire, so as to be near me work.

It was the first week in November, an' a lonesome road I had to travel, an' dark enough, wid threes above it; an' about halfways along there was a bit of a bridge I had to cross, over one o' them little sthrames that runs into the Doddher.

I walked on in the middle iv the road, for there was no toe-path at that time. Nor for many a long day after that. But as I was sayin', I walked along 'til I came nigh upon the bridge, where the road was a bit open, an' there, right enough, I seen the hog's back o' the old-fashioned bridge that used to be there 'til it was pulled down, an' a white mist steamin' up out o' the wather all around it.

Well now Mr. Harry, often as I'd passed by the place before, that night it seemed sthrange to me, an' like a place ye might see in a dhrame. An' as I come up to it I began to feel a cowld wind blowin' through the hollow o' me heart.

"Musha Thomas," sez I to meself, "is it yourself that's in it? Or, if it is, what's the matter wid ye at al at all?".

So I put a bold face on it, an I made a sthruggle to set one leg afore the other, until I came to the rise o' the bridge. And there… God be good to us! In a cantle o' the wall I seen an ould woman, as I thought, sittin' on her hunkers, all crouched together, an' her head bowed down, seemingly in the greatest affliction.

Well I did pity the ould craythur, an though I wasn't worth a thraneen, for the mortial fright I was in, I up an sez to her, "That's a cowld lodgin' for ye, ma'am"

Well, the sorra ha'porth she sez to that, nor tuk no more notice o' me than if I hadn't let a word out o' me, but kep' rockin' herself to an ' fro, as if her heart was breaking'.

So I sez to her again, "Eh, ma'am, is there anythin' the matther wid ye?" An' I made for to touch her on the showlder, on'y somethin' stopped me, for as I looked closer at her I saw she was no more an ould woman nor she was an ould cat.

The first thing I tuk notice to was her hair, that was sthreelin' down over her shoulders a good yard on the ground on aich side of her. O, be the hoky farmer, but that was the hair! The likes of which I never seen on mortial woman, young or old, before nor sense. It grew as sthrong out of her as out of e'er a young slip of a girl ye could see; but the colour of it was a misthery to describe. The first squint I got of it I thought it was silvery grey, like an ould crone's; but when I got up beside her I saw, be the glance of the sky, it was a soart iv an Iscariot colour, an' a shine out of it like floss silk. It ran over her showlders and the two shapely arms she was lanin' her head on, for all the world like Mary Magdalen's in a pitcher; and then I persaved that the grey cloak and the green gownd undernaith it was made of no earthly material I ever laid eyes on.

Now, I seen all this in a twinkle of a bedpost. So I made a step back from her, an' "The Lord be betune us an' harm!" sez I, out loud, an' wid that I blessed meself. Well, Misther Harry, the word wasn't out o' me mouth afore she turned her face on me. Aw, but 'twas that the awfullest apparition ever I seen, the face of her as she looked at me! God forgive me for sayin' it, but 'twas more like the face of the 'Axy Homo' beyond in Marlboro Sthyreet Chapel nor like any face I could mintion – as pale as a corpse, an' a most o' freckles on it, like the freckles on a turkey's egg; an' the two eyes like sewn in wid thread, from the terrible power o' cryin' the' had to do; an' such a pair iv eyes as the' wor, Mister Harry, as blue as two forget-me-nots, an' as cowld as the moon in a bog-hole of a frosty night, an' a dead-an'-alive look in them that sent a cold shiver through the marra o' me bones. Be the mortial! Ye could ha' rung a tay cupful o' cowld perspiration out o' me head that minute.

Well, I thought the life 'ud lave me intirely when she riz up from her hunkers, till, bedad! She looked mostly as tall as Nelson's Pillar; an' wid the two eyes gazin' back at me, an' her two arms stretched out before hor, an' a keine out o' her that riz the hair o' me scalp 'til it was as stiff as the hog's bristles in a new hearth broom, away she glides – glides! Round the angle o' the bridge, an down wit' her into the sthrame that ran indernaith it. "'Twas then I began to suspect what she was.

"Wisha, Thomas!" sez I to meself; an' I made a great struggle to get me two legs into a throt, in spite o' the spavin o' fright the pair o' them wor in; an' how I brought meself home that night the Lord in heaven only knows, for I never could tell; but I must ha' tumbled agin the door, and shot in head foremost into the middle o' the flure, where I lay in a dead swoon for mostly an hour; and the first I knew was Mrs. Maguire stannin' over me with a jorum of punch she was pourin' down me throath, to bring the life into me, an' me head in a pool of cowld wather she dashed over me in her first fright.

"Arrah, Mister Connolly," shasee, "what ails ye, to put a scare on a lone woman like that?"

"Am I in this world or the next?" sez I.

"Musha! Where else would ye be on'y here in my kitchen?" shasee.

"O, glory be to God!" sez I, "but I thought I was in Purgathory at the last, not to mintion an uglier place," on'y it's too cowld I find meself, an' not too hot."

"Faix, an' it may be ye wor more nor half-ways there, on'y for me," shasee, "but what is it that's come to ye at all? Is it yur fetch ye seen, Misther Connolly?"

"Aw, naboclish, never mind it," sez I. "Never mind what I seen." So be degrees I begun to come around a little... an' that's the way I met the Banshee, Misther Harry!"

"But how did you know it was really the Banshee after all, Thomas?"

"Begor, I knew the apparition of her well enough, but then 'twas con-firmed by a sarcumstance that occurred the same time. There was a Misther O'Nales come visiting ye must know, to a place in the neighborhood – one o' the ould O'Nales iv the county Tyrone, a rale ould Irish family – an the banshee was heard keening round the house that same night; be more then one that was in it; an' sure enough, he was found dead in his bed the next mornin'. So if it wasn't the banshee, I'd like to know what else it could ha' been".

"How Thomas Connolly Met the Banshee", by John Todhunter.
John Todhunter was an Irish poet and playwright, born 1839 in Dublin and raised as a Quaker. He received his medical degree from Trinity College, and also wrote seven volumes of poetry and several plays. He was an early participant in the Gaelic literary revival. He also wrote a poem about the Banshee, published in a collection of his, *The Bamshee and Other Poems*. Although a well-respected scholar and professor of English literature in Dublin, he resigned his post to travel in Europe and Egypt. Later he was part of a small community of writers and artists that included W.B. Yeats, a close friend and neighbor, and he helped found the Irish Literary Society.

LAILA TOV
~ GOOD NIGHT ~

Robert B. Finegold

from the *Sefer Yehudi min ha-Galut*

א

When the world was younger and the moon still inspired wonder, there was a lamia so low among the lilin that she had no name. In service to Samael, the demon king, she shepherded all living creatures within the beylik of east Eretna, which crafty Mutaherten once ruled. She loyally performed her duties: collecting the seed from men who lusted in their sleep; snatching the breath from infants swaddled in their cribs; drying up the milk within mothers' breasts be they of beast or daughter of Eve. She freed each – seed, breath, and milk – from their mortal constraints.

One evening in the waning of the year when the chill winds blew down from the Armenian Highlands and the moon's Cyclopean eye cast glints from the snows of distant Mt Ararat, the lamia was drawn to the cot of Bilchek the cripple, a tailor of some skill though near blind.

Near the west bank of the sluggish Ahern, his small broken-fenced yard was a lake of frozen mud strewn with tiny islands of brittle grass, nibbled short and capped with the first snow. His hut held only a simple plank table and chair, a cold stone hearth and equally cold tin bedpan, and an empty hope chest of boot-scuffed pine with dull and dented brass hinges. To one side an overturned bucket huddled near a strawmat bed, its mattress crushed so flat that even the fleas rubbed elbows. A fat goat slept at the foot of the bed chewing on the edge of a patchwork blanket that covered the crumpled form of the sleeping tailor. In spite of all, the hut was a pauper's castle, for there was nothing poor or dull about Bilchek's dreams.

He dreamed of his youth, long-passed, and of young women, grossly and inaccurately imagined, for he'd never stood under the wedding huppa, nor dallied in the autumn fields at harvest when the grain was high and the elders could not see, nor had he any sisters as a child to share the family bath barrel. What lay beneath kaftan or hirka, when his few lady clients permitted him to measure, was unknown to Bilchek; thus, the lamia who wove her cloak of desire from the vivid lust-laced imaginings of dreaming men, found naught but vague visions of cotton softness and felt-covered curves, and of warmth; warmth to be shared under a patchwork blanket during the long nights as the year neared its frigid end. It was the latter that gave her pause.

This man's longings were not as those of other men, of struggle and moist release, but of pairings and sharings. However, his urgent need drew her as strongly as that of any man rutting in his sleep, and she never shirked her duties.

Bilchek was a challenge, for the fire was more in his heart than in his beytsim. Yet Bilchek's God had empowered the urge to engender even among the ignorant; and the lamia caressed him in his dreams, successfully raising the pride and embarrassment of men, and coaxed his seed from him as he slept.

Unlike the innumerable others who upon attaining their release turned and ran back to sleep's depths, Bilchek awoke. He rested his hand upon her waist as she moved off of him.

"By *Hashem*, please don't go."

She turned to rake him with her claws, but there is power in the Holy Name said in love and need. His words were like a prayer, and they were answered.

"Why should I not go? Why should you not wish to be rid of me? Why don't you cower in horror and shame?"

"I am familiar with all these things. I see them in others' eyes at the sight of me."

"You're blind!" she declared.

"And crippled," he replied.

"You're a fool."

"And poor."

The lamia had no answer. She longed to strike him and flee. Yet she stood by the bed, the man's hand at her waist. The few of her herd who'd seen her.... they were the ones who fled. Not her. And not Bilchek.

"Help me, please," he said. "My spectacles. Pass them to me."

She looked and saw them upon the floor. They had fallen from the overturned bucket he used for a nightstand. She hooked them with the claw of one finger and passed them to him. They were of frail bent wire and small mismatched circles of thick glass.

He hooked the stems around his ears, the wires nearly encircling them to help support the weight of the lenses that over the years had left a permanent furrow upon his nose. Then he looked at the lamia.

Her skin from her waist down was of fine iridescent scales like a mountain viper's, her feet were owls' talons, and her wings.... from the bony spines of her shoulders rose nearly translucent wings of soft leather on long bony fingers. They curved over her thin muscular arms and thick-fingered claws like a long black cloak. Her eyes were large and contained no white. Instead, a deep black filled them, like mountain tarns on winter nights when the moon was hidden. She had ebon hair that fell in waves to below her breasts, two small pale cones crowned with tightened nipples the color of amethysts. Her chin was delicately pointed; her lips thin, drawn inward with ire; and her nose was as subtle as an infant's. Her skin from forehead to navel was so pale that she seemed to float upon the ripples of her black hair and enfolding wings like moonlight on dark water.

He did not scream. He did not flinch in fear. He did not flee.

Instead he begged, "Stay."

"Stay?" The word, the suggestion, so strange to hear.

"Yes. Please stay."

She blinked and pulled away from his hand. It had merely rested upon her and had never grasped her in possession. She spread her wings.

"I am a demon!"

"Is that your fault?"

"You are a mere mortal!"

"Is that mine?"

She leaned toward him and opened her mouth to display delicate fangs like small scythes. "You are prey!"

"To every mocking word and pitying stare," he said in calm reply.

Her fangs retracted. She stared at the crippled tailor in confusion.

He stared at her with longing and.... something else.

"You would forswear a mate of your own kind?" she whispered.

He spread his hands wide, displaying his shallow chest and protuberant belly, and how the curvature of his spine made him seem stuck in mid-dance, belly over right hip, shoulders over left. Extending his arms to either side he bared his breast and the soul rhythm of what beat beneath. "What woman would have Bilchek?" he said. "They love my skills but loathe my looks and know not I have a heart that loves."

And with this she relented. She sat on the strawmat cot and tentatively took his sure hands within her claws, careful not to wound him.

When Bilchek asked, "Be my wife," she did not strike, she did not mock, she did not flee.

"If you will have me, then let us wed," she said.

As it was the Sabbath eve, and they had consented to one another, it was so.

Bilchek broke no wine glass, but instead filled it with the wine saved for the Sabbath and shared it with her.

"What is your name?" he asked.

"I have no name. I am a daughter of the Night."

"Then I will call you Laila." And he smiled, "My Laila Tov, my Good Night."

ב

Snow as fine as confectionary sugar was falling upon the frozen village lane outside the shop of Melis, the baker's wife, when she first heard the suppressed laughter and whispers that Bilchek the cripple had a woman. The widow Tansu scolded her nieces. "Ansa, Trelip, stop tittering like dormice." The two girls, heads bent together with hands covering their mouths, tried to stifle their laughter.

"What's this?" asked Melis, placing hot braided loaves of bread upon the counter. She pressed her hands firmly upon them. "Bilchek has a wife?" The widow's nieces giggled.

"Tshah," said Tansu, tugging at the loaves. "Who said anything about a wife?" She leaned forward and whispered, "We were out for a stroll..."

To pass the home of the widower Nathan the moneylender, Melis knew.

"...and we took the Farmer's Way by the river..."

To avoid being seen by good folk.

"...when we heard a woman's voice, sweet as a spring lark, coming from the shack of Bilchek!"

Melis shrugged. "Some low-born wife seeking a new entari or feraçe to please her husband. Bilchek is as gifted with cloth and thread as he is ugly."

"No. No," Tansu said. "I know every voice of our village. It was no voice ever heard before in Kirkatel."

"A traveler. A stranger, then. Where was her husband or escort?"

"Exactly what I thought. 'A stranger is danger,' no? I crept to Bilchek's window, a single filmy pane like ice with bubbles. Even so, I could see the crooked form of Bilchek... dancing! I imagine only the demons in Gehinnom cavort so grotesquely. And he was dancing with a woman!"

Melis leaned forward, nose to nose with the old gossip. She said, "What did she look like?"

"Like a Musselman's woman," Tansu whispered.

"No!" Melis straightened, releasing the loaves.

"Yes!" Tansu snatched the bread and a sweet roll as well, passing them behind her back to her nieces. "She was tall. Well, taller than Bilchek, and covered head to toe in black, hiding her shape as they do. Formless, sexless, except for that voice. A woman's voice, strangely accented, but young and sweet." She leaned forward again and slid another sweet roll off the counter as she kept her eyes on Melis' face. "And she called him 'husband'!" Melis dropped onto the stool behind the counter. "God forfend. If the Musselmen discover one of their women with a Jew! The village could be burned!"

The widow Tansu chewed a sweet roll wearing a satisfied smirk, sugar paling her upper lip like a cat that'd got into the cream. She turned and left, her giggling nieces trailing her like ducklings.

The door to the shop closed, and Melis looked through her window of pristine glass. Flakes of snow landed upon the panes, a myriad of tiny stars, melting, running together, and blurring the world without.

ג

Bilchek released Laila, and they fell to the floor with laughter. The floorboards creaked, unused to such gay tread.

Laila had sought to cover herself, to conceal her form that caused aurochs to tremble, wolves to howl, and babes to shriek. She'd taken a sheaf of black drape, the one thrown out by the rich widow Liat at the end of her year of mourning (on the same day she announced her engagement to Tilc, who was half her age and half her weight and as poor as a flea on a hairless cur). The drape was black as night and she found comfort within its folds, hidden from the glaring beam of sunlight that thrust through the melted glass eye of Bilchek's window and determinedly sought her, gazing accusingly from one side of the hut to the other as the day passed from dawn to dusk.

She found haven for her shame under the dark cloth, hiding her owl's feet, scaled pale flesh, long taloned fingers, bat's wings, and gaunt vulpine face and fangs. She found herself ugly compared to the swayback slant-toothed balding Bilchek, who was radiant in his love for her. And this love was both foreign and enticing, like a strange new fruit from a distant land, one both sweet and tart and odd of texture yet delightful upon the tongue, even hers which was forked.

Love. She had yet to understand it or know how to accept it or reciprocate. But she desired it. She who was mistress of desire in others had never herself felt its ache. Perhaps she sought to hide from this as well within the comforting dark under the mourning drape.

When Bilchek had come back from his goings about the village, a hem to fix here, a feraçe to mend there, he had found Laila sitting under her drape, the eye of the sun winking with the passing of clouds and worrying a knot of wood on the floorboards in front of her. He laughed.

"Excuse me, Drape, have you seen my lovely Laila?"

From the concealment of the cloth, the demoness replied, "Your Laila is a hideous creature of the Night. She is not as human women. She need hide her ugliness from the day, unless she be discovered and forced to leave her husband."

"You don't know my Laila then, Drape. She is lovely, my greatest delight of both night and day. And though other women pale to her, she is not unlike them in this needless fear."

The black mound of drapery shivered. "How so?"

"Do not all women, at some time, mistake their treasures for ugliness? Cover them in the day only to reveal them to their loving husbands under the concealment of night?"

"Perhaps. But one man's treasure is another's offal. And I would not be so seen and thereby disgrace you or, worse, bring man's hatred and fear of me upon you. Other women have clothing, I have nothing."

"You are clothed in my love."

"For the night, and for when we are alone. But for the day..."

Bilchek placed one long finger upon the side of his bulbous nose. "You shall have all you desire, day or night, or I'm not Bilchek the Tailor." Looking though at the hill of black drapery on the floor before him, he could not but laugh again.

"My wife has become a tent, like that for the Purim festival dance."

He ran his long thin fingers, almost needles themselves, down her drape-covered shoulders until he grasped her hands through the cloth and raised her to her feet.

"Though I have longed to dance under the festival tent, I never thought to dance *with* the tent."

And with that he turned with her and capered upon the hut floor that squeaked and drummed under his wood-soled shoes. Her feet made no noise except the scratch of her talons upon the wood, like the scrape of a chair pulled across the floor.

Laila knew not what to say or do. She did not protest, nor resist, nor assert, but let him lead her in turns around the small hut as he bobbed and weaved and spun with her, making two become one in a way new and different yet not unlike the binding of lovers she knew far better and had perverted for her Lord Samael these many centuries of Men.

His eyes held hers even through the veil of cloth, and as they brightened with his smile, with his joy of her, she felt herself smiling in return, and not in the delight of anticipated or conquered prey. From shuffling her feet as he turned her, she first raised one clawed foot and put it down, and then the other, first in an awkward stumble, then more and more in harmony with the rhythm of his own.

He laughed and urged her on. She bumped the table with a cloaked wing and a tin cup clattered to the floor, causing the goat, who'd been watching the antics of his master and mistress with patient disdain, to bleat, scamper around them, and burrow under the bed. Laila laughed.

It was a laugh unlike any she had ever voiced. It was a laugh not at the wail of a mother who found her child pale and cold in its crib, or a man who woke with dreams of guilt and his nightshirt soiled. No. She laughed because *she felt joy in another who found joy in her.*

Bilchek stuck his large head through a cleft in the drape, joining her in her shadow, seeing her as she was. "My lovely wife," he said.

Her joy made her laugh again, a songbird's trill as sweet as a cool gurgling highlands stream. "My loving husband," she said.

And they laughed and danced more wildly until the black drape slipped from her shoulders and tangled their feet. Hands still clasped, they fell to the floor, their breath mingling in mirth. The floorboards boomed like the staccato of a drum, the rumble slowly fading like echoing thunder.

Bilchek held her hands. She noted thin scratches where her nails had cut his flesh, a few welling with blood, and she jerked her hands from him. She grabbed the black drape in her claws and clutched it to her chest, drawing her wings around her, hiding her face.

"Ah, no, my Laila Tov." He reached again for her hands, gently placing his upon hers. "There is nothing to hide from. There is nothing for which to feel shame."

She let one wing slide back just enough that her left eye, dark and shiny as obsidian, looked at him from beneath silken feathers of raven hair. "I... I hurt you."

He shook his head. "Love always leaves marks. Man bleeds for love, as does woman, but when love is returned there is only joy, my rose of Sharon."

He kissed her, and she leaned forward and encompassed him in the shield of her wings and returned his kiss, dropping the black cloth drape and letting it flow like Night to puddle upon the now silent and sated floor.

ד

The first crystalline snow came and passed, leaving the eaves and lintels and roofs and lanes of Kirkatel to sparkle like gems in the late autumn sun. A second snow soon followed leaving a half-foot of powder as fine and dry as flour. When winds came, light for the season, ribbons of snow flowed down the narrow ways and wider lanes buffeting the villagers as they walked like waders in a swift-moving stream. The last of the traveling merchants and tinkers passed through Kirkatel, their horse-drawn carts like small houses that clanged and drummed as pots banged and barrels rolled. The tinkers remarked at how the village had been blessedly spared from the ice and snow now deepening to the west, the north, and particularly among the eastern highlands.

Melis stormed the lanes of Kirkatel, the village women in her wake. Snow scattered away from the hem of her kaftan like hens from the butcher's wife. While the women of Kirkatel remarked on the strangeness of the unusually mild weather, Melis worried at the knowledge of the ugly cripple's Muslim wife like a cur with too large a bone, unable to get to the marrow.

Melis had seen her.

For three restless nights, like Jonah tossed within the belly of the whale, she lay abed next to the bulk of her snoring husband. Then, on the following morning, she stole from the shop, leaving her husband to serve any late breakfasting customers. She cloaked herself in an old tattered wool kaftan and a plain brown yasmak that veiled her nose and mouth. No one called to her in her disguise as she slipped along the narrow ways down the hill to the farmer's track. She stopped in the shadow of Pilpul the tanner's shed, wrinkling her nose at the foul smell, and waited. When Bilchek hobbled past, his large multicolored pack of fabrics and rags upon his back, she'd scuttled to his small yard.

For a moment she stood amazed. While snow lightly rested upon the packed earth and small islets of twisted winter grass, small violets and peonies like tiny amethysts and sapphires poked their heads above the canopy of snow. Not a single icicle hung from the edge of the thatched roof, and swathes of grass, green as spring, huddled against the walls of the hovel. She scuttled to the ramshackle of a window where she felt the warmth of the hut radiating through her mittens. The heat caressed her face as if she had raised it to the summer sun. Bilchek and his foreign woman must be burning all his winter's store of firewood. Was the stranger from the Arab or African sands to require such warmth? Was she one of the black-skinned Muslims? She heard they were the fiercest. She shivered and noticed, despite the warmth, her breath still steamed the air and frosted the single melted pane of the window. She wiped it and peered in as the widow Tansu claimed to have done.

And Melis saw what Tansu claimed to have seen. She could not tell her bear of a husband. He abhorred gossip. After the death of Joseph, their infant son, he became fiercely religious, spending evenings at studies with the rabbi and his students. Every Sabbath eve he was atop her, doing his duty as she did hers. For all the good it did them. The only thing that rose in the ovens of Melis and Reuven the baker was his breads.

Melis gave Tupi the beggar half a loaf of day-old bread to fetch Bilchek to her. The tailor came, bowing and smiling, his large bag of rags lifted high over the curve of his spine like a turtle shell.

She gave him a robe. "The fur lining is parting at the hem, Bilchek. And winter deepens."

"I can mend this, Dame Melis."

"And I require a fur muffler. My hands are fair."

"Truly fair. You shall have it."

She offered him the other half of the loaf of bread that she had given Tupi.

He thanked her, but he placed it in his pack rather than wolf it down as had the beggar. He took out his needle, sat upon the bench by the window where the light was best, and began mending the hem.

"You are well, Bilchek?"

He nodded, kissing needle to thread, joining them.

"You are keeping warm?"

He nodded again, his head bobbing in rhythm with his hands that pierced and pulled, pierced and pulled, drawing the edges of the fur-lining and the woolen robe together seamlessly.

"I often wonder how you and your little goat can survive in the winter in your hut by the river. The winds from the highlands blow unhindered there, and the snows drift like ocean waves. How do you keep warm on winter's nights? How do you light your fires, care for your animals, cook and wash and clean, and tailor? Who watches over you when you are ill? Who warms you in your bed when the nights are long and the days are cold? Surely not your goat?"

Without looking up, Bilchek answered, "God provides. Baruch HaShem."

"Baruch HaShem," Melis' husband repeated as he entered from the back room, his face red and beaded with sweat from the heat of the ovens.

Bilchek stood and displayed the repaired lining. It looked as good as new, even better than when she had taken a knife to it and pulled the hem loose an hour before. Her husband admired it as well, "Good hands, good heart, Bilchek," and gave him a few copper manghirs and a fresh loaf of bread still warm from the ovens.

Melis said nothing.

Three weeks passed, and winter remained mild, at least for the village of Kirkatel. No further travelers came and none were expected until spring, when the town would be full of people passing to the Highlands with their flocks, or taking the old Roman roads upon oxen-drawn wains carrying winter-made goods to the tiled cities of the west and south. The Sultan's tax collector would come to collect the jizya, slapping lightly each man of the eyil of Kirkatel upon the face as he collected the Sultan's due from the Jews of Anatolia.

And he would come with his soldiers, Melis told Tansu and her nieces. If he discovered a Jew had taken a Muslim to wife, he would burn the village. To discover the Jew was the ugly cripple Bilchek... he could burn them all *with* the village.

Melis' words sparked fear in the gossip Tansu and, like a smoldering fire, soon ignited small flames that whispered among the other women of Kirkatel.

Fat Esther crossed her arms over her breasts and rested her chins upon them. "Why would a Musselman woman marry Bilchek?"

"Why would *any* woman marry Bilchek?" asked Miri.

"He's got good hands," said Huddle and tittered.

This evoked outrage and exclamations of disgust.

Huddle shrugged. "Just saying."

They squawked at one other, all but Melis. They're as flighty as hens, she thought; someone needed to be the fox. "I saw her as well. She will be the death of us all!"

The women quieted.

"She could just be a girl from another village, possibly betrothed long ago."

"Poor thing."

"Could you imagine lifting one's veil to kiss...that?"

The hens clucked and squawked until Melis stated, "We must know!"

A cool wind, tinged with the scent of snow, gusted and sent the hems of their kaftans flapping.

"We should visit her."

"Yes," said Tansu. "We have a duty to welcome her to Kirkatel."

"We should leave well enough alone," Esther said.

"We should be a comfort to her," said Melis. She smiled, and it was a smile as cold as the wind that gusted and made them shiver.

Gathering together, they walked down the hill. When they reached the farm track that led to the tailor's hovel, Huddle asked, "I wonder if Bilchek's pitzel is as nimble as his hands?"

The hens squawked.

ה

Laila was combing burs out of the goat's pelt with her fingers. It lay on its side upon the slatted wooden floor and raised its head with a look of disdain when a knock came at the door.

She rose, and the folds of her black robe flowed over her like night. The silver veil that covered her face, barely visible beneath the dark hood, rose and fluttered before settling. The robe hid both her hands and feet, and silver moons and stars were embroidered along its hem.

She stood a moment, indecisive. Except for her husband, none before had knocked upon the door in the weeks since her marriage, but his knock was a respectful tap followed by a cheerful "Shalom!" She had asked him why he knocked to enter his own home, and he had answered it was her home now.

The knock repeated, more insistent. She suddenly feared for Bilchek, and the little goat nudged the back of her knee.

Opening the door, Laila saw five women in rich kaftans of green, blue, maroon, magenta, and purple. One said, "Shalom aleichem."

"Aleichem shalom," said Laila.

They seemed to study her words as they stood looking at her. The one in blue shuffled her feet. Suddenly remembering human customs she invited them to come in. They all did, except the fat one in purple who merely asked for a chair so she could sit outside the door. The woman in magenta and the old one in green had already taken the hut's only two chairs, including the new one Bilchek had made for her from scraps of old wood purchased from

Isaac the carpenter. The two young women sat on the cot bed, the moon-eyed one locking eyes with the goat. Laila took the bucket and placed it top down outside the door. The fat woman looked at it distrustfully but settled her weight upon it. The bucket gave a muffled creak.

Introductions were made. "Laila?" said the old woman Tansu. "What sort of name is that?"

"One my husband gave me."

"What's your true name?" asked Melis.

"Any which my husband calls me under God."

"Some names my husband calls me at night he wouldn't speak before God," said Huddle. That set the two on the couch tittering. Melis and Tansu frowned.

"May... may I offer you tea?" Laila asked, and in the chorus of first nays and then, "If it would not be too much trouble," she poured water in the kettle and placed it upon the nail within the hearth, then looked for cups. She saw only the two tin cups she and Bilchek used, but also four clay bowls. When Miri added, "A slice of bread to dip would be lovely," Laila felt dismay at what little she had to offer, of bringing dishonor to her husband, but took the single loaf of bread she had saved for the Sabbath and placed it upon the table along with a knife and small pad of butter.

"Where are you from dear?" asked Melis, slicing the bread.

"From over the hills and under them. East Eretna is my home."

"Were you promised to Bilchek?" Esther asked from the doorway.

"He holds my promise."

Huddle shuddered.

Laila poured tea, grasping the handle of the kettle through the hem of her robe. Melis held a tin cup, gazed sourly at it, and put it down to watch Laila serve the other women. She had not an inch of skin exposed. "Why don't you loosen your veil, Laila. We are all women here. Even among you Musselmen, women may gaze upon one another."

The crackling of the hearth flames filled the hut. The goat snorted.

"I am not a Muslim," Laila said and continued passing cups of tea to Tansu, Miri, Huddle, and Esther.

"But are you a Jew?" blurted Esther.

Laila lifted her head and gazed at her through her veil. *"'I am my beloved's and my beloved is mine.'"*

Esther nodded.

"You have a wonderful voice," said Miri, "like a nightingale."

"Perhaps that is where she got her name," said Esther at the door.

Laila took up the wooden plate of sliced bread and offered it first to Melis, who waved her away, and then to the widow Tansu.

"When God gives one gift, it is in balance for another," said Tansu, worrying a slice of bread between her gums.

Miri leaned forward and whispered, "Do you cover yourself because you are scarred or ugly?"

Laila straightened and stood still even as Esther barked at her to save her the heel of the bread. "Come on, girl. Bring it here before I starve."

"Is that it then?" Melis said. Her voice was accusatory and held no compassion. "An ugly bride for an ugly tailor?"

"Bilchek is not ugly!" said Laila.

"And I'm not fat," said Esther. The women laughed.

"He has a heart of gold!" Laila felt herself flushing.

"It's the only gold you'll ever have from him," said Tansu and sipped her tea. That set the others laughing again.

Laila turned to face the hearth. The flames therein began to roil and snap.

"His hands have never been raised against me in anger nor left bruises upon my flesh, Tansu. Only caresses. I will never feel the need to place belladonna in his wine to win free of him."

Tansu choked, tea spluttering from her lips.

"He never calls me names nor looks at me with disgust, nor seeks the embrace of other women, Esther. Isn't that right Miri?"

The fat woman howled and Miri's eyes widened until she looked more frog-faced than moon-faced.

"He has strength in his flesh and joy of me. I need not find solace rutting with strangers, nor recall their different visages each day upon the faces of my children, Huddle. Nor lie each Sabbath under a man I abhor with a penis as small as his belly is huge and find pleasure only in my hand while he snores, Melis."

"Lies!"

Melis leapt from her chair. Her face was as red as the fire and her eyes matched its sparks. "Ugly words from an ugly whore! Let's see if you are uglier than Bilchek!" She grabbed Laila's robe and pulled. The cloth tore, and Melis flung it toward the door. The robe floated and rippled as it fell, silver stars and moons fluttering on fabric black as midnight until it pooled upon the floorboards like a shadow in the morning sun.

And Laila was revealed.

A slender woman, pale of skin, with long black hair, and gowned in white muslin. Her slender hands and slippered feet were like a dancer's; her face was oval and flawless: full lipped, peg-nosed and hazel-eyed -- human eyes, large and piercing beneath long dark lashes.

"Lies," Melis repeated as if to reassure herself, but her words were a whisper. "Disgusting lies."

"Ugly truths," Laila said. "We all possess them. Yet they are past. While I am here, you'll never need fear their repetition."

ך

The lamia Parosh -- Flea, a name she detested -- sat upon a gnarled branch of a leafless oak on a hill overlooking the village of Kirkatel. The village was silent beneath the stars. Wisps of smoke rose from chimneys and made the stars dance. Snow climbed the trunk of the tree and piled in tall sway-backed hillocks that ringed Kirkatel like fortifications. But Parosh sensed the snow was not a barrier but instead barred from the stone and mud brick homes and packed earth lanes. There was a power in Kirkatel that forbid winter's harsh incursion.

Something was not quite wrong. Not as it should be.

Though much of east Eretna seemed the same, there was a tense yet content susurration across the beylik. An anticipatory quiet. How was it no mothers wailed, no children screeched in tantrums. The old fostered the young with memories of pleasant times. There was still gossip, there would be as long as there were men, but it was like dry snow that failed to cling and was dispersed by the lightest breath of wind. Men still cursed, but more out of habit than rancor. A patina of snow and ice coated village lanes like melted sugar and crunched like the crusts of crisp breads and sweet crackers beneath the tread of boots as neighbor visited neighbor and taverns stayed alight and echoed laughter until the winter moon passed its zenith. Contrarily, there were too few footprints cracking the lace of ice on the paths to mosque, church, and synagogue; and fewer still marring the snow that blanketed the cemeteries.

She spread her wings and leaned forward. A passing breeze lifted her from the branch and into the night air. The wind currents were unseasonably warm and gentle, cool caresses rather than bitter bites, kinder than the wintry gusts that ruled her own beylik leagues to the south.

She drifted over Kirkatel, gliding low across the rooftops. She let her talons scrape and mar snowy parapets and roof ridges, grasping and releasing, as she propelled herself in a tightening circle toward the center of the perturbation.

She alighted on a ramshackle hovel, small and odd in its haphazard construction of mud brick, raw stone, and broken wood. She readied herself to spring up again in fear the roof would collapse under her weight; but despite its decrepit appearance, it was sturdy, firm and unyielding. The roof was bare of snow, as was the yard from doorway to crooked fence. Grass ringed the home and small flowers grew like a scattering of rubies, sapphires, and agates. A garden in winter?

The lamia sidled across the roof. Grasping the eaves with her feet, she swung her body over the edge to hang face down and peered into the hut through the mottled single glass eye of its window.

There was darkness within, tinged only by the glow of coals slumbering in the hearth. Wan red light and still shadows bathed two intertwined forms asleep under a patchwork blanket. A goat lay at the foot of the bed chewing on the blanket's tattered edge as it slept. It twitched an ear then opened one eye.

Parosh bent her knees, lifting her face from the window. She waited until starred Kesel the Hunter nodded his head toward the horizon before lowering herself again. The goat was asleep but had pulled the blanket off the foot of one of its bedmates. The foot was that of a young woman, slender and smooth and yet...

The lamia blinked and nictitating membranes slid over her eyes. Through them, she could see the ghostly outline of iridescent scales and hooked talons surrounding the human foot. She pulled herself back up to the roof and crouched.

Her sister was not dead as had been feared. She had lain with the sleeping man. The smell of sex was evident. But why did her sister stay? She gazed again at the strange town, held in spring rather than mid-winter. She started. Was her sister held as well? Was the hovel's occupant a mage who had bound her? The thought of being so constrained ignited her anger, as sudden and fierce as lightning. She leapt into the air, claws extending, her wings spreading wide.

She would kill the man. A hand grabbed her ankle and pulled her to the roof. She gave a stifled cry and fell onto her back as a black shadow with eyes scarlet as the hearth's coals fell over her.

"You overstep your border, sister," Laila said.

The lamia snarled and made to rise, but to her surprise found she could not. That delicate semblance of a human foot rested on her chest, and it was as if it held the weight of all Creation. How? Parosh was larger, stronger, higher in the cloud of lilin who served their Lord Samael. But she let not this wonder defeat her. It was a lilin's nature to use craft and wiles where strength and power alone did not serve. She lay back displaying her throat and palms in a gesture of submission.

"The cloud grew concerned, sister," she said. "For a moon, no Eretnan seed, breath, nor milk has been brought before Lord Samael; and neither wing nor claw nor fang seen of you."

"Was I missed, or just my tithes?"

"I...don't understand." Parosh gasped as the weight of the foot increased, pinning her to the roof. Her wings fluttered like a trapped moth's against the tiles of interwoven broken pottery, adobe, and thatch.

Then the weight eased and her strange sister spoke, "No. You wouldn't."

Hazel eyes now met obsidian. Parosh rose to a crouch but found she still could not stand, her bindings had been loosened but not released.

Laila turned and gazed skyward. The moon was near full and ringed with ghostly light, a necklace of ice crystals trapped high above Kirkatel.

"What do you know of love, sister?" Laila asked.

"Love?" The lamia smiled and moonlight glistened off her fangs. "Love is taking pleasure from others."

Laila shook her head. "Love is giving of oneself to please others."

"Giving is lessening. We are gatherers. We take, we collect."

"And then?"

"We bring all to Lord Samael."

"And he takes everything from us. How does this make you feel?"

"Feel?" Parosh frowned. "I am emptied. I need get more!"

"And yet what you take does not last. Love...love is stronger than lust. It persists when lust abates." Their eyes met again. "With love, the more you *give*, the more you have. You always feel full."

The lamia crouched in Laila's shadow, a shadow cast by the moon that silvered the outline of this strange sister who had assumed the form of their prey, who mouthed such odd words with the certainty of Lord Samael himself. Again Parosh made to rise and spread her wings, but found she could not. From where did this least among her sisters acquire such power? She spoke in the tongue they shared, but Parosh did not understand her.

"There is a wonder in love," Laila said, looking over her shoulder at the moon. Her eyes once onyx, then hazel, now glowed bright with reflected moonlight. "A wonder which Samael has taught us to deny and ridicule without ever tasting. He fears if we did, we'd be free. We'd know joy. We'd have lovers' names." She looked back at the crouching lamia and said with a rush, "Seek it, sister!"

The words struck Parosh with the force of Command, but they also seemed a plea. Words with power that did not pierce her flesh, but bathed it, then passed behind her into the night.

The lamia blinked, flicking her nictitating membranes over her eyes. She narrowed them and asked, "What power does love have over our own that I should seek it?"

"Mercy," Laila answered in a whisper.

Parosh felt the weight upon her dissipate. She rose. "I will consider all you have said," she lied. Stretching her wings, she launched herself into the night.

She flew south almost to the border of her beylik of Dulkadir before arcing westward, flying faster than the wind toward Mount Ericyes and Samael.

She joined a murder of crows as they winged toward **Karamanoğollan**; but when she smiled, they fled from her with panicked squawks and cries.

As a reward, perhaps Samael would grant her a new name.

ד

Melis dreamed.

Egg yolks slid between her fingers like tadpoles as she strove to mash them into the flour. She grabbed a wooden spoon and fiercely beat the inside of the bowl, raising a cloud of white dust. She stopped, breathing heavily as the cloud settled. Intact yolks slid like golden galleons over waves of flour. They came to rest, staring up at her with accusing eyes.

Reuven sat on the floor in front of an oven that was cold and bare. He sobbed quietly, his face buried in his hands.

The door to the shop banged open, so startling Melis that she dropped her spoon. A parade of customers entered, Tansu at their head, a bloom of nightshade in her hair.

Her nieces rolled Reuven onto his back. Taking their hands, she stepped onto Reuven's belly before the open maw of the oven, now fiery red and exhaling a fierce heat.

Tansu cast one disapproving look at Melis then lowered her head and walked into the flames. Her screams were stifled by the oven's roar.

Her nieces followed and were consumed with two small squeaks. The oven belched a cloud of gray ash.

Huddle urged her children forward. They sprung nimbly into the oven laughing, bouncing off Reuven's belly, thinking it a game, their laughter bursting into brief cries of pain cut short. Long tongues of flame lapped them up.

Melis coughed, covering her nose at the sickly smell of burning flesh, too reminiscent of caramelized butter. The heat in the shop was stifling. Melis' sweat-drenched hirka clung to her body, binding her.

The oven became a living thing, growing muscled arms of baked adobe. Large-knuckled stone hands grappled Esther. She fell forward, filling its throat that stretched to accommodate her like a serpent swallowing a rat.

Each villager was swallowed in turn with bursts of flame and ash until only the rabbi remained. He regarded Melis accusingly; then he lowered his head, shaking it once side-to-side, and followed the rest of his congregation into the flames.

Smoke and ash stung Melis' eyes. She blinked away black tears and... the oven was just an oven, and the room was cold and empty save for wisps of snow curling through the open shop door.

"You could have stopped this," said a familiar voice.

Reuven stood by the washbasin in his nightshift preparing for bed. With a cloth, he wiped flour and soot from his face. "You could have said something."

"I wanted to!"

"But you didn't."

He turned and looked at her. Melis stepped back, catching her breath.

Reuven's eyes were black, deep black orbs, cold wells of utter darkness save for motes of tiny flames floating like sparks above an evening fire.

"They're all gone," Samael said. "Friends, neighbors..." He paused, "...our son Joseph. All dead. All your fault."

"It's *not* my fault!"

His eyes held hers. She feared she'd fall into them as Tansu, Huddle, and fat Esther had fallen into the maw of the oven.

"Then whose fault, is it?"

His words were a sibilant purr. She shuddered and recalled the face of Bilchek's woman, her pale alabaster skin, so young and smooth, unmarred by time, eyelashes long as a fawn's, and hair as black as the dark between the stars. It was an abomination to imagine her beauty with the ugly tailor when

Melis' own beauty had faded; an abomination for Laila to find joy in such a poor uncomely husband and he in her when she and Reuven now shared naught but cool acceptance.

It had been so different once.

"And could be again," Reuven-Samael said and placed his hand upon her breast.

Melis started. Reuven's hair had lost its gray, his beard was now close-cropped and neat, his belly flat and firm, his chest and arms muscled as they were in his youth.

Where had his shift gone?

Where had hers!

"Who is this Laila, this cripple's wife? Where did she come from?" he asked.

"No one knows. She's not of the village. Tansu says she's a Musselman woman." She groaned as Reuven's hands began to wander upon her. His hands were warm, feverishly hot.

"And if she is discovered by the sultan's tax-collector?"

Melis gasped, though she was uncertain if it was from the image of the villagers consumed by the holocaust of the oven or from the trembling aroused by Reuven's hands. "We'll all burn! All because of that woman."

"Woman?" He leaned forward and his breath curled around the soft hairs of her ear, caressing it before entering. "She's no daughter of Eve."

And Melis again recalled the slender form of Laila standing in slippered feet upon the uneven plank floor of Bilchek's hut. The figure shimmered, blurred, then twisted into a creature of horror: talons, claws, fangs, and bat's wings black as midnight draping her from her fox-like face to owl's feet.

"A demon!"

"A lilin," Reuven said. "The very one who took our child Joseph from us." He pushed her back upon the bed.

Melis cried even as she opened herself to receive him. "That sorceress," she sobbed as tears flowed down her cheeks. "That witch!"

"And what does the Lord command concerning witches?" Reuven asked, lowering himself upon her, filling her unlike ever before.

"*Thou shalt not suffer a witch to live!*" She cried and shuddered against him as pleasure took her.

But she was uncertain if this pleasure was from the ending of their long unshared intimacy or from anticipation of the revenge she would bring upon the disgusting cripple and his demon bride.

ח

So it was that when Bilchek opened his door one morning, he saw his neighbors gathered at his broken gate, old Rabbi Pinchas at their head looking distressed, as if he had yet to complete his morning ablutions. The crowd muttered, some pointing to the garden of violets and peonies and belled snowdrops, others to the rich growth of grass that flowed across the yard like a sultan's carpet.

The tailor smiled. "Yom tov! How may I be of service?"

Did he seem taller? Was his back straighter? Rabbi Pinchas raised a hand to hush the whisperers.

"We hear you have taken a wife, Bilchek," he said.

"This is true, Rabbi. HaShem has so blessed me."

"But you have not stood under the huppa before the community and declared her your wife." The rabbi shook his finger. "It is not good for a man to be with an unwed woman."

"*It is not good for a man to be alone,*" Bilchek replied. "Like Adam and Eve, my Laila and I have wed under the canopy of Heaven and declared ourselves for one another. As this sufficed for God for His first children, shall it not suffice for us all? But come, rabbi, for my neighbors and friends, I would have you marry us for *shalom.*"

The rabbi looked relieved and nodded, turning to the crowd. Frowns greeted him, none deeper than that of Melis the baker's wife.

Someone called out, "Is she a Jew, Bilchek?"

Another added, "What have you brought upon us?"

The rabbi felt the bony finger of the widow Tansu prod his back. Discomforted, he shrugged, turned his palms upward and asked the tailor, "*Is* she a Jew, Bilchek?"

At that, the door to the tailor's hut opened and out stepped Laila. Gone was the ebon drape of mourning. She was gowned in a feraçe of many colors, lovingly crafted by her husband, and embroidered with birds aflight and beasts afield. A ring of goats capered along its hem, some beneath trees and others upon hills. Her yasmak veiled the lower half of her face like spider silk affixed with small stars. The crowd gaped, some in wonder, some making the sign to ward the evil eye.

"*Thy people shall be my people, and thy God shall be my God,*" she said. She stood respectfully a step behind Bilchek.

Some slowly nodded, their frowns fading, but someone murmured loud enough for her neighbors to hear, *"where thou diest will I die, and there shall I be buried."*

"There is concern that your woman is a Musselman's daughter, Bilchek" the rabbi said. "It would not go well with us if this be true. The Muslims forbid our marrying their women."

Miriam called out, "Is she a Saracen, Bilchek? Will her people seek revenge upon us?"

Another said, "Things are finally good! Will you bring war and death upon us?"

And a third shouted, "Bilchek, she must go!"

Many nodded assent.

Bilchek took Laila's hand. "'

"'Her ways are ways of pleasantness, and all her paths are peace.'"

The crowd's voices rose like squabbling crows until the rabbi raised a veined hand and they quieted. "That may be, Bilchek," he said, "but the world turns as it will, not as we desire. Is she a daughter of Ishmael?"

But again a voice muttered just loud enough to be heard, "...or of Samael!"

"Look at the yard!" said Huddle.

"Unnatural," said Miri.

"Sorcery," said Esther, and the villagers again began to talk and argue in a cacophony of noise.

The rabbi raised his arms to quiet them, but it was like holding back a flood with an unfurled Torah scroll. People began to shout at one another.

"She's a witch! A demon!"

"Superstitious nonsense! She's just a girl!"

Laila stepped in front of Bilchek and lowered her veil.

The crowd fell silent.

Thereafter, none could agree on what they saw. Those who looked upon her with malice said she was hideous, those who viewed her with wonder said she was angelic.

Laila met the eyes of each in turn.

They had been the herd she had shepherded for Samael. Now they were her neighbors. Meeting her eyes, many felt lost, confused, recalling her visage from some past night, some past dream. The rabbi (whom she also had known as Lilith had known Adam) averted his gaze as did most of the men, but the women (her flawed competition) grew stern, feeling inexplicable rage mixed with loss, and it was one among them who cast the first stone.

Bilchek swept Laila behind him, and the stone struck him upon the brow with a crack as sharp and loud as a tree snapped by winter ice. He fell to his knees.

The rabbi cried, "Tah'ana! Stop!" and others, "Hold!" and still others, "Kill them!"

And Laila changed.

With a mournful cry, she spread her wings around Bilchek. They were like Joseph's rainbow coat to some (eliciting shame), angel's wings to others (inspiring awe), and devil's wings in the eyes of the rest who bent to raise stones of their own.

Laila flowed around Bilchek like the Ahern in summer flood, pressing her body against his, enfolding him between her arms and the shield of her wings. He collapsed inward, limbs curling fetal-like. Her lips touched his, soft, warm, and sweet. The stones fell upon them like hail.

And winter returned to Kirkatel.

ט

The small sward of earth and patchwork hut where the crippled tailor and his demon bride once lived was shunned for its evil, or so the villagers would claim; but whether it was for the evil that once dwelt there or the evil that was inflicted upon it none would say. It was not fear but some other emotion they displayed, averting their eyes and hurrying past, when they need take the farmer's path.

The Sultan's soldiers arrived in the spring and the jizya was collected, each man of Kirkatel receiving the light slap on his cheek in token acknowledgement of the Prophet's words, yet the humiliation they felt did not abate. No war came to Kirkatel; but slowly, as is the way with all things from empires to eyils, more left the village than were there born. With them like scattered seed went the story, first told in whispers, of Bilchek and Laila. In time, only the heat and rain and snow swept the lanes and broached the shadowed doorways and open windows of Kirkatel.

At the foot of the village near where the slow Ahern curled, a swath of green grass covered the splintered wood and cracked brick of a fallen hut, and upon the grass a single cloudy eyelet of glass winked in turn at the passing sun and moon. There among the violets, peonies, and snowbells grew a juniper tree.

And people began to return to Kirkatel.

The young mostly, but also old soldiers and widows cherishing memories more than new trials. But not one stayed, for one does not take residence near, for fear of soiling, the places where wonder has touched the earth.

The juniper tree and the small swath of grass by the river became a place lovers met to make secret betrothals and pray for a love strong and lasting. And while the village is long gone, and its people dust or scattered among the Gentile Nations or, Baruch Hashem, in Eretz Yisrael, the moon still shines, the mountains still stand, the wind still blows, and the tree grows there still.

Of the three known copies
of the
Sefer ha-Yehudim min ha-Galut,
two end here,
but one,
rescued from the Nazi burning of the Rashi synagogue in Worms,
contains the following hand-written script in the margins:

27 MARCHESVAN. I came at night upon the place the Turkamen claimed had been Kirkatel, and rested there. Snow glistened atop far Mount Ararat under the full moon, a reminder of this day and G-d's Promise. "'*The Eearth had dried.*'" Rubble was strewn in patterns hinting at the foundations of homes that once were. Betwixt moonlight and shadows I could imagine their walls and roofs, and the people who had lived within them, greeting friends, comforting children, and raising their voices in Psalms. All gone, except for the memories in stone.

At the foot of the village, I found the tree as promised. Tall, thrusting upward as if to ward against the Night, standing as a sentinel, or a memorial. The ground was uncannily warm and there was grass, soft and full for so late in the season. Perhaps a hot spring lies beneath, though the nearby stream was cool to drink. I sat to take my rest and recalled the tales of the cripple and his demon bride until I fell asleep.

Past midnight I awoke to a rustle in the tree above me, as if some night creature had alighted and stirred restlessly. Looking up, I was shocked to see a woman crouched upon a high branch, her skin pale and glowing in the moonlight. She whispered to herself, but her words carried in the still air.

'What was it like, sister? What was it like?'

She stood with a cry, unfolding leathery wings that blocked the moonlight as she leapt into the sky.

Then I fled.

"Laila Tov", by Robert Finegold   robertbfinegold.author@gmail.com   October 18, 2016

Robert B. Finegold MD is a retired radiologist, a former major in the U.S. Army, and a consulting editor for Cosmic Roots & Eldritch Shores. Since 2011 Bob's stories of science fiction, fantasy, and Yiddishkeit have appeared in magazines, e-zines, and anthologies. He edited the *3rd and Starlight Anthology* and was twice a finalist in the Writers of the Future contest. He resides in Maine. Find his occasional musings at robertbfinegold.com and on facebook at RobertBFinegold Kvells and Kvetchings.

Many generations of Bob's forbears lived in the Kyiv Oblast of Ukraine within the historical Pale of Settlement. His beloved paternal grandfather, John "Jack" Finegold, of blessed memory, was born in Zhytomyr. After surviving the Zhytomyr pogrom of 1905, he lived in Bratslav for 14 years before immigrating to the U.S. in 1914 to escape increasing anti-Jewish violence. His memoir of his youth in Ukraine and early years in Massachusetts is a cherished family possession. Papa Jack lived as Rabbi Nachman of his native Bratslav urged us all in the face of adversity: «*It is a great mitzvah to be constantly joyous.*» Being the big-hearted, big-souled, gentle man that he was, Papa Jack would have been pleased and, Bob believes, unsurprised, that Ukraine's heroic, well-spoken, and *elected with 73% of the popular vote* president, Volodymyr Zelensky, is also a Ukranian Jew.

...and Always

Joan Stewart

Never again and always
Will we dance upon the green,
Where the midnight lights of wandering wights
Are imagined to be seen

Never again and always
Will I burn in the light of your soul
'Til the fire in our bones cracks open the stones
In the hardest and cruelest of hearts.

Never again and always
In the dark past all that is known
Will the book of Night in our candle's light
Share the Truth of the love we have sown

Whitby Abbey, North Yorkshire, 1910, Albert Goodwin

The Listeners

Walter de La Mare

'Is there anybody there?' said the Traveller,
   Knocking on the moonlit door;
And his horse in the silence champed the grasses
   Of the forest's ferny floor:
And a bird flew up out of the turret,
   Above the Traveller's head:
And he smote upon the door a second time;
   'Is there anybody there?' he said.
But no one descended to the Traveller;
   No head from the leaf-fringed sill
Leaned over and looked into his grey eyes,
   Where he stood perplexed and still.
But only a host of phantom listeners
   That dwelt in the lone house then
Stood listening in the quiet of the moonlight
   To that voice from the world of men:
Stood thronging the faint moonbeams on the dark stair,
   That goes down to the empty hall,
Hearkening in an air stirred and shaken
   By the lonely Traveller's call.
And he felt in his heart their strangeness,
   Their stillness answering his cry,

While his horse moved, cropping the dark turf,
  'Neath the starred and leafy sky;
For he suddenly smote on the door, even
  Louder, and lifted his head: —
'Tell them I came, and no one answered,
  That I kept my word,' he said.
Never the least stir made the listeners,
  Though every word he spake
Fell echoing through the shadowiness of the still house
  From the one man left awake:
Ay, they heard his foot upon the stirrup,
  And the sound of iron on stone,
And how the silence surged softly back,
  When the plunging hoofs were gone.

Published 1912. Walter de la Mare was born April 25, 1873 in London. Considered a leading writer of the romantic imagination. His works include poetry, short stories, and novels, weaving together romantic themes: dreams, death, rare states of mind and emotion, adult and childhood fantasy worlds, and the pursuit of the transcendent.

Bolaji Has A Heart

Osahon Ize-Iyamu

When Bolaji's husband died, people cast her aside as if she were dead. They stepped around her like she wasn't there, and turned their heads, like she didn't exist anymore without her man, that dead woman.

Did she kill him? was the first gossip she'd heard, after the funeral, when everyone cast wide-eyed glances at her while his ashes were put atop his gravestone, afraid of what she'd do next when she was only grieving. It made a raging fire beneath her bones; like she wasn't in her own skin, just shifting around inside their fears and imaginings. Surely, it couldn't be her they were referring to? She'd bought from their markets, laughed with them during outings in the forest. How could this now be her story?

Like hot water cooling, she'd since eased into it, gotten used to walking alone to fetch water, to sitting down alone after the farm work was done, the whole day hiding in her thoughts, floating in the void where no one could hurt her.

It's dark in here, her thoughts whispered, and she jolted, looking around. Day was beginning to fade. She'd done the farm work, weeded and watered and harvested and swept away sand. She cooked, and ate with ravenous hunger.

A knock on her door. Obioro, She'd expected one of her in-laws They came looking for trouble, looking to complain, another reason she preferred they didn't enter her home. *Her* home, not her *dead husband's home,* as they called it. They tried to overshadow her, when their shadows were mice in sunlight.

Obioro tipped his hat then scowled, running his eye over her empty food dishes."Bolaji, I thought you were a damn fine woman, but we've noticed you're not following custom,"

"Only now custom has meaning for you? Do I see you working the farm with me? No. I hear you all whispering: 'Oh a good woman! Who's gonna take her next? Who's gonna pay her price? Look at the way her round—' "

Obioro's pointy ears reddened, but he raised his head. "How about some food for your brother-in-law?"

She shrugged, brushing sand off her coat. These were the cold, strange periods, when sand flew in the eyes in waves, and people had to protect themselves while the sands did as they pleased. "There's no food for those who don't work."

She wanted to shut the door, like she was in control of the conversation.She wanted to release all the burning rage inside her but that wouldn't fit with people's sense of proper custom.

Obioro removed his hat, rubbing at the dark wet spot along the inside;

his sweat didn't stop in cold or heat. "You'd do well to remind yourself there are things we brothers own, and that many other families have gone about torturing their widows. Now," Obioro laughed, "you're not the first to have a dead husband. Live a little." He leaned in against the door.

Bolaji kept a shoulder to the door against the pressure. "I've never been that social." She rubbed her palms together, watching the black sand, like gunpowder, fall from her fingers.

He pressed the door harder. "But you should have friends. You need them. Makes the pain ebb."

He tried to grab her hands but she pulled them away.

"The hell are you two doing here?" a woman called.

Bolaji's eyes widened, darting around to every house and hut. Empty. Nothing. . Dark. A tumbleweed blew by. Then she saw a woman in the street, holding a stiffened slip of paper.

"They're drawing lots tonight?" Bolaji gasped at her forgetfulness.

The woman just placed a hand to her hips and raised an eyebrow in answer.

Bolaji rushed out of the house, twisting the key in the lock, and brushed past her brother-in-law, holding her coat close, her sandglasses firm against her nose.

"You'll be sweeping the market square this week," the woman laughed.

Bolaji winced, at the thought of how she'd fit it in between selling and farming and the best part of her day -- rest and thought, when she leaned back into that empty space free of frustration or sorrow.

"I think you should take my shift, too," Obioro adjusted his collar. "I'm a busy man. I have a family to feed. What do you got? No child, spirit--"

She stopped.

What? What did he say? *What?*

Barren woman, empty woman.

Something slammed inside her. She wanted to slap him, she wanted him as broken as his words, and yet the rage stayed unfinished within her raised hand.

He saw her intent and grabbed her hand so that one movement would snap a finger. "We had that talk about respect. Remember?" He pressed down and she ground her teeth. "Say you remember so I'm sure you've learnt."

Bolaji closed her eyes tight. She took a cool breath. Her body stirred, hitting with each heartbeat, that calm anger. She let it flow. "Go ahead"

He stared at her, faltered, black skin paling.

"Go ahead" she said again, voice level, eyes still shut as a smile crept onto her face. "Because I know your mother didn't wait eighteen years to have you and your brothers without hearing that song, 'barren woman, empty woman.' I know she sat me down and spoke with so much anger at how they treated her, how she suffered, and one word to her of what you're doing, whatever spirit or hand in me you're trying to break, she'll crack you twice as hard, and I'll join her."

She opened her eyes, let him see her eyes.

Obioro let go, using his hat to almost cover his face. "I'll do my shift." He looked in her eyes again. "And yours. This once."

People were lost in daily gossip and conversation about bets from last night's Masquerade dance. Her town was a melting pot; cultures twining and turning and bringing out hybrid flavours.

"Kind of you to join us," Afang, the census taker, remarked. His brows were burnt off so if his words held any witticisms or sarcastic undertones they were hard to decipher.

Obioro distanced himself from Bolaji. "How much did I miss?"

"Constable did opening statements," Afang said as he moved through the crowds. "And he wanted to do the lots today, so I let him. I need a break."

"You do a fine job," Obioro flashed his teeth.

Bolaji rolled her eyes.

"Your watch doesn't do a fine job keeping you on time," the census taker raised a burnt-off brow.

"You can't put a clock on family matters."

"And this community is not your family?" Afang almost spat.

Obioro faltered.

Bolaji chuckled and they both stared at her in irritation.

"Now, last I checked, we didn't come here for no party!" Constable Edu boomed gruffly. Everyone snapped up, like a sudden prickle against their skin. Voices died down as sand rose up, dancing around the square. The sun drowned in quicksand and the world turned blue, as if to mourn the sun's disappearance.

Timing was key.

"Tell 'em, Edu!" Mansima, one of the market sellers, shouted. Bolaji remembered the woman's laugh during visits when their husbands would have long talks. Now Mansima turned narrowed eyes at her. All the things, the people she'd loved, had withered away. Bolaji paused. She forced a smile, and spoke, eyes twinkling. "Remember that time at my house you offered to go get the pepper, but you made a mistake and brought ashes?"

Mansima stared hard at her, unsmiling. "Remember that time your husband died?"

Bolaji closed her eyes. She didn't take a breath. Her body froze. Then she opened them. Unraveled, fire within.

Bad woman, senseless woman, hard wo--

"Afang, collect their lots." Constable Edu held up strips of hardened paper then stared at the latecomers.

"I thought I had a break," Afang muttered, moving through the late attendees bringing out strips from their pockets. "Not here to be your damn assistant." Afang handed him the last strips.

"I'll throw a name, it will be true," the constable said, like chanting a wish, then whipped out one strip. "Nonso. First day."

There were groans, and sighs of relief.

"Now, now," Afang told them, raising his hands. "We don't make the call."

Only one person turned off the lights. This was the way of it. People liked lighting them, the fire close to their eyes. They said it kept the witches away, if only for a few hours. But nobody wanted the job of turning them off, scurrying home in darkness.

Turning off the lights came with the fear of all things unseen in the dark and the loneliness of the task. Tales were told about Masquerades and pacts with demons and their forest babies that needed meals each week. Stories of evil forests and monstrous marauders and spearrangs that had a little too much fun spinning up people's insides. You heard things that shook you and made you spin. And there were all the people that took their turn and came back different, never came back at all, died in strange ways. Like the man who came back with seven scars that slowly ate him whole over the course of days.

"Bolaji. Third day."

Everyone looked at her, like how they watched her at the funeral. Her heart stopped pumping for a moment. The constable's voice melted into the background. She could manage it. She had to manage it. There was no option. Just turn off some lights. They couldn't be left on all night. That was the tradition. It had been that way forever.

"Okay," she said to her spirits. "Okay."

It was all right because it was just lots, because no one made the call, because it would help her fit back in to the life of the town.

Either that, or they were hoping that the night would bless them and rid them of her.

In three days…

She placed it in the order of things, scheduled it, and got back to work. Her scythe cleared another portion of field as she sang, the weeds swinging away to the wind with a promise to come back. And when they reappeared once more, she would root them out again.

In her darkest days, Bolaji had allowed the farm to grow reckless and wild, but she was back now.

Barren woman, empty woman, hollowed woman, drained woman.

She refused to sell the farm, and the men saved face by saying she wouldn't be able to handle it, so she wanted to show them how well these crops would thrive.   Her husband's brothers would come in when the work was done to chop the food. And she had to give them some battles to win so they didn't look like utter fools and invite people to put "the widow" in her place.

Like Afang, giving his sister-in-law a proper dressing after her husband died, one night while the lights were still on. He made a red dress for her out of the cuts he gave, a suit of many colours painted flesh and blood, slicing the skin nice and thin to cover her body in scars that matted up and wrinkled to scarred messes. They took him to the constable, but he got off because he counts good and after all that's just how men grieve. Pity him, poor man lost a brother. Woman only lost a husband; she'll get another.

Dirty woman, cursed woman, witched woman, childless woman.

Bolaji toiled in the hot sun. Her hand gripped the sickle firmly, so no one would tell her she wasn't doing it right. She dropped it and mixed sweat with the ground as she applied manure and searched for pests. She sprayed her husband's concoction to keep the insects away, put up the Masquerade she'd stitched to scare the birds away.

She reminded herself to spread rumors that her Masquerade danced in the night and knocked at the houses of children who came to steal her yams, placing charms on them. And just like that, there would be another story to be superstitious about, adding to the problem, but woking to her benefit.

Naughty woman, harlot woman, sloppy woman, no woman.

She clutched her stomach, stabbed a hand into it like she was plucking herself out.

Her eyes wide, she took a breath. Breathed long and deep, hard and soft, ragged and smooth.

The words were not new, and she had a shield against these things. But.

It ate at her, tore at her, screamed right in her ear. And every once in a while, she flinched. And her wall came down.

And it chewed at her insides, pulling out stumps of tissues and muscles, belly engorged on the pink fat inside her, bones rattling in their shells. She fell into the trap. Time slowed itself down, told her of the hours to be spent washing clothes and cleaning plates and serving tickets and sweeping sand and weaving mats for the market, but she couldn't get up, she felt heavy, full.

When time gave up on her, and when the sun stretched down and out and away, she still stood there, watching as the world went purple then dark.

Weighted, Bolaji went home.

The days passed by faster than she expected, and soon it was time. She told herself it was going to be no dramatic thing; she was going to get it over with and carry on, but it was the first thought she had on waking.

Her eyelids struggled to open, and part of her felt dead. She tasted bees in her mouth. Sweat rolled down her body. Her throat burned, and her heart fluttered.

Falls away.

Dies away.

Screams away.

Never stays.

Eventually, she had to lift herself up, dust herself off, fix herself up; do it anyway.

Bolaji had a soul; barely living, but not dead yet.

Obioro knocked on her door in the pattern she recognized.

She groaned, rubbing her temples. Her vision was blurry, but behind Obioro she could see a raven perched on a house across the road.

He tipped his hat then stared. "Damn, you're sick? And that's not the only omen I've seen today…"

"Omen?" She shifted, bones screaming with each movement.

"Bad dreams. Woke up to a murder of ravens. And the scarecrows aren't dancing for your health, those fore-bringers of death. Figure you're not a witch though 'cos you've got death on the way. I regret not taking my brother's property. Now you'll die and we'll have to burn the house down. You make things hard, Bolaji."

She scrunched up her face. "You think so, in-law? So, I should just fetch my noose?"

He glared at her. "You think you can be smart with me. No way now you're getting buried with my brother, unless…" he rubbed his hands. "You're been so difficult about choosing another of us --"

"I choose no one. Women can be alone you know."

"Ain't a good thing to test a man's patience. Just because my brother didn't give you a scratch. That dark skin of yours could use a lash or two. 'Cos of you there's not a trace of him left behind so we're not even family anymore. Why are you here? Who are you fighting for?"

For a minute her heart stopped. Silence, rising with the winds, taking up sand with it, falling with the winds. She breathed with the motion.

"If you die, Bolaji, make it easy for yourself and don't struggle, because your battle is long over."

It was only the early hours of the evening and she was already hearing owls and dead children calling out to her. Her husband's face, reaching for her from the grave, his ashes forming flesh again, touching her.

Falls away.

Dies away.

Screams away.

Never stays.

Time dragged, chipping away at the day then taking a breath. Holding a breath. When it exhaled, with the world transformed in its darkness, the oil lights came on. The lights made the place shine as people hurried to their houses.

With a sigh, Bolaji opened her door, closed it behind her, and waited.

She would be the last one outside, but it was good to feel the cool night breeze while the night fell deeper into sleep. Her father turned off the lights one time, and her heart was up waiting for him. But he did come back. Whistling, in fact, like it was just another day's work.

Who taught them to fear the night? Who taught them this darkness was evil, sinister, a hand trying to bind them? Why did the fear persist? She stood, shoulders high and back tense, eyes alert. She had been alone for so long, it didn't faze her that the crowds thinned with each passing moment.

And when everyone was shut in for the night, when it was pitch black with a full moon that didn't have a pregnant belly, she chanted and moved past the fires, fanning out flames, ending the day.

Full woman, good woman, precious woman, blessed woman.
Again.
Full woman, good woman, precious woman, blessed woman.
Again.
Full woman, good woman, precious woman, blessed woman.
Gracious woman, glorious woman, hearty woman, strong woman.
Fine woman, best woman, first woman, all woman.
You are loved.
You are loved.
You are loved.

There was a laugh in the darkness. "I knew you'd gone mad, Bolaji, but this is a whole new low," a voice whispered. She turned to see Obioro, standing with folded arms. She tucked the song under the folds of her skin.

"What are you doing here?"

"I started thinking 'what if you die and people decide our family is cursed?'"

"Thought I wasn't family."

"Not to me, but to them you are."

"Your mother send you out here?"

He shrugged.

They proceeded under the guise of never ending time, night revealing nothing. The air stood still, and the temperature dropped, leaving them in shivers. Every now and then, a night bird broke out in song.

Something shuffled in the darkness. Messy steps and movements, like a bull moving toward them. She looked back, body burning with chills. Obioro brought out his pistol, making it dance in the air.

"Drop it," the thing commanded.

They turned to see Afang, holding his dressing knife, eyes wide, hands shaking. Surrounded by Masquerades, faces full of light and shining, full of breathes of air, no costume about it. Nothing human underneath or in the gaze. Pale woven skin in abstract forms, body parts in all directions, but hands holding the census taker, embracing him, leading him.

The night revealing itself.

"Hell," Obioro dropped his gun and stiffened.

"F-f-f-fool," Afang pointed at Obioro. "We drew lots for this. Only one person to come."

"Buuuut…," Obioro's eyes followed the Masquerades. "It's just…"

"Lots." Bolaji brought the words down. It was decisions not made by humans, but by fate, or something else. Like Masquerades. Like Keepers of the night. Superstition kept in check. Lots.

"How do we fix this?" Obioro asked.

The Masquerades smiled and looked at the lights.

The lamps responded, fading and glowing, fading and glowing, fading and glowing. then flaring on fully to life.

They let go of Afang, released him from their grasp. Bolaji's body wished to run, wished to flee, but she stood held in place under the gaze and shadows of them, like they weren't done with her.

The Masquerades stood, then took a step back. And forward. And back. Again. And again, until she realized they were making a pattern.

"Hell," she said.

Their bodies spun as they began to dance, the lights playing out a strange music. Their legs spread out then fell again while they moved around the three of them, dancing, locking them within this space.

Making a big circle like Bolaji's mother's cooking pot.

She looked at the two men, their bodies lost to fear. Bodies contorting, flesh screaming, pulling apart then coming back the way a rubber band snaps, like their ghosts wanted to depart. They let out blood in their screams as eyeballs shook in their sockets, rupturing and losing fluid then coming back. Veins expanded then burst, spitting themselves out. Skin rolled up and out then scarred itself down, in the process of destroying and mending, destroying and mending; all things a pattern. All the while, the Masquerades went on dancing, smiling, loving, embracing.

And Bolaji?

Bolaji had a heart, the bones of it, the flesh of it, pumping blood as it fell from her chest. Bolaji had lungs, increasing with a pressure that just wouldn't allow her to breathe. Bolaji had skin, skin that remained intact as she let out her anguish while her insides suffered, churning, her body acids eating her whole.

And she was tired of being out of control, so she fought, searching for a strength in her body. The Masquerades gave her a pitying look as they moved; they knew her story, they had been watching all this time -- and when she felt a little strength, a little free, less locked in position though still reeling in pain, she clutched a Masquerade and clawed her hand through its raffia skin, squeezing, screaming, and pulling it apart. The Masquerades made her body lock again, no pity now, but the damage was done, and the one she'd ripped open fell into the bushes, hiding itself away with inhuman cries. The sharp night music grew louder and she stood again, ready for her torment, feeling relief for the bit of control she'd finally taken.

Did they expect her to give up without a struggle? To owe obedience? To feel indebted? She was done with that.

And with that, the circle broke for her, only her, the Masquerades bunching to the side, and in relief she fell to her knees, then got back up, her shadow increasing as she stood tall and gave the Masquerades one last blazing look. Then she ran, not afraid of this night or what came of it. And if the men survived, or if she only came back alive, there would be another story of the night to keep fears alive. And maybe she would tell it, make it her own, her tale.

Her heart was racing, but she was alive, fully formed, and whole. And Bolaji was safe.

Whole woman, living woman, lucky woman, brave woman.

End

"Bolaji Has a Heart", by Osahon Ize-Iyamu   First published in Cosmic Roots and Eldritch Shores on October 18, 2017

Osahon Ize-Iyamu writes speculative fiction novels and shorter fiction. He lives in Nigeria. He is a graduate of the 2017 Alpha Writers Workshop, and you can find his fiction in The Dark. You can also find him online @osahon4545.

The illustration "Star-Filled" uses Mo-Nabbach's *Stock Model 33*.

A Possession of Magpies

E.E. King

Catherine Linton has lived above the cemetery on Drakes Bay Lane for as long as she can remember. It is a beautiful old cemetery, edged with slender poplars that grow golden or sprout green as the seasons turn. The whitetail deer wandering between the graves clip the grass, prune the willows weeping over stone angels, and lick the salty tops of the white marble tombs. It is full of bird song and the cooing of mourning doves, the only harsh notes struck by murders of crows and parliaments of magpies.

People picnic there -- young lovers sharing bottles of red wine, old widows and widowers eating sandwiches at the graves of their departed. Catherine wonders if the dead appreciate these visits, if the smell of old grapes and fresh bread salted with tears and memories is welcome food for their hungry souls.

She'd lived on the lane when it ended at the graveyard. Now widened and connected to the state highway, it has become a teeming throughway of the living passing the land of the dead. But Catherine's hearing is dim, and her eyesight cloudy. She tunes out the roar of the cars. She sees Drakes Bay as it was, a small ribbon of pavement, edging past silent tombs and mausoleums.

Winter has been cold. Now that spring is here, she passes the warming days on the porch, on a rocker as stiff and creaky as her bones. She watches the magpies swoop down and gather the souls rising from the graves of the newly dead, curling up from the freshly-turned earth like the soft smoke of extinguished candles. Her eyes are milky with cataracts but she can focus on the magpies because they are so black and white. And on the souls because she's so close to joining them.

What do the birds do with the souls they so carefully collect? Carry them to another world? Soar above the clouds and set them free partway to paradise? Line their nests with these softer-than-featherdown souls? Feed them to their young? She shivers.

Thinking how someday she'll be buried in Drakes Bay, she expects a magpie will claim her. She wonders if a magpie had taken her betrothed, Tommy, when he died so long ago on a battlefield in France. She had been heartbroken, but now the memory is soft and gentle.

As she sits swaying in the sun one afternoon her eyes drift closed. Her breathing grows sonorous, and Catherine dreams of Tommy. It has been so long since she has dreamed of him it seems a visitation.

He stands before her, young and elegant in a black and white tuxedo. He passes beneath a chandelier and the black tails of his jacket catch the light and shimmer with a hundred iridescent rainbows. Tommy opens his mouth, but instead of his melting baritone, out comes a harsh caw and a thud.

She awakens with a start.

A young magpie has smashed into her window and lies near her feet. His right wing is bent oddly. A breeze ruffles his feathers into a glittering kaleidoscope of colors.

Though she can barely take care of herself, she cradles the fallen bird in her withered hand and listens to its shallow breathing.

She remembers how she used to nurse all manner of injured wild creatures -- birds, squirrels, foxes, deer. Tommy had called her Florence Nightingale of the Animals. She smiles at the memory, cracking her face into a million wrinkled folds.

She wraps the bird in a blanket, sets him near a heater, and searches for a place to house him. Beneath her bed she finds a shoebox. The dust rises from it like fog off distant mountains, like souls out of tombs. It's filled with old photos. She empties them onto her bed. The top photo is one of Tommy.

She puts the bird in the towel-lined box and searches out some dry cat food, a relic from an old feline companion. She soaks it in water, placing it and a water bowl in the box.

When the bird wakes, he eats slowly, cocking his head and looking at her with one bright eye, much too knowingly for such a young bird.

Catherine straightens his wing and binds it to his chest with an old ace bandage. She wonders how she manages the delicate work with her knobby arthritic fingers, almost like claws themselves. The bird lies quiet in her hands.

"Smart bird," she says. "You know I'm helping you."

She cares for the bird for weeks, binding and rebinding the wing as needed. It heals whole and strong, though slightly bent. She wonders if his flight will tilt to the left, if he will fly in circles.

The day the bird hops off the table and flies to the old upright piano she knows it's time to let him go, though she flinches at the thought. It seems like forever since she has felt deeply. Now love and loss come crashing back down on her like a wave.

Catherine looks at the piano. Instead of the magpie's dark feather's glistening in the sunlight she sees Tommy in a shining black tailcoat. He is playing "Jeanie with the Light Brown Hair," just like he used to, but instead of Jeanie he sings "Cathy."

He was a real musician. He would play and sing, and she would join in, harmonizing with his smooth baritone. Her throat aches at the memory. Everything she has forgotten comes back - the way Tommy held her in his arms, how it felt like flying when they danced, the lightness in her soul when he told her he would never leave her.

"But you did," she whispers. "You left and never came back."

And now, somehow, Tommy is both at the piano and right beside her, holding out open arms, offering to surround her.

Catherine feels young and weightless. She does not care that this is impossible, she falls into his arms. They waltz round the room in sweeping circles. She wheels around, arms wide. Her heart races. Her head spins.

Her eyes darken, and her legs fold beneath her. She lies curled on the floor gasping for air. The magpie flies to her. His feathers brush her face, but Catherine feels Tommy's black sleeve grazing her cheek. The bird pecks her wrist. Her chin. But now she lies still. He flies out the window, catches an updraft, and is gone.

Catherine isn't found for a week.

A notice appears in the paper. Neighbors whisper how this is a tragic reminder of what can happen when the old live alone. And the house sits empty.

Catherine is buried in the cemetery below her house. No one sees her soul rising like smoke from her grave. No one sees as it is snatched by a magpie.

The magpie swallows her soul. For a moment there is darkness as long and silent as eternity.

So, this is what death is, she thinks. No light, sound, sensation. Only emptiness, never-ending nothingness.

And then she is seeing the world again, but through the eyes of the magpie, circling the boneyard, skimming the treetops, rising towards the clouds on currents of warm air. She is weightless. She is free. For the first time in so long everything is clear.

Magpies are drawn to the cemetery by bugs, berries, the occasional picnic, and souls. And the souls? They have always been drawn to wings and feathers. That's why there are birds. That's why there are angels.

From out of the slender poplars a magpie flies up. His right wing is slightly bent, yet he sweeps through the air as smoothly as a melody, black feathers catching the sunlight and shimmering with hundreds of iridescent rainbows.

He joins Catherine and together they fly into the rising sun.

"A Possession of Magpies" © E.E. King   First published on December 23, 2019 in Cosmic Roots & Eldritch Shores

E.E. King is an award-winning painter, performer, writer, and naturalist.

Ray Bradbury called her stories, "marvelously inventive, wildly funny, and deeply thought-provoking."

She has been published in over 100 magazines and anthologies. Her stories are on Tangent's 2019, 2020, and 2022 year's best stories. Her novels include *Dirk Quigby's Guide to the Afterlife: All You Need to Know to Choose the Right Heaven,* as well as several story collections. She's been nominated for a Rhysling and seven Pushcart awards. www.elizabetheveking.com,   https://twitter.com/ElizabethEvKing,   facebook. com/pages/EE-King   and amazon.com/author/eeking

Still Life

Adam Stemple

The cathedral loomed over the wide Edinburgh street,
its gothic architecture all vaults and spires, gargoyles and chimeras.

Despite its foreboding presence, it went largely unnoticed by the passing crowd more intent on revelry than reverence. I felt an affinity with the old building. We shared the same corner, standing stock still, waiting for fickle Fringe-goers to drop their coins into our collection plates.

Today, I was Rodin's *Thinker*. Fist on chin, my right elbow and left forearm sharing my left knee, bare feet at slightly different elevations as I sat forward on my small wooden stool. My skin was darkened to bronze with theatrical make-up; bicycle shorts the same color gave the illusion of nudity.

I was immobile.

"Wow. Is he real, Mum?"

"Don't touch him!"

"Think he'll move if I do?"

"I said no!"

A few coins clinked into my cup.

Unlike some in the living statue craft, I never went for the cheap laugh, jumping out at tourists after mere minutes of stillness. I never broke for the bathroom or lunch or tea -- if it was daylight during the Fringe, I was a statue on High Street. And I never thanked the punters for dropping coins into my cup. Breaking character for a mere 50p?

Not me.

"Take my picture with him, Jimbo. Wait, wait, OK, now!"

Click. The jingle of more coins.

I learned stillness young, to be like a rabbit freezing in the tall grass, predators soaring overhead or slithering along the ground. Or living in your house. My reflexes were to freeze, though my father would have preferred fight, my mother, flight. Those were certainly their tendencies.

Sometimes, I thought I was part stone. I'd have to be.

"Olé, olé, olé, olé..."

Football supporters.

"Oy! Look at the git in the shorts."

From the south.

"Think he'll move if we tip him over?"

"You tip him. I'll piss on his head!"

Real original thinkers, too.

"All right lads. Move along."

Enter the constabulary.

"Bloody pols."

Police 1. Arsenal 0.

The shadows were stretching all the way across the street now, just tickling my feet, and I knew the day didn't have much left to it. These were the hard minutes, fighting the shakes and twitches that had been building all through the day.

One of the shadows broke away, and a long silhouette glided towards me. Its owner took a position behind my right shoulder, unseen unless I turned my head sharply.

Obviously, I didn't.

"I have been watching you." The voice was old, graveled, unknown. But it triggered a memory from my childhood of a dark corner where my father never looked, an unseen voice soothing me, "Be still, child. Be still and it will be all right."

It was not the same voice, but it was of a type.

A lot of people have been watching me, I thought back, unsettled by the memory, though it had not been an unpleasant one. *And most of them were polite enough to toss a few pence into the cup.*

The shadow rejoined its fellows as the speaker returned to the crowd. As the sun ducked out of sight, I creaked and popped to an upright position, took my tip jar, and headed home. The Shadow and the crowd were long gone.

A few days later and I was on to my second pose of the festival, a standing one this time. I was Michelangelo's *David*, steeling himself for his coming battle, left knee cocked, right arm almost straight at my side, left hand holding an imaginary slingshot over my shoulder. My hair was curled into Grecian ringlets. I was alabaster from head to toe.

"Feck's sake, look at 'im. Is he naked?"

"Cover the wee ones' eyes!"

"Christ, the flippin' Fringe."

I wasn't naked. But the illusion was, shall we say, alarming. And my take was down, accordingly.

"Ooh. Nice body on that one, eh Lizzie?"

"Give him a few bob then, why don't ye?"

Clink. Some patrons of the arts still out there, it seemed. Too bad more like them hadn't been at the World Living Statues Championship in Holland. Maybe then I wouldn't have had my title stripped for being a "poor ambassador of the art form."

Enough, I thought. *Don't obsess over past grievances. Don't worry about the individual reactions. Just. Be. Still.*

Then, with the sun once more sending shadows slanting across the cobblestones, The Voice again.

"I have been watching you." Old and cold. It went on this time. "You understand stillness. But do you understand stone?"

No pleasant memories accompanied it this time.

I understand you're a cheap bastard, I answered silently. I just couldn't help myself.

Shadows merged. Footsteps faded. I was alone.

I played out the David saga over the next two days. Bernini's *David,* lips thin and determined, body twisted, having just released the sling's stone; then Donatello's post-1432 *David,* cockier than the others, perhaps because his foot rested upon the severed head of Goliath. Continuing along in the same vein, I followed with Cellini's *Perseus,* right hand holding aloft the head of Medusa, before going in the other direction completely with Vecchietta's *Christ Risen.*

With each new pose, I could feel myself closer to the ideal. Breathing slowed, eyes blinked rarely, heartbeats grew separate and weak. And when breath was too soft to mist a mirror, when I couldn't remember the last time I'd blinked, when I could no longer feel the imminent tremors and pain -- then I would make the attempt. I would stop my breath, freeze my eyelids open...

And try to stop my heart.
Then,
 for one brief moment,
between one beat of that treacherous organ and the next,
I would be completely, perfectly,
Still.
Until the next heart beat.
The next breath.
The next blink of an eye.

And at night, as I lay in bed, I asked myself, I understand stillness, but do I understand stone?

On the eve of the final day of the Fringe, the image of my father's gravestone came to me, as solid and serene as the man himself never was, and an inspiration for the profession he had unthinkingly beaten into me. *But had he? Had he given me my profession?* The voice from my childhood came back again, and this time I recalled a single cold finger touching my chest.

Be still, child.

This couldn't have happened, but suddenly I had a clear memory of a sliver of cold breaking loose from that stony finger and lodging in my young chest.

The final day of the Fringe arrived and for it I was a doomed saint. *The Execution of John the Baptist* was a tricky and demanding pose: half-crouched, torso twisted, head turned back over my shoulder. I was practically inviting cramps and seizures. But it was worth it. This Fringe had been a journey toward true stillness, the closest I'd come. And I'd brought the crowds with me. There were no more snide comments, no more threats. Just awed silence and the soft clink of coins. To end with a simple pose would be a disservice to them, to me, and to the art itself.

Saint John spent the day waiting for the headsman's axe; I spent it waiting for The Voice. It came at sunset.

"I have been watching you."

I know.

"Do you yet understand stone?"

I thought about the cathedral towering behind me. It was the true stone on this corner: immovable, unchanging.

Unchanging?

I resisted the urge to turn my head the few inches necessary to see the cathedral. There was no need; I knew how weathered and worn it was. In my mind's eye I could see how the years had softened its lines, blunted its spires, drawn tracks in its ancient stone walls. How very different it was from the rough rock dug from the ground! And after being carved and set in place, did it not keep mutating, though its speed was imperceptible to the eye? I finally had an answer for The Voice.

Stone is immobile but not immutable.

"Yes! Never moving, ever changing."

I nearly leapt from my pose. Nearly.

"Meet me tonight," The Voice rasped. "Behind the cathedral. After the moon goes down."

My heart beat fast but unnoticed beneath the folds of my toga. My breath quickened, but my chest stayed firm. Ten minutes remained until sundown.

I kept still.

I lay sleepless in bed, staring out my window as the stars began their slow march across the heavens.

Had The Voice really read my mind?

It had certainly seemed so. I lay still, thinking it would be dangerous folly to meet a total stranger behind a deserted cathedral in the dead of night. Yet I meant to go.

Never moving, ever changing.

The moon made its entrance, robbing the stars of their brilliance. I tracked its passage across the night sky and when it just touched the horizon, I rose.

I dressed, slipped down the steps, and was on the street. A slow walk to Princes Street Gardens, passing by the piked stone monolith of the Scott Memorial darker black against the night sky. Then up the long stone stairs to the Royal Mile. High Street was abandoned. The echoes of my footsteps in the soft silent night air brought with them the memory of my father's footsteps in the hall, after he'd locked the dog in the basement, sent my mom to the store. I was frozen in my room, listening to his approach, trying to stay so still I would disappear.

Be still, child. Be still and it will be all right.

And the soothing voice had been right. Eventually. My father was a force of nature, a wild storm of a man. But like a stone, I weathered him. And eventually, he battered himself to death on the rock face of my stillness.

The thought of myself as stone buoyed me. No longer weighted down by memories and regret, I quickened my pace. The setting moon slipped down behind the hills just as the cathedral rose from the darkness. I circled towards the rear, through an iron gate, and into a walled courtyard of old graves. Shadows and silence greeted me. Then…

"You came," said The Voice.

This time, I spun around. Scanning the darkness, my eyes came to rest on a squat figure standing by the cathedral wall. Gray and still, almost a part of the building.

I nodded. The figure took a slow step forward. I could see now it wore a voluminous cloak with a Benedictine cowl that covered its face with blackness. I took a step back, my earlier buoyancy making a swift and cowardly exit.

"I have an offer," rasped The Voice.

I didn't want to hear any offer. I wanted to be back home in my bed.

"I offer you stone."

The Voice took another step forward but I held my ground this time. What terror could this creature hold that I couldn't stand before? I was sure to have been still in the face of worse.

Be still, child.

My body was a rock as my eyes tried to pierce the darkness in the shadowed folds of the cowl.

"True stillness," The Voice continued. "The silence of centuries."

Be still, and it will be all right.

One more step, and I could almost discern features beneath the hood. But their alignment added up to something I wasn't ready to accept.

"I offer you the passage of time as a furrow the wind carves in your cheek," said The Voice, low and slow.

Be still.

They were not the same voice, but they were of a type. Somehow, this hooded apparition was linked to the voice from my childhood. Linked to me.

It was just yards away now, the shadows clearing from its face.

"And what do you want in return?" My voice sounded thin and fearful compared to their basso profundo confidence.

The Voice lifted unnaturally long fingers to its hood and pulled it back.

Beautiful.

She was gray and worn, with lichen spotting her cheeks. Canines, dulled by centuries of wind and rain, still extended well past her cracked lips. She threw off her cloak, revealing broad veined wings. She spread them out, pumping them in the still air. I felt the rush of wind on my face. It smelled of rough-hewn boulders and hidden caverns deep below the earth.

"Companionship," she said. Folding her wings, she leapt forward, landing catlike on all fours in front of me. "Even stone gets weary of being alone." She sat back on her haunches and ran a taloned finger down my jawline.

I searched her eyes for a spark, a glint. There was nothing. Eyelids, iris, pupil--all stone.

The passage of time as a furrow the wind carves in your cheek...

I nodded to her. "Yes."

"Then be still."

Be still, said the voice in my memory.

I froze as still as I'd ever been. Stiller than the frightened child. Stiller than the broken youth. Stiller than the lonely man.

She placed a heavy stone paw on my chest. I heard the snick of claws extending and felt five sharp points pierce my skin.

She locked her stone eyes onto mine. "Be still."

Then she raked her claw slowly down my chest and I could feel my skin peeling away. The pain was immense yet somehow I knew moving would mean my death.

I kept still.

My chest open, I felt her paw on my sternum, then my ribs, and through the haze of agony I felt her forcing herself through. I swallowed a scream as she touched my heart.

Hot pain turned cold as the one part of me I'd never been able to fully control finally stopped. And did not restart.

"Look," she said.

I looked down at my bleeding torso and saw gray spreading from my quiet heart outward, ribs petrifying one by one. I felt hips, legs, arms, all turn from bone to stone. My flesh curled away like paper before a flame and granite grew in its place. She released me, and I fell forward onto hard knuckles, felt my shoulder blades crack and split as wings sprouted from my back, creaking and groaning.

Then silence.

I spread my wings gingerly, feeling the wind breathe across them.

She sheathed her claws. "Come."

She leapt toward the cathedral and I followed, stone wings defying gravity and dragging my new bulk high into the air. We alit close together and settled against the cool wall. Stone on stone, my eyes ground in their sockets as I looked her way, admiring the strong lines of her feline form, wings half-folded, predatory grin on her long face.

Be still, child.

I was still.

But not for fear and not for my father.

I was still for her.

And for myself.

And for what I had been transformed into.

Moments passed, or possibly years, as there was darkness and light and the cold touch of snow on forehead, the blaze of summer sun on my face. The damp ground scent of spring filled my nostrils and the sweet rot of autumn, too. I saw the stars shift in the night sky and the moon flash past, taking its Sisyphean journey circling the Earth. Then, the feel of rushing, bitter rainwater sluicing through my mouth to the street below, I hear her call to me again.

Reluctantly, I move.

Adam Stemple is an award-winning author of fantasy and fiction. He can be found online at www.adamstemple.com, his site for books, music, art, and more. Check out the Mika Bare-Hand Books Available in paperback and ebook.

Emissary

Joshua Grasso

Then fell a stillness such as harks appalled
When far-gone dead return upon the world

The Unreturning, Wilfred Owens

From out of the cold grey morning mist, a spare, weather-beaten figure moved slowly toward the gates of the Wooden City. He passed through the laborers' quarters, people staring as he limped by. Those that were not too afraid began to follow. He wended his way through a maze of log houses and smoking tenements, pausing sometimes before an old soldier or beggar huddled on the ground, and murmuring to him. No one caught the words, but the old and the wounded would look up with a flickering moment of recognition before their eyes unfocused into the distance again. The fearful backed away, crossing themselves quickly and whispering the names of saints.

As he neared the spires of the White City some of the crowd fell back. He walked on through its mud-caked streets teeming with stalls and horses, as well-to-do Muscovites peered down from their windows in wonder. He clearly wasn't a pilgrim. He wore a long soldier's jacket, the collar turned high, and an old hat that looked to have been pecked by every bird from there to Yaroslavl.

He stopped. "I seek the Kremlin," he said, his low voice dragged up from the depths of his chest.

"Ah…that way!" a drunken man flung out a tremulous arm. "Through Basket Town -- watch your purse! Then you'll see St. Basil's and Red Square."

With a slow nod he moved on, leaving the White City behind him, drawing on more followers. They tramped through the earthy stench of Basket Town, where children caught sight of him and took up the cry, "the devil's come to Moscow!" Merchants came to their doorways and gaped.

A burly, well-fed man stepped into his path. "Who are you? What do you want here?"

"I am a soldier. I seek an audience with the tsar," he said tonelessly.

"No one approaches the tsar. He sits on a gold throne in Heaven by God's right hand and together they look down and rule us."

"God does not rule this city, and the tsar's throne lies in another place. I have come many long versts, and my mission demands I speak with him."

The man gasped. "Leave fool! You'll only cause trouble for us and death for yourself." And then he fled.

An old beggar in a tattered soldier's coat limped forward. "I'll show you the way, brother."

So two ragged men and their ragged followers walked dung-laden paths and log-paved roads until the spires of St. Basil's rose through the mist. The bustle increased, as old women hawked their wares along the street -- silks and cabbages, icons and onions. But the stranger looked only to his prize -- the Spassky Gate, flanked by guards and pikes.

"Now, brother, if you have any fear of God, go no further!" the beggar whispered.

"God is not here, and it is not He who is to be feared," answered the soldier.

The crowd held back, nervous, as the soldier marched forward, like a moth to the flame. He stopped before the guards and stared blankly at the rooftops covered with snow, the gleaming cupolas spinning like tops. The silence grew, and the guards, usually so brave and contemptuous of those few who approached, shifted nervously. The way he stood, straight, arms at his sides, eyes upon them, as if expecting an invitation to enter.

"What business do you have here, stranger?" one young guard asked.

"I seek an audience with the tsar," he said.

The young guard laughed, "Begone, and quickly! My captain would already have responded with this." He waved his spear.

There were gasps, and the crowd shrunk back.

But the soldier was implacable. "I am sent to speak with the great tsar! He will not deny me entrance, for I have fought these fifteen years against our enemies in grueling campaigns. I've fought on the western front, on the eastern steppe, in the southern marshes, in the northern wastes. I've watched my comrades fall by the hundreds, in single battles or over long months and years. I've lain in my own blood at the bottom of a ravine and felt the approach of death like a raven. And I have thought to myself: *Who is this man I live and die for? Whose commands have left thousands torn and dead in the mud of foreign lands? Whose very name I bow to and yet never once have I set eyes upon him. Never once heard his voice.*"

The soldier's words swept through the crowd. A few fell to their knees and removed their hats and kerchiefs. Some wept. The guards lowered their spears at the dread implication: had he bought his confidence with his life's blood?

The captain stepped forward. "Soldier, we applaud your service and welcome you as a brother. But no man can petition the tsar. If he does not summon you not even the greatest can darken his doorway."

"Then strike me down and scatter my bones to the winds. For I have no home to return to, and will fight no more battles in the name of the tsar."

Soft murmurs swept through the crowd.

"You are no holy *yurodivy*," whispered the captain, "appointed by God to speak before the tsar. You are a common soldier, so," he sighed, "go on men, send him to meet his fellows. And may someone claim his corpse!"

The guards advanced, averting their eyes and thankful he seemed to be half-dead already.

"*Stop in the name of the tsar!*" a high voice called from above.

The guards looked up to the battlements, shielding their eyes against the glare of the morning sun. And there, pointing down at them, was the young tsarevna, Ekaterina Alexandrovna. The guards bowed their heads and awaited her will.

"Send him in at once! I'm coming down!"

With creaking and groaning the gates swung wide under ancient ropes and pulleys. The guards parted to make way for the soldier.

Soon the tsarevna swept up, her Cossack Escort close about her.

The guards, the entire crowd, bowed low, their foreheads touching the earth. But the stranger stood impassively.

"Fool! The tsarevna approaches! Bow!" the captain hissed.

Yet he remained unmoving.

The tsarevna paused, then smiled "No, captain. A man who has fought for years, and shed his blood for his country, and watched his own comrades die, has a right to stand before me. Brave soldier, your name?"

"My name has left me, as all those I loved are no longer here to say it. But you may call me Ivan."

"Ivan…" she prompted, searching for his patronymic.

But he only stood, silent, patient.

"In that case, *Ivan*, please follow me. I'll bring you before my father. I'm sure he'll be glad to meet one of his dedicated soldiers."

So Ivan followed Ekaterina, surrounded by her Cossack Escort, into the Kremlin. She breezed through hallways heavy with icons and tapestries, glories never to be seen by most citizens.

Ivan was not bedazzled by the gleam of gold, and his dark eyes looked right through the puzzled glances of servants and boyars.

"Papa's tired," Ekaterina whispered, "from the long work of the wars. He needs someone from among the people who can let him know what is happening in our lands. Whenever I talk to him he says I'm just a child.

He looked at her, his eyes reflecting nothing in the candlelight.

"Don't be shy," she urged him, as they approached the tsar's receiving chamber. "My papa loves his subjects."

Two enormous Cossacks bowed to the tsarevna and opened the door, glaring at Ivan. She led him into the room, plush with Astrakahn carpets and shining with icons of gold.

The tsar relaxed upon a gold throne, as a gusli player plucked solemn notes. A crush of boyars ran to intercept them.

But the tsar roused himself. "Let her through! Katya! And who's this you've brought? Another miserable soul you've taken pity on?"

"Papa, this is Ivan, one of your brave soldiers! He's fought for you on the Western front, the eastern steppes, the southern marshes, and… and somewhere in the north."

"Indeed?" the tsar said, sitting straighter. "Who's your commanding officer, soldier?"

"I've fought under many, your majesty. Most recently General Oleg White-Hair defending the gates of Saratov."

"Katya, you remember General Oleg. He always gave you candies."

"They tasted bitter," she said, "from the mean look in his eyes."

"My dear, you don't become a general by plucking daisies," the tsar laughed. "So how is he, old white-hair?"

"Dead, your majesty. His skull was split open by a Tatar sword,"

"Unfortunate. But you kept Saratov, I take it?"

"Saratov stands, your highness, on the bones and blood of my entire regiment."

"A worthy sacrifice. And those who die fighting for Russia go straight to Heaven."

"That I have not witnessed, your majesty."

The tsar snorted. "You are a simple man! And you fought in the East?"

"Yes, under Vorkuta, and before that, Kashkin."

"Mmm, fine men. They are well?"

"They are both well dead, your majesty. Kashkin was beheaded by a Livonian giant. Vorkuta drowned in the Dnieper with hundreds of men. Only a handful escaped, I among them."

"Yes. The cost of war." the tsar frowned, signaling for the musician to stop. "Would you like some refreshment? French wine, Circassian tea?"

"I haven't come to sip tea," Ivan said, to the astonishment of all. "I'm sent here on a mission of dire importance. And my time is short."

Was the man insane to speak to him like this? "And what is this dire mission?" the tsar asked, like a cat circling a mouse.

"To end the wars."

This man was more than just a soldier, and had a look in his eyes, a snake on his tongue. The tsar gestured for Ekaterina to come to his side. But she crossed her arms and made the same face her mother did when she held her ground. He ordered the boyars out of the room, and a glance at his guards had them move closer. Then he leaned forward and spoke as if unburdening himself of a secret.

"Would that it were that easy. But we do not fight for our own sake! We fight to avenge this and that dishonor, to honor a pact with another land to avenge *their* dishonor. It would take entire books to unravel all the reasons we fight."

"Pacts and honor are great things... but what of human life? Recall the armies, declare a truce, make reparations. Give the survivors leave to mourn and bury their dead. To live and make good lives for their families."

The tsar narrowed his eyes. At this rate Ivan would leave the room like Kashkin, his head in a basket. "Declare a truce? ...I wouldn't know where to begin, whom to speak with. I've tried. Messengers have been sent... and they return to us in a box, sometimes in pieces this small," he said, holding up his pinky. "Recalling the armies would be weak and foolish. And it is they who must make reparations to us."

Ivan's dark eyes stared into the tsar. "Life is the dearest thing a man has, yet you have us risk all while you sit in splendour and drink tea and guard your power."

Ekaterina gasped. The Cossacks put their hands to their sword hilts.

"I humored you for my daughter's sake. No more."

The tsar gestured to his Cossacks. But when they had grabbed Ivan's arms and pulled him back, his coat swung open and revealed the gaping hole in his chest where his heart should have been, and a shirt stiffened with old blood.

The tsar stood. His Cossacks backed away. Ekaterina covered her mouth, eyes wide.

Ivan spread his arms wide, displaying his mortal wound.

"And now you see I am in deadly earnest. Offer yourself as hostage, return with me to World's End until the wars are stopped, or we will come as a flood through the city. In our many thousands -- the dead from all your wars: the Russians, Livonians, Tartars, Circassians... they're waiting for my return, and for you. You see, I cannot simply take your word -- it was you who slaughtered messengers. Yes! I learned it from their own lips when they came to World's End. In the secret councils of the Kremlin you told them peace and promises could be damned. Then you watched as their throats were slit. And you sent them back in pieces."

"Papa! No! No...?"

Ivan's voice tolled out. "The dead can no longer sit idly by and watch their comrades slain for pride and greed. Even as we stand here a thousand lives, a thousand worlds of hopes and dreams are ended, crushed needlessly underfoot. How many worlds must you extinguish to widen your empire?"

"This is witchcraft! Magic! If God wanted me to make peace He would speak in visions, portents. *Retreat is weakness!* I didn't become Tsar of all the Russias by covering my mouth with a handkerchief and averting my eyes. War is proof of strength. This is the business of being tsar – to spill the blood of thousands to uphold the will of God. I am God's chosen on earth!"

"We stared into the face of mindless hell and still did our duty. We died like loyal dogs for you. And this is your answer?"

Ekaterina's eyes shimmered with tears. "Come outside the palace, papa, among the people, as I have, and see the suffering, the tears! We have lost so much!"

The tsar rounded on his daughter. "We have lost nothing! One day this war will end, when we have set the terms, and all the realms bow at our feet! Better to set the entire kingdom aflame, butcher every man, woman and child, than lose."

Perhaps here for once the truth would serve him. "If I were taken as hostage, if I were not here, my generals would not stop the wars, they'd war on each other to take my place, and conveniently find it impossible to make peace and bring me back."

""Then who is dear enough that you will keep a promise?" Ivan's dark eyes turned towards the tsar's daughter.

""No!"

Ekaterina stepped forward, shaking. "I will go. To save you, to save Russia, I will go with him to World's End until you have brought peace."

"No! Take someone else. Take… my chief advisor. Or, his daughter. Yes, take Dragovitch's daughter."

"No, papa, she's my dearest friend!"

Ivan shook his head. "She is not dear to the tsar."

The tsarevitch moved to Ivan's side. "I'll go. I trust you, father. For me you will stop the wars."

She put her hand on Ivan's arm and he walked her to the door while the tsar and his Cossacks stood frozen. As she left, she looked back and smiled at him, her face now dim and indistinct to his eyes.

Wary negotiations slowly untangled terms, territories shifted, but the tsar signed treaties, withdrew his scattered forces.

Soldiers returned home from the Eastern front; cities in the West opened their gates unmolested; trading resumed in the south, as far as spice-laden Samarkand.

At the same time, he called in fierce and powerful shamans from the Siberian forests. Once his daughter was back he'd have them ward all his lands against approach by the dead, and resume his attacks when they were least expected.

But his daughter did not return.

The tsar stalked the parapets, muttering.

His staff and guards seemed to know the deal he had made, the deal with the dead, the deal of a weak man.

How? He wondered, when he'd so carefully had all witnesses put to death?

Then one night as he slept he struggled for breath, and felt a weight upon his chest. He opened his eyes and saw his daughter standing by his bedside.

"Katya! You're back!"

"Not yet. World's End is so far away, such a long, frightful journey, and I have only your love to guide me. Once you honor your promise though,

I'll be back."

"But, I did, child. It's all done. For you." Reaching for her he felt only cold mist.

"But you called for the shamans. To undo it all. You must send them away. It's your only chance Papa."

"They are my only chance to still win."

"You don't need to win now!"

"You don't understand the ways of power child."

She faded away.

The tsar dwindled. He felt sure everyone, his chief advisor especially, was watching him. He was seen, indistinctly, roaming Red Square by the light of the moon, speaking to statues, trailed at a cautious distance by his Cossacks.

Another night, again the pressure on his chest. Greater this time. Katya was near his bedside but he could barely see her pale form.

"Papa, if you don't send them away, you will not be safe."

"The shamans are my safety."

She shook her head and was gone.

Servants grew more fearful of him. They glanced at him out of the corners of their eyes, trembling, wondering if a kikimora was haunting him. But Dragovitch now looked at him with a little smile.

The tsar looked into mirrors, wondering when they had gone so dim.

Another night, and the weight upon his chest was so great he cried out. His daughter, barely a mist, was again by his bedside. "Will you not, for me, send the shamans away?"

"You don't understand child!' He gasped through the pain. "They'll ward the lands, protect us from the dead!"

"If you do not war again, you have no need of their protection. This is my last time, Papa. If you don't send them away, I will not return."

The tsar shook his head and struggled for breath. "Return I say! And I will not war again once the realms are mine."

Pale tears gleamed faintly on her cheeks and she disappeared like mist into the darkness.

And then in a rushing wind out of the void came Ivan, and his voice rang like a leaden, far-off bell. "It is no fulfillment to give with one hand what you take with the other." He reached out for the tsar. "Now you have lost everything."

Neither the tsar's commands for help, nor later his screams and pleas into the empty air, brought any response from his guards.

Next morning, when they found him, stiff, eyes huge, his hands tightly clutching his throat, Dragovitch had the shamans take him with them back to Siberia.

And in the frozen tundra, in the grey of late winter, the shamans buried the tsar of all the Russias, with a stake through his heart, and they salted his grave.

And as Spring returned, Ekaterina, daughter of all the Russias, walked in through Spassky Gate. Quiet. Pale. Living.

THE END

"Emissary", by Joshua Grasso, © Joshua Grasso. First published in Cosmic Roots & Eldritch Shores, November, 2022.

Joshua Grasso is a professor of English at East Central University in Oklahoma, where he teaches classes in subjects ranging from Beowulf to Batman.
In his academic persona, he has published many articles on 18th century novels, Gothic literature, science fiction and fantasy, and comics. But when academia gets him down, he enjoys writing fiction stories that have appeared in publications such as Daily Science Fiction, Metaphorosis, Allegory, Penumbra SF, and Tales to Terrify.

Estevan of the Children

E.E. King

The spirit children, the Angelitos, find their way home following the paths of marigolds, leaving their small footprints in the golden petals. That was why parents made impressions of their newborn's feet even before they were baptized, pressing sole, heel, and each tiny toe tenderly to the ink, then rolling the little feet over white paper, learning by heart the curves and mazes of their children's feet. Then if they were unlucky enough to have their little ones die, they would recognize the tracks their ghosts left when they came home on the eve of Dia de Muertos to spend one day with their families.

When the children's spirits returned to their graves at twilight each November first, the paths between the cemetery and the homes of their grieving parents were filled with golden swirls of marigold petals imprinted with each tiny foot.

But Estevan lost his way. Something he'd rarely done in his ten years on earth. He'd been adept at finding lost children, animals, and objects. His mother Maria Leticia said it was because he'd been born on the feast day of Saint Jude, patron saint of those desperate, helpless, and alone.

He found a grieving widow's wedding ring glistening down in the limestone arroyo. When Señor Diaz's youngest daughter, Magdalena Maria waded into the river and got swept away, Estevan found her downstream clinging to a willow branch and helped her to shore.

So when he heard plaintive cries from an old dry well and found a small white dog looking up at him with eyes as brown and soulful as his own, he naturally slipped over the side to save him. But a stone came loose and he fell. They found his body at the bottom of the well, the dog curled protectively around his still form. His mother kept the dog and called him Vite, little Estevan.

Now, almost a year later, Estevan awoke, slipped from his grave, and in the gray twilight wafted after the souls weaving their way around headstones and grave mounds heaped with flowers, candles, and incense. Gliding past the old, black metal gates of the graveyard, Estevan headed for home, drawn by the yipping of Vite, the scent of sorrow, and the gentle tendrils of loss winding from his home.

Vite leaped joyfully as Estivan's spirit passed through the heavy oak doors. In the kitchen his mother was placing aatole, his favorite sweet agave drink, and a dozen tiny loaves of pan de muertos beside the flowers and candles on his altar. The loaves were made with fresh eggs, blood oranges and wild anise seeds but salted with his mother's tears and sweetened with her longing. Tiny sugar-bright, icing faces peeped from between the folds of dough like hidden sorrows.

Estivan stroked Vite and drifted to the altar, inhaling the essence of the bread into his hollow body, strengthening his spirit with his mother's love. The bread's inner substance filled him with happiness and made his drowsy.

He watched as his mother finished freshly making up his bed with newly laundered sheets scented with lavender and devotion. He nestled into it and drifted off to a sleep different from the slumber of death. Floating on memories, he dreamt of sugar skulls and flying, of mother's kisses and morning light, of playing fetch with a small white dog. Vite snuggled next to him, warming the memory of his bones.

The days were overcast and he was so deep in the dreams of home he didn't awaken until after Dia de Muertos had ended. Vite was nudging him and returning sunlight was flickering in his eyes. He leapt up, called out his farewells, and raced from the house, seeking the path of marigolds, but it was gone, blown away in the breeze, trampled by burros, cart-wheels, and feet.

Estevan whirled about like a leaf in a whirlwind, dazed by the light and noise and motion. The papel picado, the paper pictures blowing in the wind, dizzied him. The sun came pouring down through him and he began to fade. If only he could find home again and hide until next year, but spirits navigate by the pull of darkness that rises in the dust of their bones like a tide, and Estevan could not find that beckoning call. Too much time had gone by. He was lost and the world was a haze.

He drifted through the days and nights fading to a wisp of cloud, dimming until he was paler than a mist. By winter's solstice, he was less than a twilight haze over still water. He knew his time was done. By morning, he would be gone. Even his mother would forget the boy she loved so much, for though memory helps the dead live on, who can remember a ghost that has dwindled to nothing? As he began to disappear, dwindling into darkness, a voice rose out of the night, quavering like light through a storm.

Estevan drifted toward the sound, pulled to something for the first time since he had awakened too late. He found the small spirit of a young boy.

"Why are you crying?" Estivan whispered, his voice soft as a tickle in the wind.

The boy looked up, transparent tears running down his face.

"I can't open the door," he sobbed. "My mother won't let me in. She doesn't want me!" He sobbed, each tear washing away more of him.

Estevasn shook his head. "No, she loves you, she just can't hear you. Because.. because you've died."

The boy's eyes opened so wide Estevan could see into his soul.

"But it's alright! You can rest. Sleep quiet in your grave. It's peaceful in the cemetery. Then, next October thirty-first you can spend the whole day with your family."

"A day! I want forever!"

"Forever it will be. Someday. For now sleep quiet."

"I don't know the way!"

Estevan laid a hand lighter than a gentle breeze on the ghost boy's shoulder. And as he did he could see about him, see a phantom echo of the bright pathway of golden marigolds. Their scent filled him with longing, and strength. He took the boy by the hand, lucent fingers interlacing like braids of mist, and led him gently to the graveyard. With a grateful sigh the boy slipped into his grave.

Estevan readied himself to lay down and sleep, but he heard a cry, soft as sunset, from outside the gates. He drifted out and there knelt a small translucent girl.

"Why are you crying?" Estevan asked. "Are you lost?"

The girl gazed up at him out of wide, night-black eyes and nodded.

"I tried to go home," she whispered. "But Mommy didn't let me in. She... she didn't even see me."

"She can't see you. Just for now." said Estevan. He explained why, gently took her hand, and led her to her grave.

"It's okay," he said. "Now it's time to rest."

"But I'm cold," she whispered.

"If you lie down in your grave, the love of your mother will cover you like a blanket and each November first you can return home and let her memories fill you like a sea of hot chocolate and warm you for another year, until the time we're all reunited." He kissed her softly and she faded back into the earth.

Thus it was that Estevan did not return to the earth that year, or the next, or the next. He stayed behind to guide the lost and the newly dead down the path of marigolds to sleep. Years later, when Vite died, he joined Estevan in searching out lost ones and leading wandering spirits to peace and slumber.

And from that day to this, mothers tell their little ones that if ever they lose their way, in this life, or the next, there is a ghostly boy with a little white dog who will lead them to safety.

The End

"Estevan of the Children" by E.E. King. First published October 31, 2018 in Cosmic Roots & Eldritch Shores

E.E. King is an award-winning painter, performer, writer, and naturalist.
Ray Bradbury called her stories, "marvelously inventive, wildly funny, and deeply thought-provoking."
She has been published in over 100 magazines and anthologies. Her stories are on Tangent's 2019, 2020, and 2022 year's best stories. Her novels include *Dirk Quigby's Guide to the Afterlife: All You Need to Know to Choose the Right Heaven*, as well as several story collections. She's been nominated for a Rhysling and several Pushcart awards.
amazon.com/author/eeking   www.elizabetheveking.com,
https://twitter.com/ElizabethEvKing facebook.com/pages/EE-King

Ice

Diana Silver

Translated by Ashley Cowles

It was on the Ice and in the Storm that I crossed paths with Edmund Hawkings. Had I known how much he'd give up for my sake, I wouldn't have tried so hard to kill him.

Snow blew into drifts across the ice fields. The howling wind
made the ropes sing and tents shudder. A young man in a thick fur coat
plowed through the drifts, face hidden deep in his hood. Edmund. He undid
a tent flap and ducked into Stevens' tent.

The expedition leader sat warming himself by the camp stove. He
looked more at home now than in one of the Royal Geographical Society's
leather armchairs back in London, more suited to the infinite ice fields than
London homes with mounted trophies and the clink of china tea cups.

"Don't bother with your coat, lad. I won't keep you. I just wanted you
to know first."

Edmund stopped fumbling with the clasps of his mitts and looked up.

"When the storm lets up, we're heading back to the ship."

"We're giving up? We can't. Not now."

"I know what this means to you, Edmund. And your father was my
good friend, but the storms will only be increasing now, and the ice shift lost
us miles of progress overnight. I won't let this mission suffer the same fate
as your father's."

"Sir, please, we have to find him!"

Stevens stood and looked down at the young man. "Not in this life, lad.
Now get back to your tent before the worst of it hits."

All I had ever known was the law of the Storm. It raged where it
wished, unstoppable, and I rode with it, whipping the wind across fields and
against glaciers, their edges straining and splintering under the power of it.
I reveled in snow falling so thickly it whited out the world.

From across the stretches of ice, my first impression of Edmund was
that here was a wounded animal, howling its last. Those who give up belong
to the Ice. Riding the wind I slammed into him but he stayed upright. The
boy wasn't giving in. He raged on -- against the Ice that had taken his father,
against the Storm that had torn them apart. Something about him made
me pause. He howled at the Storm? I would send it howling back into his
face. I gathered the currents and circled round. I dove down, battering
down on him.

Then my world shifted. The wind escaped my grasp. I was pulled into
darkness, I was weighted down, confined. I saw the world through a film
of tear-filled eyes. The wind lashed at exposed skin, the cold was as solid

as a wall of ice. I hurled myself about the darkness of my prison, roaring through his mind, while the Storm raged on without me.

"Stop. Stop!" Edmund sank to his knees in the snow, clutching his temples. I shrank back -- he had ripped me from the Storm. If he could do that, what else could he do?

He pushed himself to his feet. I could feel muscles straining, finding balance. His thoughts tumbled over me, an avalanche of alien words and images and meanings.

He tried to head for a tent. Toward *shelter* and *heat,* anathema to me. Panicking, I fought, pushed him away from camp. He swayed and fell. Through his coat the cold sucked the warmth out of him. *Cold* was *danger, freezing, death.* Good, let it help me escape. I fought his attempts to rise. I kept him pinned in the drifts. Soon I could feel the cold creeping up through his fingers and toes, first piercing him like knives, then numbing him. His body was failing.

But Edmund would not surrender. He clung to hard to life, raging and confused, convinced the law of the Ice wouldn't apply to him. So I held him fast and gradually his coat froze stiff. Crystals of ice formed on his lips and eyelashes. I could feel the life seeping out of him and I wondered how someone like this could have pulled me from the Storm.

And why had the Storm abandoned me to him? Traitor! I circled through the dying boy's mind. No, I decided, this time the Storm would not get her due. I wrapped still air around him. I wrung out warmth from the wind's power and shielded him with it while the Storm raged, until the last flakes fell and the last gust of wind whipped the clouds from the pale sun. I was left behind, clinging to Edmund and the barely visible haze of his breath.

Men probed the snow, their search line as solemn as a funeral procession. But this one didn't end as they usually do.

I could hear their shouts as they found him. I could feel his numb limbs move as they lifted him. They carried him and laid him down in a warm place, covered him with furs. I was with him while he slept, felt his fingers tingle with returning warmth. Outside was the creak of ice under men's boots, and muffled voices. Canvas rustled, and for a moment, the sounds became clearer. We weren't alone. Someone nearby was breathing deeply. The visitor stood beside the bed for a long time. Then he touched the boy on the shoulder.

Edmund opened his eyes. "Sir…" he croaked.

"Welcome back, lad."

"What happened?"

"We found you outside the tent ring," Stevens said. His eyes bored into Edmund's. Distress and relief were put aside. "What were you doing outside the camp?"

"The wind… the storm…" Edmund shook his head.

Stevens sat beside the bed. "The men are saying it's a miracle you survived. He sat silent for a moment. "I've seen many strange things in this country. You should be dead, yet you barely have frostbite…" His tone shifted. "It would have meant more delay, and being two hands short the rest of the expedition. When I give an order, obey it absolutely. We're not in London. This is the Pole, and we must trust each other with our lives. If we can't count on you, you're not cut out to be a polar explorer."

I could feel the immense respect Edmund had for Stevens. But those final words struck an angry undercurrent in him.

"As if you could count on my father."

Stevens rubbed his hands together. "Your father was… different. Strange things happened when he was out there. With the Ice." He got up. "We're breaking camp. I gave the men an hour's rest. That's all the time we can afford. We need to be well underway before the next storm hits."

Then he left. Edmund stared blankly at the tent wall.

"Who are you?" he said.

I had no name. I'd been one with the wind.

"You came from the storm," he said. His mind conjured up danger, darkness, bitter cold, destruction.

No. I showed him soaring over peaks and through drifts of powdered snow, gliding across the ice fields and howling through ravines, making the water tremble. Freedom, power.

"The Pole," Edmund said. "You know the entire North Pole!"

The Ice. It seemed the most suitable of the words his mind contained.

"Then you know where my father is!"

What?

"My father. We're looking for his last camp."

His thoughts were of separate places, single viewpoints. But the Storm lives throughout the wind and snow and ice, across the vastness of sky, rising, falling, compressing through narrow crevasses and widening out across the ice fields, always moving.

Edmund threw off the covers. "I'll show you."

Stiffly, he wrapped himself in his coat, pulled the hood up and stuffed his hands into his mitts. He ducked out through the tent flaps. The men readying to break camp gave him measuring looks as he walked past the tent ring.

Edmund plowed up a slope, the snow dry as sand. The snowdrifts didn't swirl with us. They worked against us at every step. The freezing air stung his eyes and further stiffened his limbs. He lived within the frail world of a single body. And I was trapped within it.

The top of the slope was a peak thrust up by colliding ice sheets. He looked down. "Our camp." Little thin tents, sledges, dog teams.

He turned to face the ice field and flung his arms wide. "My father's camp is out there."

What lay before us was an endless expanse of white stretching out to the Pole. The Ice as I'd known it had been filled with dancing wind, but now I looked out over the plains as humans saw it - pure, stark, pitiless. An empty land, frozen and unrelenting. Only the sight of the clouds racing high above seemed familiar. They laughed as they tumbled in the wind, free, unburdened by thoughts. Would I be free of thoughts again? My memories were already being reshaped, impressions from Edmund's senses tumbling over me in waves.

"Ice! My father's camp. Where is it?"

Ice? I am not 'Ice'. I swirled through the darkness of his mind, looking for a way out.

Edmund held his head. "Stop!" Dizzy, he stumbled over a fault. The ice beneath us groaned and creaked and gave way. Edmund yelped. We slid for a long moment, then slammed to a stop, wedged into ice, surrounded by smooth walls. He looked up but there was nothing to give him a handhold. His shouts were dampened by the walls of ice.

He stared up at the tiny patch of sky, his breath becoming ragged.

Can't you see there's no way up?

"Get out of my head if you won't help!"

If only I could.

"They'll never find me. Maybe they won't even look."

I felt too bleak to bite back at him.

Time passed. He began shivering.

"Ice?"

...I'm not 'Ice'. But I'm here. Can you not feel the air? It flows down.

Edmund looked down. Near his feet was a slit, barely high enough for him to fit through lying down.

"Enter that? That ice coffin?"

Feel the wind. It's being pulled down, through to a large open space. Why was I helping him?

With an empty laugh Edmund searched desperately above him again. And still found nothing. His breath hissed out.

"Alright." He gritted his teeth. He slowly wedged himself through the slit and began to slide down.

The gap narrowed and he almost stopped moving. Edmund breathed in ragged gasps. I only understood his fear now. The gap had to narrow but the slightest and he'd be helplessly stuck.

The draft strengthened. The gap widened and we slid down into a cavern, hollowed out and polished by endless wind. High above us, the icy roof glittered in shifting light, lit from above in a multitude of greens and blues flickering across it. Bright patches alternating with recesses in intense darkness. It was a beautiful sight, though it did nothing to make up for what I'd lost.

The beauty of our surroundings had a similar effect on Edmund. He was practically snarling as he looked around the breathtaking cave. He stood atop a shallow ice mound in the center of the cave.

"He was always gone. Always here. He left us again and again. And Mother would cry, but he wasn't there to see it. And I… I needed him!" His hands had curled into fists. "When I finally was old enough for expeditions, he stopped me. 'Too dangerous,' he said, 'Never set foot on the Ice.' Why did he get to leave? Why did he get to risk his life?" His voice was cold and hard. "And now he's dead."

Then what are you doing here?

"I told you, I'm looking for him."

So once you find his camp?

He shrugged.

Then why are you here?

He was silent a long while. His shivering came back. "Whenever he was planning to leave, he'd get this look. As if he were seeing right through us, to something else. His eyes seemed lighter then, the color of ice. I want to know what he was seeing, what he left us for all those times." His eyes swept over the sparkling ice all round us.

"But this…" he said bitterly. "This couldn't be it."

The light changed. The bright colors of the cave siphoned off in just an instant, leaving dark gray. Edmund thought the sun had set then remembered it wouldn't be dark for weeks yet. The air changed too. A strong wind pulled through cracks and hollows in the wall, the power of the sound vibrating through Edmund's body. My spirit leaped.

It was the Storm.

"No!" Edmund stumbled his way past scattered chunks of ice to a way out, but quickly drew back from the roaring wind. He stared at the ice fields becoming obscured under a thick fall of snow. It got steadily colder. He thought darkly of Stevens' intention to break camp before the Storm returned. The fear of being left behind, alone, sapped his willpower.

"Ice. You saved me from the Storm last time."

I don't know if I can do that again.

Edmund's despair was palpable, but he turned to face the outside and set out, as grim at the prospect of being in the Storm as I was excited.

But trapped inside Edmund, the Storm was a different creature. It whipped by us with immense power. It lashed out mercilessly at Edmund. His clothing froze stiff. The bitter cold and dry snow chafed his skin raw. He searched for a way through the peaks and chunks of ice as big as houses. He climbed ice and pushed through snowdrifts, making it over the peak. But the cold began to win out, even as he reached the foot of a familiar slope. He stumbled across something. He reached into the snow and pulled up a broken tent pole. A little further on lay shallow indentations in the fresh snow where the tents had been.

Edmund stopped and stared. They had broken camp. His legs gave way. He lay unmoving in the snow.

Get up. Go after them.

He slowly shook his head. "Catch up with the sledges? I can hardly move." His whole body shook, battered by the blistering cold. "Besides," his voice cracked. "When I die, you'll be free."

Edmund...

"The Storm is here. Go with it."

Until now we'd only fought each other, but now we looked up at the Storm together, his resignation and my sorrow mingling.

If I rejoined the Storm would I be as I had been, part of the winds, a drifting swirl and little else? I only had thoughts after hearing his. How astonishing *to think!* I only discovered desires after feeling his. I was not just of the Storm now, I was also of Edmund.

I moved, reaching with his arms and stretching with his fingers. I'd only been a spectator, vaguely aware of his physical sensations, but now I looked for myself, made myself *feel*. I recoiled instantly. Pain was no minor inconvenience. The biting bitter cold was agony, the exhaustion completely overwhelming, the stiffness of his limbs frightening. I shook -- what courage it took to face the Ice in a body this fragile and defenseless! There was a grandeur in how he resisted death, in the rebellious way he clung to life.

Edmund's thoughts were almost incoherent. I felt openings for me to slip away. But this wasn't how I wanted to leave him. Not while I could act. I'd see him safe first. The Storm howled at us, but I rebuffed the wind and chased the snow until it swirled around us, leaving us untouched. But that wouldn't be enough.

Edmund. You need to get up.

He blinked.

The Storm won't hurt you, I promise.

He couldn't speak. *Ice...* He wanted to tell me he couldn't go on, but stopped. *Okay.*

I helped him struggle to a stand.

I was as aware of the Storm as I'd been before, but now I could lead it. I stretched out his hands. I took his arm and swept it around. The wind understood us, changing direction. I turned it further and it was at our back. It cleared a path through the drifts for us.

Edmund looked around in wonder. It was his turn to see through my eyes. *This is the Storm?* he asked. *It's beautiful.*

He could feel it gliding around us, he could sense the vast expanse of never-ending Ice -- in the glaciers, beneath our feet, beneath the struggling dog paws pulling the sledges scraping through the snow further down the ice fields, tracks covered as soon as they were made.

"The expedition!"

Edmund had a sense of direction unknown to me, alien to the Storm. Slowly, stiffly, he pointed, and the Storm turned. He strode forward, pushed along by the wind.

He was panting and shaking, but exhilarated.

Dying here would mean becoming one with the Ice? His breath steamed out as he laughed. *I don't think I'd want to die anywhere else.*

We shared a smile.

But we had a long way to go. Yet, our spirits soared. When the Storm raged off past us we glimpsed a line of black dots against the white expanse of Ice. Someone must have spotted us, as they halted. We drew closer and a figure broke away from the group: Stevens, coming back to meet us.

"Edmund Hawkings," he said as we stood face-to-face. "Welcome back."

Edmund expected to be admonished. This time even Stevens had to be astonished by this miraculous escape from death. But Stevens was quiet for a long time. He searched Edmund's eyes.

Edmund wanted to look away.

No! We moved the Storm. We needn't cast our eyes down for any man.

"Your father had the same look in his eyes," Stevens said finally. Then he lent Edmund support and they headed for the expedition.

Edmund was dimly aware of the other men watching and waiting. For the first time, he understood his father.

He looked back over his shoulder.

Ice, we will always come back here. This is home.

A gust of wind blew across our face. A silent *'Until next time'* from the Storm.

The Ice stretched across the horizon. The sight stays clear in our memory, even for the short times we're away in those strange places built by humans, where softer winds reign.

Diana Silver lives in an old Dutch town where old ghosts never stop whispering their stories. She has written historical fantasy which has been published in the Netherlands.

from Sir John Gielgud portraying Prospero, in The Tempest

excerpt from

The Tempest

William Shakespeare

You elves of hills, brooks, standing lakes, and groves,
And you that on the sands with printless foot
Do chase the ebbing Neptune, and do fly him
When he comes back; you demi-puppets that
By moonshine do the green sour ringlets make,
Whereof the ewe not bites; and you whose pastime
Is to make midnight mushrumps, that rejoice
To hear the solemn curfew; by whose aid,
Weak masters though you be, I have bedimmed
The noontide sun, called forth the mutinous winds,
And 'twixt the green sea and the azured vault
Set roaring war; to the dread rattling thunder
Have I given fire, and rifted Jove's stout oak
With his own bolt; the strong-based promontory
Have I made shake, and by the spurs plucked up
The pine and cedar; graves at my command
Have waked their sleepers, oped, and let 'em forth
By my so potent art. But this rough magic
I here abjure, and when I have required
Some heavenly music, which even now I do,
To work mine end upon their senses that
This airy charm is for, I'll break my staff,
Bury it certain fathoms in the earth,
And deeper than did ever plummet sound
I'll drown my book.

for
Young People of All Ages

Witch on a Broom, by Ida Rentoul Outhwaite

Puck, Arthur Rackham

excerpt from

A Midsummer Night's Dream

William Shakespeare

Over hill, over dale,
Thorough bush, thorough brier,
Over park, over pale,
Thorough flood, thorough fire!
I do wander everywhere,
Swifter than the moon's sphere;
And I serve the Fairy Queen,
To dew her orbs upon the green;
The cowslips tall her pensioners be;
In their gold coats spots you see;
Those be rubies, fairy favours;
In those freckles live their savours;
I must go seek some dewdrops here,
And hang a pearl in every cowslip's ear.

Eternity, Stephanie Law

The Lady & the Moon

Matt Dovey

Ella raced up the forest path and dropped her armful of branches and twigs in the firepit. Granddad was still a ways down the hill, his creaky legs making him slow, so Ella lay down at the cliff's edge, the long grass tickling her chin. The salty summer wind blew her hair into twists like rope as she looked out over the sea. Small white clouds floated below, skimming over the surface of the water, their tops picked out in copper by the setting sun.

A huffin' and a puffin' behind her meant Granddad Judd had made it to the clifftop, so she sat up and turned to face him. He eased hisself onto a weathered log by the firepit. A large conch shell on a length of twine swung loose from his baggy shirt as he leaned forward and took a bottle of seaweed wine out of his bag.

"Ella," he said, bottle shaking in his hands, "how old are you now, girl?"

"Nearly eight," said Ella, puffing her chest out to look as grown up as she could.

"Nearly eight," he chuckled. "Back in my day, we called that 'seven'." He took a gulp of the wine and put the bottle back into the bag, and pulled a tinder box out in its place. He knelt down and tried to strike a spark into the kindling. His fingers fumbled the steel half a dozen times afore he gave in. "Ella, girl, light the fire for an old man."

Ella rolled her eyes and took the flint and steel. She lit the fire in two clean strikes.

"Thank you, girl. Now, do you know why you're up here tonight?"

"'Cos mother told me I had to come."

Granddad's eyes wrinkled up as he smiled. "I'm sure she did. And why did she tell you to come?"

"I don't know. Is it 'cos I said I wanted to be a fisherfolk, like Henry? Henry always said you knew lots about fishin' 'cos of how you'd done it so long."

"Leastways your brother learned some manners from his mother. Do you truly want to go out onto the sea?"

"Yes, Granddad. All the boys say it ain't for girls but I don't see how that matters none to the sea."

"You know, I don't reckon it does neither. I reckon all that matters is you know how to respect her."

"How'd you mean, Granddad?"

Granddad Judd got a funny look in his eyes, like he did when he told his old stories. When he spoke his voice had gone kind of odd, as if he was reciting something important, and it rumbled like the waves.

"Ella... do you see the sea?"

"Yes, Granddad."

"Do you love the sea?"

"Yes, Granddad."

"Do you know why you must love the sea?"

"No, Granddad."

"Then let me tell you of the Lady... "

"The Lady used to sit in the sky with the Moon, a brilliant white glow trailing her as she danced around him. The Moon hisself was a smooth and flawless disc in those days. Anything done beneath their light was seen as blessed, and many a child was conceived and born under their gaze, as the stars themselves were born to the Lady and the Moon.

All the world knew her, and all the world loved her, and she bore a hundred different names across every country: Whisperer of Stars, Swain of Moon, Ember of Life; She Who Births Light, She Who Gifts Goodness, She Who Sees All and Ever; Singer, Giver, Lover, Bringer, Mother, Wife. For thousands of years the Lady and the Moon watched the fortunes of men turn through hope and tragedy and joy and grief, but you see we were only a curiosity to her and nothing as compared to her true love.

"Yet one man looked up and saw not love or grace, but opportunity. Opportunity for hisself, with no thought as to the cost.

"We do not speak his name where the sea might hear us. He was a sorcerer of an old lost empire, a man with the power to direct and divert the weather as suited his ends. But the problem with power is there's no satisfying that particular thirst, and no matter how much he had, he never had enough. And so he came to devise a plan whereby he could make hisself king of all kings, paramount authority in all the world.

"Pleading a secret quest to his Emperor, he organised hisself a great ship crewed by mutes, a crew that could tell no tales, and set off from the shores of the known world. He sailed out to the farthest part of the known oceans, where no birds glide for fear of the distance, and he used the Moon hisself to guide his way. In those days, you see, the Moon sat still in the sky, and sailors everywhere would navigate by him. And so it was this way that the Moon betrayed his love, without malice, without knowledge, but to his eternal sorrow.

"As the ship came to rest beneath the Moon, he sent all the crew sent below, and stood on the forecastle with a cloth across his eyes. He spread his arms wide," Granddad spread his arms, "and sent great threads of thought out into the sea around him. With a vast effort he pushed his will out down the threads and calmed the sea all round, turnin' its surface flat as glass for an enormous distance. Then he tilted his head back and began chantin' and singin', a high, keening note that he sent up through the sky to catch the ear of the Lady.

"Now, nothing had ever called to her like this, and naturally she was curious. When she looked down to the world to see what was callin', she saw her love, the Moon, reflected perfectly upon that still ocean, with his bright light hiding the ship. Astonished and delighted, she dove down, wanting to dance in this new night sky.

"The sorcerer prepared hisself, eyes shielded from her beauty by his blindfold, and waited his moment. As soon as the Lady pierced the surface of the water he snapped tight his threads," Grandad *clapped* just then, and Ella jumped, "and he tied them about the Lady, binding her to the sea.

"It had been in his mind that he should subdue the Lady and use her glamour to bring kings to their knees, prostrate before her. But he had not reckoned on her wilfulness. As soon as the filaments of her imprisonment wound around her, she knew what had happened, and she raged. Oh, how she raged! She struggled to break free of his trap, but it was all in vain.

"As she twisted and writhed so too did the sea twist and writhe, and the sorcerer's ship was smashed and upturned and lost to the depths. And so the Lady undid herself, for in drowning him she drowned all hope of ever escapin' her bonds, and doomed herself to forever be tied to the sea, parted from her love.

"There were storms that night the likes of which have never been seen since. Grief tore at the Lady and the seas tore at the coasts, wrecking boats and villages and families alike. Whole towns fled inland to escape her wrath, leaving behind all their homes and livings so that they might survive the night."

Granddad fell silent, and Ella guessed he was thinking of Grandma, who'd died in a storm before Ella was born. Now that Granddad wasn't talking none, Ella noticed how hard the ground was where she'd shuffled closer, so she shifted her legs to try and get comfortable. Granddad noticed her again, blinked back his tears, smiled a sad sort of smile, and continued in a cracked voice.

"The Moon was still high in the night, and had seen all this happen. He began to weep, and his tears fell across the sky, great streaks of fire across the heavens. Ever after was his face scarred, as you see it now, witness to his torment.

"Seeing his anguish the Lady subsided, wracked with guilt at the loss she herself had caused, her own tears filling the sea with salt and regret.

"The Moon travels endlessly above the world now, searching in vain and unable to see through the waters that tie the Lady down. And as he moves across the sky, so she strives to be with him, the oceans swellin' and shiftin' so they can be closer. So were the tides begun and named: yearning tide and weeping tide, lovers' tide and mourners' tide.

"When you ride upon the ocean, girl, you ride upon the Lady, and to love the sea is to love her. She'll always repay that love if you keep it true.

"As you head out into deep waters you'll see the great whales of the oceans, and hear how they call to the Moon with a song of love that she taught 'em.

"As you watch on a calm night you'll see the Moon reflect perfectly as she tries to gather him close to her.

"You'll stand on sandy beaches and see turtles come up to lay their eggs where the Moon will watch over them.

"And when storm clouds cover the night sky and hide the Moon you'll learn it's time to batten down the hatches and huddle 'neath decks, for the Lady will cry when his face is hidden from her, and in her sorrow she will forget you ride upon her. But when the storm has passed she'll repay your courage with gifts, and never is the fishing so sweet as when the Lady feels she owes you.

"This is how it is, girl. This is the truth of it and the heart of it, and for your sake I'd have you learn it well. You must truly love the Lady, for when you're out there she's all that's lookin' after you, and all that'll bring you home safe.

"You'll love others, aye, in time of course, but you'll love her first and above all, and when your time comes to go you'll not be set in the ground like most folk but set free to swim with her forever in the moonlight, held deep in her bosom and swayed into the everafter with her song in your heart. This is our life, girl, our way, and it is hard, but by the Lady and the Moon, it is ours."

Ella sat in silence. The red of sunset had given way to the deep blue of night, though the breeze was still warm and heavy with salt. The Moon hung low on the horizon.

"You still want to be a fisherfolk then, girl?"

"Yes, Granddad."

Granddad Judd nodded in satisfaction. He started to root around in his bag, and when he didn't immediately produce anything, Ella reached over and fished out the bottle of wine by its neck, gently proffering it up for him.

"No girl, not that. This."

Granddad pulled out a beautiful conch shell similar to the one he had round his own neck. A piece of twine was threaded through a hole by the opening. He tied it round the back of Ella's neck and let the shell rest against her chest.

"It's a bit big isn't it, Granddad?" she asked, holding it up in front of her face.

"You'll grow into it, girl. You'll need it for a lot of years yet."

"What's it for?"

Granddad grasped his shell in thick fingers and held it against his ear, motioning for Ella to copy him. She did as he showed, eyes widening as she heard a soft whooshing sound inside.

"This is a piece of the sea, girl. Now, the Lady loves every part of her domain, and she won't ever let go of any of it. That's her you're hearing right now. So you wear that shell, and the Lady knows you're hers."

Ella nodded solemnly, shell clutched tight to her head.

Granddad pushed hisself up from the log, in that stiff way he always moved when he'd been sitting too long. "Come on girl, give me a hand. I want to sit and watch the sea a while."

Ella jumped up and took hold of his arm, steadying him as he took a shaky step towards the cliff's edge. They sat themselves down on the grass with legs dangling against the rock face, their feet over empty air, and backs warmed by the fire. Together they watched the Lady churn beneath the light of the Moon, the smell of her salty tears in the air and the yearning tide rising up the beach beneath them.

"The Lady and the Moon" © Matt Dovey First published June 2016 in Cosmic Roots & Eldritch Shores

Matt Dovey is very tall, very British, and probably drinking a cup of tea right now. Though his surname rhymes with "Dopey", any other similarities to the dwarf are purely coincidental. He lives in a quiet market town in rural England with his wife and three children, and cannot adequately express his delight in this wonderful arrangement. He is the host of PodCastle as of 2022, and has fiction out and forthcoming all over the place: you can keep up with all this at mattdovey.com, and find him timewasting on Twitter as @mattdoveywriter.
Art: "Eternity", by Stephanie Puiman Law https://www.deviantart.com/puimun/art/Eternity-260427094

Tree With Chalicotheres

Vicki Saunders

First, there was the tree. When it was very small, builders ran a bulldozer over it. The tree retaliated by sprouting eleven trunks and uncountable branches. Forty years on, it loomed over the house. Trunks sprawled into mossy platforms, twisted and joined, leaving gaps like parted lips.

Then, there was the house: old growth cedar nailed into a rambler. In 2005, it belonged to Carla. She fought the house's straight lines with frilly lamps and splashy wallpapers.

Last, there was the girl. Magda, just thirteen, dark hair, dark eyes. Lanky. Wiry. Strong. She had a bed in the house, but spent most of her time high up in the tree.

Carla explained to visitors that "The child has no" (her mouth made a big lipsticked 'O') "one. My ex-husband's -- who dropped dead after I dropped him. His batty old mother kept the kid 'til she dropped dead. Then -- no one. What else could I do but take her in?"

Magda would cover her ears, run out the door, and climb into the tree. She'd built her own place there: plywood walls, big soda bottles for windows, blue plastic wading pool for a roof.

"An eyesore," Carla would say. "Like you. You ever consider wearing something besides a ratty t-shirt and jeans? Like something the dog chewed. You could at least comb the sticks outta your hair."

Magda looked down at Carla, chewed up by the beauty parlor, with eyelashes like centipedes. She looked up into the tree. "Feathers, not sticks," she said under her breath. "Braided into my hair."

One afternoon she overheard Dillon, Carla's boyfriend, down on the deck. "I'm sick of cleaning leaves out of the roof gutters. You should cut that tree down before I break my neck."

Magda admired Dillon for his craggy looks, slow drawl, vast t-shirt collection, knit hat, peppery smell, and lovely way of sorting Carla out. But the tree was none of his business.

Carla nodded along. "Without that tree, we could have a lawn. That tree sucks the life out of everything."

"Plenty lives under it," Magda shouted down through the branches. "Just not what you want."

Nothing happened for a while, which was how things normally went for their household, except the tree kept growing. When branches began to scrape the roof, Carla called in Harris Davis, a born-again Christian with a biblical beard and a chainsaw.

Magda climbed the tree when he arrived.

Harris said, "I can't cut this tree until you remove that child."

"I'm not coming down till Harris leaves," she announced.

"You'll be down by dark. Nasty things come out in the dark. Things with teeth," said Carla, showing her own extra-white ones.

But Magda was still in the tree the next day, and Carla called the fire department. They didn't possess a ladder truck though, so the firemen hauled out an extension ladder. Magda climbed into branches too slender for the weighty child-rescuers. Frustrated, they milled about below, cajoling Magda through a bullhorn until Dillon said, "Leave her be. She might fall."

The firemen left.

The following day, Carla called in the police, but they didn't attempt a climb. They knew their limitations, and called Child Protective Services, which sent a woman too skinny for her suit jacket and hair scragglier than Magda's. Magda was reluctant to come within conversation distance. The woman looked like she could climb.

"Hello, Magda. My name is Leah. Are you afraid to come down?"

"No!"

"Is anyone hitting you?"

"No one hits me!" A lie, but a true lie. No one hit her for the joy of hitting. Carla hit when Magda did things she considered bad. This was hard to predict, but Magda didn't think it would help if Leah-like persons told Carla to quit.

"Dillon…has he ever…"

Magda shouted, "No." She climbed higher, losing herself in tender new leaves. Leah withdrew. The daylight faded. Rain set in.

Magda slipped into the tree house and wrapped herself up in her grandmother's quilt. If she stared at that quilt long enough, she could see stars or baby's blocks. Rain pattered on the wading pool roof. She slept.

Magda spent the next day reading, but ran short of provisions. The morning after that, she stared down at the north-side neighbor's hounds, wondering how bad dog food tasted. On the south-side, a brown-haired, brown-skinned boy about her size sat on a deck, slurping cereal from a bowl.

"Psst," she said.

The boy looked around.

"Up here."

He looked up with wary eyes. Carla would say shifty.

"You got any more cereal?" called Magda.

"Oh, you," said the boy. "The girl who won't come down. Why not?"

"They'll cut down the tree. You know how old this tree is? It took a long time to get this way. They shouldn't just cut it down. It's older than them. It was here before them."

"Can I come up and see it?" he asked.

"Can you bring food? And something to drink?"

He went into his house, reappeared soon after with a backpack stuffed full, and almost leapt up the trunk. He hunkered next to Magda, handing her a corked stoneware flask.

She pulled the stopper and sniffed. Ginger beer. "Nice. Thanks."

He looked all elbows and knees, scabby, skinny, and a little dodgy. His eyes, now that she saw him up close, were streaky brown-green, like the crowns of trees.

"I'm Tycho," he said. "Like the astronomer. He could see farther than anybody. Most people call me Ty."

"I'm Magda."

They settled into the tree house to eat.

"How old are you?" she asked.

"How old are you?"

"Thirteen."

"Me too."

"How come I never saw you before?"

"Homeschooled," said Ty. "And we don't get out much. Okay if I look around?"

"Sure," said Magda.

Ty climbed up to a dark cavity in one of the trunks. Bits of bark rattled down.

"Watch it," Magda shouted. "Something nests in there." She'd heard scuffles and thrums, and she left that trunk alone.

But Ty swung himself in.

When he didn't pop out right away, Magda climbed over and peered inside. The top of his head was sinking out of sight. She hadn't realized the hole was that deep.

"What's down there?" she called.

Sneakers thudded. "Wow," his voice rose up from below. "Lookit."

She boosted herself in, braking her downward slide with her arms, stirring up an earthy, musky smell. She squeezed through a tight spot, ear pressed against wood. Tiny ticking, crawling, and chewing noises startled her, and she slid to the bottom, catching herself on a network of roots when the hole opened to a low dry-stone chamber.

There was an arched door in the winding courses of stones. Something bugled from the other side of it and the door cracked open. They scrambled backwards. A horse-like head emerged, A coppery blaze ran down its nose, and a blue mane sprouted from its shoulders. It lumbered out the door to reveal a heavy, potbellied body. Long forelegs ended in hooked claws like a sloth's. Its back slanted down to short, muscular hind legs. The beast was the size of a llama and moved like a gorilla, knuckling on its huge claws. It raised its head and bugled again, wiggling a flexible snout.

They fled, scrambling back up the hole. Once out, they climbed into the highest branches that would hold them.

The creature snuffled and thrummed and slowly clambered out after them. It settled into a low, fat crotch, curled its upper lip, sniffed, reached out with its hooks and pulled leaves into its mouth, making a humming noise through its nose Its mottled brown and yellow pelt blended seamlessly with sun-dapples. Surrounded by leaves, it was nearly invisible.

A chainsaw drowned out the hums. Harris was back. But before the saw could touch the tree, the beast flicked out a long arm fast as a striking snake, hooked the saw, and tossed it. The blade sunk into the ground and the engine stalled. The beast carried on stuffing itself and chewing loudly. A heavy musk wafted from it.

Harris Davis shouted, "Dear Jesus, child. Be careful!"

Carla shrilled, "Magda, what are you doing? You could have killed Harris!"

"I didn't do it," said Magda.

"Don't give me that. Get down this instant! Harris is going to cut down the tree."

Harris said, "Not 'til you remove that child." He pulled his chainsaw out of the ground. "'An undisciplined child disgraces its mother.' Proverbs 29:15. I'm going home to reset my saw."

Carla clicked across the deck on her espadrilles, shouting and waving her arms, "You're Incorrigible!" She swayed back into the house.

The beast suspended itself like a hammock, resting its head on its chest, hidden again amidst the leaves. It started to growl -- no, snore.

Magda climbed just a little lower. Its ears, spotted and fuzzy, flicked a bit. She scrambled back up and turned to see Ty with a wide grin splitting his face.

"What's so funny?" said Magda.

The beast sighed and shifted its rear.

Deck doors slid open. Pizza smells drifted out. "Magda, sweetie, I got your favorite: pizza marinara," said Carla in a syrupy voice. Something bad always happened when she used that voice. She put a platter down on the deck table. "And lemon-lime soda."

The beast opened its eyes.

"Melted mozzarella. Soda-in-a-bottle." Carla clicked her nails on the glass, then swiveled around and went back inside.

The beast whinnied and climbed down, dropping onto the deck.

"Maybe it will eat her," said Magda.

"He's vegetarian," said Ty.

The beast sat on its haunches and grabbed a soda, popping off the cap with a claw and sticking its long blue tongue inside. It swallowed a few times, hooted, swung back up the tree and scooted down the hollow trunk. Through the deck doors, Magda could see Carla, turned away from the deck, on the phone, coral-pink lips flapping.

Ty said, "I gotta go. You can come with me if you like. Just... my gran's a little... different."

"I lived with my gran. Old ladies... " Magda shrugged. "They're weird."

"My gran likes to keep things."

"Like a hoarder?"

"Kinda."

"I gotta stay with the tree," said Magda.

When the light turned long and golden, the beast returned to the low branches, and so did Harris, revving his chainsaw. Magda moved into view. Harris cut the engine and roared, "Mrs. Fiascuro, you said the child was out of the tree!"

"She can take care of herself. That tree is ripping my roof off. Plus it has vermin."

"It's not, and it doesn't," said Magda.

"It has you, doesn't it?" said Carla. "Get down now. Or we'll girdle the tree. That'll kill it." She moved toward Harris's chainsaw.

Harris Davis said, "Excuse me, ma'am, but you cannot touch my chainsaw."

"So I'll get an ax!" She went round back toward the woodpile.

"Harris," Magda said. "Don't cut it down, please."

"What's your name? Mary?"

"Magda."

"All due respect, Magda, but there are lots of trees in the world, and some of them are in the wrong places. You should respect and obey your mother."

"She's not my mom," said Magda.

"I'm happy for you. But it's just a tree. There's plenty others. Ponder that, Mary." He hefted his chainsaw and drove off.

Carla returned with the ax, raised it, and struck. Magda screamed. The ax bounced off the trunk. As Carla raised the ax for a second blow, the beast swung its arm, flicking the ax into Ty's yard in a motion too fast to follow.

Carla howled, "You want blood? I'll give you blood!" But she just retreated to the house and locked the door behind her.

Magda hoped Carla had seen the beast. That would teach her. She took refuge in the tree house and wrapped her gran's quilt around herself. Eventually, she slept.

When Magda emerged next morning, the beast had gone, but below Carla was pacing the deck. It was like being above a snake's pit

When Carla disappeared into the house, Ty climbed up and joined Magda. He brought cold pizza and soda.

A car pulled up. Ty scrambled out of sight. Leah pattered onto the deck, craned her neck, and said, "Good morning, Magda. Carla tells me you're incorrigible. She's requesting mediation. You'll need to come to the agency."

How foolish could Leah be? Harris Davis could have the whole tree down by the time she and Carla got back.

"You realize you could be declared a Child in Need of Services? And if you're declared incorrigible, you might be adjudicated? Detained? The mediation is scheduled for tomorrow. If you don't come, we'll only hear Carla's side."

Magda just looked up into the crown of the tree: branches rising over branches, drifts of leaves soughing in the wind. Ty was scrambling into the hollow trunk.

Leah shook her head and left.

Magda followed Ty down into the tree. At the bottom, light poured from the open doorway. Through it they could see smoke curling through the gaps in a dome-shaped hut of huge interlocking bones. Beyond the hut stretched a treeless plain, the horizon lost in a yellow haze.

The light from the doorway turned Ty's eyes an elvish leaf-green. He extended his hand to her and drew her through. The air poured over her skin like syrup. Everything slowed, heartbeat, and thought, and breath.

The beast shambled out of the hut, knuckling along on its hooks, and bugled.

From the hut a voice as dry and cracked as old book bindings called to them. "Come in. Come in!"

"My Grandmother," Ty said.

"But the beast!"

"He's fine. He's hers. Come on, the beast will look after the tree." He led Magda through a gap in the bones into the hut. Sunbeams shot through colossal ribs, lighting an old woman bent over a fire. Like Magda's gran, she wore a cardigan, but hers was sleeveless and long past her knees. Tattoos laddered her bare arms and curled over half her wrinkled face, shadowed by dozens of short braids stiff with red clay. She smelled like wool and pitch, smoke and ancient dust.

"Grandmother Nal, Magda," said Ty. He sat on the earth floor and Magda sat beside him.

Nal held out a rounded ivory cup with uneven edges. Magda held it close and looked. The inside was imprinted with the marks of delicate veins. Tight, wiggling lines joined the bits of ivory together, and when, all at once, she recognized what she held, she trembled, and nearly dropped it.

"This is a human skull!"

"The cup belonged to grandfather. This cup was grandfather. She's honoring you. Drink."

Grandmother Nal's black eyes snapped at Magda. Magda took a sip of the smooth pale liquid and relaxed. Like yogurt. Pungent, sour, bubbly. And a taste of almonds and sun-warmed grass. Warming.

"Pass it," nudged Ty.

Magda handed the cup to him. Someone's thoughts had been inside there once....

Ty turned the cup, sipped, and passed it back to his grandmother. She turned it, sipped, and placed it in a hollow in the floor. She smiled at Magda, showing crooked, yellowed, but strong teeth.

"Gran, we can't keep Magda..."

The old woman nodded. "Time's a-moving."

Magda stared as they passed back through the door. It had been morning, but moonlight shone down the trunk. "It's night!"

"They say time is a river. My gran stores things in the backwaters. Time eddies. Slowest of all in Chaco's place. She's held on to him a long time..."

"Why didn't you tell me you knew the beast? What is it, anyway?"

"A chalicotheres. They're mostly extinct, since um... probably since the early Paleolithic? I don't remember exactly," said Ty. "Like I said, Gran's a hoarder."

"What is your gran that she can do that?"

"Just Gran," said Ty.

In the tree house, Magda wrapped herself in her grandma's quilt, spent. She heard Ty's door slide open and shut, and then sleep took her.

She panicked when she woke up, but the tree was fine. Ty showed up with dried figs, bread, and cheese.

"So you live in a time eddy?" she asked.

"Gran doesn't like me growing up too quick. She admires how you won't come down, but you can't stay up here forever. Come stay with us."

"Maybe I could stay here forever, with the eddies."

"You can't use them that way. They don't go steady. And Gran can't keep letting Chaco out. She'll lose him. She doesn't like me being out too much either. You saw the tattoos on her arms? She cuts those lines when she loses someone. Rubs their ashes in the cut, makes the mark."

"Too many cuts and the tree falls."

"Gran heals. Nal means pine needle, a part of the whole tree, the forest, all connected. Like this tree. Its roots go deep and wide. They'd have to kill the forest to kill it."

Ty left and Magda sat, thinking about her tree twining with an entire forest.

The deck door clattered. Carla stood below, wide-legged, hands on hips. "Time for our mediation, sweetie."

"You can't kill this tree."

"Suit yourself," shrugged Carla, and drove off.

Harris Davis showed up minutes later. Magda waved to him.

"Still holding out," he said. "Well, 'Blessed is the one who perseveres under trial.' James 1:12." He put on his climbers.

"Harris, you said you wouldn't cut the tree down with me in it."

"And I keep my word." He looked past her.

She caught a movement and was starting to turn when Dillon grabbed her round the waist from behind.

"You're not the only one who can climb," he said.

She kicked and howled. Dillon hung on. She kicked again, hard.

"Dang it, Magda, that hurt. Look, we're going to take down the tree. You can make it easy or hard, but you can't stop us."

She went limp.

"That's not easy," said Dillon.

"It's not hard, either," retorted Magda.

Dillon and Harris bundled her into what Carla termed "Magda's room," a loft at the top of the house with a cot, a dresser, and racks stuffed with Carla's clothes.

She gave them the filthiest look she could muster.

"You don't want to get in the way of a chainsaw," Dillon said. "I've left you pizza and soda." They locked her in.

Harris Davis started his chainsaw up. It roared. Branches crashed. Magda looked out the window at the two-story drop right into Harris's growing branch pile. She unzipped the vinyl covers of Carla's clothes racks and tore down camisoles, capris, pants suits, fake pashminas; Lycra, linen, silk, spandex; tangerine, turquoise, cream and leopard-spotted; all reeking of Carla's perfume. She ripped them into strips and braided them into a technicolor rope.

Another look out the window made her speed up the destruction. Finally, she anchored the finished rope to the dresser, cinching it with bras and yoga pants. The men had seven trunks down by the time she'd got her escape route set. Beneath the branches, she spied the wreckage of her tree house.

The tree-butchers were intent on their work. Magda dropped the rope out the window and shimmied down. As the saw revved, she retrieved her quilt.

She took a last look at Carla's wardrobe, hanging from the window in a festive braid. The butchers were still engrossed. Magda scrambled over onto Ty's side of the fence, clutching the quilt.

She wriggled through thick rhododendrons to Ty's deck, drifted over with dead leaves. She tapped on the door. No answer. If Harris or Dillon looked up, or if Carla returned, they'd see her. Magda dropped down into a basement window well and pushed at the window frame. It opened just an inch and then stuck.

The whoosh of an approaching car. She pushed harder. It gave all at once.

She slipped through and dropped down to the floor. Honeyed air, slow heart, long breath. A time eddy. They didn't go steady. She might never get back.

But at that place in time, where they were killing the tree, where she had destroyed Carla's clothes, where she'd be adjudicated, detained, locked up, Magda had nothing to lose.

In the dim light, she made out pots and figurines; axes -- copper, bronze, iron, single, double, corroded green and red; potshards and bones curling around a forest of standing stones, amphoras, spindle whorls, and jeweled crowns all spilling into each other in swirling interlocking heaps, blocking the way, blocking the light. After working around dozens of piles, she found herself back where she started. Maybe. She shivered and called, "Tyyyychooooo."

A muffled hoot. She stumbled toward the sound, found wooden steps, stumbled blindly up, and fell into Ty as he opened the door.

"They cut it down," said Magda.

Ty pulled her into a hall lined with chests. He took the quilt from under her arm and spread it out on a wooden, iron-banded chest. "Sit. I'll be right back."

He came back with a plain thick mug of steaming brown liquid.

She sniffed. Cocoa. With marshmallows. "I lost the tree," she said. She felt like a treeless plain, horizon vanished in a yellow haze. She put the mug down and cradled her head in her hands.

Carla's shrill scream from next door came like the whistle of a train. A small smile flickered across Magda's face. "Is your gran here?"

"She'll be back. She likes it here. This house, it's made of the bones of old trees. Old friends. Your house too -- cedar and fir, a thousand years old. But young to Gran. She remembers.

"Gran asked me to give you this." Ty pressed a walnut-sized orange lump into her hand. Like a rock, but warm and light. "Rub it between your hands," he said. "Then sniff."

Magda rubbed and sniffed. It smelt like a pine forest on a sunny day. She held it up and it glowed in the light. "There's a face on it," she said. "Huge wide eyes and a mouth with a slight smile."

"Yeah," said Ty. "That's amber, fossilized from a forest alive back when Chaco was born. Like a time eddy. The face was put on later. Gran says it's supposed to be her. She said to tell you nothing lasts forever but some things last a long, long time.

"Some things come back."

Magda spent the night in a feather bed under her gran's quilt, the amber strung round her neck. If she stared at that quilt long enough, she couldn't tell which way was up. She could see stars or baby's blocks.

Ty pulled her out on the deck the next morning. They looked up into the crown of a tree: branches rising over branches, drifts of leaves soughing in the wind. She counted, twice. The tree had sprouted twenty-four trunks.

<<END>>

"Tree With Chalicotheres" © Vicki Saunders. First published July 21, 2017 in Cosmic Roots & Eldritch Shores

Vicki Saunders lives on an island in the Pacific Northwest where you can't see the houses for the trees. You can find other stories by her at Three-Lobed Burning Eye, and archived at Ideomancer. She distracts herself from writing by laying out publications, cooking, and gardening.

The High Priestess, by Howard David Johnson

The Book of Winter

Caroline Friedel

A snowstorm howled around the cottage that night like
a wild beast on the prowl. Having fed and milked the goat, Lentetje sat with

her straw dolls by the fireplace. Her parents' gloomy whispering filled her with worry. There was so little food left. When she caught the words "goat" and "slaughter", she covered her ears.

Just then a knock echoed through the cottage. The family turned to stare at the door. There was another knock, more urgent this time.

Lentetje scrambled to her feet and pushed a chair to the door. She climbed up and opened the small lookout window.

Beneath a thick hood, frosty blue eyes the colour of a frozen lake gazed at her. A white beard hid most of the man's face, but there were dark shadows beneath his eyes. At the sight of Lentetje, his face lit up with a smile.

As she smiled back her father lifted her away from the door and stepped to the lookout. Seeing the old man, he relaxed a bit. He searched the darkness behind the man, but the whirling snow was impenetrable.

"You're alone?" her father asked.

"Alone, and old and tired. Just looking for shelter for the night."

"Papa," Lentetje whispered, "let him in, please. It's so cold outside."

Her father's hand went to the bolt.

"Pieter, again?" Lentetje's mother twisted her hands together. "We've barely enough for ourselves."

He turned to her. "We can't leave him in the storm, Lieke. He'll freeze to death."

With an apologetic look at her, Pieter shut the lookout and unbolted the door.

The old man stamped his boots, brushed the thick snow from his coat and slowly made his way in. "Thank you, sir. I'm Talvi."

Pieter pushed the door shut against the wind and snow. "I'm Pieter. This is my wife Lieke. Please, come sit by the fire."

"Thank you," Talvi said. "First though…" he lowered his heavy sack to the floor with a sigh of relief, pulled out a bag, and held it up. "Food."

Lieke took the bag as if it were treasure. When she looked inside and saw the turnips, onions, parsnips, and cheese it held, she drew a breath. "So much. We can't take this much from you."

"Don't worry," Talvi said. "I'll soon reach home."

"Where it will also be needed."

"They should still be well stocked."

"Where's home?" asked Lentetje.

"Lentetje, let him rest," Lieke told her.

Talvi pulled off his heavy coat and Pieter hung it by the door. With a contented sigh, he sank into the chair by the fire and closed his eyes.

Thanking him, Lieke went to prepare a meal and Pieter stoked the fire. Lentetje planted herself cross-legged on the floor before Talvi.

"I'm Lentetje," she said.

"It's an honour to meet you," he said with a small bow of his head.

"Where's home?"

"On the far side of the hills. I haven't been back for years though, not since the end of autumn."

"Much will have changed, I'm afraid," Pieter said. "These long years of winter have left their mark everywhere."

"That's what I fear."

"We were well stocked from the years of summer," Pieter said. "But if winter doesn't end soon… "

"We'd have more if Pieter hadn't been so generous with our harvest," Lieke said. "Everyone who laughed at us for stockpiling in summer came begging once winter dug its claws in." The parsnips danced about under the vigour of her chopping.

"I couldn't let them starve, could I?"

She said nothing but now the parsnips nearly flew.

Talvi turned to Lentetje and gestured toward his sack. "Would you like to see something I carried with me on my travels to the north?"

Lentetje nodded eagerly, jumped up to get the sack, and dragged it across the floor to him. He drew out a package wrapped in waxed cotton. The whole family looked on as he unfolded it layer by layer to reveal a heavy book bound in blue linen.

The cover said *The Book of Winter* in frosty blue letters edged in silver. On the title page, it was written again, encircled by snowflakes, ice crystals, and icicles that shimmered and sparkled in the firelight. Lentetje's eyes widened. Talvi smiled and turned the page.

Lentetje gasped. A fiery red, violet, and gold sunset was mirrored in the smooth ice of a frozen lake. Behind the lake rose a forest of spruces and firs capped with snow. Talvi turned the page to reveal a vast snow-covered plain, the snow crystals sparkling like diamonds in the winter sun.

"All the ways winter can be," he said. "So beautiful and so terrible. So magical and so merciless."

Page after page, the beautiful images drew them into the book. They saw cottages with fluffy coats of snow and warm light in their windows, frozen waterfalls gleaming in the sun, and savage blizzards. Christmas roses and holly berries, red against the white snow, deer, kestrels, snowfinches and grouse, next to barren, wind-swept ice fields.

They took it all in with widened eyes. When Talvi turned the last page, they were startled to find themselves back in the cottage.

"I wish there were a Book of Spring too," Lentetje sighed.

Talvi gazed softly at her. "Perhaps there is."

"She has never known Spring," Pieter explained. "She was born at the end of the last one."

"I remember autumn," Lentetje said. "The trees had leaves like fire, red and orange. I want to see leaves again. And flowers."

"Spring will return," Talvi said. "Soon."

"You can't know that," Lieke said.

"But it's true! Just as the legends of the North tell, Spring, Summer, Autumn, and Winter are not just seasons, they are humans as well. And each of them has a book that is the source of their power."

"Why hasn't Spring taken their turn then?" Lentetje asked.

"There was a witch, a very powerful witch--"

"Hmm." Pieter looked sceptical.

"Truly! She lived far to the north, where on the coldest nights even the air freezes. But she wanted warmth and green living things. So she stole the Book of Spring."

"Spring should have guarded it!" Lentetje cried.

"Oh he tried. He fought bravely. But he was no match for the witch, and in the end, though she didn't mean to, she killed him."

Lentetje hid her face in her hands.

"But she soon found it's not the book that makes one a season. One must be born to it. When the witch killed Spring, a new Spring was born. But..." Talvi sighed.

"But what?" Lentetje asked fearfully.

"A new season was always born well before the old one died. But now, this new Spring was just a baby. So the other seasons drew out their time to let Spring grow, and they searched for the book until they had exhausted themselves."

"Seasons get tired?" Lieke raised an eyebrow.

"Of course. Summer and Autumn did their best, but each had to rest in the end. When Winter's turn came, he searched for years, though weariness crept into his bones. He yearned to go home, but he knew without the book everything would die beneath endless ice."

Lentetje wrapped her arms around herself. "He has to find it."

"He has! The witch had it hidden in an ice castle high in the sunless frozen north. But he found her. And under the flickering Northern Lights,

Winter and the witch fought. She raised ice dragons. He shattered them with hailstorms. She called forth an army of frozen ghosts. He blew them away with a blizzard. She shaped giants out of frost crystals. He brought down an avalanche on them and on the witch. He almost left her to suffocate…"

Lentetje stared at him wide-eyed.

"…but he didn't. He pulled her free, and built a prison of ice to hold her in."

"Perhaps the ice in her heart will melt if she's brought to where the seasons change," Lentetje said.

Talvi smiled. "That's a good idea for all the Seasons to talk about. But first Winter has to take the book to the new Spring."

"And then it will be Spring?" Lentetje asked.

"And then it will be Spring."

"That was a good story," Lieke said with a smile as she carried the stew pot to the fireplace. "And soon, we'll have good food."

That night in her small attic bed, Lentetje dreamed of things she had never seen -- fat buds unfolding into blossoms and young leaves, soft green grass sweeping the hills, delicate flowers unfurling.

When she woke in the morning, the storm had passed. Through her small window the clear cold dawn sent new light.

Lentetje climbed down the ladder to the first floor where her parents slept and then down the creaking steps to the ground floor. The fire had burned low and the armchair by the fireplace was empty. Talvi's coat and sack were gone and the bolt on the front door was drawn back.

Tears burned her eyes as she looked at the empty chair, then she gasped. On the table -- his book!

But no, though it was shaped the same, the colour was a soft green. Was this… She held her breath and looked at the cover.

'The Book of Spring' was written on it in white letters outlined in gold. Inside, the book's name was encircled by blossoms in soft, bright colours and green vines twined around the letters. She recognized them from her dream!

Her fingers shook as she turned the page. It was blank. She searched the whole book. Blank. All blank. Her breath trembled at the edge of tears.

-- *You have to fill it.* It was Talvi's voice, soft and far away.

Lentetje looked around. "Where are you?"

-- *On my way home. But if you need me, ask in your thoughts, and I will answer.*

-- *The book is empty.*

-- You have to fill it.

-- I? You mean I... I am... Spring? Her hand shook as she reached out to touch the page. It stayed blank. *-- Nothing happened!*

-- Give it your dreams.

She closed her eyes and in her mind the strange, beautiful shapes from her dreams came to life.

A picture formed on the page to the soft scratching of an invisible quill: icicles melting and snow sliding off the roof of a cottage just like their own. She cradled the book and hurried outside. Icicles were dripping in the first warm sun Lentetje could remember.

It would be long before their roof lost its burden of snow, but in her mind and on the next page the retreat of snow began to reveal pale green grass sprinkled with clusters of small white flowers. Their delicate white bells trembled above the melting snow.

"Snowdrops," she whispered. Her mother had told her about them. As the invisible quill swept across the page, flowers in yellow, white, red, and purple unfolded, sketched out petal by petal and leaf by leaf. Bright blue star-shaped blossoms spread across the green meadow.

With the rush of images appearing in the book, she began to tire. She needed rest, but she knew that as the days passed Spring would spread through the book and the land. She could glimpse it all, in memories she never knew she had and in fleeting images of dreams to come.

"Blooming trees, green fields filled with wildflowers," she whispered. "Hyacinth, daffodil, primrose, bluebell, lilac, peony. Animals! -- sparrow, stork, rabbit, deer, fox. Fish jumping in lake waters. Dragonflies, lightning bugs, bees, butterflies. Warmth, growth, life."

On the other side of the valley, Talvi looked up. The sun had come out from behind the clouds and its golden rays washed over him and the fields all round. A laugh of joy escaped his lips. He opened his heavy coat, raised his arms and danced slowly in the melting snow.

END

Caroline Friedel, a scientist by heart and by training, is currently associate professor for bioinformatics at the LMU Munich. She has published >60 scientific articles and two other short stories: "The Tale of the Storyteller", part of the anthology "In Memory: A Tribute to Sir Terry Pratchett", and, in MYTHIC Magazine (issue #4), "The Anthropomorphic Personification Support Group".

Artwork: "The High Priestess", by Howard David Johnson. David works with oils, acrylics, pastels, colored pencils and digital media to create his realistic fantasy and mythological paintings. His website is filled with beautiful work on many different themes. https://www.howarddavidjohnson.com/

Star Falls by Toshio Ebine

A Ladder to the Moon

Naoko Awa

translated by Toshiya Kamei

Keiko was given a rabbit for her birthday. Not a toy, a real rabbit. Small and cuddly, she had snow-white fur and brown eyes. Keiko loved her and named her Mimi.

She was a gift from Keiko's great-grandmother, who walked with a cane and lived in a nearby town. She told Keiko, "It's easy to care for a rabbit. But there's one thing you must remember. Rabbits love the moon. And the moon also loves rabbits. So make sure Mimi doesn't escape on a full moon night."

Keiko nodded, stroking Mimi's silky fur. Mimi gazed up at Keiko.

Autumn came. Time to celebrate the Moon Festival, with dango dumplings, susuki grasses, and gentian flowers were placed in the windows. But Keiko was a little worried. And when a round peach-colored moon rose and loomed large in the eastern sky, she became more worried. It seemed to stare at her and say, "Your rabbit will be mine."

"Oh no, this is serious!" Keiko ran into the yard and peeked into the hutch. The rabbit sat quietly in a furry bundle, legs tucked under, her eyes gleaming mysteriously.

"Mimi!" she called. But the rabbit kept gazing out into the sky. Her heart began to pound. She gathered Mimi into her arms and hurried back to her room.

Keiko laid Mimi on her bed. "You'll sleep here tonight." She locked the window and closed the curtains, but still she worried. The moonlight might seep through a narrow gap in the curtains. She covered Mimi with a blanket. "No need to worry now. You're safe." She went to sleep cradling her rabbit.

But a strange song woke her at an odd hour.

> *"Lula, lula, lula,*
> *I weave a ladder from my own silver light*
> *Lu la la la*
> *Come, bunnies, from home take flight.*
> *Lu la la la*
> *Climb the ladder to me on this moon-lit night."*

Keiko sat up. The room was dimly lit. The curtains were swaying in the breeze. Mimi was gone.

She jumped out of bed and pulled back the curtains. The window she had locked tight was open, just enough for a rabbit to slip through. The moon's song was spreading across the night sky.

Keiko climbed out the window and ran in search of her rabbit. She looked behind the shed and in the shadows of the thickets, but no bunny.

"She must have gone past the gate!"

Keiko mustered her courage and opened the back gate.

And gasped. There, instead of the apartment building, post office, and supermarket, she saw a field of silver susuki grass swaying under the moonlight, spreading as far as she could see.

"I must be dreaming," she thought, yet she couldn't help but step out into the field.

"Mimi-chan! Mimi-chan!" she called.

A chorus of voices said, "Hurry! Your rabbit is running away!" It came from Gentian flowers blooming nearby. "Look. She's climbing a silver rope ladder."

Keiko saw a narrow path winding through the field. It led to a silver ladder woven of moonlight trailing down from the sky.

Keiko thanked the gentian flowers and ran towards the ladder.

Rabbits were lining up and climbing. She spotted Mimi in the line. She had a white ribbon around her neck.

"Mimi-chan, don't go!" Keiko shouted.

But moonlight-enraptured rabbits pay little heed to humans. By the time Keiko reached the ladder, Mimi was already climbing.

Keiko touched the ladder. It was soft and supple. She began to climb. The higher she climbed, the lighter she became, and the larger the moon became. Her hair danced with the wind, her pajamas swelling out like a sail. She felt as light as a flower petal.

Just as she thought she was close enough to touch the moon, she heard a rifle shot.

She shut her eyes in fear. When she timidly opened them again, she was standing in a vast field. Gold susuki grasses stretched as far as she could see, their tassels tossing like horses' manes, and a new, larger, golden-yellow full moon hung above the field. The stars were larger too. Moondrops were falling like dew, onto the field, onto Keiko's hair and pajamas. But where had all the rabbits gone?

Then she heard a sound behind her. She turned and saw a bearded man. She could tell he was a hunter. He was wearing a fur vest and had a rifle slung across his shoulder. He was holding a rabbit he had just shot.

Keiko turned pale and began to tremble.

"Finally, I've shot one," the hunter said with a smile. "I want one more because I've got two daughters." Then he ran off through the field, singing:

"Rabbit magic in the full-moon light
Their fur is velvet delight,
Their eyes are rubies bright,
Their meat delicious stew alright!"

"Oh no, that's terrible!" Keiko thought. Panicked, she ran, calling "Mimi-chan! Mimi-chan!" After a long while she came upon a small tent and heard girls laughing.

Softly she asked, "Excuse me, have you seen a white rabbit?"

A black-eyed girl popped her head out the tent door. She was about the same age as Keiko. Behind her was another girl who looked just like her. "We're waiting for rabbits, too," they said in unison.

Inside the tent was a large steaming pot on a stove.

"The pot is ready," said one of the girls. "We've chopped vegetables.

"We're just waiting for rabbits," said the other.

Keiko stood silent in shock.

"Have you seen our father? He carries a rifle. He'll bring us rabbits.

"You can stay for dinner if you like. Rabbit stew is delicious," said the girl softly.

Keiko stared silently at the girl. Do such sweet girls really eat rabbits? she wondered. I can't believe it.

The girl flashed her a friendly smile. "Did you know you can become pretty if you eat rabbit meat? Once a year, on a moon-lit night, we climb the silver ladder with our father to eat rabbits. He makes us vests from the fur. On moon-lit nights, their fur is smooth as velvet. That's because they want nothing but the moon. If you catch them on their way to the moon, their fur is velvet, their eyes are rubies, and their meat makes a delicious stew."

Keiko turned pale and walked away before the girl finished. She searched desperately for Mimi.

On the breeze came a gentle voice asking, "Who are you looking for?"

She followed the voice to a cluster of evening primroses.

"My rabbit," Keiko said, hoping for help. "She wears a white ribbon around her neck."

The flowers nodded, "Ah, we have seen her. She just jumped out of the susuki grass and has started to climb the ladder woven by the moon of golden moonlight. Look!"

Keiko turned and looked out over the fields. She spotted the golden ladder leading up into the sky towards the moon, and saw a small white ball of fur climbing it. Mimi. Keiko started to run.

The flowers called in chorus, "Wait! Wait!"

The tallest evening primrose said, "Rabbits are too fast to catch on a moon-lit night. If you just chase her there's no way you can catch her. You must make your rabbit sleep."

"How?"

"Cover her with a yellow handkerchief."

Keiko checked her pajama pockets, but found she had only a white handkerchief.

"I'll tell you what," the evening primrose whispered. "Pluck a lot of our petals, put them in your handkerchief, and rub. That will tint it yellow. Hurry, hurry!"

Keiko hesitated. She didn't know if she should pluck petals from such warm-hearted flowers.

As if the flowers had read her mind, they said in unison:

"Don't worry about us. We'll bloom anew tomorrow. We're evening primroses on a moon-lit night."

The hunter had killed rabbits to make his daughters beautiful. She would be hurting flowers to get her rabbit back. Her heart trembled with sadness and regret.

"Close your eyes. Hold your breath." Keiko quickly plucked petals and wrapped them in her handkerchief. Because she knew the pain the flowers felt, she too closed her eyes and held her breath as she rubbed the handkerchief. When she gently opened it, it had turned from plain white to yellow, imprinted with flowers.

"Thank you!" Keiko said. She ran to the golden ladder, and climbed. More and more golden dewdrops covered her the higher she climbed.,

"Stop looking at the moon!" Keiko called, but Mimi kept climbing and staring up, moon-struck. Then Keiko waved the handkerchief. Mimi stopped and looked back at her. She caught up quickly, wrapped Mimi in the handkerchief, and held the rabbit softly in her arms.

Suddenly Keiko heard the hunter and his daughters singing in the distance and the susuki grass and evening primroses were nowhere to be seen. There was only the moon and the stars, and herself on a long golden ladder holding Mimi quiet in her arms.

Hurry! Keiko told herself. She started back down the long ladder. One hundred steps, two hundred, three hundred… When she reached the ground, she was at the back gate of her home. The empty lot she always played in was there again. She could see the apartment building and the post office. She stood in her pajamas, bathing in the moonlight and a cool breeze, Mimi sleeping peacefully in her arms

She opened the gate quietly, stood on tiptoes at the window of her room, and slipped in.

As she snuggled into bed, Mimi in her arms, she thought of calling her great-grandmother in the morning and sharing the secret of how to keep rabbits safe: "Great-grandmother! I've learned how to keep rabbits from escaping on a moon-lit night. Before the moon rises, cover her with a yellow handkerchief and she will fall fast asleep."

the End

Naoko Awa

Planet Plain by Toshio Ebine

We are pleased that the first publication of this story by the much loved children's author Naoko Awa was in Cosmic Roots & Eldritch Shores on Sept. 15, 2019, with the kind permission of her estate.

Naoko Awa (1943-1993) was a much loved, award-winning writer of modern fairy tales. Born in Tokyo, she grew up in different parts of Japan. As a child, she read fairy tales by the Brothers Grimm, Hans Christian Andersen, Wilhelm Hauff, and *The Arabian Nights*. In 1962, while in college, she made her literary debut in the magazine Mejiro jido bungaku. She earned a degree in Japanese literature from Japan Women's University, where she studied under Shizuka Yamamuro (1906-2000) During a literary career that spanned three decades, she published numerous books, including *Mahō o kakerareta shita* (1971), *Kaze to ki no uta* (1972), *Tōi nobara no mura* (1981), *Kaze no rōrā sukēto* (1984), and *Hanamame no nieru made* (1993).

Translater Toshiya Kamei has an MFA in Literary Translation from the University of Arkansas. He is the translator of books by Claudia Apablaza, Liliana Blum, Carlos Bortoni, Selfa Chew, Espido Freire, and Leticia Luna.
His translations have appeared in The Magazine of Fantasy & Science Fiction, Clarkes world, and Strange Horizons.

Artwork by Toshio Ebine. *Planet Plain*, July 22, 2013, and *Star Falls* Dec 30, 2011 By Ebineyland. Toshio Ebine, ebineyland@gmail.com

Autumn Leaves by Franklin Booth

ZEPHYR'S FAIR CHILD

Scott J. Couturier

Fickle sprite of middle air: your blue hair
& azure eyes dazzle me to delight.
I spot the surplice of sunlight you wear,
sparkling as you spin in dizzying flight:
a crown of acorn for your elfin brow,
stout sword of thistle-sting strung at your side.
I see you strut upon a willow bough,
then – disappear! with effervescent glide.
Ever have I craved the Perilous Call,
hearkened for Mab's overture, stood in rings
of mushroom on eves when evil things crawl,
yet no sight have I had – save of your wings!

Fitful faerie of cloud, zephyr's fair child;
you vanish, but my soul remains beguiled.

"Zephyr's Fair Child" © Scott J. Couturier. First published in Cosmic Roots &
Eldrtich Shores October 23, 2020
Scott J. Couturier is a Rhysling-nominated poet and prose writer of the weird,
liminal, and darkly fantastic. His work has appeared in numerous venues, including
*The Audient Void, Spectral Realms, Tales from the Magician's Skull, Space and Time Magazine,
Cosmic Horror Monthly*, and *Weirdbook*. His collection of Weird fiction, *The Box*, is
available from Hybrid Sequence Media, while his collection of autumnal & folk
horror verse, *I Awaken In October*, is available from Jackanapes Press.
Currently he works as a copy and content editor for Mission Point Press, living an
obscure reverie in the wilds of northern Michigan with his partner/live-in editor
and two cats.

ACKNOWLEDGMENTS

As Carl Sagan said, to bake an apple pie, one must first create the universe. This is also true of an anthology. It rests on so many nested levels of support, it's turtles all the way down.

I'd first like to thank all readers of this book; where would we be without readers? Then, with great appreciation, thanks to the writers and artists who generously donated their wonderful work. I am grateful to our great team of first readers and editors at Cosmic Roots & Eldritch Shores, our online magazine, where most of the stories in this anthology were first published. I'd also like to thank Andrew Burt, for his very helpful advice at various stages of the project. I'm grateful too for the publisher's group started by B. Morris Allen, where the idea for creating benefit anthologies was first discussed. Thanks to Eugene Sadko; his font store is where I found the Ukrainian fonts used at various points for titling.

I am grateful for the internet and the people who created it and those who maintain its open and free use, allowing ideas, news, and creativity to spread and connect around the planet. Thanks to those who write code, worked printing presses, carved out the first letters, spoke the first word... stretching on back eventually, to yes, the creation of the universe. We live not only in this moment, but also within the outpouring bestowed on us by untold generations and millennia, and with luck we get to add something from our own self to the stream. So fundamental thanks to our universe, to its kaleidoscopic potentials, and to the chances we each have to unfold potential in our own individual way and breathe it to life.

WRITERS & ARTISTS

THE WRITERS AND ARTISTS IN THIS ANTHOLOGY DONATED THEIR WORK IN SUPPORT OF UKRAINE.

Cover Art: Tempus Fugit, by Artur Rosa
Artur S. Rosa began working with computer graphics in 2006. You can find him on twitter at https://twitter.com/ArturSRosa and on deviantart at https://www.deviantart.com/arthurblue

394   Acknowledgements

Non-attributed images by Fran Eisemann with stock from Omnia

SCIENCE FICTION

Front page: Illustration for "Red Planit", published on November 30, 2019 in Cosmic Roots & Eldritch Shores

"The Abraxas Conjecture", by Akua Lezli Hope, akualezli@gmail.com. First published here in this anthology, To Ukraine, With Love.
Akua Lezli Hope uses sound, words, and materials to create poems, patterns, stories, music, sculpture, adornments, and peace. She has been in print since 1974 with over 400 poems. Her collections include *Embouchure: Poems on Jazz and Other Musics* (Writer's Digest award winner), *Them Gone*, Otherwheres: Speculative Poetry (2021 Elgin Award winner), and *Stratospherics* at the Quarantine Public Library. A Cave Canem fellow, her honors include the NEA, two NYFAs, an SFPA, and multiple Rhysling and Pushcart Prize nominations. She has won Rattle's Poets Respond twice and launched Speculative Sundays, an online poetry reading series. She is the editor of the record-breaking sea-themed issue of Eye To The Telescope #42, and of *NOMBONO: An Anthology of Speculative Poetry by BIPOC Creators*, a first of its kind, from Sundress Publications (2021). She won a 2022 New York State Council of the Arts grant to create Afrofuturist, speculative, pastoral poetry. She exhibits her artwork regularly, sings her favorite anime songs in Japanese, practices soprano saxophone, and prays for the cessation of suffering for all sentience, from the ancestral land of the Seneca, the Southern Finger Lakes region of New York State.

"The Resonance of Light" © Geoffrey A. Landis, First published in ReVisions, Czerneda and Szpindel, eds., DAW Books, Aug. 2004 Geoffrey A. Landis is a science-fiction writer and a scientist. He has won the Hugo and Nebula awards for science fiction. He is the author of the novel *Mars Crossing* and the story collection *Impact Parameter (and Other Quantum Realities)*. As a scientist, he works for NASA on developing advanced technologies for spaceflight, and is a member of the Mars Exploration Rovers science team. He was the 2014 recipient of the Robert A. Heinlein Award "for outstanding published works in science fiction and technical writings that inspire the human exploration of space." More information can be found at his web page, http://www.geoffreylandis.com.

"Glory Whales" © Marc Criley. First published August 23, 2020 in Cosmic Roots & Eldritch Shores
Marc A. Criley began writing in his early 50s, and his stories have since appeared in Cosmic Roots and Eldritch Shores, Beneath Ceaseless Skies, Galaxy's Edge and elsewhere, so one can rest assured it's never too late to start writing. Marc and his wife "manage" a menagerie of cats in the hills of North Alabama. He maintains a blog at marccriley.com and carries on at Mastodon as @MarcC@Wandering.shop. Slava Ukraini!

"Spicer's Modest Success" © Jared VanDyke. First published November 27, 2018 in Cosmic Roots & Eldritch Shores.
Jared VanDyke is a deaf librarian who met his true love through Japanese crime dramas. He earned his MFA in Creative Writing from Goddard College, which taught him how to write the fun, quirky, and touching tales featured in Cosmic Roots and Eldritch Shores. Feel free to contact him at WriteVanDyke@gmail.com regarding any collaboration or information requests.

"Watchers", © David Gray. First published December 15, 2017 in Cosmic Roots & Eldritch Shores.
David A. Gray is a Scots-born creative director and writer living in Brooklyn, NYC. His first novel, *Moonflowers*, came out in 2019. He doesn't tweet, and is too private to be a natural with The Facebook, but his Instagram account (david_a-gray) is an obsessive compilation of random things he finds as he wanders Red Hook and environs. Also, of the real-life locations that end up in his stories and novel.
Artwork: *Tau Ceti*, Giovanni Palumbo. He has loved drawing and painting since he was a child. He designs 3d projects and produces technical drawings.

"One Good Turn" © Alan K. Baker. First published April 27, 2021 in Cosmic Roots & Eldritch Shores
Alan K. Baker is a British expat living on Florida's Gulf Coast. He has published six novels with independent presses in the United Kingdom, including *The Lighthouse Keeper*, a supernatural thriller inspired by the Flannan Isles mystery; the Blackwood & Harrington Steampunk mysteries; and *The Martian Falcon*, a Dieselpunk noir adventure. His latest novel, the SF thriller *Dyatlov Pass*, was published by Lume Books. His short fiction has appeared in Analog.

"Boomerang Zone" © Robert Dawson. First published February 27, 2016 in Cosmic Roots & Eldritch Shores
Robert Dawson teaches mathematics at a Nova Scotian university. Interests include writing, cycling, and fencing, and he volunteers with a Scout troop. He is an alumnus of the Sage Hill and Viable Paradise writing workshops, and on the executive of SF Canada. He believes the world needs more bicycles."
Make a Wish, digital painting © Karim Fakhoury.
Karim is an illustrator and designer based in Montreal, Canada. He has turned his passion for the world of visual arts and design into a profession. He specializes in image making, digital illustrations, and branding identity.
photograph courtesy of NASA

"Weatherbuns", © Diana Hauer. First publ;shed April 26, 2017 in Cosmic Roots & Eldritch Shores
Diana Hauer is a writer of words, both technical and fantastical, who lives in Beaverton, Oregon, with a dog and a fiance, both of whom she adores. When she's not writing, she enjoys gardening, reading, gaming, and martial arts.

"Sensoria" © Andrew Burt.   First published in this anthology, To Ukraine, With With Love, Benefit Anthology for Ukraine.
Dr. Andrew Burt is founder & moderator of the first writers' workshop on the web, Critique.org; founder of the world's first internet service provider -- Nyx.net, donation funded and still going strong; CEO of Reanimus Press -- specializing in bringing out of print books back to life; former Vice President of the Science Fiction & Fantasy Writers Association; professional science fiction writer; retired computer science professor at the University of Denver (research in AI, networking, security, privacy, and free speech/social issues); and CEO of TechSoft, https://www.aburt.com.

"Danged Black Thing" © Eugen Bacon & E. Don Harpe. First published in Jagged Edge of Otherwhen by Interbac, July 2012

Eugen Bacon is an African Australian author of several novels and fiction collections. She's a 2022 World Fantasy Award finalist, a Foreword Book of the Year silver award winner, and was announced in the honor list of the 2022 Otherwise Fellowships for 'doing exciting work in gender and speculative fiction".
Danged Black Thing, by Transit Lounge Publishing, was a finalist in the Foreword, BSFA, Aurealis, and Australian Shadows Awards, and made the Otherwise Honor List as a 'sharp collection of Afro-Surrealist work.' Eugen's creative work has appeared worldwide, including in Award Winning Australian Writing, Fantasy Magazine, Fantasy & Science Fiction, and Year's Best African Speculative Fiction. Eugen has two new novels, a novella, and three anthologies (ed) out in 2023, including Serengotti, a novel, and the US release of Danged Black Thing. Visit her website at eugenbacon. com and Twitter feed at @EugenBacon
E. Don Harpe has had a varied career, ranging from military service in the 1960s to industrial engineering. A published Nashville songwriter, he is a real descendant of the Harpe Brothers, America's first serial killers. Harpe has nearly forty short stories, including two in the Twisted Tales II anthology that won the Eppie Award for best science fiction anthology in 2007. Harpe lives in South Central Georgia, USA, and devotes his time to his family and his writng.

"Bubbles", © David Brin. First published 1987 in The Universe, edited by Byron Preiss.
David Brin is a scientist, speaker, technical consultant and world-known author. His novels have been New York Times Bestsellers, winning multiple Hugo, Nebula and other awards. At least a dozen have been translated into more than twenty languages. See more about him at https://www.davidbrin.com/biography.html

"Waiting for Mother" © Glenn Lyvers. First published here in Benefit Anthology for Ukraine.
Glenn Lyvers is a writer, editor, and head of Prolific Press. You can find out more about him at https://glennlyvers.com.

FANTASY

Front page: *Allegory of Power*, Georg Janny

"A Witch's Junk Drawer" © Rebecca Buchanan, 2022. First published 2022 in Cosmic Roots & Eldritch Shores.
Rebecca Buchanan is editor of Eternal Haunted Summer, a Pagan literary ezine, eternalhauntedsummer.com, and is a regular contributor to evOke:witchcraft*-paganism*lifestyle, evOkepublication.com. Published in a variety of venues, she currently has three short story collections and one poetry collection out, with two more collections expected by the end of the year.

"The River's Daughter and the Gunslinger God", © Matthew Claxton. First published March 15, 2017 in Cosmic Roots & Eldritch Shores.
Matthew Claxton is a reporter whose career has allowed him to encounter magicians, con artists, philanthropists, lemurs, robots, stunt pilots, Mounties, live bears, and politicioans. His stories have previously appeared in Asimov's Science Fiction and MothershipZeta. He lives near Vancouver, British Columbia. He has a newsletter, Unsettling Futures, at https://www.getrevue.co/profile/ouranosaurus.

"The Trial of St. George", © Andrew Jensen. First published April 23 2022 I Cosmic Roots & Eldritch Shores.
Andrew Jensen lives in rural Ontario with his family and too many dogs and cats. He is the minister at Knox United Church, Nepean. Over twenty-five of his stories have appeared in the USA, Canada, the UK, and New Zealand. Andrew plays trumpet, impersonates Kermit the Frog, and performs in musical theatre. You should have seen him as Henry Higgins...
Andrew grew up in Terrasse Vaudreuil, near Montreal, during the Cold War. Many of his neighbours were from Ukraine, Latvia and Estonia. They worked tirelessly for years to help the folks "back home" living under Russian occupation. Andrew is proud to have "The Trial of St. George" included in this benefit anthology.
Artwork: *St. George and the Dragon*, © Scot Gustafson. All rights reserved. For more information please visit www.scottgustafson.com
It is in illustrating children's books that Scot finds the greatest satisfaction, with such classics as *Peter Pan, The Night Before Christmas*, and more recently, *Classic Fairy Tales, Favorite Nursery Rhymes from Mother Goose, Classic Bedtime Stories*, and his novel for young readers, *Eddie: The Lost Youth of Edgar Allan Poe*, which he also illustrated. Scott's most recent book, **Classic Storybook Fables**, was released by Artisan after two years (and 49 new oil paintings) in the making! Artisan has also reprinted *Classic Fairy Tales, Favorite Nursery Rhymes from Mother Goose* and *Classic* Bedtime Stories For more information please visit www.scottgustafson.com

"Cloud Tower Rising", © Ian Pohl. First published January 31, 2020 by Cosmic Roots & Eldritch Shores
Ian Pohl grew up on a homestead in Alaska surrounded by books, snow, tree forts, and northern lights. Today he works as an oceanographer in the Pacific Northwest. When not diving or at sea aboard research ships, he is typically reading, writing, coding in Python, or messing around with cameras above and below the water. This was his first fiction publication.
Artwork: *Lingering in the Golden Gleam*, © Artur Rosa.
Artur S. Rosa began working with computer graphics in 2006. You can find him on twitter at https://twitter.com/ArturSRosa and on deviantart at https://www.deviantart.com/arthurblue

"Love Potion", © Anne E.G. Nydam. First published February 14, 2022 in Cosmic Roots & Eldritch Shores.
Anne E.G. Nydam has created imaginary worlds since she could hold a crayon, bringing them to life in both art and writing. A former middle school art teacher with an undergraduate degree in linguistics, she makes relief block prints celebrating the wonders of worlds real and imaginary, and writes books about adventure, creativity, and looking for the best in others. Her most recent book is *On the Virtues of Beasts of the Realms of Imagination*. See her art and books at NydamPrints.com.
Artwork: *Love Potion* and *Ineffable Feathersquid* by Anne E.G. Nydam,

"The Memory Bank and Trust", © Patrick Hurley. First published April 30, 2019 in Cosmic Roots & Eldritch Shores.
Patrick Hurley has had fiction published in Factor Four, Deep Magic, Paizo's Pathfinder, Flame Tree Press, and Abyss & Apex. Patrick is a graduate of the 2017 Taos Toolbox Writer's Workshop and a member of SFWA. Find out more about his work at www.patrickhurleywrites.com.

"Cat and Mouse", by Lara Crigger. First published May 30, 2018 in Cosmic Roots & Eldritch Shores.
L.C. Brown lives with her husband and two kids in a secret volcano lair just outside New Orleans, LA.

"Maggoty Meg Flies Up the Mountain", © Jonathan Lenore Kastin. First published February 25, 2022 in Cosmic Roots & Eldritch Shores.
Jonathan Lenore Kastin (he/they) is a queer, trans writer with an MFA in Writing from Vermont College of Fine Arts. His poems have been published in Mythic Delirium, Goblin Fruit, Liminality, and Abyss & Apex. His short stories can be found in Cosmic Roots and Eldritch Shores, On Spec, and Galaxy's Edge, and the anthologies *Ab(solutely) Normal*, *Transmogrify!*, and *We Mostly Come Out at Night*. He lives with two mischievous cats and more books than he could ever read.
Artwork: Vintage illustration, artist signature "KG"

"The Quiet", © George Guthridge. First published, July, 1981, by F&SF. Reprinted in Far Frontiers (1982), Year's Best SF (1982), Nebula Awards Stories (1982), and Under African Skies (1993). Latest reprint: Speculatief (in Dutch), April 2022. A Nebula and Hugo finalist.
George Guthridge is Professor Emeritus at the University of Alaska Fairbanks. An expert in indigenous cognition, he was named as one of America's 78 top educators for his work with Alaska Native youth. His fiction has appeared in Amazing, Analog, Asimov's, F&SF, and many other places. A Hugo finalist and twice Nebula finalist, he was co-winner of the Bram Stoker for year's best horror novel, grand prize winner in the Las Vegas International Screenplay Competition, and national finalist for the Benjamin Franklin Award for year's best book about education. He has retired and now lives in Thailand. Email: glguthridge@alaska.edu

"The Witch of Atlas,"excerpt, by Percy Bysshe Shelley
Artwork: *Night*, Edward Robert Hughes

Myths, Legends, and Fairy Tales:

Front page: *Circe Invidiosa*, John William Waterhouse

"The Song of Wandering Aengus", by W.B. Yeats
Artwork: *The Silver Apples of the Moon*, Margaret MacDonald MacKintosh

"Following the White Deer: on Myth and Writing" © Terri Windling   First published in The Journal of Mythic Arts, 1996
Terri Windling is a writer, editor, painter, and folklorist specialising in fantasy and mythic arts. She has published over forty books, receiving ten World Fantasy Awards (including the Life Achievement Award in 2022), the Mythopoeic Award (for her novel *The Wood Wife*), the Bram Stoker Award, and the SFWA Solstice Award. She has edited fantasy fiction since the 1980s, working with many of the major writers in the field, and co-edited *The Year's Best Fantasy & Horror* anthologies with Ellen Datlow for sixteen years. She writes fiction for adults and children, nonfiction on folklore and fairy tales, and a long-running blog on myth, nature, and creativity: *Myth & Moor*. She delivered the fourth annual Tolkien Lecture on Fantasy Literature at Pembroke College, Oxford (2016); participated in the Modern Fairies folklore and music project (Oxford and Sheffield Universities, 2018-2019); served on the Advisory Board for *Realms of Imagination*, a major exhibition of fantasy at the British Library in London (2023-2024); and has been involved with The Centre for Fantasy and the Fantastic at the University of Glasgow since its founding in 2020. Born in the U.S., she now lives in a small village full of artists in south-west England.
https://www.terriwindling.com/books/author-biography.html
For her mythic arts blog: https://www.terriwindling.com/mythic-arts/

Artwork: detail from *Allegro*, from the Stag Cycle, by Stephanie Law.
Stephanie Law's images trace the boundary between dream and reality. She delves into allegory, explores mythology, interweaves te xture, watercolor, gold and silver leaf, ink, and creates intricate layered pieces with resin and custom designed frames. Archetypes are one of the defining inspirations for her imagery. She has been a dancer for almost two decades, and not only do the humans dance across the page, but the branches of her trees move with a sinuous grace, and the arrangement of inanimate elements has a choreographed rhythm and flow. Her early career moved through the illustration and gaming world, but in recent decades she has focused on her own body of work, gallery shows, and publications. https://www.shadows-capes.com/index.php and https://www.patreon.com/StephanieLaw

"The Witching Hour", © Oghenechovwe Ekpeki. First published April 23, 2018 in Cosmic Roots & Eldritch Shores. A Nommo Award Winner.
Oghenechovwe Donald Ekpeki is an African speculative fiction writer, editor, and publisher in Nigeria. He has won the Nebula, Otherwise, Nommo, Locus, British & World Fantasy awards, and was a finalist in the Hugo, Sturgeon, British Science Fiction, & NAACP Image awards His works have appeared in Asimov's, F&SF, Uncanny Magazine, Tordotcom, Galaxy's Edge, and other venues. He edited the *Bridging Worlds* and *Year's Best African Speculative Fiction* anthologies, and co-edited the *Dominion* and *Africa Risen* anthologies.
He was a guest of honor at CanCon and at the Afrofuturism-themed ICFA 44, where he created the term/genre Afropantheology. You can find him in Twitter https://twitter.com/penprince

"Out of Brambles", © Leenna Naidoo. First published March 5, 2016 in Cosmic Roots & Eldritch Shores.
Leenna wanted to be a witch when she was little, but decided to be a writer instead.   She loves writing cross-genre suspense, romance, and dabbling in sci-fi/fantasy. Her books include *Settle Down Now* and *Here Be Monsters*. Her short stories have appeared in Mad Scientist Journal, SciPhi Journal, and Cosmic Roots & Eldritch Shores, where she is editor for the Myths, Legends, & Fairy Tales department. She also reads the tarot and tries her hand at any-thing vaguely artistic. Her most unnerving experiences include interviewing Alan Dean Foster (even though it was by email) and teaching a hellhound to share biscuits. Blog: https://leennanaidoo.wordpress.com. Patreon: https://www.patreon.com/LeennaNaidoo/   Website: https://leennascreativebox.com. She wanders down net and real world rabbit-holes, looking for her next story idea.

"Rapunzel – A Re-Winding", © Joan Stewart. First published August 30, 2018 in Cosmic Roots & Eldritch Shores.
Joan Stewart first thought of rewinding the tale of Rapunzel years ago when she read Paul O. Zelinsky's note on his beautifully illustrated retelling of the fairy tale. She had what she thought was a flash of insight – how much a story can be funda mentally altered even while retaining its essential elements, and evolve (or devolve)

along with the cultures they are formed in. But then she read Joseph Campbell's *Transformations of Myth Through Time*, and even the title let her know that this fact… had been noticed long ago. She hopes her version is a good evolution and will be enjoyed. To Em, The Kingdoms, and the ties that bind them
Artwork is based on a vintage illustration, artist unknown.

"Major Difficulties", © H.B. Stonebridge. First published on March 20, 2022 in Cosmic Roots & Eldritch Shores
H.B. Stonebridge is actually the writer team Helena and Byron.
Helena pursues her obsession with the magic of words by studying literature and philosophy. When she is not trying out new recipes for exotic sweets, she is reading her stories to her prime audience – her brown spotted Dalmatian.
Byron is a writer, history professor, and Game Master who lives in Florida with his two sons and two dogs.
Artwork: *Papa Legba Final*, © NiaDaiyo, https://www.deviantart.com/niadayo

"How Thomas Connolly Met the Banshee", by John Todhunter..
John Todhunter was an Irish poet and playwright, born 1839 in Dublin and raised as a Quaker. He received a medical degree from Trinity College, and wrote seven volumes of poetry and several plays. He was an early participant in the Gaelic literary revival. He also wrote a poem about the Banshee, published in a his collection, *The Banshee and Other Poems*. Although a well-respected scholar and professor of English literature in Dublin, he resigned his post to travel in Europe and Egypt. Later he was part of a small community of writers and artists that included W.B. Yeats, a close friend and neighbor, and he helped found the Irish Literary Society.

"Laila Tov", © Robert B. Finegold, MD. First published October 18, 2016   in Cosmic Roots & Eldritch Shores.
Robert B. Finegold MD is a retired radiologist, a former major in the U.S. Army, and a consulting editor for Cosmic Roots & Eldritch Shores. Since 2011 Bob's stories of science fiction, fantasy, and Yiddishkeit have appeared in magazines, e-zines, and anthologies. He edited the *3rd and Starlight Anthology* and was twice a finalist in the Writers of the Future contest. He resides in Maine. On facebook at RobertBFinegold Kvells and Kvetchings. _
Many generations of Bob's forbears lived in the Kyiv Oblast of Ukraine within the historical Pale of Settlement. His beloved paternal grandfather, John "Jack" Finegold, of blessed memory, was born in Zhytomyr. After surviving the Zhytomyr pogrom of 1905, he lived in Bratslav for 14 years before immigrating to the U.S. in 1914 to escape increasing anti-Jewish violence. His memoir of his youth in Ukraine and early years in Massachusetts is a cherished family possession. Papa Jack lived as Rabbi Nachman of his native Bratslav urged us all in the face of adversity: «*It is a great mitzvah to be constantly joyous.*» Being the big-hearted, big-souled, gentle man that he was, Papa Jack would have been pleased and, Bob believes, unsurprised, that Ukraine's heroic, well-spoken, and *elected with 73% of the popular vote* president, Volodymyr Zelensky, is also a Ukranian Jew.

"…and Always" © Joan Stewart. First published here in *To Ukraine, With Love*
Joan Stewart is a writer and artist who lives with a lot of trees, plants, and animals
and works at making a few small constructive contributions to the world.

Eldritch

"The Listeners" by Walter De La Mare. Published 1912.
Walter de la Mare, born 1873 in London, is one of modern literature's chief poets
of romantic imagination and themes: dreams, death, strange states of mind and
emotion, fantasy worlds of childhood, and the pursuit of the transcendent. He
began writing while working as a bookkeeper from the 1890s until 1908, when a
pension allowed him to turn full time to writing, short stories, poetry, and novels.
Artwork: *Whitby Abbey, North Yorkshire, 1910*, Albert Goodwin

"Bolaji Has a Heart", © Osahon Ize-Iyamu. First published October 18, 2017 in
Cosmic Roots & Eldritch Shores.
Osahon Ize-Iyamu writes speculative fiction novels and shorter fiction. He lives in
Nigeria. He is a graduate of the 2017 Alpha Writers Workshop, and you can find
his fiction in The Dark. You can also find him online @osahon4545.
Artwork: "Star-Filled" uses Mo-Nabbach's Stock Model 33. Mo-Nabbach is a hair-
dresser and fashion photographer. He can be found on deviantart, where he provides artists with stock photos, at https://www.deviantart.com/mo-nabbach, also
at www.exposurebox.com/ and https://mandmhairacademy.com/

"A Possession of Magpies", © E.E. King. First published December 23, 2019 in
Cosmic Roots & Eldritch Shores.
E.E. King is an award-winning painter, performer, writer, and naturalist. She'll do
anything that won't pay the bills, especially if it involves animals. Ray Bradbury
called her stories, "marvelously inventive, wildly funny, and deeply thought-provoking." She's been published in over 100 magazines and anthologies, including
Clarkesworld, Daily Science Fiction, *Chicken Soup for the Soul*, Short Edition, and
Flametree. Her novels include *Dirk Quigby's Guide to the Afterlife: All you need to know
to choose the right heaven*, and several story collections. Her stories are on Tangent's
2019, 2020, and 2022 year's best stories list. She's been nominated for a Rhysling
and several Pushcart awards. She's shown paintings at LACMA, painted murals in
numerous locations, co-hosts The Long-Lost Friends Show and Metastellar story
time, and spends her summers doing bird rescue and her winters planting coral in
Bonaire. Paintings, writing, musings, and books at: www.elizabetheveking.com and
amazon.com/author/eeking E.E. King

"Emissary", by Joshua Grasso, © Joshua Grasso. First published in Cosmic Roots
& Eldritch Shores, November, 2022.
Joshua Grasso is a professor of English at East Central University in Oklahoma,
where he teaches subjects that range from Beowulf to Batman. In his academic

persona, he has published many articles on 18th century novels, Gothic literature, science fiction and fantasy, and comics. But when academia gets him down, he enjoys writing fiction stories that have appeared in publications such as Daily Science Fiction, Metaphorosis, Allegory, Penumbra SF, and Tales to Terrify.

"Estevan of the Children", © E.E. King. First published December 23, 2019 in Cosmic Roots & Eldritch Shores.
See E.E. King's bio under "A Possession of Magpies", above.

"Ice", © Diana Silver. First published January 14, 2018 in Cosmic Roots & Eldritch Shores, in English and in the original Dutch version.
Diana Silver lives in an old Dutch town where old ghosts never stop whispering their stories. Her historical fantasy has been previously published in the Netherlands. Translation from the original Dutch was done by Asley Cowles.

The Tempest, excerpt, by William Shakespeare
Artwork: based on Sir John Gielgud portraying Prospero. 1950

FOR YOUNG PEOPLE OF ALL AGES

Front page: *Witch on a Broom*, Ida Rentoul Outhwaite

A Midsummer Night;'s Dream, excerpt, by William Shakespeare
Artwork: *Puck*, Arthur Rackham

"The Lady and the Moon", © Matt Dovey. First published Spring 2016 in Cosmic Roots & Eldritch Shores.
Matt Dovey is very tall, very British, and probably drinking a cup of tea right now. Although his surname rhymes with "Dopey", any other similarities to the dwarf are purely coincidental. He lives in a quiet market town in rural England with his wife and three children, and cannot adequately express his delight in this wonderful arrangement. He is the host of PodCastle as of 2022, and has fiction out and forthcoming all over the place: you can keep up with it at mattdovey.com, or find him timewasting on Twitter as @mattdoveywriter.
Artwork: *Eternity*, Stephanie Law.
Stephanie Law's images trace the boundary between dream and reality. She delves into allegory, mythology, interweaves texture, watercolor, gold and silver leaf, ink, and creates intricate layered pieces with resin and custom designed frames. Archetypes are one of the defining inspirations for her imagery. Stephanie has been a dancer for almost two decades, and not only do the humans dance across the page, but the branches of her trees move with a sinuous grace, and the arrangement of inanimate elements has a choreographed rhythm and flow. In recent decades she has focused more on her own work, gallery shows, and publications. https://www.shadowscapes.com/index.php and https://www.patreon.com/StephanieLaw

"Tree With Chalicotheres", © Vicki Saunders. First published July 21, 2017 in Cosmic Roots & Eldritch Shores.
Vicki Saunders lives on an island in the Pacific Northwest where you can't see the houses for the trees. Many of these trees may be the very same kind of huge, many-limbed, many-trunked, fast growing tree featured in her story. Perhaps one of them even contains a chalicotheres. You can find other stories by her at Three-Lobed Burning Eye, and archived at Ideomancer. She distracts herself from writing by laying out publications, cooking, and gardening.

"The Book of Winter", © Caroline Friedel. First published December 23, 2018 in Cosmic Roots & Eldritch Shores.
Caroline Friedel is a scientist by heart and training and currently an associate professor for bioinformatics at the LMU Munich. To date, she published >60 scientific articles as well as two other short stories: "The Tale of the Storyteller" in the anthology *In Memory: A Tribute to Sir Terry Pratchett* and "The Anthropomorphic Personification Support Group" in MYTHIC Magazine (issue #4).
Artwork: *The High Priestess*, by Howard David Johnson
David works with oils, acrylics, pastels, colored pencils and digital media to create his realistic fantasy and mythological paintings. His website is filled with beautiful work on many different themes. https://www.howarddavidjohnson.com/ With a background in the Natural Sciences Howard David Johnson uses traditional media including oils, pastels & colored pencils and also embraces leading edge digital media in the creation of his realistic depictions of fantasy, folklore, mythology, legend, religion, and heroic history.

"A Ladder to the Moon", by Naoko Awa, © estate of Naoko Awa. Translated by Toshiya Kamei.
We are pleased that the first publication of this story by the much loved children's author Naoko Awa was in Cosmic Roots and Eldritch Shores on Sept. 15, 2019, with the kind permission of her estate. Naoko Awa (1943-1993) was an award-winning writer of modern fairy tales. As a child, she read the Brothers Grimm, Hans Christian Andersen, and Wilhelm Hauff, and *The Arabian Nights*. In 1962, while still in college, she made her literary debut in the magazine Mejiro jido bungaku. In 1965, she earned a bachelor's degree in Japanese literature from Japan Women's University, where she studied under Shizuka Yamamuro (1906-2000). During a literary career that spanned three decades, she published numerous books, including *Mahō o kakerareta shita* (1971), *Kaze to ki no uta* (1972), *Tōi nobara no mura* (1981), *Kaze no rōrā suketo* (1984), and *Hanamame no nieru made* (1993).
Toshiya Kamei translated "A Ladder to the Moon" from its original Japanese language version into English. He holds an MFA in Literary Translation from the University of Arkansas. He has translated books by Claudia Apablaza, Liliana Blum, Carlos Bortoni, Selfa Chew, Espido Freire, and Leticia Luna, and a number of short stories by others. His translations have appeared in Clarkesworld, The Magazine of Fantasy & Science Fiction, and Strange Horizons.

Artwork: *Planet Plain,,* and *Star Falls,* Toshio Ebine is a painter; his works are from his imagination. His painting technique is self taught. He began creating art work in around 1998. He uses gouache paint. His themes are nostalgia, fantasy, clouds, landscapes, animals, insects... He began working digital in 2022.
https://www.ebineyland.com/ and https://www.deviantart.com/ebineyland

"Zephyr's Fair Child" © Scott J. Couturier. First published in Cosmic Roots & Eldrtich Shores October 23, 2020
Scott J. Couturier is a Rhysling-nominated poet and prose writer of the weird, liminal, and darkly fantastic. His work has appeared in numerous venues, including *The Audient Void, Spectral Realms, Tales from the Magician's Skull, Space and Time Magazine, Cosmic Horror Monthly,* and *Weirdbook.* His collection of Weird fiction, *The Box,* is available from Hybrid Sequence Media, while his collection of autumnal & folk horror verse, *I Awaken In October,* is available from Jackanapes Press.
Currently he works as a copy and content editor for Mission Point Press, living an obscure reverie in the wilds of northern Michigan with his partner/live-in editor and two cats.
Artwork: *Autumn Leaves,* Franklin Boot

I especially thank the team at Cosmic Roots & Eldritch Shores, our online magazine of science ficiton, fantasy, myths, legends, fairy tales, and eldritch stories, art, articles, and podcasts.

Over the years their hard work, critiquing skills, and thoughtful, helpful comments have brought to readers of Cosmic Roots & Eldritch Shores good stories by authors new and known, and it is on our pages that most of the stories in this anthology were first published.

Over time our team has included many wonderful members:
Casey Honebrink, Joel Roosa, Leena Naidoo, A.J. Cunder, Aaron Gudmunson, Robert Finegold, Warren Brown, Wayne Martin, Will Shadbolt, Douglas Dluzen, Tara Grimravn, Chris Yona, Brendan T. Stallings, Eugen Bacon, Lee Melling, Asch, George Guthridge, Oghenechovwe Donald Ekpeki, Erica Ciko Campbell, Eric Fromley, Rebecca Glazer, John Baumgartner, Cory Diagnault, Tyra Tanner, John Eckelkamp, Amy Fontaine, James Blakey, Mike Wyant, Evan Mullicane, Ben Hennesey, and first of all team members Ien Nivens.
Our podcast crew is Lauren Jane Delaney and Emily Rose.
Our tech support guy is Glenn Lyvers.

I would also like to thank the editor/publisher group started by B. Morris Allen, where the idea of a benefit anthology was first discussed and inspired me to put together *To Ukraine, With Love.*

Aside from myself at Cosmic Roots & Eldritch Shores, the editors/publishers who participated in initial discussians included:

B. Morris Allen, Metaphorosis magazine -- Beautifully made speculative fiction. https://magazine.metaphorosis.com/

Joshua Fagan, the editor-in-chief of Orion's Belt, which publishes speculative literary fiction and poetry. orions-belt.net

Ádám Gerencsér, co-editor of Sci Phi Journal, a Belgium-based quarterly which is dedicated to the intersection of speculative fiction and philosophy, and winner of the 2022 European Science Fiction Award for Best Magazine.

E.D.E. Bell from Atthis Arts

Tyler Berd, managing editor for Planet Scumm, is a musician, educator, and poet. planetscumm.space is an indie sci-fiction magazine collecting short stories from visionary, thought-provoking authors the world over.

Andrew Leon, Mythaxis, https://mythaxis.co.uk/, focused on fiction, free to read, and free of ads.

Monica Louzon, is the Acquiring Editor for The Dread Machine, a magazine, publishing house, and community where fans of dread-inspiring fiction and poetry can read and connect. (www.thedreadmachine.com)

Selena Middleton, Publisher/EIC of Stelliform Press, speculative stories regarding climate change and environmental justice. www.stelliform.press.

The main body of this book is printed in Baskerville.

Cover and some interior titles are in Zahar. This font family is based on lettering by the famous Ukrainian graphic artist Georgi Yakutovich and designed for Ivan Franko's book Zakhar Berkut.
Zahar is good for the design of famtasy books, folk tales, songs, etc. Zahar is easy to read in short texts. It supports Extended Latin and Cyrillic (including Old Church Slavonic). A special OT-feature is added to support the Old Church Slavonic alphabetic numeral system. The typeface was designed by Victor Kharik and Gennady Zarechnyuk during 2011–2019, and their font foundry is Apostrof.

ZLUKA TITLING is also used on the cover and interior titling, and is based on the lettering of Petro Kholodny. Kholodny probably relied on the work of Heorhiy Narbut and Mark Kyrnarsky, who began an expressive style of Ukrainian typography but whose work was cut short by the troubles of the Ukrainian nation. The project is a full-fledged font family with 6 font styles, and is named after the reunification of the country into one independent Ukrainian People's Republic in 1919.
The typeface contains modern Slavic Cyrillic that allows for the possible use of accents, modern European Latin, historical and stylistic alternatives, Macedonian-Serbian italics, some decorative elements. Zluka is designed for purposes from logos and corporate identity to body text in newspapers, magazines, books and their websites.
This typeface was also designed by Gennady Zarechnyuk and Victor Kharyk, with the support of Serhiy Tkachenko in 2018.

Zahar and **ZLUKA TITLING** typefaces are licensed from Eugene Sadko, at rentafont.com

For more great stories, artwork, reviews, articles, and podcasts, Cosmic Roots & Eldritch Shores online magazine can be found at https://cosmicrootsandeldritchshores.com
We hope to do more benefit anthologies.

Peace and Freedom to All Sentient Beings